Hillbrooke
God's Rewrite

Beverly Joy Roberts

Illustrations and design by Erin Mohrman

This book is dedicated to those
who serve on the frontline who sacrifice
to help improve the lives of wounded children!
You are heroes.

Social Workers
Foster Care Parents
Court-Appointed Special Advocate (**CASA**)
Advocates
Mediators
Attorneys
Judges
Medical/Mental Health Personnel
Adoptive Parents

Acknowledgement

Dear Reader,
This is the third and final book of the fictional city of Hillbrooke in my beloved home state of Michigan. The pastor and the people in the community are all characters that I make up in my overactive imagination, but somehow, over the past three years, they have become very real.

I hope you will be challenged and blessed as you read book three, *Hillbrooke God's Rewrite*. Who knows, maybe God will move on your heart to expand the borders of your tent and make room in your home and heart for one or many who need to be loved and protected.

My heartfelt appreciation to the *New Life Book Club* ladies, thanks for your feedback and help with the grammar, punctuation, and my endless spelling mistakes. All of you are a blessing and encouragement to me. The open discussion and positive feedback are fuel to a writer's gas tank!

Also, to Diana Wiehe, Sharon Chambers, and Marianne Siefert thank you for giving of your time to read my manuscript. Your contribution was a blessing. And to my dear sister, Barb Cody, who has given of her time to read each of my books out loud to help me made corrections, you are a treasure.

And of course, my husband Bob, who is my biggest fan—I love you more than words can say. And that's saying a lot since I'm a writer!

Thank you dear reader for taking another chance on me and buying this book.
God Bless,
Beverly Joy Roberts

List of Characters

Returning Characters:
Snake—Zak Parker (Carl Fields)
Fauna Parker—Snake's wife
James and Marilyn Fields (children Snake and Emily)
Dr. Stuart Hayes M.D.
Samantha Hayes—Stuart's wife
    Children: Isabelle and Baylee Hayes
Rey Douglas—Pastor Community Outreach
Callan Douglas—Rey's wife
    Children: Zander and Ty Douglas
Tom Brown—Widower (Wife/Jean Brown passed away)
Ms. Laura Klingburg—Social Worker
Kota and Emily Edwards (Emily, sister to Snake)
    Children: Maddie and William

New Characters:
Helen Franko—social worker
Griffin Walsh—college student
CeCe Jefferson—foster child

Places:
Community Outreach Church
Hillbrooke Counseling Center
Christian Family Services (CFS)

1

...He listened! He heard my prayer! He paid attention to it!
Blessed be God, who didn't turn away when I was praying
and didn't refuse me His kindness and love.
Psalm 66:19-20 (TLB)

Zak Parker held the steering wheel with one hand and mindlessly massaged his bushy beard with the other. His beard partially covered the once prominent tattoo on his face, that gave him the nickname, Snake. The tattoo was much less threatening, now, with just the head of the hissing snake poking out of his thick beard.

Snake wiggled his fingers free from his thick facial hair and a smile formed on his lips as he recalled how Fauna giggled the first time she noticed his beard covering all but the snake's head. It had caught her off guard. A warm and happy sensation rushed through his body at the memory of that moment and the sound of her laugh.

Snake used the steering wheel to pull himself up from his relaxed position and pressed down on the gas pedal.

Zak Parker was Snake's legal name, but neither he nor those in his circle of friends ever called him Zak. Snake was once a man to be feared, but since his transformation in Christ, the Snake tattoo that previously defined him was barely noticeable to those in his circle. The tough guy persona had been replaced by the image of a big hairy guy with a heart as soft as a marshmallow.

The black SUV seemed to know the way home as Snake robotically steered the car.

Shortly after Snake and Fauna married, he sold his starter home to buy a four-bedroom fixer upper. They wouldn't settle for anything less than four bedrooms. They dreamed of one day having a house that was filled with as many children as the Lord would bless them with.

Snake came to a stop in the driveway of the house he and Fauna had shared for two years. He exited the car and rushed towards the front door with long strides. In one seamless motion, he opened the door and shouted in a breathless voice, "Did you wait?"

The screen door slammed shut behind him. He breathed in deeply through his mouth making a quick gasp as he looked at the empty room.

Fauna poked her head into the kitchen with a half-smile that bordered on a smirk, "Did you think I'd do this without you?"

Snake heard a hint of excitement mingled with apprehension in her tone. His eyes focused on the small flat rectangle box on the kitchen table. Over the past 18 months, Snake had seen boxes like this one before. His eyes were locked on that little box while he answered Fauna's question. "No. I guess I knew you wouldn't do it without me." He took a few steps towards her. "I just didn't want you to be alone in case—I just wanted to be with you—whatever happens."

Snake picked up the container from the table and held it like all his hopes and dreams were locked away in that little box. He felt his stomach tense up like he was anticipating a punch to the gut. He looked directly at his wife and asked. "Are you okay?"

Fauna walked towards Snake and timidly said, "Hopeful." Then she reached for the box in Snake's hand. With one swoop, Snake drew her into a full hug and held her there longer than usual. Fauna rested her head on his chest and relaxed against him—the best she could.

Snake felt the tension in his wife's body. He gently stroked her back with his free hand.

Fauna pushed back from Snake, and he reluctantly released her along with the box. He gently squeezed his wife's shoulder before she moved towards the hallway.

Fauna glanced back over her shoulder. Their eyes met. No words passed between them, but Snake could read all the emotions wrapped up in that one moment.

The sound of the bathroom door closing caused his shoulders to tense. He inhaled deeply holding his breath for a few seconds then he exhaled. He waited. The thought of another disappointment filled his thoughts with worry. Snake walked into the living room and plopped down in his favorite recliner.

Why was this taking so long? He wondered. It seemed longer than usual.

Only a few minutes had passed when Fauna returned holding a white, plastic stick wrapped in tissue. She placed it on the end table between them and set the timer on her phone for five minutes. The silence in the room was deafening.

Over the past months, they both had learned to speak the language of silence very well—too well.

Snake eased up from his recliner and slipped next to Fauna on the couch. He reached for her hand and cupped it gently with both of his hands. He couldn't bring himself to pray out loud, but in his heart, he pleaded with God for the chance to be a father and for Fauna to be a mother.

***

Emily Edwards, Snake's little sister, rocked her three-year-old son, William, as he drifted off to sleep. Her six-year-old daughter, Maddie, was now in school giving Emily more time to lavish love on *The Little Gentleman,* as William was affectionately nicknamed by his father, Kota.

The Little Gentleman both acted and looked like Kota's father, Bill Edwards, who had passed away over seven years ago. Bill's death had been the domino that started a chain reaction that God used to transform the lives of many of the members of the Community Outreach Church including Pastor Rey and Callan Douglas.

5

Emily remembered how *The Little Gentleman* would blurt out a kind word or an idea to help someone who was sad. His nightly prayers always included someone less fortunate, who was struggling or sick. This little man brought their family so much happiness.

Emily softly patted her son's back as she pushed her feet against the floor with a steady rocking motion. She hummed softly, *Jesus Loves Me This I Know*. Tears welled in Emily's eyes as she held her son a bit tighter while fighting the urge to sob. They had planned on two children, a boy and a girl. They thought they were done—their family complete.

Emily caught her breath as she tried to hold back the emotion and the tightness in her chest. Her conflicting thoughts waged war on the peaceful moment. She and Kota weren't *unhappy* about the news. It was just…what about Snake and Fauna? Here, she and Kota had two precious children and now an unexpected blessing was on the way while Fauna had none.

Emily brushed the tears from her cheek as she wiggled her way out of the chair with her sleeping child in her arms. She walked down the hallway and laid William in his bed.

Closing the door behind her, Emily placed her hand low on her belly. The bump was there. She could feel it and soon others would notice. The news needed to be shared with her family and soon. A whispered prayer eased from her lips, "Lord, please give Fauna a family too. Fill her empty arms with life."

***

Laura Klingburg hit the down arrow on her laptop to scroll through the names of children needing emergency placement. She stopped on the name CeCe Jefferson. The picture of the three-year-old girl with light brown skin and greenish eyes looked back at her from the screen. CeCe was a beautiful child who had lived through unthinkable things in her short life. She never asked to be born to a drug addicted mother who was unable to put a father's name on the birth certificate. Many men had passed through her life, most of them—nameless.

CeCe's mother had considered abortion, but she was in denial about her condition until abortion was no longer viable. Adoption had been discussed, but in the hospital, holding the small baby she believed she could be a better mom than her mother had been. CeCe's mother tested clean for drugs at the hospital much to her own surprise. A mix-up of tests results released a helpless child into the care of an unfit mother. This careless mistake would cost CeCe so much.

Laura glanced again at the photo on her computer screen. CeCe was meant to be born, just not into the messy life of this mother. She ran her fingers over the screen and read the details of CeCe's life: difficult placement, emotional problems, not toilet trained, violent outbursts, dislikes women, unable to bond, present foster home wants her removed immediately.

Laura rested her face in her hands and prayed silently. *Lord, give me wisdom. Help CeCe to find a safe and forever home. Help her bond with her new family. Please heal her broken spirit.* A knock at the door brought Laura Klingburg's short prayer to an end.

Ms. Klingburg looked up at the sheepish looking young woman standing in her office doorway. "Yes Gina?"

"Ms. K, a voice mail message on my phone this morning sounded urgent. The foster home of CeCe Jefferson says that they are done. They are dropping her off this morning. They even said that if you don't like it, then pull their license. They can't take her issues one more day."

Gina stopped to take in a gulp of air and continued. "The foster mom said that she must consider her *own* children. The message said that CeCe's not a good fit for their family." With the last word, Gina leaned against the door frame of Ms. Klingburg's office and waited.

Gina had been the office receptionist for only four

months and still wasn't fully sure how protocol worked at Christian Family Services.

***

Eighteen months ago, Ms. K took the director position at Christian Family Services (CFS) leaving behind more than 20 years of service with the state of Michigan. She also left behind a bitter and judgmental attitude. It had been more than two years since her conversion at the close of the healing service at Community Outreach Church.

Laura Klingburg saw with her own eyes a true physical miracle—the healing of Baylee Hayes. She heard with her own ears what Pastor Rey had said from the pulpit before the healing. These were things only God himself could have known. Pastor Rey spoke these words over the entire congregation, but Laura knew they were a love letter to her from God. That night, she felt for the first time in her life she knew true forgiveness—given and received.

Whenever she recalled that day, it still caused the hair on her arms to tingle. That was the day she was born again. She had been contaminated by the business she was in. She had been a vengeful person and at times outright cruel. Rarely did anyone ever rise above her low expectations, neither the inept birth parents or the demanding fosters.

Since Ms. K's conversion, her heart was open to them all equally. She wanted to find solutions for the betterment of the child first, the hope of reunification for the qualifying parents and give the foster parents the respect and appreciation they deserved. Their sacrifice was great. These were grueling tasks to accomplish especially working through the restrictions of government red tape.

When the door opened for Laura Klingburg to become the director of the CFS, she walked through and began a new chapter in her life. For her, it was a ministry opportunity opening more than a job advancement.

***

Ms. K seemed to be deep in thought. Gina cleared her throat and shifted from one foot to the other. "Should I have given this to one of the others?" Her voice sounded worried with a touch of impatience.

"No Gina, I'll handle it. CeCe was already on my radar. Could you pull up a list of emergency placement homes and call to see if anyone will take her? We need to place her with a temporary family today while I look for something long term."

Gina timidly walked into Ms. K's office and laid the note on the pile of brown folders that cluttered the top of the desk. "You probably already have these, but here are all the details." Then she hurried back to her desk at the front of the office.

Gina's desk was the first one behind the bulletproof glass with the little opening under the glass for people to transact business without any personal contact. Gina thought the place didn't look as friendly as its name, Christian Family Services (CFS). She opened her computer and located the emergency placement file. She scanned over the short list of names and began to randomly make calls. Four calls later she had secured an emergency placement for CeCe.

Within the hour, true to her promise, a large woman walked into the office of CFS with a small girl in tow. The child had big wild curls all over her head. At first glance, the little girl's beauty was striking. Her skin was tan. Her hair was a unique two-tone brown almost like it couldn't decide if it was dark or light. Her eyes were big and round with thick black lashes that drew you into the pale green center of her eyes. But the child looked straight ahead. Her face was void of emotion. Her beautiful eyes were empty.

The foster mom had enough attitude and expression for both, plus some. She snapped her fingers and pointed at the chair. The child moved in slow motion, but not fast enough. The woman snatched the child up and plopped her down in the chair with just enough force to speak the unspoken.

The large woman scowled at the child while she extended one knuckle and rapped on the bulletproof glass instead of using the buzzer that was clearly marked to the right of the window.

The child sat motionless.

Without a word, the woman tossed a small plastic shopping bag in the general direction of the chair where the child sat. The bag holding all the child's possessions slid across the floor and stopped when it hit the leg of the chair.

The woman returned her attention to the window and readied her hand for another series of rapping on the glass. Then the security door buzzed, signaling the door was open.

Gina peered out from behind the door and smiled at the gruff woman. Gina asked the question to which she already knew the answer. "May I help you?"

"Here! She's your problem now." The foster mother nodded in the general direction of the small girl. "I'm done. Is Ms. Klingburg here? I'd like to know if she wants to pull our license which I'd be fine with at this very moment."

Gina propped the door open, returned to her desk and buzzed Ms. K's office. "CeCe and her foster mom are here. How would you like to handle the transfer?"

"I'll be right out. Thanks Gina." Ms. K pushed out from her desk and slipped her bare feet back into her shoes. As she passed through the main office, she couldn't help but notice the six social workers, five women and one man, were busy on phones, computers or doing paperwork. She wished for the day that there would not be a need for this type of business or at least for the day things would be slow. It would be great to have a day where children were safe and not in fear of death or bodily harm. A day when people were willing to help even when it meant sacrifice.

The foster mom had moved just inside the security door and saw Ms. K coming towards her. With an angry tone the woman's voice bellowed through the office, "You didn't prepare me for this." The workplace came to an immediate halt.

Ms. K continued to the front of the office without saying a word. She passed by the incensed foster mother and stepped into the waiting area. When she saw CeCe, her heart was heavy. She knelt down using the empty chair beside CeCe to carefully ease herself to the child's eye level.

Ms. K was careful not to touch the child before she evaluated CeCe's mood. "It's always good to see you CeCe. I'm going to make sure you have a good home very soon. I'm sorry things didn't work out again. We'll keep trying until we find you a match."

CeCe never looked at Ms. K—not once.

Ms. K gently patted CeCe's mop of hair and pushed herself up from the floor with the help of the chair. She walked over to the foster mom whose body language shouted hostility.

"Come into my office where we can talk privately." Ms. K motioned for the foster mom to follow her.

Gina took CeCe to the playroom that was set up for situations just like this one. It was a holding room. A place to occupy children until their new families could arrive or they could be delivered to their new home.

The foster mom followed Ms. K, not making eye contact with any of the social workers as she passed through the busy work area. Once they were both inside the private office, Ms. K closed the door and pointed at the chair in front of her desk. The disgruntled foster mom sat down with a heavy plop.

Before Ms. K could be seated, the angry woman spoke. "You have no idea what that child has put me through. She is damaged goods. She may look all cute and pitiful at first sight but she's the devil. You need to put her in a group home or institution. She is damaged beyond repair." The woman huffed. "When we first saw her, I thought she looked like a little angel, but she is a demon from the pit of hell."

The woman repositioned herself in the snug chair, then

continued. "She destroyed the bedroom, smeared her poo on the wall and threw food in my face. I have my own children. The situation was beyond impossible, and the nightmares with screaming." The foster mom put her arms out in front of her and nodded with her head at her extended arms. "Look! Just look how she clawed my arms." The woman lifted her head and met Ms. K's eyes, then drug out the words with a snarl on her face. "Sheee's a DEMON."

Ms. K was nearing the boiling point. She held her tongue, but her inner monologue was fierce. Are you kidding me? You're the adult. What did you think you were signing up for...summer camp? Ms. K drew in a deep slow breath—then spoke. "Thank you for your three days of service, Mrs. Glass. We'll keep your license on file if you'd like us to, but we'll give you a month or two before we call on you again. How does that sound?"

Mrs. Glass pushed herself out of the chair with enough force to cause the chair to teeter. "Fine. But my own dear children have been traumatized by this experience. We are heading to the park, then McDonalds for ice cream. Let's say four months before you call me again." She paused at the door, turned back and looked directly at Ms. K. "At least four months. Maybe longer."

Ms. K's left eyebrow arched as the woman left her office. As Mrs. Glass disappeared from her line of vision, she shook her head in disbelief at her empty office. She whispered a prayer for the Lord's help and immediately her attention was refocused on CeCe's needs. She picked up her desk phone to finalize the arrangements for pickup, but before she punched in the number, she laid the receiver back in its holder.

Next to her computer, she reached for her cell phone and scrolled through her personal contacts until she landed on Fauna Parker. She laid her cell phone aside and buzzed Gina.

"Yes, Ms. K."

"You remember the couple that applied for foster care named Zak and Fauna Parker. He was a huge guy with a ton of tattoos and she had a butterfly tattoo on her face."

"Well, of course. They would be kinda hard to forget. They still have a few more hoops to jump through. I'd say maybe two weeks before they're licensed."

There was a thoughtful pause before Ms. K spoke. "I may still have a few connections at the state level. I'm reasonably sure my friend will help move them to the head of the line."

"You're the boss. Just say the word and I'll do all I can to expedite their licensing, and if you have friends in high places, then maybe this could happen in a week—maybe."

Ms. Klingburg replied. "I'm thinking more like a few days. I think they will be a good match for CeCe."

A moment of silence proceeded Gina's cautious voice, "Really? Rookies again for CeCe?"

A knowing smile rested on Laura Klingburg's face, "Let's not underestimate what God can do."

"I know—but CeCe?"

"I'm going to make that call to Lansing now. You get busy on the remaining paperwork and I'll do the rest." Ms. K hung up the phone and resumed her prayer from an hour ago...*and Lord if Snake and Fauna are the right home for CeCe help this to happen for all of them. It is in the powerful name of Jesus that I ask this. Thank you, Lord for hearing my prayer.*

* * *

The alarm on Fauna's phone rang, signaling the completion of the timer. She reached for the pregnancy test on the end table. She turned the results into view. Snake strained his eyes to read the tiny words. The word NOT came into view first, followed by PREGNANT. Snake reached for Fauna's hand but didn't speak. Silence was less painful than words.

2

Do two walk together unless they have agreed to do so?
Amos 3:3 NIV

Snake embraced Fauna until she gently pushed away. "You gotta go and so do I. Our lunch hour has come and gone."

"Okay, but I feel like we need to talk about this more if you want. Maybe tonight?" Snake tried to read her facial expressions. "You do want to talk?"

"No, thanks! I'm done talking about this. I've got nothing left to say. Nothing! Nor do I have any words left to pray." Pointing one finger at Snake and putting the other hand on her hip she scolded, "And if one more person asks me when we're gonna have a baby, well, I can't be held responsible for what I might say." She forced a smile, hoping to pass the outburst off as a joke, but her face began to quiver as more words spilled out.

Fauna's eyes pooled with tears. Her voice cracked, "I'm aching to be a mother. Surely one day I'll be able to face one of these negative pregnancy tests without being reduced to a bucket of tears." But that wasn't going to be today, and Fauna gave way to her pain.

Snake drew her back into his arms. He was going to be late for work. He checked his watch behind her back, but he didn't let go. He wouldn't let go.

***

Callan Douglas, the pastor's wife at Community Outreach Church, dialed her husband's cell number, placed the phone on the countertop and turned on the speaker. The phone rang three times before Rey's greeting filled the kitchen.

Without returning his greeting, Callan began her interrogation. "Rey? Did Snake call yet? What did you hear? Tell me everything. I want details. I'm crazy excited. This has to be it." Callan loaded the dishwasher while she spoke to the phone on the countertop.

Rey cautioned, "Wait a minute. Remember, we aren't asking them any questions or talking about this. He told me in confidence. No one is supposed to know."

"I know. I know. I'm talking to you not posting on social media. So, did you hear anything?"

"No. All's quiet here." Rey's cell phone on the desk buzzed. "Snake's calling me now on my cell. I'll let you go and see if there's any news."

Rey said goodbye to his very persistent wife and answered his cell phone. "Hey Snake. Any news?"

"Pastor, negative. It's negative again. She's crushed." Snake's voice cracked with emotion. The line went quiet.

The silence was uncomfortable while Rey waited for Snake to speak.

Snake blurted out, "I wish she'd reach out to Callan for support, but she can't. She won't. She's hurting, and I don't know how to help."

Silence.

"Pastor?"

"I'm here." Rey tried to be a listener instead of a fixer.

Snake reassured himself. "It has to be her idea to talk to someone. At least she's still pushing through with the fostering. Fauna's whole life is helping hurting people, so fostering seems like a great fit for us until the Lord sees fit to give us a family of our own. I think this will help take her mind off..." Snake gripped the steering wheel, pinching it tighter, as if that would stop the emotion pushing in.

"Snake. It's okay. I'm here. Take all the time you need."

Snake got out the words. "I'll call you later. I can't do this right now. I gotta go to work."

Rey heard the sound of the call disconnecting. He dialed

Callan's cell phone while thinking how disappointed she would be to hear the news.

***

Fauna threw her purse into the passenger seat, plopped down behind the wheel and checked her face in the rearview mirror. She shook her head in dismay at the face looking back. How could she cover up the red eyes and blotchy marks? Not even a tattoo would draw people's eyes away from the fact that she'd been crying—a lot. She swallowed a gulp of air and fought back the overpowering emotions. She gave her cheeks a hard pinch, hoping the pain would help numb her heart and give a bright glow to her cheeks to downplay the redness of her eyes and nose.

As Fauna backed out of the driveway, an incoming call sent a loud ringing through the car's speaker system. She glanced at the caller I.D. on the car dashboard. The words *Christian Family Services* showed on the screen. Her first instinct was to let it go to voicemail, but she dutifully pushed the accept button.

"Hello, this is Fauna Parker."

"Oh great. This is Gina from CFS and Ms. K, I mean Ms. Klingburg, is interested in placing a child in your home, but there are a few more things we're gonna need from you. Could you stop by sometime today to speak with Ms. Klingburg and we can finalize everything while you're here? Also, the placement is an emergency and we'd need to place the child by the end of the week if you and your husband are still interested."

"Uh. What? A child? When? Do we both need to come? Do you need Snake, I mean Zak too?"

"You should be able to complete what's left without him. Then we can set a final meeting for both of you in a few days. Could you be here by 3 P.M.?"

"I'm on my way to meet with a client right now. I'll call you back after I check my schedule. And thank you. Thank you."

"Mrs. Parker. You do know these children come with baggage and not the kind that has clothes in it."

"Of course. I'm a counselor." Fauna breathed in deeply and continued. "I was one of 'these children' myself. I'll call you when I get to the office and check my afternoon appointments. You said Gina, correct?"

"Yes. When you call, ask for Gina, but don't worry. I'm the one who usually answers the phone."

Fauna touched the end button on the dashboard screen disconnecting the call. She waited for the screen to clear, then touched the phone button to place her call.

A robotic voice responded through the car speaker system, "Your phone is ready."

Fauna replied, "Call Snake at work." The car repeated back to her the same words in the form of a question, and she replied, "Yes."

The sound of ringing filled the car again, but this time, with each ring a feeling of expectation grew in Fauna's heart. She said out loud, "This must be what hope feels like."

***

Isabelle Hayes sat on the window seat of her second story bedroom. From her position, she watched Baylee, her younger sister in the backyard. Baylee was just a few months away from being an official teenager, but she still loved to sit on the tree swing and pump her legs while the wind blew through her hair.

The first ten years of Baylee's life, she had limited mobility, but since her miraculous physical healing, Baylee was trying to squeeze in all the things she had missed. She was enjoying life to its fullest—as much as an almost 13-year-old was allowed.

Isabelle watched her sister and smiled. She pulled out her phone and opened the calendar app. She scrolled backwards through October, September, August, and then she paused in the month of July. That was when it happened. She had missed four months. Once, she thought she was in the clear, but it only lasted a day. Sickness had been her constant companion at the beginning of the school year, but she passed that off as food poisoning and nervous stomach. Having a father who was a doctor, you'd think he'd be a bit more observant, but two years ago everything in the Hayes' family changed.

Isabelle had evolved into an obedient and pleasant daughter. She hadn't given her parents a moment of worry. Until now. She looked out the window again. Baylee was walking back towards the house. Issie leaned closer to the window and pressed her forehead against the glass.

Baylee stopped. She looked right and left as if she were about to commit some sort of crime. Then she threw her arms straight out to her side and spun around in a circle a few times.

Issie smiled at her sister's spontaneity and envied Baylee's freedom to spin as if she were a child in a princess dress. Isabelle stood up. In the privacy of her bedroom, she opened her arms wide and twirled in a full circle—then sharply stopped. In one quick movement she put both hands over her mouth and hurried to her bathroom.

A few minutes later, Issie stepped out of the bathroom wiping her mouth with a washcloth and there on her bed was Baylee with her chin resting on her drawn-up knees.

Baylee looked at Isabelle and said, "What are you going to do about that?"

"About what?" Isabelle asked with a little sass in her voice.

"You do know that your bathroom is right up against my bedroom wall. I'm not as naïve as you may think even if I'm 13—almost."

Isabelle frowned. "Said the girl who moments ago was spinning in the backyard like a ballerina." Issie used her head to point at her window and nod, then she looked directly at her sister like she held the smoking gun in a murder case.

Baylee half-smiled. "Oh, I guess I forgot to look up." She giggled at herself for being caught. It was sweet and even more revealing that she was young and carefree. Baylee asked again, "But—what are you going to do about *that*?" With the emphasis on the word THAT, Baylee pointed to the washcloth that Isabelle clutched near her mouth.

Issie scolded, "You think you know something…so…out with it already!"

"I'm not saying it for you. You're gonna have to say it first—when you're ready." Baylee paused, "Mom and Dad are gonna find out. You *do* know they're not the enemy. Right?"

"What in the world are you talking about?" Issie rolled her eyes. "And why are you acting like you know some big mystery? Bay—just talk to me."

Baylee loosened the grip she had on her legs. "*You* talk to me. First, you have to admit it to yourself and then to me. Go on—say it."

"Say what?"

Baylee slid her legs down and dangled them at the end of the bed. Then she pushed off the bed with her hands and landed on the floor like a gymnast. She turned and took one step towards the door. "Whenever you're ready, I'm just one door away."

"Wait Bay! Don't go. Why do you have to be so cryptic?"

Baylee reached for the doorknob.

"Stop!" Issie's voice changed from demanding to a whisper spoken through clenched teeth. "I'm pregnant…maybe four months." She lifted her bulky sweatshirt to reveal a tiny baby bump. Isabelle quickly covered her stomach and sat down in the window seat. "I don't know what to do. Or if I should keep it. I'm 17, so technically, mom and dad don't even have to be involved if I…"

"Kill it?" Baylee gasped. "Would you do that?"

"It would be the easiest thing to do." Issie pulled her

legs up under her and sat crossed-legged. Baylee returned to her place at the end of the bed. "I could declare myself emancipated. Lots of girls at school have done it. They even brag about it." Issie looked right at Baylee and said, "I'm not bragging about this. I haven't told anyone. Not even Mrs. Parker. And she'd be the only one I'd trust, other than you, of course."

"Iss, please talk to her. She will know what to do and the sooner the better. Do it before you make any decisions or talk to anyone else." Baylee pursed her lips and twisted them from side to side. "Hey, you don't even have a boyfriend, so who's the dad?"

"That sounds so weird coming from your mouth. You're nothing more than a baby yourself." Isabelle used a mocking voice to repeat Baylee's question, "Who's the dad?"

Baylee frowned.

With a matter-of-fact tone, Isabelle stated, "He's not in the picture."

"Well, he was in the picture or there wouldn't be a baby." Baylee raised her eyebrows in a cute way to signify disbelief.

Isabelle tried to clarify her previous statement with, "It was once. Last summer. We haven't talked again since."

"You do know that Mom and Dad are gonna want to know everything." Baylee laid back on her sister's bed, rolled to one side and propped her head up to keep Issie in her line of vision.

Issie gazed at the floor in front of the window seat and spoke to the floor. "Bay, you're not helping. All these questions just reinforce the fact that it would be easier not to have to tell them at all. I'd rather just take care of it by myself and keep it private."

Baylee shot back. "Have you even watched a teen movie in your whole life? I've never seen one that ends well for mother or child where they 'take care of things privately.' There is always emotional and physical pain and besides that, I thought you believed that was murder. You even did a project on that last year." Baylee sat up and pointed towards the walk-in closet across the room. "Isn't that poster board with all the pictures from the internet still in your closet?"

Isabelle stretched her legs out on the seat cushion, leaned her back up against the wall and turned towards the window. With remorse in her voice, Isabelle blurted out, "My God, what was I thinking. I shouldn't have told you any of this. You're not even 13." Turning back to face Baylee, Issie questioned. "How do you know all this stuff?"

"I watched a lot of unsupervised TV and had free reign of the internet when I was a sick kid…remember!" Baylee had a smirk on her face that brought a smile to Isabelle's.

Issie's smile quickly faded. "I'm not ready to talk about it with anyone. Please don't tell."

"Like I said before, this isn't mine to tell." There was a moment of silence between the sisters. Baylee broke the silence, "Can I pray with you?"

"Of course, you can." Issie threw her hands up in the air, making a grand gesture, "Pray away."

Baylee walked across the room and sat by her big sister in the window seat. She prayed a prayer that surprised even Isabelle as an unspeakable peace poured over her that soothed her troubled spirit.

***

Callan hung up the phone and went to her quiet place in the family room. She curled her legs up under her and leaned her head back against the sofa.

In a shallow voice, she sighed. "Jean, why did you leave me? I need your wisdom right now. It's been two years and still, I haven't found anyone who can fill your shoes. I hate knowing things about people that I can't even talk to them about." She shook her head and sighed. "Lord, You know what's going on with Snake and Fauna. This isn't a surprise to You. No way. Help them. I can't stand seeing her hurting. Give her strength to reach beyond her borders."

Callan stopped praying. She grabbed her journal that was close by and began writing.

Everything Fauna needs is near at hand. It's only a hand grasp away. It's close. It's almost within her reach. But she won't be the one to reach out. Someone will be reaching out to her. Lord, I don't have a clue what that means, but I know You gave it to me and that's what I'm going to be praying about especially for Fauna. Lord, I know You are doing something wonderful for Fauna and Snake. You are orchestrating everything. You're putting pieces together to make ugly beautiful and You are doing it for them—in Your way and in Your time. I love You, Lord.

Callan laid her pen down and closed her journal. A peace engulfed her that started from within. It immersed her. It was a confirmation more real to her than a certified letter in the mail.

***

Snake tried desperately to concentrate on the computer screen in front of him. Fauna's feelings were foremost in his thoughts. He could still feel her head pressed against his chest and feel her sobs as his arms wrapped around her small body.

He closed his laptop and looked out the office window towards the workers who knew nothing of the weight of the pain he carried. He mechanically began to stroke his beard as he rebuked himself. Get back to work. Get focused. Trust the Lord. What good does worry do? God is in control.

Looking down at his desk again, he opened the laptop and went to his Bible program. The scripture for the day poured healing oil on his weary soul. It was a personal invitation from God to cast all your cares on Him. Not some, but all, not because God is nosy, but because He cares.

The scripture wasn't a new one to Snake's eyes, but it was the reminder that he needed.

With his eyes open, he prayed, "Jesus, things are about as bad for Fauna as they've ever been. We could use some help here. We are feeling overwhelmed and discouraged and invisible. We could use some good news any time. Any chance You could throw us a bone? Anything! Something! And if it's not asking too much, how bout sooner than later?"

Snake stopped praying. A pencil on his desk distracted him. He picked it up and began to maneuver it back and forth between two of his fingers. His thoughts were consumed with Fauna. He picked up his cell phone and scrolled through his list of favorites and found the number for the Hillbrooke Family Counseling Center. He touched the screen to place the call.

"This is Fauna Parker. May I help you?" Her voice sounded strong and professional.

"Fauna. It's me. Just wanted to see how your day was going."

"I tried to call you earlier, but there was no answer. I didn't want to leave a message, but hey it's you. I'm so glad you called. I don't want to get my hopes up, but Ms. Klingburg called about a placement. I'm going there today to finalize our remaining paperwork. We could have a child in our home within a week. It doesn't seem possible."

Snake dropped the pencil he was fiddling with and sat straight up in his chair. "A child? Is it a boy? Do you know anything yet? Have you seen a picture? How old?"

"Snake! Stop. Ms. K only said, 'a child.' Beyond that I know nothing. Maybe I'll find out more when I go there in about 20 minutes."

"You're going there? Do you need me? I can join you. I'd like that, if you want me, need me. I can meet you there. What time exactly?"

Fauna giggled a bit at the excitement in Snake's voice. "She said 3 P.M." Her heart felt so light it fluttered.

"We're in this together. No matter what. I better let you go so I can close things up here." Snake hung up the phone with one hand and closed his laptop with the other. He thought, okay, I'm all closed up. He stood up and pushed his chair to the desk and walked towards the door.

3

Be strong and courageous!
Do not fear or tremble before them,
for the Lord your God is the one who is going with you.
He will not fail you or abandon you!"
Deuteronomy 31:6 (NET Bible)

Ms. Klingburg looked out the window of her second story office at the gray cement of the Christian Family Services (CFS) parking lot. In her thoughts, she made a mental list of the things she needed to accomplish before the end of the day.

Fauna would be arriving within the hour to finish up the needed paperwork to expedite their foster care license. CeCe needed an emergency placement and she couldn't ignore the stress in the office that a certain social worker was stirring up any longer. The sound of footsteps caused Ms. K to turn away from the window.

Helen Franko, the senior social worker in the office, entered with a stack of files that rested in her arm. "Sorry to bother you, but I need you to sign off on these placements." Helen bent down towards the desk and began sliding the files from her forearm on to the top of Ms. K's desk. Helen's action pushed the open files Ms. K had been working on towards the other side of the desk.

Ms. K lunged forward to grab her coffee cup as it teetered. With cat-like quickness, she snatched it before it fell to the floor. "Helen, stop! Put the files over there." Ms. K could not mask her feelings which appeared to please Helen very much.

Ms. K pointed to a workspace across the room.

Helen appeared unable to stop her motion which caused the open files on Ms. K's desk to cascade to the floor, landing in disarray. Ms. K looked helplessly at her feet while one hand held her coffee cup and the other still hung in the air pointing across the room. The files she had meticulously worked on earlier that day were now in disarray scattered around her feet.

"Oh, let me help you pick those up." Helen walked around the desk, stooped down and slowly began to stack the papers while observing each item with interest.

Ms. K knelt down and touched Helen's hand. "No, don't bother. I'll have to reorganize everything. Just leave them."

"No, it's my fault. I'll help." Helen insisted.

Ms. K placed her hand over the remaining papers and held them in place on the floor. "You need to stop. I'll take care of it."

"Well, fine." Helen stood up and placed the few single sheets of paper she was able to snatch from the floor on Ms. K's desk with just enough force to make a point. She turned to leave the office with a flair, but her theatrics came to a quick halt when she saw Zak and Fauna Parker standing in the doorway.

Helen recognized their type from her many years in social work. They were untarnished, optimistic novices about to be devoured by the dark underbelly of the foster care system. They had obviously never housed a single foster child in their home—ever! If they had, they wouldn't be so bright-eyed, abounding with expectation and wearing big hopeful smiles.

***

It had not been an easy adjustment for Helen Franko when Ms. K arrived as the new director at Christian Family Services. Helen had applied for the directorship and was passed over for an *outsider.* They were both the same age and had equal experience in social work, but the head of the nonprofit seemed to connect with Ms. K on a level that

ROBERTS

Helen could not understand.

At one point, Helen thought the board director and the applicant might be related because they seemed too friendly. They were on a first name basis and laughed like old friends when they shook hands at the interview. Helen could see it all from her vantage point in the office. It seemed much too cozy for a first-time meeting, but she was never able to find the backstory to connect the two, not on the internet, nor by asking tons of questions to each of them about the other, nor by listening to private conversations whenever the head of the foundation came calling. And it seemed to Helen that he came more often than before.

When the announcement was made that Ms. Klingburg would be the director, Helen felt the loss deeply. She was not a fake and found it difficult to hide her disappointment or give any congratulations to the winner. The old regime was dwindling one by one leaving her and one other social worker as the only ones left who Ms. K had not hired.

Helen found out the hard way there is a fierce loyalty felt towards the person who hires you compared to a coworker.

***

Gina finished compiling the documents that still needed to be processed for the Parkers to receive their foster license. She closed the file on her desk and felt someone standing close behind her—too close. She turned her office chair slowly and let out a soft yelp. "Helen, you scared me."

"Sorry, I was just wondering what is going on with that little CeCe child. I saw her in here earlier today. She's a real piece of work. If she were one of my clients, I'd place her in a group home. What's Ms. K's plan for her?"

"You'll have to talk to Ms. K about that. I'm not comfortable discussing the case files with anyone."

"Come on. We all do it. I know there are rules in place, but you hear us talking all the time about cases. No biggy."

Gina tucked the file into her drawer and kept her head

down. "I'm not comfortable with that, Helen. I'm not a caseworker."

Helen shifted the conversation. "I saw those two rookies are here talking to Ms. K. Is she considering those two for a kid like CeCe?" She rolled her eyes and shook her head in disbelief. "That's a greenhorn mistake to place a troubled kid in the home of newbies. A client with a file as big as that kid should be placed in a group home where she can learn that the whole world doesn't revolve around her."

Helen glanced back over her shoulder at Ms. K's office, then leaned closer to Gina. "She needs to buck up and move these kids on or they'll be playing the victim card their whole life." Helen's voice lowered to a whisper. "Ms. K's a bleeding heart." Helen put her hand on the back of Gina's chair and leaned uncomfortably close, "We should report her. I mean, *you* should report her, since *you* have all the info."

Gina listened to the rant for as long as she could, but this was too much. She blurted out, "But CeCe's not even four years old. You'd really recommend a group home for a child so young?" Gina shook her head in disbelief, "Poor thing has been through so much in her short time on this earth."

Helen patted Gina's back in a motherly way. "Gina, Gina, you can't get emotional about these kids. Once you let them in they will control you. Don't look at them as children. They are clients. Use their names as little as possible. Don't get attached. Warning…if you do, they will break you. Most of them are beyond repair. It's a hopeless, helpless system. The kids can't win, and neither can we. So, protect yourself above all else."

"Does Mrs. K know how you feel about the kids?"

"Don't you mean clients?" Helen sneered.

Gina swallowed hard. She had only been employed at CFS four months, but she didn't want to end up like Helen. She was going to have to take a stand for what she believed, and she wasn't about to call a three-year-old a client. CeCe was a child. She was wounded, damaged and broken, but she wasn't beyond the reach of God. She had watched Helen make other workers lives miserable with her negativity and accusations. If she had to choose between Ms. K and Helen, well, that would not be a difficult choice for her.

Helen shifted from behind Gina's chair to sitting on the edge of her desk. She frowned, "Well?"

Gina silently prayed—then answered. "I'm not a social worker, just a receptionist. To me they are children. Children that need a ton of love, care and understanding and I hope I never forget that."

Helen leaned in so close to Gina that she felt the air on her face from Helen's nose as she snorted. Then Helen stood with her shoulders back, turned on her heels and walked towards her own desk.

Gina knew this little encounter would not go well for her in the days to come. She had witnessed the wrath of Helen spewed on others in the short time she had sat at the receptionist desk, and now it seemed she was in Helen's crosshairs.

***

Fauna and Snake held hands as they exited Ms. K's office. As they walked past the other social workers, they were oblivious to everyone around them. Gina opened the security door for them and waved as they passed by her desk.

Fauna stopped and gave Gina a quick shoulder hug before exiting. "Thanks for all you are doing to help us. We couldn't be more excited to meet this little girl."

"It should only be a few more days. I know you think you're prepared but be ready. She's gonna need an abundance of love and patience."

Fauna smiled. "This is what we've been waiting for. We're ready."

Snake took Fauna's hand as they left CFS and walked to the parking lot happier than they'd been in months.

"Should we drop off one of the cars at home before we go to your parents' house for dinner?" Fauna asked.

"Yes, then we can talk on our way over there. Do you think it's okay if we tell my family tonight?"

Fauna's voice was ecstatic. "Absolutely. I know your mom will be over the moon excited for us." A brief pause followed, "But, what about your dad?"

Snake unlocked his car doors and turned to give Fauna a kiss on the cheek. "Ten years ago, I'd have been able to tell you exactly how he would respond, but now? Since we've reconnected, well, all I can say is he still surprises me. So, I'm not going to venture a guess one way or the other. Let's wait and see how it all plays out tonight, shall we?"

"Agreed, let's see. Meet ya at home." Fauna leaned in and gave Snake's cheek a quick kiss.

"It's been awhile since you did that. I think I'll hold on to that for safekeeping." Snake laid his hand over the kiss and held it there while he opened his car door with the other hand.

***

Helen Franko jotted down Zak and Fauna Parker's names in a spiral notebook. She dated the entry and added a notation that said: *the potential foster parents were interviewed for a matter of minutes. There appears to be a personal relationship between them and the director, Ms. Klingburg. She requested that their file be expedited to accommodate a difficult child that has been placed in numerous foster homes that are far more capable than first time foster parents. None of these homes could handle the difficult child whose name is CeCe Jefferson. I tried to warn Ms. K that this was a bad idea. I recommended that the child be placed either in an experienced home or group home to handle the severity of the child's need, but my suggestions were dismissed.*

Helen closed the notebook and unlocked her drawer. She fingered through the files until she reached the one marked PRIVATE. She slipped the notebook into the file. The file held crumpled up pieces of paper that had been discarded by Ms. Klingburg or left unattended. Helen

29

collected anything she could find to build a case against Ms. K with the hopes of having her fired.

Helen turned the key in the lock on her desk drawer. Her lips formed a catlike smirk, and a contentment settled on her. Her own thoughts kept her company. I don't care how cozy and friendly Ms. K is with the director of the board. Facts are facts and he won't be able to dismiss her incompetence when the evidence is laid out.

I can bide my time. Maybe this CeCe case is just what I need to drive the last nail in her coffin. A snarl formed on Helen's lips as the smirk faded. Rest in peace, Ms. K. Helen chuckled out loud, then quickly gathered her decorum. A flashing message light on her phone reminded her that she had her own cases that needed attention.

Helen touched the voice mail button on her desk phone and listened to a birth parent's pleas to regain custody of her three children. Helen shook her head and rolled her eyes as the woman's voice became emotional, begging for her case to get attention, so her children could be reunited with her.

Helen jotted down the weepy woman's name on a piece of paper and placed the note at the bottom of a pile of notes the same size. Then she moved on to the next voice mail message.

***

Emily, Kota and their two children walked up to the grand entrance of her childhood home. She glanced back over her shoulder at the sound of an approaching car.

Snake pulled into the driveway and revved the engine in a playful manner. Emily waved and shook her head pretending to be disgusted with her older brother's antics.

Emily reached for the doorknob on the massive front door. She felt a bit emotional as she remembered that this house had not been a happy place for her brother growing up.

James and Marilyn Fields could provide every material

thing imaginable for their children, but when their children were young, they grew up behind the affluent walls of this stately house with one child who could do no wrong and the other one could do no right.

Emily's relationship with her parents throughout her childhood and adult life had been wonderful, but not so much for her brother, Snake. He had grown up privileged with a doting mother and a critical overbearing father that drove him out of the house at the young age of 17. Snake was born Carl James Fields until he became emancipated and took the name Zak Parker.

He was given the nickname Snake because of his tattoo. Snake seemed like an obvious name for someone who had a coiled snake tattoo around his neck. The snake's tail draped down one arm to the elbow. On the opposite side, the snake's head was tattooed on the side of his face hissing just below Snake's eye.

Through the constant prayers of Snake's mother, along with Pastor Rey visiting him in prison, Snake's life was changed. At that time, the path Snake was on was leading him down a road to destruction.

Shortly after his release from jail, Snake attended a service at Community Outreach Church. It was at the altar that Snake humbled himself and accepted Christ as his Savior. This act of submission brought Snake's once cruel and overbearing father back into relationship with his son and the Lord.

**

Fauna and Snake were a few steps behind Emily, Kota and the kids. Marilyn greeted them as they entered the house. James stepped out from his study when he heard the voices of his family. Three-year-old William ran with all his might and jumped straight up in the air in front of his granddad. It was something they had done for as long as William could remember.

James buried his face into his grandson's neck and William's laughter filled the foyer. It brought a smile to all their faces. Dignified James Fields being silly with his grandson was not something Marilyn, Emily, Kota, or Snake could have ever imagined seven years ago. And the fact that this grandson was also the grandson of the late Bill Edwards made the whole scene even more amazing.

James Fields had done everything in his power to bully Kota's family out of the Community Outreach Church, but not even a bully can stop God's plans and promises. And even bullies can change—if they want to. James Fields was living proof of that.

The twice-a-month Friday dinners at James and Marilyn's house had been going on since Fauna and Snake married. These had become wonderful times for the Fields' family to continue to heal from their stormy past. God had done amazing things in each of their lives to bring restoration.

***

Emily fought the urge to touch her stomach. It was almost impossible not to stroke it unconsciously knowing she carried life. This child was without a name or known gender, but she knew the life she carried had a purpose and a plan. This child's life story was already written, and she inwardly waited for the moment she could share her good news.

Fauna and Snake seemed exceptionally cozy. They held hands and sat close. They had not stopped shooting secret glances at each other since they arrived which did not go unnoticed by Emily.

"Snake, anything new going on with you two?" Emily stroked her daughter's hair as she snuggled next to her on the couch.

"Why do you ask?" Snake let go of Fauna's hand and put his arm around her shoulder to pull her closer.

"Oh, no reason, except I've known you my whole life, and I think I know you well enough to know—you have something you want to share. So out with it. We are all ears here!" Emily felt sure in her heart that this was going to be the announcement she had been longing to hear.

Marilyn stopped preparing dinner and walked into the family room. James set William at his side on the couch and looked back and forth between Snake and Fauna. Kota put the TV on mute and Fauna fought a tight-lipped smile.

"So, what's going on?" Marilyn stood next to the loveseat where Emily was sitting. Emily stood up and locked arms with her mom in anticipation.

Snake looked at Fauna.

She nodded.

Snake spoke. "Well, fine. We were going to wait until dessert but might as well share our news now. I will start out by saying Fauna is not pregnant."

Emily's disappointment was obvious when she let out a deep sigh. Marilyn squeezed her arm a bit to help her daughter refocus.

"Then what is the news?" James asked.

"We are getting a little girl next week through foster care. We don't know much about her because they want to wait to fill us in on the details once our licensing stage is complete. We are beyond excited and know that there will be difficult times ahead. We could use *all* of your support." Snake glanced in his father's direction when he said *all*.

Marilyn dropped Emily's arm and hurried across the room. Fauna and Snake sat hip to hip in an oversized recliner. Marilyn spread her arms open wide to reach around both of them and pulled them together with a hug. With her head pressed between Fauna and Snake she whispered, "We will love her like our own. Thank you for opening your home and hearts. I always wanted to do this. I'm so proud of both of you."

Emily choked back her tears. "I don't know why I'm so emotional these days. I cry over everything." The tears trickled down her cheeks and she quickly brushed them away. "Congratulations. We want to help however we can. I'll babysit or whatever. I still have some girl clothes. You can have them or borrow them. Whatever we can do to help."

Fauna piped in. "I'm holding you to that Em."

James didn't say anything. A frown formed on his face then he went back to the book he had been reading to William.

Snake looked at his mom and said, "We know it's going to be hard. Laura Klingburg at CFS gave us a few books to read to prepare us for what we are going to face. Fauna is far more prepared than I am seeing she's a counselor, but I hope I can be some help. We are excited to say the least."

Fauna gave Snake a poke with her elbow. "You will be an awesome dad. What three-year-old little girl doesn't love a bearded man with a snake tattoo?" Then she laughed, and everyone followed. Everyone but James.

4

...the destroying locust... ate everything you had.
But I will pay you back for those years of trouble.
Joel 2:25 (ERV)

Monday morning between classes, Isabelle found a quiet spot in the school entrance to make a private phone call. The walls of the foyer were lined with numerous window seats. Each seat was separated by a brick wall partition. Issie chose the seat nearest the school office where she had a good vantage point to see people coming and going.

Isabelle pulled her phone from her pocket and dialed the Hillbrooke Counseling Center. Three rings later an unfamiliar voice answered the phone in a professional, but cold, manner.

Isabelle didn't have time to question the stranger answering the phones, so she decided to get right to the point. "Is Ms. Parker in today?"

The curt voice replied, "She is in, but unavailable at this time. Would you like to make an appointment, or would you like her voice mail?"

Isabelle had hoped to set up a lunch or dinner meeting but thought an appointment may be better, considering the circumstances. "Yes. Does she have any appointments today after 3 P.M.?"

Issie could hear the sound of someone typing on a keyboard.

The receptionist answered, "How about 4 P.M.? Will that work for you?"

"I'll take it. This is Isabelle Hayes. I've seen Ms. Parker before."

"Okay, Ms. Hayes. We'll see you at 4 P.M." There was

no farewells or goodbyes—just dead air on the other end of the phone.

Issie felt panic rise in her chest as she clicked the end button on her cell phone. It was real. It was happening. She was really going to talk about it with someone other than Baylee. She knew her parents would be the next in line after Ms. Parker.

Issie took the palm of her hand and pushed it hard against her chest moving it in a circular motion. It didn't release the pressure she was feeling. She thought, do babies give people heart attacks, because that's how I'm feeling. I can't catch my breath.

It had been awhile since Issie had prayed but sitting there in that moment with an elephant sitting on her chest she whispered, "Lord, I'm sorry. I've messed up. Help me make this right."

The pressure began to subside under the palm of Issie's hand. Her breathing slowed down, and she felt almost normal. She patted her chest, looked upward and whispered, "Thank you."

The bell rang so loudly behind Issie that she let out a yelp and immediately regretted it. Her eyes darted around the large empty foyer. No one was there. She jumped up, tucked her phone back into her pocket and headed to her next class.

Issie glanced at her watch as she walked down the hallway. It was 10 A.M. She had six long hours before she would be able to finally talk to someone. Now that she had made the appointment, she was ready to talk, not wait.

***

Callan answered the parsonage phone in mid-ring. "Good morning, this is Callan."

"Well aren't you all formal this morning." There was a lightness in Fauna's voice that brought a smile to Callan's face.

"Fauna, what's up with you? We need to go out soon

and catch up. I've missed our lunches and talks the past few weeks."

Callan already knew that Fauna wasn't pregnant, but she couldn't let on that she knew anything about anything. She coached herself to keep her voice sounding upbeat and void of any sympathy. Even though she knew—she must not let on. Yes, she knew the heartbreak that Fauna and Snake were going through. Callan reminded herself…discretion is the life of the pastor's wife.

Fauna's voice broke into Callan's thoughts, "Well, it just so happens that's why I'm calling. Are you available for lunch today?"

Callan shot back, "How about I pick you up at the counseling center, and you can choose wherever you want to eat—my treat?"

"How could I say no to that? Will 12:30 P.M. work for you?" Fauna asked.

"Perfect, see you in 90 minutes." Callan hung up the phone and did a quick inventory of the things she needed to accomplish before walking out the door.

***

Fauna laid her cell phone to the side of the unfinished paperwork from her last counseling appointment. This mother and teen daughter who left her office minutes ago couldn't find any common ground to resolve their relationship that was spiraling out of control. Fauna had sat through many sessions exactly like this one.

Sometimes Fauna wanted to shake both clients and say, why can't you just love each other? Why can't you be kind? Why can't you see the other person's side for a moment? She wished they could see the future and understand for a moment what their lives would really be like if the other person were gone.

She knew only too well what a void the loss of a mother can be in a young girl's life. Once your mom is gone, so is all the history about you. The person who gave life to you, cried with you, held you is gone from your life. You will never hear her opinion—on anything—ever again.

Fauna took a deep breath, closed her eyes and whispered. "Mom, you weren't perfect, but I miss you." She fought back tears by clearing her throat and tapped her pen on the desk a few times to refocus. She checked her watch, arranged the papers on her desk then opened her laptop and focused on business.

***

Callan rinsed the raw chicken in the sink before placing it in the crockpot with cut up potatoes and carrots. She covered the food with water, added her favorite seasonings, placed the top on the pot and said out loud, "Dinner's done. Check that off my list."

Callan thought of Fauna while she put a few dirty dishes in the dishwasher hoping that she'd be ready to talk. She wasn't sure how much longer she could pretend she didn't know they had experienced yet another disappointment. The fact that Fauna called her was a great sign that she was ready to talk. Callan reminded herself that she needed to be a listener today, not an interviewer—no questions. Well, maybe a few.

Callan finished putting on her lipstick, took a few steps back from the mirror, gave herself a nod of approval and headed down the hallway towards the garage. When she reached for the doorknob, a knock at the front door caused her to stop in mid-motion.

She glanced at her watch. She had twenty minutes, and not a minute more before she had to leave the house to be at Fauna's by 12:30 P.M. She knew it was impossible to back out of the driveway with someone on her front porch. Whoever was out there knocked again.

Callan's shoulders drooped as she dutifully walked to the front door. Her lips formed the words—*Oh man!* She pressed her eye to the peephole on the door to see the intruder and to plan her next move. Her eyes focused on Samantha Hayes who stood outside anxiously looking from side to side.

Callan opened the door. "Hi. Samantha. Is everything okay?" In the three years that Callan had known Samantha, never once had she stopped over without calling first.

"I'm sorry for being so impulsive. I knew if I didn't come now I wouldn't come at all. I'll only take a minute of your time—promise."

"Oh, come on Samantha. You are always welcome. Come in." Callan opened the door and motioned for Samantha to have a seat in the formal living room.

"Really, I don't even need to sit." Samantha looked longingly at the waiting chair in the direction of Callan's extended hand but didn't move from the doormat. Turning back towards Callan, Samantha blurted out, "I'm concerned about Issie." Samantha placed her hand over her stomach area and continued talking. "I have a gut feeling that something's not right with her. She's not confiding in me for some reason. I was wondering if maybe you would ask her to go out for lunch or even dessert. Just to see if she would open up to you. I can't put my finger on it, but I've been watching her. She's been withdrawn. I don't know if she's depressed or what. I've tried to talk to her, but she shuts me down. I don't want to go back to where we were before Baylee was healed."

Samantha paused, then added with emotion in her voice. "Before we *all* were healed."

Callan engulfed Samantha in her arms and held her for a moment before she spoke. "I'd love to do that. How about if I call her tonight after school to set something up?"

Samantha's eyes were moist. "That would be great. Issie's gaining weight." Samantha swallowed hard. "And I read online that weight gain can be a sign of depression in girls her age. They are at a higher risk than boys that age to experience things like that. If they don't get help, some will attempt..." Samantha's voice fell quiet. She couldn't even form the word.

"Samantha, come on. Don't think like that. That doesn't sound like the Issie I know. I saw her last week at youth group. She seemed to be happy and engaged with her friends. Let me talk to her. Don't go to such a dark place. Issie's a teenager for goodness sakes. What is she now—16?"

"No. She's 17. Thanks for doing this, Callan." Samantha sighed. "I never want to go back to where we used to be as a family."

Callan placed her hand on Samantha's arm. "Has Stuart tried talking to her?"

Samantha's jaw tightened. "Yes, he tried. But when it comes to his girls, he's a dad first and doctor second. He got nowhere."

Callan tried to sneak a glance at her watch.

Samantha blushed. "Oh, I'm sorry. You must have things to do and I've barged in here without calling first. We can talk later. Thanks for taking time to hear me out."

Before Callan could protest, Samantha was gone.

***

The afternoon sun cascaded through the blinds of Ms. Klingburg's office window. Ms. K traced the shadows on her desk from the sun with her finger. Her thoughts were centered on the child, CeCe Jefferson, along with her own decision to place the child with Fauna and Snake. She silently questioned, Are they ready? Can they do it? Am I setting them up to fail?

Looking out into the misty fall morning, Ms. K silently prayed. *Lord, help me know this is the right thing for all of them, and especially for CeCe. How can this child sustain yet another placement? Jesus! Please, let the Parkers be the ones who will care enough to climb a mountain and cross a river for CeCe. Lord, let them be the ones who CeCe will come to trust.*

Gina buzzed Ms. K's office. Ms. K picked up the phone

and responded with her usual one word greeting. "Yes?"

Gina heard a slight edge to Ms. K's voice, like she interrupted something. "Ms. K, I have CeCe Jefferson's temporary foster mom on the line. Are you available to speak with her?"

"Is there a problem?"

"If there is, she didn't say. She just asked to speak with you if you were available."

"Go ahead and put her through." A sinking feeling swept over Ms. Klingburg as she touched line one. She shot a two-word prayer from her heart to God's ear. "Please Lord."

Ms. K breathed in and cleared her throat before extending her greeting. "Hello, June. Everything okay with CeCe?"

With a sweetness that always caught Ms. K by surprise, June McNeil answered. "Oh, Ms. K, did you have any idea what a mess this little girl is?" June's question wasn't mean-spirited or judgmental.

Ms. K replied with trepidation. "Yes. We are aware that she's in a critical situation. How are things going?" So far, there didn't seem to be a white flag going up the pole from June's voice inflection, yet the child in question *was* CeCe. If June, a seasoned expert was concerned, how could she throw Snake and Fauna to the little wolf. She quickly told herself…*so to speak*.

The foster mom answered, "You said she'd be here until Friday—correct?"

"I'm doing everything I can to place her with her forever family. Are there any specific concerns I can address in the meantime?"

"Well…" June's voice trailed off followed by an uncomfortable pause. "I know there are a lot of emotional issues at play but has CeCe been checked for any type of physical issues?" There was a thoughtful pause before the foster mom resumed. "She's a beautiful child, but she seems to be deeply traumatized. She won't allow me to come close to her. I haven't been able to find a way inside the stone walls she has erected to keep herself safe. For one so young, I don't believe she fears for her very life. I haven't been able to connect with her in a way that will help her understand consequences, danger or empathy."

The foster mom stopped talking. The phone line was quiet. When June resumed there was emotion in her voice. "My heart is broken for this baby. My husband and I pray over her every night once she is asleep. We know she won't be in our home for the long haul, but we are praying for God's mercies to be extended to her and whoever will be her forever family."

Ms. K's shoulders relaxed. She wasn't even aware until now that she had tensed up. "I knew you would be a great transitional home and so did the Lord. It is my prayer for CeCe as well that her next home will be her forever home. Hang in there and never stop praying for our kids—never."

"We won't. CeCe already has my heart."

Ms. K said her goodbyes to the foster mom and hung up the phone. Her throat was tight with emotion. She swallowed hard to regain her professionalism.

CeCe was just one. She was one in thousands that needed a safe place, a forever home, a family to be loved by *and to love.*

This foster mom got it. She understood. She was covering this discarded child in prayer. June McNeil was the starting point to help set children like CeCe on a better path. Her home was a safe place for difficult and unwanted children. June was one of the special people who could see past the outward and hope for things not yet seen.

Ms. Klingburg took a deep breath. As she exhaled, she felt it. There it was—peace. The kind that only comes from God. There was a verse from the Bible that she had recently learned. What was that verse?

She put her head in her hands for a moment and repeated the words out loud. "Peace, peace, peace." Her head popped up in such a way that someone looking on might have seen an imaginary light bulb floating above her.

Ms. K spoke the scripture. "A peace that passes all understanding." A smile formed on her lips. She remembered. The peace that comes from God is real. She felt it. There were people in this cruel world who cared, and who would go the extra mile to prove it. The documentation made by the state counselors and doctors declared the short life of CeCe to be permanently damaged, with behavior out-of-control, and they said that she may be a hopeless case. BUT God was preparing the life of CeCe Jefferson for a rewrite.

Ms. K turned her swivel chair towards the window and spoke out loud as she gazed into the parking lot. "Lord, I can't save them all, but give me the strength to save as many as I can. You've brought CeCe to me. Heal the broken pieces of her life. Open the locked doors of her heart to trust again. Let everything happen according to your plan, Lord. If CeCe is supposed to be with Snake and Fauna, let it happen for all of them."

The sound of someone clearing their throat caused Ms. K to turn toward the open door of her office. Standing a few steps inside the door frame was Helen Franko. It wasn't difficult to read the smirk on her face.

"Ms. K, I'm sorry for disturbing you. I couldn't help overhearing your..." Helen twisted her lips from side to side, "I mean." She paused again searching for the right word.

"Out with it Helen. What can I do to help?"

"Oh no. I don't need *your* help. I was going to offer to assist you with the case of CeCe Jefferson and the Parkers."

"Excuse me. How do you know about that case?"

Helen shifted from one foot to the other. "I just put the pieces together between the angry foster mom dropping CeCe off, and then Gina scrambled to find a new home, and the Parkers were just here last Friday. And...I heard you..." Helen stopped talking as she searched for the correct wording. "...mumbling something about bringing them all together."

Ms. K took a long breath before speaking. "Thank you, Helen, but I'm handling this case myself."

Helen's eyebrows arched upward, "Oh, do you have something personally invested in one or all of these clients?"

"Helen are you implying there is some impropriety between me and this case?"

"Well, I wouldn't want you to have anything come back to bite you or jeopardize your position as director." Helen fought the smirk that tried to control her lips. "I just thought if you wanted to give me this case then your hands would be clean."

"So, you do think I'm doing or have done something wrong?" Ms. K tipped her head to the side wondering what motive Helen could possibly have in wanting to be involved in CeCe's case. It couldn't be because she cared about protecting her position as director, nor CeCe's needs either.

And why would she be concerned about the Parkers as foster parents? She didn't even care about her own cases with this much zeal. In her two years as director, Helen had not shown herself to be a caring or empathetic person—at all.

Helen laughed nervously then tried to play the sympathy card, "Of course not! I can see that everything you do as director here is above board and professional. I thought because you have an excessive caseload that I'd offer to help you lighten your load." Helen tried her best to look the part of one hurt by having her pure motives misinterpreted. "I only wanted to help—*you*." She turned and walked away from Ms. Klingburg's office. Helen's lips were pinched tight holding back a full smile.

Ms. K sat down at her desk and leaned back in her chair and watched Helen walk away. She folded her arms across her chest. Her thoughts were conflicted. Was Helen sincere or did she have another motive? Helen had never been friendly or cared about her in the past. Why now and why this case?

Ms. K had an uncomfortable feeling in regard to all things *Helen Franko*.

She opened the whole case file on CeCe Jefferson to familiarize herself with the details of this child's short three years on this earth.

***

Callan tapped on her car horn three short times as she sat parked outside the Hillbrooke Counseling Center. Within a minute, Fauna was waving at her from the front porch. The Counseling Center had once been a place where lives were hurt more than helped. Now this old house had been turned into a place of true healing. It no longer held the memory of the past. Now when Callan looked at this place, it held the memory of her dear friend Jean Brown.

Every time she entered the center, she touched the plaque on the door and it was like she could feel the presence of her friend alive and well. Still in the business of helping broken people. That was and always would be a perfect description of Jean Brown. Even after Jean's death, her kindness and goodness were living on through the outreach of the Hillbrooke Counseling Center and other foundations Tom opened in her name.

Fauna opened the passenger side door and slid into the car. "I have some great news. You want it now, or shall I dangle the carrot all the way through lunch?"

Callan had worked on her facial expressions of grief when Fauna finally shared the fact that she wasn't pregnant, but she couldn't hide her shock at this. "What? If you have news to share—do it now. Tell all."

Fauna laughed like a teenager trying to attract someone's attention from across the room. "Well, I won't drag it out another moment. I hope you're ready for this. Snake and I are getting a 3-year old girl through foster care in a matter of days."

Callan's expression was like eye candy to Fauna. Callan didn't even try to hide her excitement at the news. She threw her arms around Fauna's neck embracing her while crying with joy. "I'm so happy! A girl! Three years old? That's as good as a baby! What do you know about her? What does she look like? Are her parents still in the picture? Will you be able to adopt her?"

Fauna held up her hand and said, "Whoa, all we know for sure right now is—the three-year-old girl part. There were some vague comments about the child being troubled, but Snake and I are all in for whatever. We are ready to love this little girl with all our hearts all the way to wholeness."

Callan pressed her back against the car seat and looked forward out the windshield. "I'm giddy with excitement for you! I'm glad you didn't wait to spring this on me in a public place." Callan softly clapped her hands together and sang in a high voice. "It's a girl." Then she laughed and said, "I can already see Snake carrying that little sweetie into church with her arms around his neck. The sweet little thing holding on to his beard and laughing. Oh, life is good! God is good!"

***

Issie found a quiet spot in the gym bathroom to call her mom before her last class. She had to let her know she'd be home later than usual. Even though she wasn't ready to tell her parents what was going on, she didn't want to upset her by causing worry—sooner than she had to. She could feel her parents' concern the past few months, but she just wasn't ready to talk. Now, the doors of choice were closing, and time was running out.

Issie felt the anxiety of what was coming. The lid was about to be blown off their happy home and all of it would be her fault for being such a dummy.

It was she who believed the lies. It was she who let down her guard. She knew exactly what she was doing. She had allowed things to go too far. She barely knew the boy. He was visiting family in town for the summer. She had pushed the *good feeling* envelope a bit too far. There were no excuses that she could give that would lay the blame at another's feet.

She had been fully informed by her parents about safe sex and abstinence. She was taught by her church in righteous living and being cautious about youthful affections running amuck. She had battled her whole life with a strong will and independent thinking. There were plenty of safe people she could have talked to, but no, she had it under control and now there is a whole other human life weighing in the balance. Isabelle had refrained from calling the bump in her belly a human life—until now.

Issie went into one of the bathroom stalls and dialed her mom's cell. The phone rang. She whispered, "Please don't pick up, please don't pick up." After the fourth ring, the phone went to voice mail and Issie gave a sigh of relief, then left her message. "Hey, Mom. I'm on my way to class and wanted to let you know I'd be home late. I made an appointment with Mrs. Parker at 4 P.M. I didn't want you to worry about where I was. That's all."

Isabelle was relieved it was her mom's voice mail. The last thing she wanted to do between classes was play the 20-question game with her mom. Now all she had to do was bide her time and get through her last class by making a list of the things she would tell Ms. Parker.

Issie was in a fog as she walked mindlessly to her class. When she entered the classroom, most of the students were seated. She went to an open desk near the back of the room and laid her books on the desktop. The bell rang, and the teacher began droning on about term papers and final grades.

Isabelle took out her notebook and began writing. First, she would break the news to Ms. Parker that she was going on five months pregnant. Then she would ask her if she wanted the details or could they just move on from there. She wrote down: #2. What should I do now? (keep, abort, adopt) #3. If I choose to abort, do my parents even need to know? #4. I haven't seen a doctor yet. #5. If I have no other choice, how will I ever tell my parents? #6. Baylee knows.

Issie began to draw flowers on the side of the page as she thought about Baylee's reaction the day they talked. It was kinda freaky how mature her little sister was in the way she doled out advice. Actually, it was really scary the way Baylee could be 100% kid and 100% adult—minutes apart.

Issie placed her elbow on the desk and rested her head on her open hand. She reread the points to be discussed with Ms. Parker. The teacher's voice was like a sound machine humming in the background. The teacher grilled the students on the upcoming test, but Issie's thoughts were not on American History. They had turned inward. What a mess I've made of things.

She looked at the classroom clock. She was sure it was broken, or time was standing still.

***

Laura Klingburg closed the file of CeCe Jefferson. She leaned back in her chair and cupped her hands behind her head. She breathed deeply through her clenched teeth to silence the need to scream. When she got home, she'd need a shower after reading this file.

Most of all, she wanted to shake Helen Franko until she fell unconscious. The motives of Helen were perfectly clear, and they were not to help lighten her load in the least. Unless the helping was in regard to cleaning up Helen's mess by removing the personal reprimands Helen had received that remain as fact in CeCe's file.

No wonder Helen wanted to get her hands on CeCe's file. She wanted nothing more than to hide the child away to keep her reprehensible mistakes a secret. How does one act so haphazardly and place children in harm's way? And then care more for themselves than the wounds of a child?

Ms. K prayed, "Lord, please restore to CeCe what the locusts have eaten."

5

Blessed are the merciful, for they shall receive mercy.
Matthew 5:7

Isabelle sat across from Ms. Parker's desk in the pinstriped swivel arm chair. The office was decorated in gray tones with two pinstriped chairs for a pop of color. Issie had been in Ms. Parker's office many times over the past few years. She had shared a lot of her life over the years with Ms. Parker in this very room. Isabelle soaked in the calm atmosphere of the office. From the day the clinic was dedicated, it was Issie's safe place. With Ms. Parker, she felt at ease to share her deepest secrets.

Issie tried to show confidence as she held her back upright and leaned away from the back of the chair. As she made eye contact with Ms. Parker, her mind raced back to their first encounter. Ms. Parker was the substitute school counselor then and she wasn't married to Mr. Snake. That was when Victor Darwin, the false healer, was still in town—the freaky-creepy pervert. And that was before Baylee was healed.

Even then, there was something wonderful about Ms. Parker with the butterfly tattoo on her face, long black hair and hippie clothes. Issie remembered how Ms. Parker could see right through all her attitude and pain—right to the heart of the issue. But this time it wasn't mom issues, sister issues, dad issues or even teen issues.

She was no longer the 14-year-old sulking teen—now she battled a profound personal failure. It dug deep into her very being. Another person was being formed within her—another life. What was she going to do?

Fauna smiled at Isabelle sitting across from her. Fauna felt that this moment needed a gentler touch. She moved from the formalness of sitting behind her desk to a comfortable spot on the sofa. Isabelle swiveled her chair to face Fauna.

"So, what's been going on with you, Isabelle?" Fauna reached for one of the throw pillows at the corner of the sofa and rested her arms on top of it in her lap.

Issie pulled out a folded-up paper from her jacket pocket. She smoothed the page on her lap and looked at the numbered questions. Her eyes focused on number one. A wave of nausea rumbled through the pit of her stomach. She closed her eyes, took a deep breath and blurted out, "I'm pregnant."

Fauna wasn't blind. The weight gain was obvious when she saw Issie walk into her office. She had decided not to jump to the obvious conclusion her eyes were pushing on her brain. In the past, she had guessed people pregnant because of weight gain and it was not so—much to her embarrassment. She decided long ago never to do that again. She told herself many times, you can *think* whatever you want, but say nothing in regard to the size of a woman's mid-section.

When Issie came in with the baggy clothes she hoped it was just a bit of puberty weight gain that she was trying to hide. But nope. She's preggers. Fauna asked, "Do you know how far along you are?" Everything in her wanted to jump up and hug the girl. She knew that she'd been carrying this for some time—alone. Fauna made herself remain seated and fought to keep her own emotions in check.

Isabelle fumbled with the paper she held. "I know when it happened because it was just once. It was July."

Fauna counted out the months in her mind resisting the urge to finger-count. "Sooo, that makes you about four or almost five months?"

"I guess. That sounds about right. I haven't told my parents or been to a doctor. I think I took about 20 of the home tests. Talk about depressing, every time I saw the word 'pregnant', or the blue line, or the word 'yes' I wanted to cry. I tried every brand on the market all with the same unwanted results. Then there was the other obvious thing…I haven't had a period since June and then there's this…" Issie took both of her index fingers and pointed at her belly area, raised her eyebrows then shrugged her shoulders. She knew she was making light of the situation, but if she didn't, the tears and shame would take her to a place she didn't want to go—again.

"Isabelle, you know the first thing we need to do is bring your parents into the loop. They need to know. You're still a minor and they love you dearly. They wouldn't want you to walk through this alone."

…and with those words Issie's best efforts to hold her tears at bay ended.

Fauna pushed decorum out the exit door and tossed the pillow on her lap to the side, leaned over to Issie's chair and swallowed the *little mother* up in her arms. This wasn't just any client telling her woes. This was Issie.

Fauna held her.

***

Emily Edwards, Snake's younger sister, stopped by their mom's house with *the Little Gentleman* in tow. Maddie was at school. This was the best time to talk to her mom without Maddie taking it all in. She was already wise beyond her years and keenly aware of adult conversations.

Emily couldn't hold the news much longer about her pregnancy. She wanted her mom to be the first one to know. Her mom had always been the go-to-person throughout her life when she had concerns, confusion or confessions.

Emily pushed open the front door of her childhood home and yelled. "Mom are you home?" It actually felt pointless to ask this question because her mom was always home. It seemed the only thing that got Marilyn out of the house was shopping for household needs, doing church business or involvement in her small group. Other than those things—she was home.

Over the past few years since Jean Brown's death, her mom had become a bit more reclusive than normal. Marilyn was happy to entertain the family on a moment's notice and her grandchildren were still the thing that brought a twinkle to her eyes, but anything beyond that didn't hold much interest for her.

Emily could tell at the last family dinner that her mom was excited about Snake and Fauna's news. She didn't question her dad's lack of excitement that night. Instead she just wrote it off. This was her father good or bad. He was slow to warm up to new ideas and new ways of doing things. Starting a family in any other way than the traditional way, would take James Fields time.

She prayed that there would not be a resurrection of past hurts between her father and Snake over her pregnancy versus the foster child of Snake and Fauna. Emily told herself that if her father was unable to shower love on a hurting child then she would overcompensate because any child in her brother's care was family to her.

The Little Gentleman bolted past his mom and made a beeline into the kitchen to the exact spot where his grandma kept the candy bowl. Emily stopped at the entryway mirror and stood sideways to examine her baby bump.

A huge crash reverberated through the house. Emily's motherly alarm rushed through her whole body as she hurried to the kitchen half expecting to see the side of the house collapsed.

William stood with both hands over his ears, a metal bowl at his feet and candy on the floor all around him. The look on his face brought a smile to Emily. "That must have been scary dropping that bowl. I think you got a bit too excited. Choose one piece for yourself, pick up the rest of the candy and put it back in the bowl." Emily knew the noise would soon bring her mom from wherever she was in the house.

Behind Emily, the basement door flew opened and Marilyn stood in the doorway with a surprised look on her face. "That nearly scared me to death. If I hadn't heard your voice, I don't know what I'd have done. My phone is charging upstairs. I would have been trapped in that dungeon of a basement thinking I had some very clumsy intruders robbing the place."

"What were you doing in the basement?" Emily questioned.

"Cleaning up a mess. Nothing of interest. What are you doing here? You are both a blessed distraction for me today."

"I just wanted to stop over and see you. Should I have called first?" Emily knew the answer to this question before she asked.

"Of course not. You are always welcome to stop in whenever you like."

"Mom, can we sit down and talk?"

"Is this a good or bad sit and talk?" Marilyn laughed, but wasn't sure what to expect next.

Emily called out over her back as she plopped down on the sofa in the adjoining family room. "It's all good— promise. But first, I gotta know what you think about Snake and Fauna's news. Did you talk with dad about it after we left?"

Marilyn put a coffee pod in the machine and pulled two cups from the shelf. She put one cup on the tray under the pot and pushed the button to begin the brew. Turning her attention back to Emily she let out a huge sigh, "Your father! He'll come around in his own sweet time. He always does. He moves slower than molasses in January when it comes to all things that touch his emotion button."

"Why can't he just be happy for them? He knows they want children and have been trying for a while. They want kids and there are so many kids out there that need good homes. It all seems perfectly wonderful to me."

Marilyn pulled the finished mug of coffee out, replaced the pod in the machine with a new one and slid her favorite mug under the spot as she responded. "On paper it may seem wonderful, but your father comes from old school thinking. He's a firm believer in that saying, 'the sins of the father are visited upon the children.' His grandfather, his father and he struggled with some of the same control issues and the inability to handle being disagreed with. Even your brother has had his own struggles. Thank God there was a bit of me in both of you to bring balance." Marilyn laughed at her own joke, but in her heart, she believed it wholly. "Come to think of it, with Zak's past, I'm surprised they can even BE foster parents."

Emily quickly replied. "Mom, Fauna told me that they checked that all out before they applied. You have to have five years without any drug violations to qualify. Also, a person's past legal issues cannot be violent in nature against another or against children in anyway. We both know that's not who Zak is or ever was."

Marilyn pulled her cup from the brewer and added an ample amount of cream to both cups. She walked into the family room where Emily sat cozied up on the sofa. Marilyn handed her daughter one cup and took the other cup and sat on the opposite end of the couch.

William had pulled out the box of toys his grandparents kept especially for his visits. He was fully occupied putting together a train set that was beginning to engulf the room.

Emily took a sip of the hot coffee then said, "Mom, the thing that I want to talk with you about is wonderful, but I'm having some concerns about how to share it with Snake, I mean Zak, and especially Fauna."

Marilyn turned her attention from the transatlantic railroad being constructed by her grandson to her daughter. "Hey, I'm all ears—out with it."

Emily shifted in her seat, pulled her legs up under her and turned her body to look directly at her mother. She took a deep breath and began. "Mom...in late March or early April we'll be welcoming another baby to our family."

Marilyn's eyes grew larger and her eyebrows arched in wonder. "You—you're having a baby?" There was a slight pause before Marilyn continued, "That means you're four, almost five months. Why didn't you tell us sooner? Is there something wrong? Did you think you would miscarry?" Then Marilyn looked directly at Emily's face. One good look spoke a volume of information. Marilyn whispered a one-word question. "Fauna?"

Emily's eyes became moist. "I kept waiting. I was hoping they would have their own announcement before me, but when nothing happened, week after week, I knew I needed to tell, and I need to tell them too. I was thinking that I should tell them sooner than later since they are excited about getting their foster child. What do you think? Would it lighten the blow?"

"Emily, every life deserves to be celebrated and that goes for the one you are carrying." Marilyn scooted down the sofa until she was close enough to place her hand on Emily's belly. "This baby shouldn't be hidden. Your brother and Fauna will rejoice with you."

"Mom, I know how they feel. Fauna and I have talked. She's shared with me how painful it has been when another person announces they're pregnant and she's not. Not so long ago, she told me about someone that she knew who chose abortion over adoption. There was nothing she could do. She couldn't even tell them that she would love to adopt the baby and now that baby is no more." Emily stopped talking and clenched her teeth to hold back sobbing.

Marilyn slipped her arms around her daughter and pulled her close. They held on to each other for a few moments before Marilyn spoke. "Since you came for my advice let me give it. Tell them. The sooner the better. Even before they get their little girl. Their hearts are full now and expectant, but regardless, I would give them the benefit of the doubt. I know they will want to rejoice with you."

Emily brushed her tears away. "I know you're right, Mom, but my heart was aching for them to the point of not thinking clearly. I'm gonna blame it on hormones." She stood up and pulled her top close to her tummy to reveal a small baby bump. "I'll talk to Kota tonight, and we'll tell them within the week."

Marilyn replied. "I think that's a great idea. Do you want to tell Dad or shall I?"

"Is he home now or at work?"

"He'll be home for lunch. Why don't you and William stay for lunch and you can tell him then. He'll be over the moon excited."

Emily felt a bit conflicted by that statement. Yes, her dad would be over the moon excited for this new grandchild, but what about Snake and Fauna's little girl? Would he be able to love her or even accept her? Emily tried to swallow, but her throat felt thick and dry.

***

Baylee Hayes sat at the dining room table with a few textbooks scattered around her. She rested her head on her propped-up hand. Focus was difficult between the noise her mom was making in the nearby kitchen and the thoughts of Issie being pregnant. And where was Issie anyway? She should be home by now. She wouldn't, couldn't, didn't go to…Baylee's thoughts were interrupted by her mother.

"Baylee, can you come here for a minute?" Her mom called from the kitchen.

Baylee didn't answer but pushed away from the table and ambled into the kitchen. She scooted onto one of the bar stools and looked at her mom anticipating what her mom might need.

Samantha looked at her little girl who once couldn't function without her physical help. Where had that little girl gone? Samantha looked at her youngest daughter observing her big eyes and maturing face. She had grown into a smart and capable budding teenager.

Baylee was able to walk and run like any other child her age since the Lord miraculously touched her. Samantha remembered the night of Baylee's healing. The sound of bones cracking back into place still stirred-up the emotions of that night.

Samantha swallowed hard before phrasing her question, "Bay, has Issie said anything to you about how she's been feeling? I've noticed she's been withdrawn lately."

Baylee listened but didn't speak.

Samantha twisted her mouth from side to side and continued. "I've been worried about her especially since, well, you know depression can be a problem for teens and she's been gaining weight. Have you noticed that?"

Baylee glanced out the kitchen window while her mom talked. Her thoughts were churning as she pondered how she would maneuver through this inquisition without compromising her relationship with Isabelle.

Baylee broke the silence. "Have you tried talking with Issie?"

Samantha's face filled with hope. Had they begun a real conversation? Samantha quickly replied, "I've tried, but she's keeping me at arm's length again." She paused, "You must remember how it used to be. I'm worried. Did she tell you that she's talking with Ms. Parker right now?"

"Really? She didn't tell me." Baylee was happy to admit she didn't know and equally thrilled to know the baby was safe—for now. Maybe this truthful admission would get her mom to stop asking her questions.

"Yeah, she is. She called me today from school and said that she'd be stopping there. She got her own ride there too. She'll call me to pick her up when she's done. So, she didn't tell you about this?"

"Nope. Not a word. But if you're worried, I'd say that Issie talking to Ms. Parker is the best news. Ms. Parker has a way of getting to the heart of an issue. I'm sure any concerns you have will all come to light very soon." Baylee wanted to put her hand over her mouth. She was sure that her chatter sounded like she was hiding something. She chided herself to keep it short.

"Baylee, you amaze me with your maturity. I hope she'll

be ready to talk when she gets home today. I spoke with Mrs. Douglas about asking Isabelle to go out for a talk. I hope Issie won't be mad at me for doing that."

Baylee swallowed hard and imagined her hand pressed tightly across her mouth. Her brain kept telling her mouth to be quiet. *Just nod, don't speak*, but her mouth won. "Issie doesn't have that kind of relationship with Mrs. Douglas. That could be awkward for her."

"Oh. How could a friendly chat with the pastor's wife be awkward?"

Don't talk, don't speak, don't engage, walk away... "Ahhhhhh."

Samantha's eyes narrowed as she met Baylee's. "You know something don't you. What are you hiding? Baylee?"

"Mom, you need to talk to Issie about Issie and me about me. Okay?" Baylee pushed away from the countertop and slid off the stool. She collected her books from the dining room table and headed upstairs. She needed separation from her mom before she became a fountain of information.

***

Fauna stopped talking. Isabelle's eyes were puffy and red. Her face was blotchy too. She passed the other throw pillow beside her on the couch to Issie. Issie reached out for it without saying a word and held it tightly against her chest.

"Isabelle does this sound like a good plan to you?" They were now over an hour into their talk together. Fauna was sitting back on the sofa embracing her pillow while Isabelle clutched her pillow in the swivel chair a few feet in front of Fauna.

"Yes, I know they have to be told. Especially since I'm a minor." Isabelle pressed the clutched pillow against her chest.

"Okay, tell me again how you see this playing out." Fauna leaned forward and rested her folded arms across the pillow on her lap.

Issie cleared her throat and began, "I'll call my mom to tell her that you'll be driving me home. You'll come in the house with me, and we'll all, Baylee included, sit together in the family room. Then I'll tell them." Tears rolled freely down her reddened face, but she pressed on. "I'll let them ask me any questions and I'll answer them honestly to the best of my ability."

"That's great Isabelle. And don't forget…" Before Fauna could finish her reminder, Issie resumed.

"I'll need to remember that they are just hearing this information and may not respond well. I'll need to give them time before we can have a real dialogue about the future." Isabelle recited the information like she was reading it off a teleprompter.

Fauna's eyes widened. "Wow! You really are a great listener. Just one more thing. Your parents may want to ask Baylee to leave the room. How do you feel about that?"

"She already knows. I'm not sure if my parents will be mad that she knew before them and didn't tell or if they will feel she is too young to be involved in this kind of a conversation." Issie sighed. The reality of what was coming was resonating in her spirit and it didn't feel good to her at all.

Fauna reached for Isabelle's hand. "Remember to extend grace to them no matter how they respond. This is a lot to take in for your parents, to hear their 17-year-old daughter is pregnant. Extend grace to them. You won't regret it."

Issie latched onto Fauna's hand like a drowning child. "Can we pray? Grace has never been my strength—ya know."

"I was just about to recommend that." Fauna took a deep breath and closed her eyes. *"Lord, we need You to be the buffer here. Please send Your Holy Spirit, to go before us and soften every emotion and every attitude. Strengthen Isabelle with Your peace and help her surrender her attitudes and any need to defend herself over to You. You are her Defender. You are her Refuge. You are her Hiding Place. You can redeem this situation from the pit of destruction. Protect the new life that is being formed and fashioned in Your image. Speak peace to the potential storm that awaits. Silence the wind and the waves before they have opportunity to cause even a morsel of damage. Lord, Isabelle and I agree together in Your precious name for this to be done. Your name is all powerful and it is able to bring healing to every situation. Amen."*

6

For judgment is without mercy to one who has shown no mercy.
Mercy triumphs over judgment.
James 2:13 (ESV)

P astor Rey Douglas stepped into the kitchen, dropped his backpack that was overloaded with study books and his laptop. Callan looked up from her dinner prep and tried to hide her glee.

"What's up?" Rey could see right through her attempt. She knew something.

"I was going to wait until after dinner to tell you, but since you asked. Fauna and I had lunch today. Did you know?" Callan was rubbing her hands together like a mad scientist.

"You didn't tell her that I told you that she wasn't pregnant, did you?"

Callan kept her emotions on task. "Ha! So, you don't know." Callan looked triumphant. There was a sing-song tune to her next words. "Finally. I know something you don't know."

"Well, you tell me what you know, and I'll confirm or deny if I knew." Rey's comeback was not convincing.

Callan gave Rey her Cheshire cat smile. "Sounds like a fishing expedition to me. I'll tell you, but I must say beforehand that…" Callan couldn't get out the rest of her sentence without laughing. "…this is highly confidential."

"Out with it Miss Sassy Pants." Rey was becoming impatient.

"Snake and Fauna are getting a little girl through foster care. She's three years old and that's all I know…except it could be as soon as the end of the week or the beginning of next. Isn't that amazing?"

Rey smiled but didn't respond to the level that Callan

expected.

"Rey, what's wrong? Aren't you happy for them?"

"Well, of course, but fostering isn't pink dresses and bows. This little girl is in foster care for a reason. I'm guessing it isn't pretty. And it may not be permanent. Kids get returned to their parents all the time and it can be traumatic, sad and ugly for everyone involved."

Callan's smile faded along with her inner joy. "Who replaced my husband with Debbie Downer?"

"I'm not being a downer, just a realist who has sat across the table from both foster parents and parents whose kids were in the system. If Snake and Fauna are brave enough to do this, I just hope they are fully prepared. It's not gonna be a Hallmark movie or a picnic in the park. Fostering will open the door to the darker side of humanity. It ain't pretty."

Callan walked into the family room, dropped into the recliner and curled her feet up under her. She really wanted to get into the fetal position, but she didn't. "Do you think they are making a mistake helping this little girl? What did that little girl ever do to deserve this life?"

"No, Callan! That's not it at all. I think fostering is the noblest of ministries for families to get involved in. I just know it rarely turns out to be everything the foster family hopes it will be." Rey walked to where Callan was and knelt on the floor next to her chair. "Really, I'm happy for them and believe they will be amazing foster parents. I just don't think it's something that I personally could do. You're not thinking about it are you?"

Callan looked at Rey with a surprised expression. "You thought I was priming the pump to see if we could be foster parents?"

"You have hinted, lately, about how much you would love to have a little girl and..." Rey felt he was treading on dangerous ground right now. If he kept moving in this dangerous direction, they could be adding another baby to the Douglas household. Back it up...back it up. "Well then, I guess we better add this little girl, whoever she is, to our nightly prayer time and of course, Fauna and Snake. If God brings this child to their home, it's for a reason. Who am I to judge?"

Callan frowned and turned her mouth to one side in a questioning way. "What just happened? Are you for or against? I'm confused."

"I'm *for*, but with a heavy dose of reality as the cherry on top."

Callan lifted her chin in the air with a contemplative frown on her face. "I feel like there's something more going on here. What are you trying to pull over on me?"

Rey leaned in and hugged his wife. A feeling of relief washed over him. He was nearly 40 and the thought of adding another child to their family didn't bode well. Snake and Fauna were much younger and more capable, in his opinion, to handle whatever challenges came their way. He hoped.

Callan interrupted his thoughts as she pushed back from his hug. "Samantha stopped over today too."

"That's nice. It seems like it's been awhile since we've socialized with them. Did you have plans with her?"

"No. It was a surprise visit. Which is not like Samantha—at all. She asked me to touch base with Isabelle. She's concerned she is suicidal or something."

Rey's head jerked back with shock. "What? Did Isabelle say it outright or is it a feeling?"

"Oh, I got the impression it was a feeling that Samantha was having. Or should I say concern. I couldn't imagine Isabelle would ever contemplate doing such a thing. Seeing all the Lord has done in her life these past years."

"Are you going to reach out to her?" Rey asked.

Callan stood up and walked towards the kitchen. "Well, of course. How could I not? Samantha came here asking. She looked so worried." Callan stopped and turned back to look at Rey. "Yet, I don't really have that type of relationship with Isabelle. It just feels awkward. Ya know?"

"How about if after dinner we drop in to see them?

Then we can assess the situation more clearly firsthand."

Callan nodded then cupped her hands and yelled down the hallway. "Boys, it's dinner time."

Two handsome young men walked into the family room. Ty was 12 and Zander was 15. Callan was amazed at their growth the past few years. Her little boys had been replaced by budding men. Much to her dismay, she had already spotted sprouts of facial hair on Zander's face.

Zander put his arm around his mom's shoulders and kissed the top of her head. "What's for dinner?"

Callan felt warm from her head to her toes and prayed to herself, *Lord, grow them to be men of God. Led by You and not by the voice of this world.*

***

Fauna pulled into the Hayes family driveway and slowed the car to a full stop. She moved the gear to park and looked at Isabelle, "Are you ready for this?"

"I don't see how I have much of a choice." Issie picked nervously at her thumbnail.

"I'm sorry Isabelle. I know this isn't easy." Fauna opened her car door and took the lead. Issie followed a few steps behind. Fauna spoke over her shoulder to Issie, "Okay, let's do this."

When they reached the door, Fauna stepped to the side and Issie opened the front door. A wave of fear, disappointment and shame washed over Isabelle.

Fauna put her hand on Issie's back, leaned in and whispered. "He never leaves us. He never forsakes us—and I'm right here too."

Isabelle crossed over the threshold into her house. Memories flashed through her mind: the anger she had felt, the meanness she had inflicted on others, spitefulness, her self-destructive ways. Then two years ago there was redemption, healing, joy, reconciliation, forgiveness, rebuilding, and so much more. She drew in a breath and softly prayed. "Jesus. Help *all* of us get through this."

Fauna heard her prayer and felt a wave of emotion. She wanted to cradle Isabelle like a baby and carry her through the next hour. However, as the picture formed in her mind, it wasn't she who carried Isabelle, but Jesus. He was there. She could feel it. He was removing rocks from Isabelle's path making what was crooked straight just as His Word said He would do.

Samantha peeked out from the kitchen. "Oh, hi Fauna. Thanks for bringing Issie home. Can you stay for dinner?"

Before Fauna could respond, Isabelle asked, "Mom, is Dad home?"

"He should be pulling in any minute. He called to say he was on his way." Samantha came out of the kitchen wiping her hands on a dish towel. Looking at Isabelle, Samantha asked, "So, did you have a nice talk with Ms. Parker?" Samantha gave Fauna a wink. A show of relief showed on Samantha's face.

Isabelle turned towards the family room, away from her mother's view and replied, "Yes, when Dad gets here, I need to talk to you both, and Ms. Parker is going to stay. Baylee too."

Samantha's smile faded. She looked at Fauna and asked, "Is this gonna be bad?"

Fauna walked into the family room and sat down next to Issie on the short side of the sectional sofa. She didn't reply to Samantha's question.

Isabelle did. "Mom, could you ask Baylee to come down here too?"

The sound of the garage door opening, hurried Samantha up the stairs. A few minutes later, Baylee followed her mom into the family room where Stuart sat chatting with Fauna.

Stuart looked around for the first time assessing the scene and asked, "Is this some kind of intervention or something?" He laughed, then noticed Isabelle's face was red and puffy. Samantha looked ash gray with worry evident on her face. Baylee looked like the cat who swallowed the mouse and Fauna kept her sight fixed on Isabelle.

Stuart spoke again, "Okay, out with it. Something is amiss here and I'm not a game player, so give it to me straight. Is something going on with you Iss?"

***

The sons of Pastor Rey and Callan Douglas, Zander and Ty, had stopped sharing a bedroom a few years back. Each wanted a bit more privacy as they entered the next stage of their lives. Zander was in his room alone when Ty tapped on the partially open door. "Can I come in?"

"Sure. What's up?"

"I saw you talking with Isabelle at school today. Anything going on with you two that a brother ought to know about?"

"Don't be crazy." Zander rolled his eyes then became reflective. "I wish. I've been trying for years to get her to notice me, but no such luck. I'm hoping if I hang around a lot and be a good listener that she might look at me like I'm more than a boy next door and more like a boy to be noticed."

"Don't go there. I can tell she's dealing with something. You don't want to get mixed up in whatever she has going on. You gotta be careful with *the girls*."

"And what do *you* know about *the girls*." Zander threw his head back and laughed in a mocking way.

Ty stepped inside of Zander's bedroom and closed the door behind him. "I listen in church and I read my Bible. We are entering a dangerous time in our lives. Pastor Eli said that we should not awaken love before it's time."

"Who said anything about love? I like her. I think she's pretty. I wouldn't mind getting to know her outside the friend circle. Maybe sit by her in youth group. I'm not looking to marry her." He paused. "At least not right now."

"Zander, I can't explain it. When I saw you two talking,

66

it was like a warning alarm went off in my head. Be careful. Just be careful. I know this isn't something you want to hear from a younger brother, but I need to tell you what I felt, especially when I believe it's from the Lord."

"Message received. Sometimes you are a freak with all this hearing from the Lord stuff." Zander grabbed his guitar that was leaning against the wall by his desk. "I'm going to practice for youth group. Good talk though." He waved a dismissive hand in Ty's direction.

Ty closed the door behind him as he left the room. His spirit was grieved. He knew what he felt, and he knew it was from the Lord. There was no question in his mind about that. He walked down the hallway mumbling, "Warnings are meant to be listened to."

Callan poked her head into the hallway. "What are meant to be listened to?"

"Ahhh, nothing Mom. Just talking to myself."

Callan smirked. "Well, don't make a habit of that. Are you boys going to be okay? Dad and I are stepping out for a bit."

"Sure, Mom. Zander's playing his guitar and I'm heading to my room."

Ty closed the door and knelt next to his bed. His heart felt grieved. This was not a new thing. He knew the Lord was about to use him to intercede for someone— something—somewhere. He buried his face in the comforter that covered the bed. First, he prayed with his understanding and then as the Spirit led.

***

"I'm sorry." Isabelle blurted out.

"Sorry for what? I don't understand." Samantha sat next to Stuart on the sofa side of the sectional. A large footstool separated them from Fauna and Isabelle.

Fauna interjected, "Give her just a minute. She needs to tell you something."

Baylee had been standing in the entryway. She slid into the chair furthest from ground zero and closest to the exit.

Isabelle told herself. *Just do it. Do it. Don't drag this thing out for another moment.* She sat up from her slouched position on the sofa and without emotion spoke the words, "I'm pregnant."

No one spoke for a long time—too long— uncomfortably long. Fauna kept her eyes on Isabelle but didn't interrupt the process going on. It was deafeningly silent, yet accusation hung in the air.

Finally, Stuart found his voice. It was quiet, controlled, professional. "Have you seen a doctor?"

"No."

"Do you know how far along you are?"

"Maybe four, almost five months."

"Okay, there's still time. Now we must think in weeks not months. The ultrasound will actually make the decision for us. Anything less than 20 weeks and we're golden."

Fauna wanted to scream. Stuart was a doctor, but he was serving up a death sentence to his own grandchild. It was cold and calculated. She kept quiet.

"Dad, I don't know if that's what I want. Maybe. But there are other options. Adoption is one and..." Issie looked down at the floor. "Me keeping the baby is another."

Samantha's voice was barely audible. "Sweetie, you're only 17 and what about college?"

"Lots of girls keep their babies who are much younger than me." There was a snappy tone to her voice and she regretted it immediately. "I'm not ready to make any decisions today."

"Tomorrow, you're coming to the clinic with me. We'll get the ultrasound and go from there." Stuart spoke with authority and finality.

Isabelle wanted to bolt from the room. Run and hide away from the people trying to run her life. She glanced at Baylee who was across the room trying to be invisible. Her face was void of emotion. Nothing like the confident Baylee who a week ago spoke to her with such assurance.

Isabelle surveyed the room. In her estimation, there was not one family member in the room throwing her a lifeline.

Then the question came that was hanging in the air. It was Stuart who asked, "And who is the father?"

Isabelle drew her lips inward and bit down. Her face quivered, but she didn't speak.

"So, you're not telling? Are you trying to protect him? I'm going to find out." Her father's voice was stern.

Isabelle kept quiet as hot tears rolled down her face and dripped onto her oversized top. She tried to brush them away as fast as they fell but there were so many of them she couldn't keep up.

Stuart frowned and with a huff exhaled, "You're not saying there was more than one guy, are you?"

This time Fauna's head jerked up. She looked directly at Stuart. With her best nonverbal communication, she let him know he'd crossed a line that he may never come back from.

The doorbell played a scale of chimes. The tension in the room caused everyone including Stuart to jump in their seats at the sound.

Samantha questioned, "Who in the world could that be? Right now, of all times." She walked to the door ready to lay into the Girl Scout or the person wanting to replace her windows. Without checking to see who it was she pulled the door open ready to engage.

"Hi Samantha. Rey and I felt led to stop over. We thought you guys might want to talk." Callan paused when she saw the pain on her friend's face. "Is this a bad time? We can go."

"No. Come in. Actually, you couldn't have come at a better time. This must be one of those God things."

***

Tom Brown finished packing up the last box of photos and decorations he had carefully stacked on the dining room table. He had already packed all the boxes that would be shipped to his daughters. They were stacked neatly in the garage awaiting the UPS. The movers would arrive tomorrow for what furnishings he had kept after the moving sale. Downsizing to a two bed/two bath condo had been harder than he ever imagined.

Seeing memory after memory piled in the back of cars and pick-ups as people bartered for items that had been a part of his life with Jean had nearly broken him. He was extremely thankful for the ladies of the church who came to help under Callan's direction. If it hadn't been for the kindness of the church ladies, he would not have made it through this painful process.

Tom's newly built condo was on a smaller lake in a gated community and near Community Outreach Church. Since Jean's passing and his recent resignation as VP of the solar energy plant—it was time to leave behind the large house that had become a sort of monument or museum to Jean's memory. That was not what she would have wanted for him. This he knew without a doubt.

Now that his business schedule had been trimmed down to the few charity boards and church activities, he felt emptier than ever. Life around him had continued after Jean's passing, but for him it still seemed recent. He could feel her presence in that house. Maybe moving from the Deer Lake house would finally give him the closure he needed to move on to whatever the Lord had next for him.

Tom's daughters had each begged him to settle near them, but his activities in the Hillbrooke community gave him the feeling of being useful and contributing to the well-being of others. Being a young 67 didn't make him feel ready to sit on a beach in warm weather when he still felt he had much to contribute.

Tom took the packaging tape and rolled it over the box that held so many wonderful memories. This particular box was going into storage. Tom rubbed his hand over the new tape as he remembered the day that he and Jean first arrived in Hillbrooke. It was a newspaper article, of all things, that brought them to the right church at the right time. The Lord answered their prayer more graciously than he ever could have imagined.

Hillbrooke was home, the church was family and Tom was well known in the community. He couldn't wrap his mind around the idea of starting all over again in a new place. He had always relied on the leading of the Lord in his life, and there was no peaceful assurance that moving to a new place was God's plan for his life. More likely, he believed that God was growing his roots even deeper in Hillbrooke. He was open to whatever direction the Lord led, but first—the move.

7

As holy people whom God has chosen and loved,
be sympathetic, kind, humble, gentle, and patient.
Colossians 3:12 (GW)

S nake was on his way home from work when his car phone rang. The caller I.D. showed Ms. Klingburg. He pushed the accept button on his dashboard then answered. "Hello."

"Hi Zak. I tried Fauna's number first, but it went directly to voice mail. I knew you'd want to have this information ASAP, so I hope you don't mind me calling you. Also, do you prefer Zak or Snake?"

"Snake is fine unless that seems awkward to you. Only my mom calls me Zak." He smiled even though Ms. K couldn't see him. "Fauna is probably with a client. She turns her phone off when she's doing counseling. So, what's the ASAP news? Is it about our little girl?"

"Yes, that's why I'm calling. We can drop her off to you later tonight or in the morning. Are you ready?"

"My whole life has been ready for this very moment!"

The excitement in Snake's voice brought a smile to Ms. K but it quickly faded. "Remember CeCe has attachment issues."

"Her name is CeCe? I love her already."

"Snake, I'm telling you plain and clear, she's damaged and will need a ton of love and patience. Are you and Fauna ready for this? Your lives are about to be turned upside down."

"Ms. K, I lived four years in prison, I think we can handle a 3-year-old."

The overconfidence in Snake's voice gave her, second thoughts. "Please call me day or night if things escalate. Don't wait until you are at the end of your rope. Please remember that."

"We got this. When should we expect her?"

Ms. K had second thoughts about a night drop. "Let's do the morning. It's a weekend and that will give you time to adjust to each other before you go back to work on Monday. We'll be there at 10 A.M. She will already have had breakfast."

"So, her name is CeCe. We can't wait to meet her."

"I'll bring her file with me tomorrow and go over the necessary information. There will be many appointments that will have to be met. I know you both have full-time jobs. Have you given much thought about how you will keep the appointments?"

"Between my sister, mother, and Fauna's flexible work schedule we will make it happen."

Ms. K thought, Oh Lord, help them succeed. "Tell Fauna to call me when she gets home if she has any questions. See you tomorrow."

Snake was one block from home but turned around in the opposite direction and headed to his sister Emily's house. He pushed the handsfree calling button in his car and responded to the promptings, "Call Emily at home." The car dialed the number and he counted two rings before Emily answered.

"Hey Snake. I was just getting ready to call you."

"I'm on my way over to you."

"Is Fauna with you?"

"Nope. She's counseling, but I need something from you."

"Oh, what's that?"

"Some little girl clothes. She arrives tomorrow at 10 in the morning."

Emily screamed with excitement. "Really?"

"Yes—really! I'll be there in a few minutes. Start pulling out the boxes that say 3-year-old girl clothes."

"This is so exciting. See you soon." A smile formed on Emily's lips. "I'm so happy for you and Fauna."

"Thanks, Em. We are cautiously over the moon, too."

"I'll have the clothes ready when you get here. You can take them home to see what fits, and don't worry about getting the clothes back to me unless you don't want them."

***

Rey and Callan followed Samantha into the family room. All the somber faces caused Rey to stop in his tracks and Callan ran right into the back of him. He quickly reached behind him and squeezed her hand a bit tighter than normal pulling her to his side, so she could see the somber faces before she said something she'd regret later.

"Rey, why'd you stop dead in front of me?" Callan blurted out before surveying the room.

Rey thought, oh well, too late. He replied, "Ahh, sorry." He gave Callan's hand another squeeze. This time she looked around the room. Her best attempts couldn't hide her embarrassment. They had most certainly interrupted something serious.

In the blink of an eye, Rey moved from friend to pastor. He sat in one of the side chairs facing the loveseat where Fauna and Isabelle sat. His eyes scanned the room. In one quick motion, he detected that the tension in the room seemed to lie with Isabelle. She was the only one with a blotchy red face, obviously due to crying. What in the world had they interrupted?

Samantha sat back down next to Stuart. Callan was the only one standing and sat next to Samantha on the sofa.

Samantha broke the awkwardness, "Pastor Rey, Callan— Isabelle just told us only a few minutes ago that she's pregnant. We are all still processing."

Callan let out a gasp she couldn't take back.

Rey sat stoic in his chair still assessing the climate of the room.

Everyone looked at Pastor Rey waiting for him to say something.

He looked directly at the mother-to-be and spoke with gentleness. "Isabelle, we all know this was not what you were planning for your life at this time." Rey turned towards Dr. Hayes and Samantha, "This must be shocking news to you both as well." He paused, "Now that this news has come to light, we must ask the hard question. Where do we go from here?" Rey let the question settle on them.

Pastor Rey knew that Stuart respected him, but at this moment, Stuart's facial expression and body language were a far cry from esteem. He looked agitated at the world. Rey knew him well enough to know that Dr. Hayes was a fixer. He wanted the problem to go away and get life back on track. Rey also understood that fathers want to make things better for their children, but making it go away as fast as possible wasn't going to bring the wholeness to Isabelle that she desperately needed.

Pastor Rey kept his focus on Issie. "Isabelle, there are two lives to consider—yours and your baby's. Both of you need to be cared for. No matter what decisions are made, the priority must be what's best for both—not one over the other. I know for most of us, we have only had moments to process, and each of us will need to deal with this unexpected news in our own way. I just want to stress that the two lives of focus right now are Isabelle and the baby. This is difficult news to handle, but let's guard our words. We can't take them back. And we all know that words have the potential of causing great pain."

All eyes were on Pastor Rey.

Fauna sat hip to hip with Issie. Sometime during Pastor Rey's sharing, Fauna placed her arm around Issie and softly rubbed her arm.

Isabelle's posture had changed from the bold announcement she had given moments before Pastor Rey arrived. Now she was slumped forward, head hanging, and eyes locked on her lap. Rey didn't have a daughter, but his heart was perplexed by the lack of compassion at the sight of this girl so wounded. Not one family member was rushing to her side. No mother embracing her in her pain, or father with his strong arms wrapped around her while speaking reassuring words that his love for her was deeper and stronger than any mistake she could ever make.

Pastor Rey broke the painful silence. "Stuart, Samantha, your daughter is in great pain right now. I want to caution you to be gracious with her over the next days and weeks as you begin to accept this new chapter in all of your lives." Pastor Rey lifted his hand and pointed it boldly at Isabelle, who was sinking by the moment into a fetal position. "This is your child, who you both dearly love. I have watched your family over the past three years and I know your deep love and commitment for one another. It's in times like these that our love is tested. This is a pass or fail moment. In years to come, when you look back you're going to want this to be a pass—not a fail."

Stuart's face softened for the first time. No one could question his love or devotion for his family. Pastor Rey wouldn't judge him for not having a perfect attitude or reaction in a time like this. Rey knew that this wasn't his daughter or his family that had just been altered forever.

Samantha moved first, edging her way between the sofa and the large ottoman that blocked her direct route to Isabelle. She glanced back over her shoulder at Baylee sitting alone and quiet away from everyone. Samantha motioned with her open hand for Baylee to join her. Baylee shot out of the chair and joined her mom as she moved in Isabelle's direction.

Fauna assessed the situation and quickly moved out of the way to allow the family to have their moment. Isabelle was unaware of the movement in her direction until her mother knelt in front of her, placed her hands on Issie's knees and bent her head down low to meet her daughter's eyes.

The moment Isabelle felt her mother's touch, she wept.

"Issie, we love you. We're gonna work through this together. Nobody is pressing you for a decision today."

Samantha felt the weight of Issie's head come to rest on her shoulder. She cupped her daughter's head with her hands and held her. Samantha whispered, "No more questions today. You tell us what you want, when you're ready. We'll support whatever decision you make."

Baylee slipped into the seat that Fauna vacated and placed her head on Issie's back. She slipped one arm over Isabelle's back and the other across her mom's.

Stuart moved to join the rest of his family and placed his hand on the top of Isabelle's head. He bent down close to her ear and whispered something to her. No one other than the family could hear what Stuart said.

Callan silently motioned to Rey that it was time to go. Without saying a word, Callan, Rey and Fauna left the Hayes family to begin the healing process—again.

8

The cold evening air bit at Callan's face as she stepped off the Hayes family's front porch. Fauna was a few steps in front of her and Rey a few steps behind. Callan announced, "Well that was awkward." Her observation was directed at no one in particular but in reference to Isabelle's announcement and her family's response.

Fauna stopped and turned to face Callan, "I'm sure it caught you both by surprise, but it was certainly God's appointed time that you came when you did. I can't thank you both enough for that. By the way, whatever caused you to stop by at that exact moment?"

Callan's eyes brightened as she told her story. "Samantha stopped over before we talked and asked me to take Isabelle out for a bite to eat hoping she would open up to me. She was concerned that she was sinking into a dangerous type of depression. You know what I mean, the kind where kids do something stupid."

Fauna listened but didn't speak.

Rey hesitated for a moment to see if this conversation was going to be short, then turned to cut across the neighbor's yard. He yelled over his shoulder, "You ladies can talk outside in the cold, but I'm heading back to my warm house."

Callan pulled her coat tight around her and continued, "After my conversation with Samantha this morning, I know this announcement has caught them all by surprise without a doubt." Callan shook her head back and forth in disbelief, "Did you see Stuart? I thought he was going to have a stroke for a moment."

Fauna smiled, inhaled slightly before speaking, but wasn't quick enough.

Callan didn't wait for Fauna to answer her question. "Anyway, I was surprised that Samantha asked me and not you. I don't even have a relationship with Isabelle like you do. I see her at church and say, 'Hi.' But to get her to open up to me? Well, thank God that Isabelle handled that all on her own and called you." Callan wrapped her scarf around her neck then fumbled around in her coat pocket looking for her gloves.

Fauna seized the opportunity to speak, "God's hand was in the perfect timing of all of this. I don't even want to think how different the evening might have been if Samantha hadn't stopped over to your house, and if you and Rey wouldn't have stopped by tonight. Pastor handled the situation like a pro. Before you arrived, things were beginning to spiral downward." Fauna remembered the moment. "It was God's perfect timing without question." A gust of wind blew Fauna's long hair up into the air like a funnel cloud above her head. She wrangled the long strands into a ponytail and wrapped it around her neck like a scarf. "Please tell Pastor how much I appreciated his ability to turn an all-out death squad attack on Isabelle into an outpouring of love on a fearful and wounded child." Fauna moved to open her car door before Callan could say more.

Callan kept it brief. "Okay, we'll talk later." Callan waved as she cut through the neighbor's yard and headed home.

Fauna pressed down on the brake to start the car but stopped when she noticed her cell phone on the passenger seat next to her. She picked up the phone and pressed the on button to see how many calls, messages or notifications she had missed while with Isabelle the past few hours. There were two missed calls from Ms. K and the most recent was a missed call from Snake and a voice mail from him. She started the car and touched the screen on her phone to hear the message through her car speaker system.

"Fauna, hey. I know you are with a client, but when you get this message give me a call." Fauna thought that was the end of the message and was ready to call Snake when his voice resumed. "I was going to wait to tell you when you called, but I can't. I'm too excited. Ms. K called, and we're getting our little girl tomorrow. We could have gotten her tonight, but I knew you'd want to be here when she arrived. Plus, we have so much more to do to get things ready for her arrival." Snake's message paused again but this time Fauna waited. Snake's voice continued, "...and I'm heading over to Emily's now to pick up Maddie's old clothes that she said we could borrow. Then I'll meet you at home." There was another pause, "Oh, and her name is CeCe. Our little girl's name is CeCe. I like it. Call me. Bye."

Fauna was in an immediate battle with five emotions all at once. She was ecstatic that CeCe was coming, disappointed that she missed the call from Ms. K, mad that Snake made the decision without her about CeCe's arrival, and appreciative that he was so thoughtful to pick up the clothes all on his own. There was also a creeping doubt that was sneaking into her heart. It was whispering that she wasn't capable or up to the challenge of being a mother to a 3-year-old child.

Fauna took a deep breath in and exhaled, "Lord, we can't do this without you. Help us." She suddenly realized she was holding her phone in a death grip. Loosening her hold on the phone, she dialed Snake's number and waited for his voice.

No answer.

Fauna hung up without leaving a message, started the car and headed home. "Why would he ask me to call and then not answer?" A deep sigh escaped her lips as she pushed her emotions down a bit deeper. There was too much to do right now to give way to emotion. She was going to be a foster mother in less than 18 hours.

***

Issie felt sick and alone. She rested her head on her pillow in the dark room. She rubbed one hand over the small bump. She felt something. It was something unfamiliar like a flutter low and deep inside her abdomen. She sat up and spoke out loud. "No. It can't be." She got out of bed, went to the bathroom and turned on the light. Standing sideways she examined her body in the mirror. She was wearing a tight tee shirt that revealed her expanding form. Her sin was now revealed to her family and soon it would be known to everyone in her circle; all the youth at school and church, extended family, adults and people on the fringe of her life would all be whispering, making up their own version of who, how, when, where. Her life was about to become fodder for the community gossips.

Issie heard a soft tapping on her bedroom door. She grabbed a big sweatshirt and pulled it over her head before saying, "Come in. I'm still awake."

Baylee opened the door. The dim light from the bathroom filtered into Isabelle's bedroom. "Hey, I wanted to give you some time to process that family meeting before we talked. How are you doing with all this?"

"Thanks for the space. Mom and Dad both stopped by earlier and separately. I'm not sure if they planned it that way or what, but I'd say it was about 90% good. Dad isn't pushing, but I get the distinct feeling he would be in favor of ending the pregnancy if it's not too late. Tomorrow morning, Mom and I will be going to the clinic. Dad said to be there as soon as the doors opened, and he'd make sure I was first."

Baylee sat on the edge of her sister's bed. "I wish I could go, but I know that's not gonna happen. Will you text me as soon as you find out anything?"

"I'll try. I think Mom and Dad are still reeling from the news, but seeing it..." Isabelle stopped talking and touched her belly. "...I mean seeing the baby on the ultrasound will bring a whole new wave of emotions to all of us."

"Man, I wish I was going to be there. I want to see the pictures." Baylee stopped. "Is it okay with you that I'm excited?"

"I guess. You may be the only one who is."

"I know we aren't supposed to ask questions, but do you think you might want to keep the baby yourself and raise it?"

"I can't even focus on tomorrow, let alone—making a lifetime commitment to something...someone...this baby that I haven't even seen. Part of me thinks tomorrow the ultrasound will say there's nothing there and I'll just go on with the rest of my life."

Baylee rolled her eyes and said, "Don't kid yourself. You have a growing human being in there who deserves to live and be loved. I know you're going to choose life—I just know it. You're already calling the 'it' a baby."

Isabelle curled her lips to one side with a mocking look of disgust. "I think the ultrasound will have a lot to say about what my next step will be!"

"Do you really think you could do it? I mean have an abortion." Baylee whispered the last word like it was a swear word that she shouldn't be saying. "Have you felt the baby kick yet?"

"I don't want to talk about it anymore. It's all depressing. The idea of ending a life or raising a baby, or even allowing someone else to raise my own DNA—I wish I could go back and handle things differently."

"I'm sure you aren't the first teenager to utter those words."

Isabelle raised her voice to just under a yell, "Baylee, stop talking like you're 40 years old. Gheeze! Be a kid already!"

Baylee smiled. "Can I touch your belly?" The question was less about seeking permission and more about warning her sister she was coming. Baylee walked towards Issie with both hands extended in front of her. Isabelle didn't resist. Baylee placed her hands on the protruding abdomen of her sister knowing that her fingers were inches from the forming child that would one day be her little niece or nephew.

***

Snake was carrying a large plastic tub from the car when Fauna glanced out the window and saw him. She had to fight her disappointment at not being consulted in the decision of CeCe's arrival. She tried to calm her inner voice that was on a hair trigger, cocked and ready to fire when Snake opened the door.

"Hey, you're here. Great. Can you believe this? She's coming. It's happening."

Fauna knew her next words would either be a fire hose blasting Snake to his knees or a gentle rain preparing the ground for future planting. Her brain was yelling…be kind, be patient, be mature but her mouth didn't get the message in time. "I wish you would have talked to me *first* before deciding for both of us when Ms. K should drop CeCe off." She immediately regretted her words, her tone and her body language. The expression on her husband's face while he stood in the doorway holding that big tub of clothes was yet another confirmation of the old saying, 'physician heal thyself' only this time it was 'counselor heed your own advice.'

Snake tried to lighten the mood. "Whoa, I'm sorry, I must be in the wrong house because my sweet, amazing wife appreciates my awesome thoughtful ways. I'm sorry to bother you Ma'am." Somewhere behind his thick beard was a full smile.

Fauna couldn't speak. She wanted to. There were many more words pushing at her closed lips, but she didn't trust herself at that moment to speak.

"Should I leave and come back?" Snake's bright smile was beginning to fade. He set the tub down. There was a lot of pink showing through the clear plastic sides of the bin. He used his foot to push the tub closer to Fauna. It resembled a foreign dignitary bringing his treasures to the Queen of the land, hoping to gain her favor.

Fauna's tough exterior broke. Her lips formed a thin line as she fought a giggle. She couldn't mask the twinkle in her eyes. It had always been a lifeline to Snake when he thought things were going south that it was safe to approach the throne.

"There she is. There's my wonderful wife. She's back." Snake stepped out by faith and hugged Fauna. At first, she was resistant. Then he felt her relax in his embrace. While he held her, he whispered, "I was trying to be helpful, not hurtful. I thought it would be better for you to have this evening to prepare, and better for CeCe to come in the light of day to a new place and not at night. Ms. K made the final decision."

Fauna slipped both of her arms around Snake's waist and locked them together behind his back. He returned her hug. For the first time, in the last 30 minutes, she thought of CeCe's feelings above her own. Snake was right. She needed this evening to prepare and it was far better for CeCe, a 3-year-old, to be dropped off in the daylight to have time to adjust to her new surroundings than in the darkness of night. With the realization that Snake was thinking more about the welfare of this child than she was, that creeping dread returned in the pit of her stomach. It was reminding her that she was not mom material. She was nothing but an imposter who cared more about herself than a hurting child.

Snake let go of Fauna and rubbed his hands together like an excited child about to open birthday presents. "Okay, let's get ready for our girl." He picked up the tub of girl clothes and walked into the living room to begin sorting. "What do you think, Fauna, should we just wash them all? We don't even know how big she is. Maybe she'll be tall and a bit full figured like me or she could be a shorty like..." As Snake turned to face Fauna, he looked at her face. "...Are you okay?"

Fauna sat on the sofa, then bent in half with her face buried in her hands. She surrendered to the emotions of the day. There was Isabelle's announcement, the joy of CeCe coming and then the truest reality that they would be parents tomorrow. It knocked her off her feet like an avalanche. What if she couldn't do it? What if the counselor couldn't help a hurting child in her own home? What if she failed at being a mother, just like her own mom?

Snake left the bin of clothes on the floor and sat next to Fauna. She was doubled over, and soft sobs shook her body. Snake placed his large open hand between Fauna's shoulder blades and gently rubbed her back in a circular motion. He pinched his lips together to resist the urge to try and verbally fix this. He knew Fauna well enough to know that her battle wasn't with him. She was fighting something far greater than taking in a foster child or not being included in the decision making. She was fighting her own feelings of inadequacy. Snake knew this adversary too. When she was ready, she'd talk to him. Right now was not the time for words.

With his hand on her back, inwardly Snake interceded for his wife until his prayer could not be contained a moment longer within him.

***

The sound of glass breaking brought June running to check on what the damage would be this time. CeCe's face was void of emotion. When June entered the room, the child didn't make eye contact. June prayed that God would grant her the skills to deal with *whatever*—then she saw it. The large mirror that hung over the fireplace laid in shards of glass on the floor. A heavy brass candle stick that had been on a shelf that June thought was out of a three-year-old's reach laid in the middle of the broken glass.

How much longer could she continue to be the patient and kind woman she wanted to be? June silently prayed as she crossed the room and took CeCe by the hand.

At the touch of June's hand, CeCe screamed while collapsing into a heap on the floor. June reached down and scooped up the mass of thrashing arms and legs and carried CeCe to the bedroom that had been the child's the past six nights. The once pristine little girl's room painted in a soft pink with every toy a child could imagine had been reduced to a bed and chair. All the toys had been removed—not for punishment, but for safety reasons.

June knew there was no reason to attempt questioning the child at this time. It would have been an exercise in futility. After CeCe's second day, June didn't phrase any question to the child with the word, "Why?"

As June walked back to the family room, she prayed, "How much longer? Lord, how much longer? Lord, give the next people inroads to the treasure that lies within this wounded child. She deserves to be loved."

June carefully began picking up the dangerous broken glass when she felt her phone vibrate in her sweater pocket. She pulled the phone out and saw Ms. Klingburg's name flash on the home screen. She pushed the accept button and said, "Great timing. Are you coming now to pick up CeCe?"

"No. Tomorrow morning at 9 A.M. Can you have her ready?"

"YES!" June knew there was a bit too much excitement in her voice.

Laura didn't respond.

In full disclosure, June decided to tell Laura about her recent CeCe incident "Moments ago, CeCe threw a brass candlestick holder at that large mirror that hangs above the fireplace. There was broken glass everywhere. I had to carry her to the bedroom to get her away from the danger. She wasn't hurt that I could see, but you know how she can be when she's touched—well, she just went crazy."

A soft moan escaped Laura's lips, "Oh, June. Thank you for your kindness and patience with CeCe. I pray that the Parker's will be able to win her heart and gain her trust. Maybe they will all be just what the other one needs."

June rested the phone on her shoulder and pressed it against her cheek while she continued to pick up the big pieces of glass. "God help them all. I am praying for them and CeCe."

Ms. K agreed. "Amen to that! I'll let you go—sounds like you have your hands full."

***

Ms. K laid her phone on her desk. It was after hours and the office was exceptionally quiet. Ms. K heard voices in the main office. They were talking quietly, but there was a tone of intimidation coming from one of the voices. Ms. K walked to her office door and looked out the window.

Gina sat at her desk with her chair turned towards Ms. K. Her face looked full of fear as Helen Franco stood over her with one hand pointing close to Gina's face in a threatening way. Ms. K couldn't hear what Helen was saying, but from the look on Gina's face, she couldn't stand quietly by.

"Is everything okay, ladies?" Ms. K called from her office doorway.

Helen spun around in surprise. "Oh, I thought you were gone." She rested her hand on the back of Gina's chair in a possessive way. "Gina and I were just having a personal conversation."

Ms. K walked closer to the two ladies and looked at Gina for confirmation. Her eyes were looking downward at the floor, but she didn't speak.

"Gina? Everything okay with you?"

Helen interjected. "Like I said, it's of a personal nature. Sorry we were having this conversation in the office—but it's private and has nothing to do with you." The last remark was spoken with a challenge attached. Helen's face spoke loud and clear—you don't control our personal lives and if you try, I'll definitely report you.

Ms. K knelt down in front of Gina. "Is this personal or office related?"

Helen twisted Gina's chair away from Ms. K's face and

said, "We're going now. Come on Gina."

Ms. K knew Gina was scared and Helen had something she was holding over her, but what? She'd have to make a note to talk to Gina when Helen wasn't around. Gina was a good girl and Helen could easily alter her whole life, if she sunk her claws into her.

Helen had hardened her heart years ago to everything church and Christ related, yet she could talk the talk better than anyone Laura Klingburg had ever met. Laura wasn't unfamiliar with people like this. The church of Laura's youth was filled with this type of "Christian." Their hypocritical ways were like a poison that blinded Laura's eyes to Christ's redemptive love and forgiveness. She didn't want to see Gina go down that dark, destructive path—not on her watch.

As Ms. K turned to walk back to her office, she casually mentioned, "Helen, on Monday we will be doing your case review. Could you have ready the past six months of cases you've been handling so we can go over those together?"

Helen's jaw tightened, and her voice sounded forced. "I'll be ready on Monday."

Ms. K looked at the two ladies. Gina was sitting and Helen standing behind her. Helen wore a sneer on her face and Gina looked gripped by fear. Ms. K attempted to keep a professional demeanor. "Good. I'll see you both on Monday." Ms. K looked directly at Gina, "Could I speak with you for a moment in my office?"

"Yes, Ms. K. Should I bring paper and pen?"

"No, this will only take a minute."

Gina practically jumped from her chair to escape Helen's presence and followed Ms. K to her office. Helen didn't move from behind Gina's chair, but watched like a cat stalking its prey. Ms. K held the door open until Gina was inside her office. Ms. K watched Helen disappear behind the closed door of her office.

Gina looked worried. She had already sat down in the chair across from Ms. K's desk and was massaging her hands like she had just come in from the cold. "Gina are your hands cold?"

Gina stopped ringing her hands and placed them flat on her lap. "Oh, I'm sorry. That's just a habit I have when…" She stopped.

Ms. K finished her sentence. "…when you're nervous?"

Gina looked like a deer in the headlights trying to decide which way to bolt.

"Gina, I'm not blind. Is Helen threatening you or holding something over your head? It's not blackmail—is it?"

Gina's eyes became moist. "I love my job here. I want to be a social worker myself one day. I'm not sure if I broke the law and I certainly don't want to go to jail."

"So, it does sound like Helen is threatening you. You better start at the beginning, so we can sort this thing out."

Gina went back over the past four months of Helen's bullying and threats. "There has been paperwork that has come up missing from my desk. I can't prove any of this was Helen, but she always had information that seemed private. When she asked me questions, she would have private information that I couldn't believe she knew unless you told her."

"Let me assure you, Gina. I have not confided in Helen about anything personal, nor work related outside her scope of responsibility."

"I know she played me, and I feel the fool for it. She's slick—that's all I can say." Gina's heart was beating faster than normal, and her voice reflected that. Gina blurted out, "She implied that you were having an affair with the director of the board. She said things like, 'Ms. K tries to act like a Christian but she's living a lie and can't be trusted.' Then she said for me to watch how you giggle like a teenager when he comes and to see how you both smile at each other." Gina dropped her head. "You did both look very comfortable together."

Ms. K felt an urge to defend her actions but didn't. She knew their personal history and wouldn't dignify accusations like this one about such an honorable man. "What exactly did you do that Helen is using to control you?"

"I don't know—exactly. She said that she has been keeping records about my activities in the office and she has documentation that could put me in jail if I don't get her the information she wants—on you."

Ms. K sighed. She felt like a lawyer for the prosecution trying to pull information from a hostile witness. "Out with it Gina. Give it to me in bullet points. I need the who and why?"

"It's the CeCe case and she believes you didn't do the paperwork processing the Parkers' correctly. She wants to use it to bring you down and wants me to help her. I don't believe it and I don't want to do it. That's when she said she had stuff on me that could send me to jail." There were tears. Lots of tears.

"Gina, think. What could she be talking about?"

"I don't know. But I'm afraid not to believe her. Look how she is coming after you."

"She isn't the first and won't be the last. Go home. Try not to worry. I'll get to the bottom of this on Monday. I've got too much on my plate right now to deal with Helen Franko."

Gina wiped her tears and started to open Ms. K's office door but peeked out the side window to see if Helen was gone. She didn't see her in the office, so she started to leave, then turned and asked, "Any chance you could walk me to my car?"

"Sure, I'll be done here in 10 minutes." Ms. K felt for a moment like she was back in high school. She wondered at what age do the mean girls go away.

Gina called back over her shoulder. "I'll be waiting at my desk."

9

In that day the wolf and the lamb will live together;
the leopard will lie down with the baby goat.
The calf and the yearling will be safe with the lion,
and a little child will lead them all.
Isaiah 11:6 (NLT)

Saturday mornings were about to change forever in the home of Snake and Fauna Parker. They used to linger in bed for a while and talk, then go out for brunch. They'd go shopping or go to a movie in the afternoon, then home for Snake to watch sports and Fauna would read. Occasionally, there would be a church activity or big event that they participated in. This Saturday morning, they were up and showered before 7 A.M. Fauna cooked a light breakfast; the dishes were done and the house spotless. For over two hours, they waited in near silence.

Ms. K sent a text to Fauna's phone. *On our way to you. 10 minutes out.*

Fauna couldn't speak. She handed her phone to Snake to read the message.

He grabbed Fauna's hand and held it gently. "This is it. Lord, help us. We can't do this on our own. We need you Lord."

Fauna looked at Snake with worry evident in her expression. "Are we ready?"

Snake got up and went to the kitchen window to look out. "I'm ready but I'm also not naïve. This won't be easy. Together we can do it, but I wouldn't want to have a go at this on my own."

Fauna joined him at the window. Together they peered out. Waiting for their lives to change forever.

Ms. K's work vehicle pulled into the driveway and rolled

to a stop. She exited the car and opened the door directly behind the driver's seat. She fumbled around for a few moments. Then a bundled up little person stepped out from behind the car door. The coat was brown with pink fur around the hood and cuffs. A mass of brown curls circled the hood. A tan-faced little girl stepped away from the car and stood still waiting for her next direction. Ms. K touched her on the back pushing her gently towards the house and front porch. The child moved without resistance in the direction she was guided.

Fauna and Snake nearly fell over each other getting to the front door. Snake knew his 6' 5" stature and full black beard with the hissing head of a snake coming up the side of his face may not be looked on as warm and fuzzy by any three-year-old child let alone one that had been traumatized. He decided to hold back and let Fauna take the lead. That little butterfly tattoo on her face would be girl-friendly and less threatening.

Fauna held the door open as Ms. K continued to guide CeCe into the house. Once the door was closed, Fauna fought the urge to be demonstrative in her desire to welcome this little girl to their home. She tried to pull from her own memories of being dropped off at a new foster home; the fear, the anger, the loneliness, the terror was all coming back to her. She let Ms. K take the lead.

"This is CeCe Jefferson. She is three years old. She loves stuffed animals and puzzles. Her favorite cartoon is Doc McStuffin." Ms. K pulled CeCe's hood back from her head and began unzipping her coat.

"Welcome to our home, CeCe. My name is Fauna and this big teddy bear is Zak, but we call him Snake. Can you guess why?" Fauna pointed at the big hairy man standing behind her.

CeCe looked past Fauna and directly at Snake. He slowly turned his head to reveal the snake tattoo. CeCe's eyes widened, and she almost smiled.

Ms. K pulled CeCe's first arm out of the coat and looked

at Fauna with big eyes. She mouthed the word, *wow*! Fauna felt hopeful and Snake gave CeCe a big smile. As Ms. K tried to slip CeCe's second arm out of her coat, the mood quickly changed. CeCe grabbed her coat back around her and slipped her arm back into the sleeve.

"Okay. No problem. You can keep your coat on until you're ready to take it off." Ms. K said as she tried to move CeCe towards the living room, but this time CeCe resisted. She would not be moved by the gentle guiding of Ms. K's hand. "CeCe, we're going to go into the living room to sit down. You can join us if you want or you can stay here." Ms. K moved a few steps motioning to Snake and Fauna to come with her. CeCe watched them leave the room, but she didn't move.

The three adults sat down, and Ms. K pulled out a file that looked like the manuscript for a short novel. I have a few pages for you to sign and I'm leaving this info for you to look over. You may want to read this as soon as possible. There are some great pointers in here for dealing with resistant children."

Fauna took the pile of papers from Ms. K. Snake stretched his neck to see CeCe from his place next to Fauna on the sofa. CeCe stood all alone in the kitchen. Something welled up inside of him. He wanted to swoop that baby girl up and hold her in his arms. He wanted to make lifelong promises that she would be safe, loved and protected from this day forward, but he knew better than to move that fast. But...one day...one day she would trust him, and he would make promises to always be there for her.

***

Samantha and Isabelle sat in the clinic waiting room. It was Saturday morning with only a few patients scattered about the room. The ultrasound tech wasn't scheduled but was willing to come in when Dr. Hayes explained the situation. At home Issie had allowed her father to measure her uterus to make a guess what month she might be. He didn't look happy, but he reminded everyone that the ultrasound would give an exact date.

A mother walked into the waiting area carrying a baby about 10 months old and holding the hand of another child about three years old. The three-year-old was obviously the sick one. The mother helped the little boy up on the chair then went over to the window to sign in.

When she came back and sat down she sighed. The baby thought the mom was playing and let out a deep belly laugh. Everyone in the room turned to look at mother and child. Even the sick little boy smiled at the sound of his little brother's laughter. The mom repeated the sigh and the baby laughed again, this time deeper and longer.

A smile formed on Issie's lips.

The sick little boy got on his knees in the chair next to his mom and attempted to copy the noise his mother had made. His little brother responded with an even longer belly laugh.

Samantha smiled and said, "Isn't the laughter of a baby the sweetest thing?"

Issie nodded and unconsciously rested her hand on her belly.

Samantha and Issie were both fixated with the laughing baby and totally missed Stuart standing behind the glass window in the office motioning for them to come back. He finally slid the glass window open and called, "Samantha, Isabelle, you can come back now."

When Isabelle stood, she realized for the first time that her hand was resting in a protective way over her baby. As she walked past the mother with her two children, the baby let out another round of laughter and again, Issie felt her hand move involuntarily to her baby. A smile followed closely by a frown formed on her face.

Issie thought, what in the world is happening to me?

The waiting room door closed behind her and she followed her mother and father to a dimly lit room where a perky young lady with pink stripes in her hair welcomed them. She patted the table and motioned with her head for Isabelle to lie down. "Hi, I'm Star. Is this your first ultrasound?" The tone of the worker's voice had the same excitement of a child bouncing up and down waiting for something exciting to happen.

Dr. Hayes and Samantha stood to the side of the room without saying a word. They let Isabelle take the lead for the first time in her life, and she didn't feel like a kid. She answered. "Yes. This is my first time."

"Okay, I'm going to put this warm gooey stuff on your belly area. I'll be pushing down to get that little one moving about. This isn't going to hurt in the least."

Issie was relieved that the tech spoke the truth. The ultrasound was painless, but when the tech pushed around on her stomach area, then stopped and punched in numbers, it did give Issie cause for concern. She wondered if there was something wrong. Finally, she couldn't hold her worry in another moment and asked. "Is there a problem?"

The tech giggled and adjusted her swivel stool, "I'm not seeing anything to be concerned about. Would you like to know what you're having?"

Isabelle looked at her mom and dad. Samantha nodded in the affirmative, and Stuart turned away.

Issie made the decision. "Yes, I want to know."

The striped-haired girl said, "Congratulations, your baby is a boy."

Stuart's head snapped towards the monitor where the outline of a baby was easily seen. "How many weeks along?" he asked.

The technician did a few more measurements and said, "Looks like 17 weeks with a due date of April 4th. Does that sound about right to you?" The question was directed at Isabelle, not Dr. Hayes.

Samantha stepped close to the table where Issie laid. She reached for her daughter's hand. Her voice was soft and thoughtful, "A boy."

Issie looked at the screen and for a moment allowed herself to smile at the perfect form of the baby. Growing inside of her was a baby boy. He was alive, moving, healthy and part of her.

Samantha re-asked the tech's question. "Does April 4th sound like the due date you calculated from your last period?"

Issie looked at her mom, then glanced in the direction of her father across the room. "I, umm, don't remember the date of my last period." But she did remember the 4th of July outing she went on to Lake Michigan.

In a professional tone, Stuart stated, "It doesn't matter. The ultrasound gives us the information we need. I'm going to my office. When you're done, we can talk about what's next." Stuart left the room and with him the unmistakable joy felt moments ago was gone.

The tech handed Isabelle a long strip of paper with at least 10 images of the baby boy she carried. She rolled them up like a scroll and tucked the only pictures she may ever have of her baby boy into her shoulder bag. Mother and daughter walked down the hallway to Stuart's office with a feeling of dread shadowing them.

Stuart was sitting behind his desk when they walked into his office. He was typing on his laptop and glanced up but didn't stop. He said, "I'm almost done. Take a seat. We have a lot to discuss."

Isabelle and Samantha sat in the two office side chairs opposite the desk in the cramped space. A few moments later, Stuart closed the laptop and said, "Okay, I sent an email to my friend who is an OB-GYN in Chicago. He will have connections. He should get back with me today and we can make plans from there. Seventeen weeks was good news, but we have to move fast." For the first time he made eye contact with the two women across the desk from him. The expression of shock on their faces was easy to read—even for Stuart.

"Dad, what are you talking about? Weren't you in the same room with me minutes ago? Did you see what I saw?"

Isabelle gripped the arms of her chair. She breathed in a prayer of courage to not succumb to pressure from anyone—ever again.

Stuart's expression was between hurt and confused. "Sweetheart, no. I'm not going to make this decision for you. I just want you to have all the information available to you to make a decision." He shifted a few papers around on his desk. "I saw what you saw. That's why I had to leave. I'm trying to stay impartial. This is your life. Whatever choice you make, you will have to live with."

Samantha reached over and touched her daughter's arm. "We talked last night, Issie. The decision will be yours and we will support you in whatever decision you make. You can stop it, give it, or keep it, and we won't judge you. Just be sure you know what you can live with for the rest of your life."

Isabelle took in a deep breath and held it for a moment before pushing it out through loose lips. "I can't—won't consider an abortion. I don't want to go away to hide and have this baby in secret. I've been doing that for the past four months." She sighed. "I'm not ready to make any other decisions yet. I want to keep my options open regarding adoption or keeping the baby until I know for sure which way to go."

A sense of relief was expressed by both Isabelle's parents. Stuart closed his eyes. His shoulders dropped to a relaxed position and Samantha cried.

Stuart spoke, "Issie, we know there is a ton of stuff that you are still going to have to go through over the next months and even years, but we are here for you. Your mom and I love you. We'll all get through this together. Please don't leave us out of the process. Because we can only come in, when invited."

Isabelle got up and walked around her father's desk. She placed her arms around his neck and kissed him on the top of the head. "Thank you—thank you, Dad. I've felt so alone. You are both a part of this from this day forward. And I give you permission to ask questions and give advice—just remember my delicate emotional state." She forced a laugh but felt a strength well up within her from the respect and trust her parents had extended to her.

***

Zander didn't usually listen to gossip at church or school. He had seen the painful results of rumors and untruths spread about people before. Living in a 'ministry home' had often made Zander and Ty feel like those three little monkeys who *hear no evil, see no evil, or speak no evil.* But in his 15 years, he had heard and seen plenty. He purposed in his heart that he would not be a person who spoke evil. When the text message from a friend in the youth group came, it was more than he could stomach.

"Ty—come here." Zander called down the hallway of the church parsonage.

Ty opened his bedroom door and yelled back, "What do you want? I'm busy."

Being the older brother, Zander usually just called, and Ty scampered to him. But something important must be going on for Ty to respond like that. Zander walked down the hallway to his brother's room and opened the door without knocking. "I need to ask you something right now!"

Ty sat at his desk with his laptop open. Zander strained his eyes to see what he was doing, but Ty quickly closed it. "What do you want that can't wait a few minutes?"

Zander sat on the edge of Ty's bed. "I don't want to appear to be gossiping, but…"

Ty turned his chair to face his brother. "…but you are about to gossip. Am I right?"

"Oh, stop it Ty. This is very upsetting."

"Fine, what?"

Zander pondered how to put the words in the least offensive order. Ty had a way of turning things on him and this was not his fault. "Ahhhh. I got this text message from someone, I don't want to say who, that said Isabelle is pregnant. Have you heard anything?"

Ty opened his laptop and pointed to the screen. On a private page for the teens at Hillbrooke High was a photoshopped picture of Isabelle pushing a baby carriage. The photo had a caption that read, "Next Teen Mom."

Zander immediately stood up. "I've got to call her. I don't want her to see that without some warning."

Ty closed his laptop. "Zander don't get involved with this. Remember what the Lord spoke to me. It was a warning. I'm sure of it. She has other people in her life, and she'll find out. Plus, I've already messaged Baylee. Let her family handle this."

"Oh, it's fine for you to contact Baylee, but I can't speak to Isabelle." Zander walked towards the door.

"I know you can see the difference, Zander. Baylee and I have been friends for a long time. You have liked Isabelle from afar for just as long. There is something at play here that we know nothing about. Don't go there and don't get involved. You're gonna get hurt or worse."

"What do you know about it?" Zander stopped at the doorway to make his final point. "I'm texting her right now and we'll just see where it goes from there. If it's true, then she's gonna need a friend."

"True, she will need a friend, just not you." Ty pleaded.

Zander left the room clutching his phone in his hand.

***

Snake and Fauna pulled up to his parent's home for their traditional Friday night family dinner. This would be the first time that CeCe would meet the extended family. The 15 minute car ride set the stage for things to come.

CeCe had howled most of the way after Fauna strapped her into the booster seat with the seatbelt. She had wanted to do it herself, but after more than a few tries, Fauna locked the belt into place. CeCe kicked the back of her seat and screamed until Snake put on a kid's music CD they had purchased. The music calmed her for the time being.

"Should we just go back home?" Fauna asked. "This will just reinforce what your father already believes to be a huge mistake on our part."

"We can't hide out inside our house for the rest of our lives and I believe it will be good for CeCe to mix with other children and adults."

"She doesn't trust anyone. When I drop her at daycare, it's ugly! I can see the horror on the teacher's face when she sees us coming down the hallway." Fauna spoke softly hoping the music was drowning out her words.

Snake turned down the street where he grew up. He lowered the volume of the music and spoke to CeCe while looking at her in the rearview mirror. "CeCe, this is where I grew up. And this was my house when I was your age." The car turned into the long circular drive and came to a stop in front of the grand house.

CeCe's eyes bugged out as she examined the big house with the pillars. "Hospital? Not sick. No go."

Fauna jumped in, "Oh, no CeCe. This is a house where people live. It's Snake's Mommy and Daddy who live here. No doctors, no shots, no medicine. Just nice people." Fauna felt like her statement wasn't completely true. James, Snake's father, had been straightforward about his disapproval of what they were doing, and now, after a week taking care of CeCe, Fauna inwardly was wondering if she agreed more than disagreed with her father-in-law.

CeCe's eyes turned from fright to anger as she kicked the back of Fauna's seat again. Fauna bent forward to pick up the bag she had packed for CeCe in case an emergency change of clothes might be needed. She had learned this the hard way when she took CeCe to her first appointment. That fiasco ended with CeCe being dressed from head to toe from the emergency clothing bin at the center.

Fauna opened her car door to allow CeCe to get out. She was making the same mistakes over and over in her desire to love this little girl. CeCe may be three years old, but she had strong opinions about touch. This little girl's number one 'no-no' was when someone tried to give her any form of uninvited physical contact. When this happened, it was reminiscent of that cartoon character called the Tasmanian Devil.

Snake met Fauna at the car door and both tried to open it at the same time. Fauna gave way to Snake. "You get her. She acts better with you." Snake didn't argue but opened the door with a big smile.

"Come—my girl, I'm excited for you to meet my family, and my nephew, William, is about your age. I hope you will like each other."

CeCe had her seatbelt off and held the door handle of the SUV as she eased herself to the ground. Snake gently guided her by placing his hand on the back of her hood. She moved willingly in the direction of the massive front door.

Even in the chilly air, Fauna's palms were sweating, and her heart raced. She tried to swallow the lump that had formed in her dry throat. This was not going to be the pleasant family gathering—the kind she dreamed of for so long. That dream was off the table with this little girl, CeCe. How was James going to react? What crazy thing would CeCe do if anyone tried to hug her or get too close to her face?

Snake was a few steps ahead of Fauna. He opened the door like a five-star hotel doorman and bowed as CeCe entered his childhood home. Fauna followed a few guarded steps behind CeCe, and Snake closed the door behind her.

Fauna had called Marilyn and Emily soon after CeCe arrived at their house to prepare them for this new family member. Both mother and daughter were kind, gentle and sweet. They loved children and would have a difficult time withholding their affection.

Fauna had warned them to be careful because this child did not welcome any physical contact and especially without warning. There wouldn't be a problem with James, Snake's father. He would not be interested in the least bit in this little girl who was desperately in need of a patient family.

Marilyn rounded the corner as Snake tried to take CeCe's coat off. Fauna could see that things were escalating.

Marilyn dropped to her knees to be at CeC's level. "I'm Marilyn, Snake's mommy. We are so glad you came to our house. I have toys for you to play with and a nice little boy named William for you to meet. Would you like to see?"

Marilyn held out her hand for CeCe to accept or reject.

She rejected. CeCe clutched her coat tightly around her body, and her normally stoic face showed signs of worry. She turned back towards Snake and spoke in a mournful tone. "No go."

Snake resisted the urge to sweep the little thing up in his strong arms and run. Instead he spoke with a firm voice. "We are not leaving you here. Where we go, you go. Fauna and I will stay with you."

Fauna quickly added, "Except daycare with your friends, but we always come back to get you, don't we? We've never left you there."

CeCe caught her breath a few times in her chest fighting back the sobs that were ready to bring the family night to an end before it started.

Fauna quickly said, "Okay, Marilyn, let's go check out those toys and see what you have to eat. Do you have any Pop Tarts? CeCe loves Pop Tarts."

Marilyn pushed herself up from the floor. "I don't know. I can check the pantry." As she and Fauna walked to the kitchen, she whispered, "I could have bought Pop Tarts, if I'd known."

Fauna scooped Marilyn's arm inside of hers. "Pop Tarts will be the least of our concerns tonight."

Marilyn looked back over her shoulder at the child standing alone—no one touching or comforting her. "How can you just not grab her and hug the daylights out of that sweet baby?"

Fauna dropped Marilyn's arm and displayed her hands in

front of her.

Marilyn let out a gasp.

Fauna replied. "I know. It looks like we got a kitten instead of a little girl." The scratches all over Fauna's hands were healing, but the evidence was plain to see. Fauna pulled back her long sleeve to reveal more proof. "It's hard to see the scratches on my arms because of my tattoos, but they're worse than my hands. Bath time, bedtime, and anytime where I have to make physical contact is the absolute worst." Fauna gulped back her emotions. "I was able to clip her fingernails the second night while she was sleeping. That was a skill I wasn't prepared for, but it had to be done."

Emily glanced up when Marilyn and Fauna entered the kitchen. "Where is she? William, come here. CeCe has arrived." A chubby little boy about the same size as CeCe jumped to his feet and headed towards the front door. Before Fauna could give him proper instructions he ran to CeCe, grabbed her by the hand, and began dragging her to the toys.

"You like trains? Grandma and Puppa have lots of trains."

For the first time in a week, CeCe allowed someone to touch her without a fight. William didn't notice she still had her coat on, nor did he care that she didn't speak to him. He chatted enough for both of them. All the adults in the room watched as one little person cut through every barrier and became a friend.

Fauna mouthed to Emily and motioned back and forth with her finger between them. "Play Date!"

James watched his grandson embrace this little girl with unbiased human kindness. The scripture from his youth came back to his memory. *And a child will lead them.*

10

'Call to Me and I will answer you and tell you
great and unsearchable things you do not know.'
Jeremiah 33:3 (NIV)

The pitiful cries of a child sounded through the quiet home. Fauna, half asleep, struggled to get out of bed. In frustration she said, "Not again," revealing her heart. A quick glance at the clock showed it was 4:10 A.M.

Snake rolled over, squinting his eyes at the clock across the room. "What's happening?"

"Another nightmare is what's happening." Fauna knew her voice was harsh. "My God, what happened to this child. She's only three."

CeCe screamed.

Between the cold night air and the scream, Fauna shivered. She grabbed her housecoat from the back of her bedroom door and crossed the hallway in her bare feet. From the doorway of CeCe's bedroom, Fauna scanned the room with only the help of the nightlight. CeCe's curly hair framed her face like a halo. Fauna walked across the room to take a closer look.

CeCe began to move about in a restless sleep, her brow furrowed like she was in physical pain. A sad moan escaped her pinched lips. She swiped at the air.

Fauna leaned down close and whispered, "It's okay, sweetie." She gently stroked CeCe's arm.

CeCe whimpered. Her eyes still pinched tight. She pulled away from Fauna's touch.

Fauna withdrew her hand and looked at the tormented child. The insecurities resurfaced, and she questioned her abilities to mother this child. As she lowered herself to sit on the edge of the bed she whispered, "Jesus, Jesus, Jesus help me...help CeCe."

Fauna reached out to stroke CeCe's arm in an attempt to reassure her. "It's going to be okay. You're safe. I'm here. It's Fauna. You're safe now."

This was not Fauna's first night sitting on CeCe's bed in the wee hours of the morning. She knew the routine from nights past, but her desire to show compassion made her ill-prepared for battle. Without warning, CeCe changed from passive moans to a fighting warrior. Her arms flew in every direction, her eyes still pinched shut. Her curved hands swiped aimlessly at the air with razor sharp fingernails.

Fauna tried without success to get out of the line of fire, but CeCe's fingernails drew blood when they made contact with Fauna's hands and arms.

Fauna winced. She stepped back from the bed creating a safe distance between them.

Fauna tried to keep her own emotions in check, but without success. The same questions that visited her each night came rushing in. Had they been too hasty becoming foster parents? Should they have visited a few more doctors before giving up the dream of having children of their own? What if she couldn't help CeCe? What if this child's issues were beyond her abilities? Might the child be damaged beyond repair? An anger stirred in Fauna's heart towards CeCe's birth mom. How could this woman inflict such atrocities on a child, a mere baby?

Maybe it was the interrupted sleep or maybe all the above. Whatever the case, Fauna gave in to her anger and her voice increased in volume, "CeCe! Wake up. CeCe! Wake up. It's Fauna, wake up!"

Fauna grabbed CeCe by the arms and shook her. "WAKE UP!"

CeCe's dark green eyes opened wide. They were mirrors of accusation looking back at Fauna. She dropped CeCe, and the child fell like a ragdoll onto the bed.

CeCe pulled her knees to her chest and turned her face away from Fauna and laid motionless.

Fauna pulled the Doc McStuffin's blanket up over

CeCe's small silent body and walked out of the room. She felt physically sick, and ashamed of her reaction. She crawled back into bed, her heart pounding. Snake was asleep. She resisted the urge to wake him. Sleep was precious these days. Snake loved her unconditionally.

Fauna knew this. But her most recent failure was a nagging reminder of her maternal inadequacies. She had counseled enough people in crisis to know that this kind of tension in a marriage could potentially cause a break if left unattended.

Fauna reached for the cell phone charging on the bed stand. The light of the phone cast a bright light into the darkness. Fauna typed in the name Laura Klingburg. Then keyed in her message; *We need to talk. I'm doubting if fostering is the right fit for us. It's been a month with not a ray of hope. Call me.* She reread the message, then pushed send.

* * *

The vibration of Isabelle's watch signaled it was time to get up. This was her last day of school before Christmas break. She rolled over and released a long sigh. The thought of 14 days of sleeping in seemed like something dreams were made of. The past month of school and even church hadn't been easy.

The fact that Zander Douglas had come to her rescue was a blessed surprise to her. Of all people, why him? She had always thought of him as a kid, but now he was over six feet tall, and while still a bean pole, he was starting to fill out nicely. He was smart, kind, thoughtful, protective and most of all interested in her—even in her present condition.

Isabelle allowed herself a moment to think about Zander Douglas. She had received her fair share of dirty looks from the girls at church and at school whenever Zander was attentive to her. Zander had received some unkind remarks and accusations, but he did not pull away from Isabelle. She warned him early on that hanging around her could be dangerous to his popularity and reputation. But Zander chose her over both of these.

During one of their many long talks, Zander had offered to say he was the father, if she wanted. As sweet and wonderful as that sounded, they both knew it would never work. Her father and certainly Pastor Rey would both insist on a DNA test and then their deceit would be revealed, and it would be that much worse for both of them.

Isabelle forced herself out of the bed to a standing position. She rubbed her protruding belly and wondered what it would be like to have the actual father involved in the process. She hadn't even given him a chance to accept her or reject her, let alone tell him about his child. Would he be mad? Would he want to be involved? She knew if she chose adoption she would have to tell him.

She certainly wouldn't sign away her rights first or he could swoop in and take the baby from a stable family causing her child... Isabelle stopped in the middle of her thought. Her child. Her son. She could feel herself connecting with the baby growing inside of her. Could she— would she really give it away like an unwanted garage sale item? Ms. Parker, Fauna, had taken in that little foster girl. Maybe she would like a baby—her baby. Then she could still be a part of his life. See him grow up and still have her life.

But the father, he was surely the wrinkle in all her plans. She had to find out how he felt. Yet, it was his own fault she hadn't told him anything. He hadn't called her or written— not even once. He could be dead for all she knew. He came into her life like a whirlwind and left just as quickly. What did she even know about him, other than he was staying with his aunt and uncle who attended her church.

He arrived the beginning of June and was gone by mid-July. They met at youth group and started hanging out— primarily outside of church. She had wanted it that way because if you even looked sideways at a boy at church— people were planning your wedding. If she had sat by him one time, there would have been a million questions. Now she was relieved she had insisted on anonymity.

Poor Zander though, all fingers were pointing at him. Her parents had not asked about who the father was since the night she revealed she was pregnant. Maybe they believed it was Zander too? There were some unkind teen gossips who defiled Zander's name on social media. He'd lost friendships, and Pastor Eli had called them both into his office. He considered removing Zander from the worship team, but without a solid confession by either one of them, the youth pastor was powerless to remove the pastor's son from ministry based on gossip.

Isabelle knew that people believed the gossip, and now the only thing that would clear poor Zander's name was a medical test exonerating him. And that wouldn't be happening for another four months. Someone had even left a note on Zander's Bible while he was leading worship. He showed her. The words still tasted bitter in her mouth. *Evil company corrupts.* She knew she was the one considered evil in that Bible quote. Who uses the Bible like that to hurt people?

Isabelle pushed all her endless thoughts to the back burner as she finished getting ready for her last day of school for this year. January would bring about a whole new season in her life. She didn't want to think about any of it right now. At her appointment with Ms. Parker today after school she had a lot to discuss. She hadn't told anyone what she was considering—not even Zander. And Zander had guessed correctly who the real father was.

***

The morning light filtered in the bedroom window of the Parker's house. Fauna's eyelids were heavy from lack of sleep. She was floating in a wonderful dream. There were two children running happily in the yard between Snake and her. They were all happy and laughing like a loving family. She suddenly shot straight up in the bed. Where is CeCe? She looked at the empty space next to her in the bed. Snake had left for work.

"CeCe!" Fauna called. The house was too quiet. There was no reply. Fauna called to her again with the sweetest tone she could muster. "CeCe! It's okay. You can get up."

From her bedroom, CeCe sighed loud enough for Fauna to know she was growing impatient. Since CeCe arrived, she would not get out of bed in the morning without permission. Fauna knew this must have been a painful lesson for one so young to learn. There were many other things CeCe did that were without fear, but getting out of bed in the morning was not one of them.

Each morning began with the same battles. First there was the removal of the pull-up. Fauna felt like she was violating CeCe when she tugged to remove the wet load, while CeCe held on tightly to the heavy diaper, kicking and screaming. Then they moved on to the washing phase.

The first few days after CeCe arrived, Fauna would fill the tub and put in a few toys, tested the water, assuring CeCe it was a comfortable temperature, but CeCe fought Fauna as if she were about to be cooked alive in boiling water. After a few days of that, Fauna surrendered and handed CeCe a wet wash cloth. She instructed CeCe where to wash, allowing her this win. Fauna decided they would only do the bath battle once a week.

Each morning, breakfast time was a struggle. Being sleep-deprived just added to the daily drama for Fauna.

Fauna mustered up her sweetest tone to pose the question to her difficult customer, "Okay, we have on the menu today two choices. CeCe, you get to pick which one you want. Will it be scrambled eggs or oatmeal?"

CeCe was sitting on a stool at the kitchen island and looked directly at Fauna and stuck out her tongue. Then she dropped her head down on the counter and hid her face under her folded arms.

She peeked up to demand, "I want a pop tart!"

"Maybe you can have a pop tart later for a snack."

Fauna gave a warm smile trying to keep her voice level and without emotion, "It's your lucky day. You get to pick between scrambled eggs or oatmeal. Which will it be?"

With her head still resting on the kitchen island, CeCe stretched her leg out and with her foot extended, toppled the bar stool next to her. The heavy crash caused the floor to vibrate under Fauna's feet.

Without reacting to the negative behavior, Fauna said. "Okay, scrambled eggs it is."

And with the menu selection made, CeCe fell on the floor screaming.

Fauna moved the bar stools that were still standing, out of CeCe's reach, put an episode of Doc McStuffin's on the iPad, and allowed the child to scream while she made breakfast.

Following breakfast, CeCe went to her bedroom while Fauna cleaned up the breakfast dishes. She was already emotionally exhausted when her cell phone pinged. She dried her hands and picked up the phone. It was a text message from Ms. K.

Rough night?

Fauna immediately texted back, *Yes! I'm questioning if CeCe is a good match for us.*

Ms. K replied, *Are you in a 911 situation with her?*

Fauna typed out her answer. *It's not 911...yet...but heading there. Her problems may be beyond my abilities.* The phone vibrated in her hand, signaling an incoming call. It was Ms. K.

"Hey, Fauna this sounded more like a phone call conversation than texting. Are things the same with CeCe since our last call or has something new come up?"

Fauna told Ms. K about last night's episode, carefully omitting her own loss of control. "I just don't think I can keep this up. This is the hardest thing I've ever done. I've tried. She hates my touch. She hates me. When I try to help her get dressed, she shakes and pulls away, as if my intent was to harm her. I feel terrible. When I attempt to make any physical contact with her, she reacts violently like she is fighting for her life." Fauna took a deep breath and continued. "I try to comfort her, but she attacks me with biting and digging her fingernails into my arms. Sometimes, her eyes are pinched closed, as if she's blocking out something terrible. My mind runs wild with the horrors CeCe must have experienced, and it breaks my heart."

Ms. K spoke in a reassuring tone. "Fauna, you know with kids like CeCe, who have been neglected and abused from birth, change isn't going to happen in days, weeks or even months. It may take years and it's possible she may never be completely okay. She may carry the scars of her first years for the rest of her life."

Fauna wasn't sure if Ms. K wanted her to try harder or give up. Either way the social worker's words were *not* reassuring.

Ms. K continued. "I know you're being baptized daily, let's say hourly, into a harsh reality. You can't view this as a sprint but more like a marathon." Ms. K waited. "Are you seriously considering having CeCe removed from your home? I can do that, if you feel you're done." She waited, "Or you could give it some more time. To see if there's any change. How is Snake doing through all of this?"

"That's the crazy part. I thought CeCe would attach to me before him, but she seems to be opening up to him just a bit and resisting me more each day." Fauna's voice trailed off.

"It's hard to know what is in a child's head or how they process the trauma they've experienced. I know this is hard to hear over and over but hang in there with her a bit longer if you can. She needs you both in her life right now. I don't usually say this to a foster parent, but I'm going to say it to you. Cover this baby girl with prayer, fast, and believe that she is viable. If you can—give it more time." Ms. K allowed Fauna a moment to absorb this cruel reality.

"It's so hard. Harder than I ever imagined." Fauna moaned. "I really do want to help her. For goodness sake, helping people get through difficulties and trauma is what I do, but CeCe has exhausted me. I'm emotionally crushed."

Ms. K's voice was like a lifeline. "Fauna, you are steering this ship, just say the word and she will be removed from your care."

Fauna thought for a moment, "I just want to see something, anything that would give me hope that all this work we're doing is making a difference. And while I'm dreaming, I'd like to not be viewed every day as the enemy."

Ms. K remarked, "You don't really sound like you're ready to give up. How about we give it some more time?"

"If we keep her much longer and it doesn't work out, it will be more traumatic for all of us, and I think Snake has already been taken in by those big green eyes." Fauna's face softened as she recalled how Snake looked at CeCe with tenderness.

"CeCe's testing you. She's looking for consistency. This cycle of her life has been played over and over again. She doesn't know anything else. Give it more time, if you can. She may continue to act out for months, but in time, she will feel safe enough to respond to your love."

Fauna could feel tears welling up in her eyes. She silently prayed. Lord, help me. Give me direction.

Ms. K broke the silence, "Let's touch base next week or sooner if you need me. We can reevaluate the situation then. How does that sound to you?"

"Okay. Is there any news on the parental rights being terminated?"

"There is a lot going on. I can tell you this, that CeCe has not seen her mother since she came back into care over a year ago. She has no other siblings. She could potentially be ready for adoption within six months."

Fauna heard a loud crash from CeCe's room. "I gotta go. CeCe just destroyed something." She abruptly ended the call. A feeling of dread washed over Fauna as she headed down the hallway to see what devastation awaited her in CeCe's bedroom.

Fauna opened the bedroom door. The disaster was epic. The dresser was knocked over with one drawer broken. CeCe's clothes were everywhere pulled off the hangers and out of the drawers. Black crayon scribbles were on every wall—they weren't pictures of shapes, letters, flowers or people—just bold angry marks. Fauna's eyes zoomed in on the scissors lying next to a cut-up Doc McStuffin's blanket.

Fauna was numb. It was more than she could bear. She didn't say a word to CeCe, just picked up the scissors, went across the hall to her bedroom and shut the door.

In the safety of her room, Fauna dropped to her knees next to the bed and sobbed. Something in her broke. She buried her face in the bed and poured out in prayer all the pride, pain, resentment and anger she was feeling.

11

*Faithful are the wounds of a friend...*Proverbs 27:6 (KJV)

Ms. Klingburg finished adding up the numbers from Helen Franko's file review. She mindlessly tapped her fingers on the desk as she pondered the numbers. Helen had placed over 150 children in the past eight months into the system. Of that 150, she reunited 97 of those children with their biological families. From those 97 children who were returned to parental care, 83 were back in Child Protective Services within the same month. While this was lucrative for the agency, it was devastating for the children. The pains and emotional trauma inflicted on these "repeat" children was often irreversible.

Ms. K looked out the interior office window at Helen working at her desk. She was going to have to meet with her regarding these numbers and review the complaints from foster parents and birth parents alike. Helen was not in line for any awards for kindness or diplomacy.

Ms. K's thoughts turned to CeCe's case. This was a perfect example of a child being removed and returned multiple times to an unfit parent. It had done grave damage to this little girl. It had been irresponsible and shabby social work that resulted in the crimes against CeCe. No price tag could ever be placed on returning a child into a bad home situation. Ms. K hoped that CeCe would be one of the success stories. She prayed this little girl would not be lost in foster care rotation until she aged out and ended up on the streets.

Now she understood why Helen was so interested in taking CeCe's case. Helen had been the first caseworker assigned to the infant, CeCe Jefferson. When the emergency room contacted social services for suspicious burns on the buttock, legs and arms of the six-month-old baby, it was Helen who handled the case with only an emergency placement of three weeks. CeCe was returned to her birth mother before her wounds were fully healed.

A feeling of disgust filled Ms. K as she thought how different CeCe's life might have been had she been rescued from the abuse at that young age. If there had been a comprehensive investigation with better parental follow up, maybe CeCe would not have been traumatized for two more years before the abuse was reported by a concerned neighbor.

Cases like this one stirred up rage in Ms. K's heart. She had been delivered from this type of rage a few years ago when she surrendered her life to Christ, but she still remembered how this job could destroy all hope in mankind if she allowed the injustice to consume her. It had nearly destroyed her when she harbored anger and revenge in her heart—always thinking the worst.

Pray, just pray before you meet with Helen. She repeated these instructions over in her mind. This can still be salvaged. I was salvaged. Helen can be salvaged too.

Ms. K pushed the intercom to Helen's desk. "Do you have a few minutes? I'd like to review your case files with you now."

Helen cleared her throat into the phone receiver—loudly. "I have a very heavy call schedule today. Could we do it later this week?"

Ms. K pulled the phone away from her ear and hit the speaker button. "I know you're busy. We all are, but this review must be done before the end of the year and we'll be cutting it close with people taking their vacation days."

Laura shifted in her office chair. "I can help you catch up after the meeting if you'd like."

Helen coughed loudly into the receiver. "Oh, I'm sorry. I must be coming down with something."

Ms. K didn't respond.

"Okay, fine. I'll be right in. If it's just the same to you, I'll handle my own cases. I'll just stay overtime—again!" Helen ended the call. She touched a key that was on a chain around her neck. She leaned forward with the key to unlock her desk drawer. She pulled a journal out of the file marked "private" and relocked the drawer, grabbed a pen from an old coffee cup turned desk caddy, and pushed away from her desk.

Ms. K could see Helen through the glass window in her office. By the slow motion in which Helen was moving, Ms. K questioned how busy she actually was, or maybe Helen was so passive aggressive she was unable to understand her own behavior.

Ms. K met Helen at the door. "Come in. Sorry to hear you're under the weather."

Helen produced a cough on demand, "I'm sure I'll be fine—soon." Helen nodded as she passed by Ms. K.

The ladies took their appointed seats.

"Here is a copy of the spreadsheet I created for reviews. There are four headings; removal date, child/children removed, parental return date, duration w/parent(s), 2nd removal date."

Helen scanned the paper and the totals at the bottom of each column. The numbers were financially favorable, but the repeat number of children returned back into the foster care system was difficult even for Helen to excuse.

Ms. K broke the awkward silence. "Helen, as you can see, your rate of children returning to care is the highest in the office. Why do you think that is?" Ms. K decided to keep pleasantries to a minimum due to Helen's time crunch.

Helen's voice was defensive. "Well, before you took over as director, *all* the social workers were encouraged to reunite families as quickly as possible."

Ms. K twisted her lips to one side before speaking. "Yes, but why would you push to have children returned to their parents before the parents were ready. It seems that some of the children lasted only days before being returned to care. Some even spent time in the hospital. Each of these cases show that you spoke in court in favor of the birth parents against the grave concerns voiced by medical professionals and foster parents."

Helen leaned forward in her chair. A snarl formed on her lips. "I did my job. It's not my fault the system is broken. If the parents do what is asked of them, my hands are tied."

Ms. K leaned forward and rested her forearms on the top of her desk. "Yes, but when you know the child is still in danger, there are things we can do to protect them. We are the voice for those who are voiceless. Returning children to known danger is…"

Helen stood up in a huff. "Are you calling me a criminal for following the law?"

"No, Helen. I'm just so tired of seeing children swallowed alive by the system. I believe if we would all try and do a bit more, maybe we could save one, two, or even three children from extended horrors on a regular basis. They're children. We have to care enough to fight for them."

Helen walked behind the chair where she had been sitting and rested her hands on the chair's back. "If you feel it's necessary to give me a bad review this year, I will fight it through the board of directors. I'm doing the job I was hired to do." Helen looked out the large window behind Ms. K then directly at her, "That's something you could watch and learn from me. You say you care, but you're willing to throw away good foster parents on hopeless cases."

Ms. K had a choice to make and she had to make it quickly. "Helen, I'm not going to get in a mud throwing contest with you. We have to care for all parties involved but I feel strongly that the children are our main focus. After all, they are children, and in many cases these children are unable to tell us what's happening in their homes or share with us the raging wars they battle on the inside."

Helen's fingers turned a ghostly white as she gripped the back of the chair tighter. "I knew when they selected you as director it was a mistake—a mistake for the parents, the kids and the business of social work."

Ms. K pushed back from her desk, stood and walked towards her closed office door. "I can see that you do not respect me or hold the same values that I do. I'll plan a meeting for next week with the director of the board and myself. You may bring any grievances you have against me at that time."

Helen smirked. "Why not make it the whole board. I'd feel like a third wheel with the *two of you*." The 'two of you' remark smacked of scandal.

Even though Gina had mentioned Helen's gossip to her, hearing the remark caught Ms. K by surprise. She kept her voice even. "I'll see what I can do to assemble the whole group, but the members of the board all serve as volunteers. If you insist on the whole board being present, we can schedule a time slot at their next meeting at the end of January."

"I do insist." With those words Helen walked by Ms. K and out the door.

Ms. K watched Helen sit back down at her desk and begin writing in the journal she had carried with her to their meeting.

Peering out her office window at the rest of the staff, Ms. K watched the atmosphere in the office shift. She could feel and see the stress Helen was causing on her and everyone else in the office. She pulled her cell phone from her jacket pocket and selected from her favorite's list. She dialed the number for the director of the board.

He answered on the first ring. "Hello, Laura. Great to hear from you."

"Well, actually it may not be so great. I'm calling because I have a problem with one of my social workers. She has made a veiled remark—maybe not so veiled—that implied…" Ms. K's voice abruptly stopped. She inhaled and spoke in a quiet voice. "She implied that you and I are somehow romantically involved."

The line was quiet.

***

Fauna moved the books and papers to the side and laid her

head on the desk. She closed her eyes and drifted into thought. Two months had passed since CeCe arrived at her home. She was working part-time at the counseling center to open up more time for running CeCe to her appointments.

The days she dropped CeCe at childcare were the highlight of her week. She couldn't admit that to anyone— not even Snake. But walking away from the preschool room was the reprieve she needed. Listening to clients tell her stories about their messed-up lives was a reprieve. It gave her hope that her own life was not the extravagant failure she believed it had become.

Why was CeCe more drawn to Snake than her? In their brief conversations, neither one of them expected that he would be the one CeCe would kinda accept. Why would she be drawn to a big hairy man with a hissing snake tattooed on the side of his face and not her? How did he become the safe one?

Fauna lifted her head from the desk top and rubbed her eyes. Why did CeCe allow him to read her books, throw a ball to her outside, and pull her on the sled around the back yard? Once she even touched his big hand with her index finger to trace the outline of one of his tattoos. That had been the only personal contact CeCe initiated with either one of them in the very long months that she had been living in their home.

Fauna covered her mouth as a huge yawn escaped her lips. She was glad Isabelle was a few minutes late. It's never a good thing for the counselor to be yawning uncontrollably during a session with a client. Fauna had not spoken to Isabelle since the night she told her parents about the pregnancy. She had hoped Isabelle would come for another meeting. She wanted to give her time for it to be her own idea, not forced on her by parents or an overbearing counselor. When Isabelle called to set something up, Fauna was thrilled.

Fauna heard a soft tapping on her door. "Come in."

Isabelle poked her head inside. "The receptionist told

me to come back, that you were expecting me."

"Yes, come in. Let's sit over here where it's comfortable." Fauna pointed at the budding basketball under Isabelle's form-fitting shirt. It was no longer hidden under an oversized sweater. "Things they are 'a changing' since your last visit."

Isabelle stroked her midsection and smiled. "Yes, there are no secrets here."

"Come on in and tell me how things have been going." Fauna motioned for Isabelle to sit down on one end of the sofa and she took the other. They both grabbed a pillow and got comfortable.

Isabelle began. "I had an ultrasound the day after I told my parents. The baby is a boy. I was 17 weeks then." Isabelle motioned to her expanding middle. "And as you can plainly see, I decided against having an abortion." Isabelle dug around in her purse and pulled out a scroll of folded paper. "Here's the pictures if you want to see them."

Fauna reached for the rolled-up paper and unfolded it to reveal ten different shots. "Well, I see a head here and there's a foot, and a hand." She folded the paper back up and returned it to Isabelle. "How are you feeling about all this? It must be a lot to take in."

"The baby is moving a lot now. For the most part, I'm not sick anymore. My parents have been amazing. No pressure at all from them. They are leaving everything up to me. I can keep the baby or choose adoption."

"Well, which way are you leaning right now?" Fauna wanted to touch the belly in front of her so badly. She kept telling herself, be professional, no touching.

"I'm all over the place. One day I believe I can raise this little guy with the help of my parents, and then the next I'm scared to death that I'll be the worst mother alive and I'll ruin his life forever."

"Sounds about right." Fauna identified with Isabelle's feelings, but for Fauna, the scales were tipped more in the direction of worst mom ever.

Isabelle continued. "I did want to talk to you about something I'd like you to consider. I haven't decided yet, but if I did choose adoption, there is someone that I would like to consider. I want an open adoption. What do you think of that?"

"Adoption isn't my area of expertise. But I do have a lawyer that I've referred other clients to. If you are seriously considering adoption, I have his card."

"I don't think it would hurt to consider all my options. But, I'd only want one couple that I know to be the parents if I chose adoption."

"I think that would be something the lawyer could discuss with you. Just be sure about your choice. Once you sign the papers at the hospital—it's permanent." Ms. Parker's face looked full of concern.

Isabelle reached for Fauna's hand and said. "It's you— Ms. Parker. You and Mr. Snake would be the only people I could ever imagine placing this little boy with."

Fauna could not mask her shock, which caused Issie to giggle.

"Isabelle. I don't even know what to say." Fauna was numb and excited, and her heart was racing.

Isabelle squeezed Fauna's hand tighter. "Please, don't say no. Not yet. We have months to go before either one of us has to make a final decision. Will you at least speak to Mr. Snake and see what his reaction is? I'll speak to my parents as well."

Fauna nodded in the affirmative. The counselor had no words.

"Oh, that was a big kick." Isabelle let go of Fauna's hand to rub an area on her round stomach. "Ms. Parker, would you like to feel the baby kick?"

Fauna reached forward at the invitation. Issie took her hand and placed it on her midsection.

The baby moved under her hand and Fauna smiled.

***

Ty knocked on Zander's bedroom door. There was no answer. He knocked a bit harder—still no answer. He casually wiggled the doorknob. It was locked. He took out his cell phone and texted. *Hey, are you in there?*

A moment later Ty's phone pinged. *Busy. Texting with a friend.*

Ty texted his older brother back. *I need to talk to you.* Ty waited.

Zander texted back. *FYI Don't have to talk to you right now.*

Ty felt the back of his neck tingle with perspiration. Why didn't Zander care about his own reputation? People were talking, and he needed to warn him. He made one more attempt to text him. *Fine-Mom and Dad will listen.*

The door handle turned, and Zander cracked open his bedroom door. "Really? I know there is gossip going around about me and Isabelle. That's been going on for over a month."

Ty whispered. "I'm trying to warn you."

"You did that months ago. And in case you didn't notice...I didn't listen then and I'm not listening now." The door closed in Ty's face.

"Fine, I'll just talk to you through the door." Ty raised his voice. "I know who the dad is." Before Ty could speak another word, the door opened, a hand grabbed his arm and pulled him inside the bedroom.

Zander pushed his brother to the wall and held him there with one hand. He spit his words at his brother through clenched teeth. "How could you know?"

Ty wiggled out of his brother's grip without moving away from the wall. "Well, I know it's not you, in spite of the rumors going around. For one thing, you lacked the opportunity, and Isabelle never even noticed you existed until you became her protector a few months ago."

Zander took a step back giving Ty a chance to breathe freely.

Zander sat down on the edge of his bed. "So, who do

you think the father is?" He didn't believe Ty knew, but wanted to find out what had his brother all worked up.

Ty glanced at Zander's desk and thought about crossing the room to get comfortable in the desk chair then thought he better not drag this thing out. He told what he knew in one breath. "It's that kid that came to youth group last summer for about a month or two. He sat alone most of the time, but I watched. I saw Isabelle and that guy smiling at each other when they thought no one was looking. They didn't look like strangers, but kinda like they had a secret that no one else knew. I may be a kid, but I'm not blind."

Zander felt his heart rate increase at the description. He had noticed this other guy too and had put the pieces together. But he decided not to bite. "Just what I thought, you got nothing."

He rolled his eyes and fell back on his bed. His phone was face up next to him. The phone pinged, signaling an incoming text. Picking up the phone, he read the message. Midway through he stopped for a moment, "Just because two people smile at each other across a crowded room doesn't mean they're having a baby together." He looked back down at the screen then began typing with his thumbs.

Ty stepped closer to Zander's bed. "If I can figure it out—others will too. Isabelle needs to tell him, and you need to step back. You're setting yourself up for a ton of hurt. She's not going to pick you over a guy who can drive a car and is almost done with his first year of college. You're 15 and you've caused Mom and Dad enough heartache."

"What do you know about it? I've talked to them already. They had questions and I answered them—truthfully."

"You think that matters when a whole community believes one thing. You're being insensitive to Isabelle and to Mom and Dad."

Zander stood up towering over his brother by nearly a foot. With his index finger extended, he pushed his younger brother backwards until he was in the hallway. The door shut with force in Ty's face. Through the door Zander shot back, "Later bro."

Ty shook his head and walked down the hallway to his bedroom. His parents' bedroom door was open as he walked past. He didn't notice his mother standing inside her bedroom out of his line of sight.

Callan's lips quivered as she mentally processed the conversation she'd overheard.

***

The Parker's house was dark and quiet. Fauna cuddled up next to Snake and recounted the details of her day. She included all her personal pitfalls, negative thoughts and each of the outright failures of her day. "Now that you've heard all the dark details, there was one wonderful thing that happened. In desperation—I prayed and by *prayed*—I mean—I PRAYED!"

Snake drew his wife in a bit closer while she shared the one positive part of her very long day.

"I poured out all my pain, and feelings of inadequacy to the Lord. Crazy thing is, while praying, these words ran through my thoughts, *you can't fix this*. Strange enough—I found this phrase liberating. *I can't fix this*. Only God can."

Snake sat up in the bed and flicked on the lamp next to him. "It's been awhile since I've heard you talk like this."

Fauna sat up and faced Snake in the bed. "I know. Right! Only Jesus can make this right for CeCe, and only He can make things right for me regarding my feelings of inadequacy."

Snake listened.

"When I prayed today, I released both of us, CeCe and me, to the Lord. I released my fears to Him." Fauna rested her head on her husband's chest and slipped her arms around him. "I'll be honest, I want to have my own children. I mean our children—biological children."

Fauna stepped back from Snake. "I'm beginning to

accept the fact that this may never happen. "

Her voice broke. "The most painful part of all this is that I feel like a fake, an imposter trying to be a mother to CeCe. I can't say for sure if we will be the parents who will always be in CeCe's life, but I prayed for whoever it would be that they would love her unconditionally."

Fauna fingered the corner of her eye to stop a tear from rolling down her cheek. "If it's not us, I pray that CeCe's pain will be gone and that she will be whole. I believe God can heal CeCe and He can heal me too, but I'm not sure if we can get to this place together."

Snake drew Fauna into a hug and pressed his lips against her ear and whispered, "We're going to get through this and I believe we will do it *all* together."

Fauna returned the hug. "I don't want to give up on CeCe. I'm just saying that it's been months and I haven't seen anything that would give me hope that she is warming up to me." Fauna pulled away from Snake. She spoke her next words slowly stressing each word, "I'm not giving up— I'm just saying—it's been hard—really hard."

Snake tried to be reassuring, "You're doing an amazing job with her and handling all your other responsibilities as well."

Fauna spoke with excitement as soon as the last word exited Snake's mouth. "One other thing that happened today. You aren't going to believe it. Isabelle would like us to consider adopting her baby boy." Fauna just put it out there and waited.

Snake didn't respond. Fauna's words hung in the air. The room was dim, but Fauna could see and hear the concern in Snake's face and voice. "Really? For real. Could she really do that? Give up her baby? And her parents? Could they let go of their grandchild? It would be painful to watch someone else raising your son or grandson right in front of you. Who could do that?"

"Lots of people do that. Would you want to consider it or talk about it with them more?" Again, Fauna was void of commitment or emotion as she shared in the dimly lit bedroom this life altering news.

Snake scratched his thick beard as he pondered his next words. "That's a lot to bite off right now. I mean, emotionally with CeCe and all. Is that what you want?" He choked out the words, "to pursue adoption. Have we closed the door on biological children?"

"No! Of course not! But that's not happening and I spoke with Isabelle today so the whole adoption thing is pretty fluid right now. I didn't tip my hand or show any interest one way or the other. At least I don't—think I did. I know she's a hormonal teenager so I'm not building my nest on any materials she is offering up—if you know what I mean?"

"Well, I don't think you could have said it any better than that. We should definitely proceed with caution if you are even thinking of moving forward at all."

Fauna laid back and rested her head on the pillow. "I don't know. A baby would give us a chance to make our own mistakes and not spend all our time correcting someone else's."

Snake laid down on his side of the bed and squinted his eyes to make out the darkened light fixture over the bed. "We have CeCe now. It seems like the Lord put her here *with us* for a reason. I'd feel if we pursued a baby we'd be..." Snake's voice trailed off for a moment. "...unfaithful to her."

"Oh, Snake. You are a pile of mush when it comes to that child. I want to believe, as we partner with the Lord, that we'll see a positive outcome sooner rather than later. I'll be honest with you, I haven't seen anything in CeCe that gives me hope. And I'm so tired."

A piercing scream caused Fauna to sit straight up in the bed. With her heart pounding in her chest, she dropped her face into her hands.

Snake touched her back. "Let me take the first shift. You go back to sleep. I'll lay on the floor in CeCe's room so she's not alone. Put your headphones on and listen to music or scripture."

Snake walked out of the bedroom and closed the door behind him. He grabbed a sleeping bag from the hall closet and carried it to CeCe's room. She laid thrashing in the bed, but he didn't speak to her or touch her. He smoothed out the sleeping bag on the floor, laid down and began praying as the Spirit led.

12

*"I will deliver you from the power of the wicked.
I will free you from the clutches of violent people."*
Jeremiah 15:21 (NET)

Youth group had not felt like a friendly place for a long time for Isabelle. She decided after her situation had become known that she would not withdraw or isolate herself from the church. She needed to be there for herself. There was plenty of judgment, side looks and lack of friends. She decided to push on, friends or no friends.

The worship portion of the youth service ended when Zander strummed in a downward motion on his guitar. As he connected with the strings, there was a loud reverberating chord that echoed off the cinder block walls. The cheers from the youth resounded their approval. Zander lifted his guitar strap over his head and propped his instrument in the stand behind him. He glanced towards the back of the room as he stepped off the platform.

Pastor Eli, the youth minister, crossed the platform and spoke into the mike. "Take a few minutes to greet each other. I've got a great teaching for you tonight, so get ready!" Pastor E was well liked by the youth. He made church fun for the kids and he had a way of talking about the Bible that brought it down to earth. He made it interesting. It wasn't just a bunch of foreign places with unpronounceable names and a boring history lesson. Whether the topic was love, sin or forgiveness, Pastor E seemed to be able to reach the youth no matter their personal level of biblical understanding.

Zander nodded his head and gave a halfhearted smile to a few girls as he passed by. The momentary nod did not deter his focus on the cute girl in the back row who was watching him draw closer with each step.

Ty stepped in front of Zander causing his brother to

bump into him. Zander's focus on the smiling girl in the back row was temporarily broken.

"Hey Zander, come and sit with me over there in the front with my friends." Ty motioned across the room in the opposite direction from where Zander was going.

Zander stepped past his younger brother, took a few steps, then called back over his shoulder. "Nope. I'm sitting with Isabelle."

Ty circled back in front of his brother. "Please, come sit with us. I invited Seth from school and I thought you could encourage…"

"Just stop it. I know what you're doing. I'm sitting with Isabelle, end of discussion." Zander glanced past his brother's shoulder and watched the smile on Isabelle's face fade. He leaned into his brother and whispered. "If you do something to ruin this, I'll never forgive you."

Ty stepped to the side and watched his brother smile at Isabelle while she returned the smile with a bit less enthusiasm than before. Ty moved to the back of the youth room and watched the other youth milling about in groups of three or more. A few girls were laughing loudly, drawing attention to their group while some of the boys watched from the safety of their own groups. It was a bit reminiscent of a 6th grade school dance.

Ty shook his head in disgust. The place was like a boiling pot of teen hormones.

"Hey everyone, find a seat. We're gonna get started." Pastor E's voice was one decibel point below screaming. The volume in the room dropped gradually while the youth moved to their seats. The seating hierarchy had begun. Who you sat next to, across from, in front of or behind was paramount to a marriage proposal in the eyes of teenagers. After all, making the correct seat choice would land you next to your person of interest for 30-40 minutes. This was nearly eternity for a teen.

Ty reluctantly left Zander and Isabelle sitting side by side in the back row of the dimly lit room. Walking to the front of the youth room he silently prayed for both of them. He didn't dislike Isabelle. Not at all, but Zander was in a dangerous place. His big brother was gonna get burned if he didn't back away from the flames. Ty wondered why *he* knew this, and Zander didn't.

Pastor E tapped his open hand on the music stand that served as his podium. "Okay, let's get started. I have a crazy, cool media presentation that will accompany this message." He jokingly said, "You're gonna love it." The words RUN FOR YOUR LIFE appeared on the screen behind him. The words came up one at a time then burst in every direction like a bomb had exploded sending the individual letters flying. The words began to reappear one letter at a time before locking on the screen RUN FOR YOUR LIFE.

"In case you haven't figured it out, we're gonna be talking tonight about running away from sin. People who get close to sin can really mess up their lives. Sometimes, one bad choice can have consequences that will affect the rest of your life. Tonight, I hope each one here will see the importance of running away from sin before it changes the course of your life—forever."

One of the boys had rested his feet on the back of the empty chair in front of him. As he repositioned his feet, the folding chair suddenly crashed to the floor. The sound was so loud a few girls screamed out in fright, which caused a series of nervous giggles to ripple through the youth group.

The collapsing chair gave some an opportunity to glance to the back of the room to see how Isabelle was handling Pastor E's sermon topic.

Isabelle moved uncomfortably in her chair, crossing and uncrossing her legs. The more her belly popped outward, more guessing about who the *baby daddy* might be grew, and many believed it was Zander.

Pastor Eli quoted his scripture text from memory. "In second Timothy 2:22, it says, run from anything that stimulates youthful lusts. Instead, pursue righteous living, faithfulness, love, and peace. Enjoy the companionship of those who call on the Lord with pure hearts."

While Pastor E continued his message, a few kids in the youth group casually looked backwards to steal an inquisitive look at Isabelle—and Zander too.

Isabelle wondered if *everyone* in the room felt the message was geared directly at her because she sure felt it.

Zander reached for Isabelle's hand. She didn't resist.

***

Laura Klingburg waited for the director of the Family Christian Services board to respond to the rumors about them. They had a warm friendship, but they had never been out for a meal together or even sat together at Community Outreach Church where they both attended. How Helen ever came up with this idea was far beyond Laura's comprehension. She was always happy to see him, but for goodness sake, the man lost his wife a short time ago and he was at least ten years her senior.

Laura cleared her throat. "Are you there?"

"Umm. Yes. I'm still here. This is so unexpected. I'm not even sure how to reply." The senior gentleman moved his half empty cup of coffee around on the table in front of him. "Did Ms. Franko give any reason why she suspected that we were intimately acquainted?"

"She has been cold to me since I began working here 18 months ago. I'm thinking it goes all the way back to my hiring. She may feel that I had some kind of inside connection with you and that's why I was hired over her for the position of director."

A smile formed on the wrinkled face of the board chairman. "Ah, Laura. Don't give any more worry to that. I've watched your life play out at church and watched you grow in the Lord. You were the type of person we wanted in this position. Someone with experience but who also was willing to place children above the bottom line. We are a non-profit—not for profit. If I recall, that was the deciding factor in the whole board's final decision."

"Tom, I'm concerned about your reputation and mine as well. It only takes one allegation to stick and it will be nearly impossible to peel that muck off of us once the insinuation has been made." Laura swiveled her chair away from the desk towards the exterior window in her office.

Tom knew Laura's assessment of the situation was correct. He had worked in the business world for many years and had himself believed false allegations regarding co-workers before he had factual information. "Would you like to meet and discuss this in person?"

Laura answered, "I think we would be playing right into Helen Franko's hand. How about if we asked Pastor Rey and Callan to meet with us at the church? That would be neutral ground and wouldn't hold any form of impropriety."

Tom agreed.

Laura continued, "I'll call Grace to see if Pastor Rey can fit us into his schedule in the next week."

There was a pause then Laura added with a soft voice, "I'm extremely sorry that your good name has been tarnished by this office rivalry."

"Don't worry. Helen Franko has been on my radar and the whole board's for quite a while."

"Thank you, Tom, for your confidence in me, and again, I am so sorry." Laura hung up the phone and returned to the review of Helen Franko's files on her desk. She fingered through a few pages and then pushed them aside.

Her heart was saddened by the actions of one person's vindictiveness and how it had spilled out into the lives of so many innocent people. Tom Brown didn't deserve to be pulled into this. He was a good and decent man. And CeCe, that poor child—her life was damaged all because of greed and Helen Franko's sloppy social work. How many more stories like CeCe's were hidden in Helen Franko's files?

***

The January thaw was underway with patches of grass poking through the piles of snow that lined the driveway. CeCe wandered around the yard in her snowsuit kicking the soccer ball the best she could with her snow boots. She pulled back her leg and connected with the ball with all her might, sending the ball sailing in Snake's direction.

The ball hit Snake in the back of the head and he playfully yelped. "OUCH! You got me." He proceeded to fall to the ground and play dead.

Fauna watched from the sliding door, as Snake lay on the ground motionless.

Nothing prepared either Snake or Fauna for CeCe's response. A gut level belly laugh burst from somewhere deep inside the child, and the sound of her laughter immediately brought Snake to his hands and knees.

Snake wasn't sure how to respond to CeCe's positive outburst since it was the first time in the months since CeCe arrived, that she expressed this unrestrained release of joy.

CeCe collected herself for a brief moment and then burst into tearful glee and yelled, "Bear! Bear!" As she pointed at Snake.

Snake responded by raising up on his knees, pawed at the air and growled like a bear. "Grrrrrrrrrr!"

CeCe copied Snake's movements and responded in kind. "Grrrrrrrrr!"

Fauna watched their playful interaction from the window, wishing she was part of this special moment. She moved the glass sliding door just enough to yell out, "Run, CeCe, run. That bear's gonna get you."

CeCe stopped laughing and lowered her bear claws. "Not playing with you." She frowned at Fauna.

Snake tried to regain the lost ground. "CeCe. Fauna is fun. I like to play with her. She could be the Momma bear. I'll be the Papa bear and you can be the baby bear."

"Momma bears mean. Momma bears hurt baby."

Fauna listened from the deck in amazement. Even

though CeCe's words were painful to hear, it was the most positive moment they had had with her since she arrived. Until now, CeCe had not verbalized anything negative about anyone in her life. Her communication was usually in three words or less, and other than emotional or violent outbursts, she had not shared her feelings, fears or happiness—ever.

Fauna counted this a step in the right direction. Even if she was still personally being pushed to the sidelines, it was a place they could begin to build on. Now, she had to show CeCe that all momma bears are not the same.

Fauna grabbed her jacket off a nearby chair and opened the sliding door. As she stepped out on the deck, CeCe's eyes narrowed. Her demeanor changed to survival mode. CeCe's eyes darted around the yard from the slightly open door behind Fauna, to Snake who was still on his knees, to the open gate that went out to the driveway. CeCe's eyes showed the desperation of a caged animal.

Snake knew he couldn't stand up. His 6'5" height alone could be terrifying at this moment. He decided to let the counselor handle this one.

Fauna took a few steps to the end of the deck and sat down on the first step. "CeCe, it's okay to tell us how you feel. We want to know. I know there are some Momma bears who are not nice and can hurt people, but I'm not a mean Momma bear. I'm nice. I don't hurt babies. I love babies. I'm nice to all kids and especially you."

CeCe frowned at Fauna, looked at the ground, and crossed her arms across her chest as best she could with her heavy snowsuit on.

Fauna scooted down another step and kept eyes on the pouting child. "You know what I think would be fun—hot chocolate. Do you like hot chocolate with marshmallows or whip cream?"

CeCe looked up at Snake. He smiled at her, winked and nodded his head.

"Snake too?" CeCe puckered her full red lips as if she were waiting for a kiss.

Fauna stood up, turned her back on CeCe and walked towards the sliding door. She called back over her shoulder. "Of course, Snake too. Hot chocolate is the favorite drink of all Papa and Momma bears."

Snake stood up and reached his hand out to CeCe. A smile was scarcely visible under his heavily bearded face.

CeCe scrutinized Snake's outreached hand. Her face revealed the inward battle of trust. Void of emotion, she turned away from Snake and walked towards the deck. In a soft voice, she spoke to no one, "Marshmallows. Snake too."

***

Samantha yelled up the stairs. "Girls, dinner's ready." The dining room table was set, the baked chicken mushroom casserole was surrounded by a tossed salad and garlic bread. The garlic aroma filled the air.

Baylee bounded down the steps two at a time. Isabelle held the railing and descended the stairs with the grace of Scarlet O'Hara in *Gone With The Wind*. It was her only option since she could not see the stairs beneath her swollen midsection.

Baylee rounded the corner into the dining room where her mom and dad were already seated. "Mom, it smells wonderful down here. I'm starved."

A few seconds later, Isabelle stuck her head in with her nose in the air. "Garlic. Why don't they make a garlic perfume? I'd buy that." She giggled. "My smells are all mixed up right now."

Stuart and Samantha looked at each other and smiled. This was the happy family sitting together around the table that Samantha had always dreamed of having. The Hayes family dinners began shortly after Baylee's healing and for the past two years had been a nightly experience. On the surface, the family smiled and laughed, but the *'pink elephant in the room'* had not been mentioned since the discussion in Dr. Hayes' office following the ultrasound.

Isabelle scooted up to the table, dropped her napkin on her disappearing lap and bowed her head awaiting her father's prayer. The mealtime prayer had become a welcome part of the Hayes' family table gatherings.

Stuart looked around the table at the bowed heads of the three women in his life. A content smile formed on his lips. He was a blessed man indeed. With his eyes open, he prayed. "Lord, thank You for another day. Thank You for Your love and protection. We need You in our lives as we each have decisions to make. We love You, adore You and are grateful to You. Bless this food to our bodies. It is in Your name that we pray. Amen."

Samantha reached for her husband's plate, moved it to the casserole dish and proceeded to fill the plate with an ample portion of the main course.

"Whoa, I'm only one person, Samantha." Stuart signaled to his wife with an open hand.

Samantha smiled warmly at her husband and slid half the portion she had dished up back into the serving dish before returning the plate.

Baylee lifted her plate next and Samantha filled it with food. Isabelle followed. The nightly table conversation began with the same dinner question that began their meal for the past three months. "How was school for you today, Issie?"

A smirk formed on Isabelle's face. "Things haven't been the same since I returned after Christmas break. Before Christmas break it was much different."

Samantha looked up. "How so? You aren't being bullied, are you?"

"Of course not. Like—I could be bullied." Isabelle laughed at her own sass. "Before Christmas, it seemed like everyone was treating me like I had a contagious disease, but now all of a sudden, I'm a celebrity. Even the teachers are treating me special."

Isabelle continued without interruption, "I have these two teachers who are single ladies in their mid-twenties.

They teach English and Business Math and are always talking to me like we're BFF's. You know? Best Friends Forever. I thought it would be the opposite. The bigger my middle expanded…" With a fork still in her hand, Isabelle moved her arms outward from her belly. "…I thought people wouldn't want to associate with me." Issie took a big mouthful of casserole and chewed. Then let out a long content, "Mmmmmmm. Mom, it's so good."

"Thanks. It's a new recipe I saw on Facebook. The picture looked amazing, so I had to try it." Samantha turned to Baylee who was sitting at the end of the table opposite her father. She looked distracted and distant from the rest of the family. "And how was your day Baylee?"

Baylee moved the food around in a circle on her plate. "Fine. Nothing new here." She kept her eyes fixed on the moving food in front of her.

Stuart chimed in, "Well, I must say, you two girls lead a very boring life!"

Samantha smiled, "Just the way we like it!"

Isabelle looked around the table before speaking. "Well…actually, I do have something I need to talk to you all about."

Baylee looked up from her plate in anticipation. Stuart and Samantha drew deep breaths, then glanced at each other.

Issie cleared her throat before plunging in. "Ah-um. I spoke with Ms. Parker recently about something I've been considering. But before I decide one way or the other, I want to bring you all into the discussion." Isabelle looked at her parents. "Thank you, Mom and Dad for giving me space over the past months while I process my options."

All eyes were fixed on Issie as she continued.

"Abortion was never going to happen. I knew that from the beginning. I don't even know why I threw that out there. Probably because I was afraid to tell you guys. I wanted to believe I could just make it go away."

Baylee twisted her mouth to the side. "I knew you couldn't do it." She looked around the room, "You did have me worried though. I will admit that."

Isabelle rolled her eyes at her sister. "I couldn't push through with abortion, but I am considering looking into adoption."

The room grew quiet. No one spoke.

Isabelle continued. "How would you feel about that..." She looked around the table and locked eyes with her mother. "...Mom?"

Samantha squirmed in her seat. She wanted more time to collect her thoughts. What if she said something wrong? What if she messed it all up for everyone? She glanced around the table at the other cast members hoping someone would jump in and rescue her. No one did. All eyes were on her.

Her answer was riddled with pauses. "Iss...that's a...big decision...and a lifetime...of possible...regret." Samantha glanced at Stuart.

They had talked privately about what Issie might decide and they had shared with each other how they hoped it would turn out.

Samantha wanted to have the opportunity to be a part of her grandson's life in a meaningful way while Stuart felt Issie was too young to fully understand what she was committing to for the rest of her life. If she chose to raise a baby at the young age of seventeen, he was sure her life would never be what she hoped. He was team adoption, and her mom was fully on board with keeping the baby.

Baylee continued to mix her food up on the plate in front of her. The next words spilled out of Baylee's mouth before she could stop them. "I hope you keep him."

Samantha looked at her youngest daughter and sighed. This was affecting all of them—not just Isabelle and the child she carried.

Stuart breathed in deeply before speaking. "Iss, I want the best possible outcome for you. I will support you, if adoption is what you want to do, but just be sure about whatever direction you choose. It's a lifetime commitment."

Stuart looked at Samantha who was trying desperately to keep her emotions at bay.

Isabelle exhaled. "I mentioned to Ms. Parker that I'd like her and Mr. Snake to consider an open adoption with…" She rubbed her extended belly. "…this little guy."

Stuart's eyebrows lifted in surprise, and a half smile formed on his lips. "How did she respond?"

"I think she was being very professional and cautious. Actually, she didn't show any interest one way or the other. I think she knows I'm still processing the whole idea. She probably was protecting her emotions too. But, I think she would be interested in talking more…after she talks to Mr. Snake." Isabelle looked at her mom.

Samantha leaned forward and rubbed her forehead then looked up and met Isabelle's gaze. "That could work. At least we'd be in close proximity to our grandson and maybe they would allow us to be grandparents—maybe?" Her smile grew. "And you Iss, could see him growing, and you could still be part of his life without changing the whole course of yours."

Baylee shook her head back and forth. Without lifting her eyes, she gave her opinion. "Don't do it Iss. You are his mother. Keep him. We are all here for you." Baylee looked up at the three family members looking at her. "Well— aren't we?" Then she looked at Isabelle. "Have you ever watched one of those adoption reunifications shows? They're brutal."

"Baylee stop adulting! You're a kid…*adoption reunification*…really?"

Stuart frowned at Baylee and raised one finger to his mouth. Then with a calm voice he said, "This is just a discussion. No decisions are being made tonight. Let's enjoy our dinner and we'll revisit this later." Stuart looked at Isabelle and asked one last question. "When will you speak to Fauna again?"

"She gave me the card of an adoption lawyer and steered me in that direction for now."

"Okay, let's make an appointment with the lawyer to get information." Stuart looked back and forth between Baylee and Samantha and said. "Making decisions without getting all the information doesn't make any sense. Let's help Isabelle make an educated decision."

Baylee mumbled under her breath. "*Hearts* will trump over *minds*—always."

13

*This is the way God's children are distinguished
from the devil's children.
Everyone who doesn't do what is right
or love other believers isn't God's child.*
1 John 3:10 (GW)

The sound of flesh hitting flesh left a smacking sound ringing in Fauna's ears. Her face burned from the multiple hits she took, as she tried to lock CeCe into her car seat. With the sweetest voice she could muster she spoke to the frightened and angry child. "I'm not going to hurt you. Please don't hit me. I am not going to hit you." She repeated her words over and over to the thrashing child.

Once Fauna heard the seatbelt click, she quickly withdrew from the line of fire. When she was in the driver's seat, Fauna rubbed the reddened side of her face. It still smarted from the child's swats. She pushed the play button on the CD player and the music quieted the angry child in the back seat. She picked up her cell phone and dialed Emily Edwards' number.

"Hey, Fauna. What time are you dropping off *the little angel?*" This was followed by a sarcastic giggle, then a tender voice. "Have you seen any signs of improvement or bonding yet? I know it's bad of me to laugh, but she seems pretty good when she's over here as long as I steer clear."

Fauna spoke quietly, "Every once in a while, I think that something wonderful is about to happen then she shuts down. And FYI, she is no angel today. Hope you can handle her. Are you sure you're up for this?"

"Of course. William loves her like a sister already. And it's good practice for me and *The Little Gentleman* since sister number two is just two months away."

"We'll be there in a few minutes." Fauna hung up and glanced in the review mirror at CeCe. She was holding a doll. The expression on her face was grim. Fauna asked, "Is that your baby, CeCe?"

CeCe dropped the doll to the floor and turned her head away from Fauna's view.

"CeCe, mommies should be gentle with their babies. We love them and don't want to hurt them."

CeCe turned her head back slowly and glanced downward at the doll that lay on the floor behind Fauna's seat. It was now outside of her reach.

Between watching the road and glancing in the rearview mirror, Fauna tried to interpret CeCe's facial expression. Usually, this was impossible to decode, but this time Fauna was reasonably sure and hopeful that CeCe was looking longingly at the discarded doll. Fauna thought she saw a sense of regret as she tried to extend her arm to recover the doll that was beyond reach.

Fauna turned the SUV into Kota and Emily's driveway. As soon as the vehicle was in park, CeCe disengaged her seatbelt and reached for the baby doll alone on the car floor.

Fauna opened the door behind the passenger seat where CeCe stood holding the doll tightly to her chest. "Okay, little momma let's go see William."

CeCe lowered herself out of the SUV and walked towards the open door where Emily and William waited. William yelled, "E-cc's here!" He was jumping up and down as his mommy opened the door. CeCe walked in and William beckoned her to follow him.

Fauna shook her head as she approached the door. "I'm gonna get going. I'm hoping I'll be done in less than two hours. Thanks for giving me this outlet to do my grocery shopping and errands in peace." She turned back around and looked at her very pregnant sister-in-law. "Please be sure and let me watch William and Maddie anytime for you too. I'm on a part-time schedule at the center right now. In a few months, when the baby comes, it will be my turn to give you a break."

Emily smiled and touched her belly with her free hand. "When this little one arrives, I'll be taking you up on that—you can count on it."

Fauna returned to her car and pulled out of the driveway. As she turned right, she noticed a car turn into Emily's driveway behind her. A groaning, ugh sound pushed past her lips. It was James Fields, her father-in-law who turned into Emily's driveway as she pulled away. As James' car disappeared behind her, a slight smile formed on Fauna's lips. Her thoughts betrayed her. *Get'm CeCe—Get'm.*

* * *

Zander yelled over his shoulder as he exited the front door. "Isabelle's here. I'm going."

There was no response to his proclamation.

To cover his bases he added, "We're going to Beantown at the mall. I got my cell, if you need me." The door slammed shut behind him as he bolted to the waiting car.

Isabelle looked like any other teen driver behind the wheel from Zander's view. No one would guess that she was seven months pregnant. The small red car was a recent gift from her parents shortly after she announced her pregnancy.

Unlike most doctor's children, Isabelle did not receive a car on her 16th birthday. The family had an extra car, but it was never called Isabelle's car until her parents gifted it to her. They were cautious to let her know it was not a reward for being pregnant, but more a means of giving them all peace of mind. She had appointments and they didn't want her to be dependent on them or others for transportation.

Zander opened the passenger door and folded his tall frame into the small space allotted for the person riding shotgun. Isabelle gave Zander a side smile as she guided the stick shift into reverse.

"Were your parent's okay with me driving you to the mall?" Isabelle asked while keeping her eye on the rearview mirror as she backed down the long driveway towards Lancaster Boulevard.

"They said, yes, and they like you. They probably feel I'm safer with you than a teenage boy." Zander looked at the side of Isabelle's face and slipped his arm over her shoulder. He wanted to take it back as soon as he did it. It was awkward but if he removed it too soon it would be even more uncomfortable.

"Zander, would you mind moving your arm. It's blocking my view." Isabelle's remark took the pressure off both of them.

"Oh sure." Zander moved his arm back to his side of the car, feeling relieved to have that clumsy attempt at affection behind him.

Isabelle took her hand off the stick shift for a moment and patted Zander's leg just above the knee. Then returned to shifting into 2nd gear as she sped up on the open road.

The consolation tap caused the corners of Zander's lips to push upward into a full smile. He asked, "What did your parents say about your adoption idea?"

Isabelle shifted into 3rd gear as she answered. "My mom and Baylee were in the 'absolutely not' column, but they promised to be supportive of my decision. My dad was trying to stay very neutral with a 'count the cost' little sermonette before you commit. He stayed very objective with his words, but I'm pretty sure he'd be in favor of adoption, especially if it was an open adoption, and I believe he likes the Parkers. He just wants me to be sure one way or the other before I sign my name on the line. Because there is no going back after that."

"Which way are you leaning *today* adoption or motherhood?" Zander folded his hands in his lap and looked straight ahead.

Isabelle took a moment before she answered. "There is one huge advantage to motherhood. I wouldn't have to tell the birth father anything, but if I choose adoption then he has to know. If I didn't tell him, he could come in later and mess everything up for the adoptive parents." The car was momentarily quiet then Issie added, "If I keep the baby, I don't even have to put the father's name on the birth certificate. If he found out later, he could push for a DNA test—I guess. But that would only affect me, not some innocent family. I haven't heard a word from him so I'm guessing he's not interested either way."

"What did Ms. Parker say about the whole idea of the adoption?" Zander touched his thumbs together and began tapping them.

Isabelle glanced at Zander's thumb movement, then returned her focus to the road. "It was a big bomb to drop on her, so I'm not judging lack of enthusiasm as an outright—not interested. She needs time to warm to the idea…" Isabelle's voice trailed off.

Zander finished her sentence. "…and maybe you have to warm to the idea too."

Isabelle looked above the treetops at the huge sign that read, Pine-Hill Mall. She down-shifted from 3rd to 2nd gear as the entrance to the mall came into view. Isabelle engaged the right turn blinker as she cleared the last blue spruce that lined the rural road before the entrance to the mall parking lot. The next words that exited Isabelle's mouth were like sandpaper on an open wound to Zander's ears. "I've been thinking that either way, keep or adopt, I'm going to need to contact Griffin. He deserves to know."

Zander's head turned and looked at the side of Isabelle's face. "Really? Why? He's the one who cut off all communication with you."

"Yes. But once I tell him—that will put an end to the wondering." Isabelle pulled into a parking space near the door.

Zander clenched his jaw tightly and rolled his eyes. He could feel his heart pounding in his chest. His mouth was at the brink of spilling over his immaturity. He willed himself to be quiet. At this moment, words were not his friend.

***

"Pastor Rey?" Grace, the church secretary's voice echoed in the empty office. "Are you there?" Still no answer. Grace touched the hold button on the church phone. "I'm sorry Laura. Pastor's not picking up. I can give you his voice mail if you'd like?"

Laura Klingburg considered her options for a moment. "I need to make an appointment to speak with Pastor and if possible, I'd like to have Callan there as well."

"I don't usually make appointments that include Callan. If you want the meeting here at the office then I'd say it would be better to set something up with me, but if you want to be sure Callan can be there, it might be better to call her at home and schedule something with her. I don't know her schedule, but she knows Pastor's. Does that make sense?"

"Absolutely. I have Callan's number. Thanks Grace." Laura hung up and opened her calendar. She needed the meeting to be soon. Laura dialed Callan's number and waited. It went straight to voice mail. "Hey Callan. It's Laura. I need to speak with you as soon as possible. Long story short, it's about Tom Brown and myself and an ugly rumor that I heard. We both would like to meet with you and Pastor to discuss the rumor as it pertains to something here at work. Give me a call when you can, and we'll set something up. Thanks." Laura hung up and felt better even though she hadn't spoken with Callan. The weight of carrying this alone was now a bit lighter. It was good to have friends who love you and cared about the things you care about.

Laura shook her head in a moment of disbelief. Three years ago, if someone would have told her she would be calling Callan Douglas, or Rey Douglas for that matter, to share personal details of her life and ask them for godly counsel, she would have burst into a fit of mocking laughter. My how the Lord changes people's hearts, passions and desires when they truly surrender to Him.

Laura laid her cell phone down and opened the file of a family of three children that needed emergency placement. The file was red-flagged. She hoped June's house would be open. She picked up her cell phone to call June, but it rang in her hand before she could place the call.

It was Callan Douglas returning her call. "Hello Callan. Thanks for calling me back so quickly."

"What in the world is going on with you—and Tom Brown? Are you kidding me?"

"No—nothing. Remember it's a rumor and I really don't even know how anyone could believe such a thing or how they could put the two of us together. Other than attending the same church and he was involved in my interview and hiring at the agency, we have never been alone together. We talk occasionally about business things only— ever. We have never ever met outside the office for a business lunch or dinner. It has been a professional business relationship only." Laura stopped talking. She knew she sounded defensive and maybe she was talking too fast— which may have sounded like guilt.

She stopped talking.

"Laura, you're preaching to the choir. I would never believe anything evil of either of you. We've known Tom for years and since you were saved your life has been changed for the better. Rey and I will meet whenever it works best for you and Tom, and it can be this week. Would you like to meet at our house or the church?"

Laura sat alone in her office. Her shoulders slowly relaxed with each word Callan spoke. "I'll call Tom and see what his preferences are. I think it would be best to meet sooner. Thanks Callan for being so accommodating."

"Well come on. We're talking about Tom Brown and Laura Klingburg. Of course, we're going to find time for the two of you."

"Thank you. I'll get back with you today or at the latest tomorrow with options for when and where we could meet. Hopefully we can lock something in."

Callan ended the conversation with, "Perfect. We'll talk soon." She sat down at the kitchen breakfast nook. Her thoughts turned to Tom. Why would anyone pick on such a godly man? He was just coming out of the dark funk he had been in for nearly two years. With his retirement and downsizing, the poor guy had been through enough changes. All this had stirred up so many memories of Jean and now he was faced with fighting off some kind of rumors about him and Laura. Rumors that could affect their reputations and possibly Laura's livelihood.

Callan slapped her open hand down on the table. She was mad. It wasn't right. It just wasn't fair!

***

CeCe Jefferson stepped inside the door of Emily Edwards home. She watched quietly as Emily and her foster mom, Fauna, spoke. Fauna left, and Emily closed the door to the cold outside. CeCe removed her coat and handed it to Emily. William, who had been awaiting her arrival, grabbed her by the hand as soon as she was free of her outerwear and pulled her in the direction of the formal dining room.

When Emily was pregnant with William, they moved into their current house. It had been Kota's idea to turn the dining room into a full-fledged dream world, playland for their daughter and soon-to-be son. On one wall, he built low shelving units where they put colored tubs. Each tub had a photo taped to the front signifying what toys should be stored in what bin. The bins were labeled Lego blocks, wooden blocks, books, dolls, train set, little people, doll house furniture, and one bin said Baby Toys. In one corner there was a fully equipped tiny kitchen and across from the kitchen was an indoor slide that sat in a pool of plastic balls. Across the room was a full-size indoor playhouse. This play area was as good, if not better than any preschool in town.

CeCe had come to play with William twice before without incident. The first time Fauna stayed and may have hovered a bit, but Emily wrote that off as Fauna being a rookie mom. The second time Fauna seemed relieved for the break and didn't even step foot in the house. Emily knew that with a kid like CeCe or any child for that matter, grocery shopping could be somewhere between disaster and devastation with kids in tow. She was happy to help out whenever she could.

There was a gentle knock at the front door. Emily wasn't expecting anyone. She leaned in best she could with her big belly to look out the peephole. It was her father. As she swung open the door, she did a quick mental inventory of her calendar. Had she forgotten something? Nope. She couldn't remember anything. "Hey, Dad. Did we have plans today?"

"No. Maybe I should have called first." James stepped in the front door.

Emily was still holding CeCe's coat. "You are always welcome. Would you like to stay for lunch with the kids and me?"

James touched the brown coat with the pink fur trim that his daughter held. "Is *she* here?"

"If you mean CeCe, then yes, she and William are having a play date while Fauna runs some errands and gets her groceries."

"Well, hmm, I guess I should have called." James voice smacked of disgust.

"Don't be silly. Those two have such a good time together, I barely know she's here."

"Do you trust her alone with him? I mean do we really know much about her. She could hurt him. He's a gentle child compared to most children his age."

Emily rolled her eyes and put CeCe's coat on a hook by the front door then walked towards the kitchen. "You want coffee, Dad?"

"Sure. But really? You let them play alone?" James walked past Emily and poked his head into the dining room where the two children were playing.

The children didn't look up at the tall elderly man watching from the kitchen doorway. "I will be the daddy who goes to work," William said as he pointed at the playhouse door. "And you will be the mommy."

CeCe stood at the sink in the play kitchen. "I cook food. Go."

James watched for a few minutes, the innocent play of the two children and then returned to the kitchen. Emily was sitting at the kitchen table with two cups of hot coffee. She tapped next to the coffee cup across from her. "Sit Dad. Those kids are fine and if they need us, we're right here."

"Did you notice that even though CeCe is older than William she talks like a baby?" James raised one eyebrow.

"Really, Dad? With everything that child's been through, you zoom in on delayed speech."

"Well, that's what I noticed. No one tells me anything."

Emily poured the half and half directly from the carton into her coffee mug. "Maybe if you showed interest, Snake and Fauna would love to share with you more about their foster daughter. You do know that they are deeply committed to this little girl."

"I'm not so sure about that." James threw that out there, hoping Emily would question him more. When she didn't—he added, "I consider myself a good judge of people and when I see this mixed-up group, I'm not seeing *deeply* committed."

"Dad, you're kidding me. You're calling your son, daughter-in-law and their foster child—mixed up. Snake is loopy in love when it comes to CeCe."

"Maybe *he* is, but I don't see the same thing in Fauna. We've had at least six or more family dinners together since CeCe arrived and I've never seen the child and Fauna touch or interact like mothers and daughters do." He took a breath, "The two of them are void of affection for one another as far as I read it."

Emily frowned but didn't immediately respond. She pinched her lips tight as she mulled over her father's words.

"I guess now that you mention it, it is Snake who does all the heavy lifting regarding CeCe. But we don't know how things are playing out at home. It could be that way because CeCe seems more drawn to men than women. You did know it was her mother that was the abuser, right?"

"No, I guess I didn't." James had not wanted to open his heart to this little girl at all. He didn't know much about foster children, but what he did know was that they were not permanent. They come. They go.

"You want to see something amazing? She won't readily accept food from me, but she will from Kota if he's home and William. You want to see how she responds to you?"

James's eyes widened. "Why would I want to do that?"

"Come on Dad, she's a wounded child not a monster." Emily got up and prepared a paper plate with two pop tarts. "Take these in to the kids and sit down at the little table and chairs. Don't say anything, just sit there and see what happens."

James reluctantly reached for the plate. "Fine. Actually, I'd like to see what all the fuss is about this little girl. Your mom talks about her like she's the reason we all exist." James stood with the plate in his hands. "You know what I mean."

"Actually, I do. And I agree with her. I think there is a scripture that agrees with us, too. It says something about helping the least of these and when we do that it's as if we're helping the Lord."

James smirked at his grown-up daughter who was so much like her mother—and he loved her all the more for it. He carried the paper plate in his large hand and crossed into wonderland. The children stopped playing and followed him with their eyes. He folded his large frame into the little blue plastic chair by the kitchen play area. There were four chairs that encircled the table. He placed the paper plate in the center of the table and didn't say a word. He watched in amazement at what followed.

William left the train set that had occupied his attention and followed his grandfather to the table. He sat down on one side of his grandpa. CeCe stopped her work in the kitchen and glanced at the two pop tarts in the center of the table. She looked at William and then James. Then she opened a cupboard door and removed two plastic play plates.

While she was gathering her supplies, William took one of the pop tarts and took a large bite. He chomped on it as he watched CeCe coming to the table.

CeCe looked at the remaining pop tart and sighed. She pulled the plate close to her and looked at James. Then she went back to the play kitchen and found a toy knife. She returned to the table and cut the pop tart in two pieces. She measured the two pieces by standing them next to each other on the paper plate. Then she placed them on the small toy dishes and from the corner of her eye she looked at James. Slowly she slid one plate in front of him and kept one for herself.

James looked at the food offering and felt a wave of emotion well up. He glanced backwards over his shoulder to see if Emily was watching.

She was.

James spoke to CeCe for the first time. "Thank you for sharing your pop tart with me."

James' hand rested on the table near the plate as he contemplated what to do next. He certainly didn't want to eat a pop tart and especially not one handled by a child.

CeCe's tan hand moved slowly towards James. She tapped the table near his hand and spoke to him for the first time since her arrival months ago. "You eat."

James glanced back at his pregnant and emotional daughter. She was wiping tears. He bit down on his own lip to hold back the moisture pooling in his eyes. He picked up the pop tart and took a bite.

CeCe's green eyes twinkled at him. The small overture the child made was, to James, equal to a bear hug around his neck.

James lifted the pop tart to his lips again and took another tiny nibble. This time, he made his best attempt at a smile. "Mmmmmm. That's the best pop tart I've ever eaten. Thank you…" He paused then added. "…CeCe."

That was the first time he had addressed her by name. In fact, it was the first time he had ever spoken to any foster child…and he didn't hate it…not at all.

14

If your heart is broken, you'll find God right there;
if you're kicked in the gut, He'll help you catch your breath.
Psalm 34:18 The Message (MSG)

Isabelle sat on the edge of her bed and reached into the drawer of her nightstand. Her hand groped about in the drawer until her fingers found a single piece of folded paper tucked far in the back. She felt the paper between her fingers to be sure it was the one. Then pulled the note out of the darkness, into the light. She laid the folded paper in the palm of her hand and looked at it for a long time. Then carefully folded back the edges. The page had been torn from her spiral notebook and the fringe was still attached along the edge.

When the page was completely unfolded, Isabelle smoothed the wrinkles and examined the few doodles she had made across the top of the page last summer during youth group. She had jotted down a few thoughts from the youth message that must have seemed worthy of notation at the moment. Then her eyes moved to the bottom of the page. In another person's handwriting was the name Griffin Walsh followed by a telephone number. And that was the day it began.

She had left her notebook unattended and when she came back Griffin had written only his name and phone number. They had exchanged a few smiles and comments before and after youth group a few times, but she had not asked for his number nor he hers. She had listened to the chatter of a few of the girls and knew that Griffin was visiting family and he lived in another state. The rumors were as innocent as an extended family visit all the way to 'he was on the run' from the law. It really was anyone's guess.

Griffin had finished high school and would be starting

college in the fall. That would make him about 18, almost 19, to her 16, almost 17. She was starting her senior year in high school in the fall. Two years apart didn't seem like much of an age difference for all the wildness of Isabelle's past. Yet, she was not his equal in life experiences. Not even close.

Isabelle laid the paper on the bed next to her, picked up her cell phone and began to punch in the numbers. She had never entered his name or information into her phone. Once he abruptly left town, he didn't respond to her one voice mail, one text message, nor the one Facebook private message, she let it go. She would not pursue a boy who didn't want her. Not possible. But, now what could she do? He needed to know and so did she.

"Hello." A mature male voice answered.

Isabelle plowed forward. "Hi. Is this Griffin?"

"Who is this?" The question sounded gruff.

"It's Isabelle Hayes from Hillbrooke. We met last summer at Community Outreach Church."

An awkward silence followed.

Isabelle questioned, "Are you there?"

A softer answer followed, "Yes." Griffin paused. "I thought you vanished off the face of the earth when you didn't respond to the messages I left."

"Messages? I never received any messages from you."

"Well, I sent the messages to..." He rattled off a 10-digit telephone number as quickly as someone recites their social security number when prompted.

The corner of Isabelle's mouth turned upward as she replied. "That's not my number. I tried to call you on this number and when you didn't reply, I just assumed you weren't interested." Isabelle could hear a sigh of frustration coming from the other end of the phone line.

When Griffin spoke this time, his voice sounded familiar. "I thought the same thing about you. I figured why should I keep calling and leaving messages when no one answered or returned my calls."

Isabelle didn't want to do this over the phone. This was

going to be difficult enough. In person was the right thing to do. "I know you're probably super busy with classes, but could we meet somewhere? I have something I need to talk with you about."

"This Saturday I'm free. It's a seven-hour drive. I'll see if I can spend Saturday night with my aunt and uncle. I could be in Hillbrooke by 2 P.M. Should we meet at that little spot where we met last summer?"

"No. That won't work for me. January isn't the best time to meet at the beach in Michigan. Call me when you're an hour out of town and we'll meet about 30 minutes south of Hillbrooke. There is a little restaurant-gas station that I know. I'll send you the exact exit number once I look it up. I'll send it to this phone number." Isabelle felt compelled to add, "Griffin don't stand me up!"

In defense, Griffin replied, "When we meet, I'll show you the messages I sent you and the dates they were sent. I hope that will help you believe me."

Isabelle did want to see each of those messages on his phone. And find out why he never received the messages she sent him. She dreaded seeing his face when he saw her. She prayed it would not reveal his heart. She was doubtful she could recover from that kind of rejection—from him. For now, she would not overthink the thing and wait until they met face to face. She ended the phone call with, "See you in a few days."

Isabelle didn't wait to hear his goodbye. She quickly hit the end button on her phone. At that moment, she realized her hands were shaking, and her heart was beating faster than normal. She rubbed the sides of her expanded middle, and the baby boy she carried kicked at her touch. A smile started at the side of her mouth, but the tears won, and the smile faded.

Isabelle laid back on her bed, curled up on her side and surrendered to the moment.

***

Tom Brown and Laura Klingburg tandem parked in the driveway at Pastor Rey and Callan Douglas' house. The decision to meet on a Friday evening was best for all parties. It was not an easy task to coordinate four separate schedules.

Tom stepped up behind Laura's car and waited for her to exit. Laura's foot hit a slick spot and her arms began to flail looking for anything to latch onto. Tom reached out to help Laura and she grabbed on to his hand to steady herself on the slippery pavement. She held tightly to Tom's wrist in desperation as her feet began to slip out from under her again. Tom placed his free arm around Laura's full waist to keep her from falling.

Laura laughed nervously as she held tightly to the man she barely knew outside his role as director of the Christian Family Service board. She couldn't believe that of all times for this to happen it would be at the very moment they were trying to squash gossip about impropriety between them. And of course, this would happen right outside their pastor's house. She rolled her eyes and fought the urge to say, geez or unbelievable.

Once Laura recovered her footing, Tom released his hand from her waist and extended his elbow to her for the short walk to the front door. Laura hesitantly accepted, knowing the option could be far worse if she grabbed at the poor man again in an attempt to keep her balance. She glanced at her stylish knee-high boots and thought—blasted heels. What was I thinking?

Laura shot a side smile at Tom as she walked closely beside him. She said, "Thank you. I thought I was going down for sure and that could have been very embarrassing."

Tom looked downward at Laura and returned her smile. "It was my pleasure. It's been awhile since I've had the honor of escorting a lovely lady anywhere." As soon as the words exited his mouth, he felt a lump form in his dry throat.

The front door swung open and Callan yelled, "Oh, my goodness! Are you two alright? I told Rey we needed to salt the driveway. I'm so sorry Laura. REY!"

"I'm fine." As soon as Laura's boot touched the step of the covered porch, she released Tom's elbow from her tight grip, glanced in his direction and said, "Thank you, Tom."

Tom waited for Laura to ascend the steps before following her. Laura kept her sight fixed on Callan whose chin was turned downward towards her chest looking at her with a questioning expression.

Once safely inside the house, Laura spotted the armchairs across from the sofa, laid her bag on it so no one else could claim it and removed her winter coat.

"Here Laura, let me take your coat and yours too Tom." Callan reached for Tom's coat and nodded her head in the direction of the sofa where Rey was sitting quietly, taking in the whole French farce.

Callan was gone for only a moment, but when she returned she blurted out, "Did I miss anything?"

Rey was more in tune with the discomfort of his guests and broke the silence. "So, I hear there are some improprieties being linked with the two of you." He looked back and forth between his dear friend Tom and Laura, with whom they also had an evolving history. "Who wants to go first?"

Laura cleared her throat and let out a deep sigh. "Me. It started with me."

Tom immediately responded like a man defending a woman's honor. "Vicious lies. Only meant to undermine the fine work Laura is doing." He gave an approving smile and nodded in her direction.

Callan blurted out, "I want you both to know that I have not heard any rumors, nor would I believe anything that put either one of you in a compromising position." Callan let out a questioning groan. "Humm, let me reword that. I would not believe any remarks that were in any way unflattering." She pondered her remarks. "Nope, not that either."

Rey interjected. "I think what we are both trying to say is, we would never believe any gossip about either one of you.

Callan and I know that each of you demonstrate a godly character that is above reproach."

Tom reached out and touched Rey's shoulder. "Thank you, Pastor. This is new territory for me. I've been working in the business world my whole life, and church work as well. This is the first time any impropriety has been linked with my name." Tom dropped his hand from Pastor Rey's shoulder and linked his fingers together in his lap like a child about to pray. He looked directly at Laura and said, "I hope it's okay if I speak for both of us."

She nodded.

Tom returned his focus to Pastor Rey and continued. "We would like to ask your opinion how we should respond or not respond to these accusations. The person making them told Laura that she has proof and documentation. I can't even imagine what that could be since Laura and I have never socialized privately nor publicly. Nor have we written or made phone calls to one another except in regard to agency business."

Callan had taken the chair next to Laura. "Well, there you have it. No evidence. No truth."

Rey's cautioned. "It's never a good idea to ignore false accusations. People will believe an untruth without proper facts if they are predisposed to believe it. I don't think we'd have to dig very deep into our own history books to see that."

Tom asked, "Pastor, how would you suggest Laura and I handle this?"

Laura rolled her lips in and bit down before speaking. "This kind of thing stirs up my old nature to fight and get even, but I have made every effort to be a good representative of Christ in my workplace and I don't want to come out swinging, if the first person I give a black eye to is Jesus."

Tom asked, "Pastor, does the scripture apply here that we should be wise as serpents but harmless as doves? I hate it when people pick and choose scripture to fit their personal fights. What do you think?"

Rey listened attentively to Tom's question and pondered it before replying. "This situation is not as much about your reputation as it is about your relationship with Christ. How you each choose to proceed is going to represent Christ in you to all who are watching. Remember it was Jesus who said pray for those who despitefully use you." Rey looked at Laura. "Pray for this lady. It wasn't so long ago that you *were* this lady and remember that someone prayed for you."

Laura blinked back tears.

Rey continued. "Everything in you is gonna want to engage in a battle of words but don't give in to that. Prayer will bring the victory, not verbal combat."

Rey looked at Tom while answering his question. "It's true that people will pull scriptures out of context to use them for their own agenda, but in this case, you are correct. In this situation, be wise as serpents and harmless as doves. There are times when someone is shouting accusations against you that the most powerful voice you can have—is silence."

***

Snake plopped down on the kitchen countertop two boxes of warm pizza. He proceeded to remove his snow-covered boots and place them on the doormat. He liked seeing CeCe's little pink boots next to Fauna's boots and his. He yelled to the quiet house, "Pizza's here. Come and get it."

Fauna stepped into the kitchen. Snake could tell at first glance that her day had been difficult.

"Hard day on the home front?" Snake's question hung in the air as he walked over and scooped his wife up in a bear hug. Fauna rested her head against his chest and wrapped her arms around his waist.

Still holding their embrace, Fauna spoke. "It started out great. Your sister Emily gave me a few hours reprieve. Funny thing too, right after I dropped CeCe off, I saw your dad pull in. He must have been shocked to see CeCe there. He has been less than interested in her since she arrived." Fauna stopped talking and pulled away. She looked up into Snake's eyes. "I really can't fault him for that as much as I'd like to. It's been hard for me too. There are days when I believe nothing is ever going to change. Then I see a tiny ray of light through the darkest clouds—like that day in the snow." Fauna's eyes glazed over in thought.

"Okay—so what happened today? I'm getting used to hearing disaster stories every time I come home. So are we looking at a $10 fix or a $1,000 fix."

"It won't cost you anything today. Just loads of attitude. I keep telling myself that a 3-year-old kid could not possibly be plotting against me, but there is a darkness in this house sometimes that feels like I'm under spiritual attack. My very worth is in question most days." She giggled in jest. "I can't believe that I find it a reprieve to go to the grocery store and stand in line at the cable company to exchange broken equipment. Standing in line, I found myself telling people to go ahead of me. I'm in no hurry."

Snake asked in anticipation, "Where is our little darling?"

"She's watching a cartoon on my iPad in the family room."

"Unsupervised?"

"She's pretty tired from playing with William today. I think most of the fight has gone out of her. It was less physical as the day wound down and more of a nonverbal attitude. I've seen a lot of narrowing eyes, stubbornness, and the occasional sass. Which I will say, her vocabulary has improved of late. She said to me, 'You an ugly thing.' That's a four-word sentence." Fauna added mockingly, "So proud."

"Okay, remember she is a 3-year-old. Let's fight fair."

Fauna's voice held sarcasm when she said, "I know. I'm sorry. I am—an ugly thing."

CeCe wandered into their conversation. "Me eat—now."

Snake went over to the cupboard and pulled down the

paper plates. He put a piece of cheese pizza and a handful of chips on the plate. He grabbed one of the sippy cups and poured bottled water into the cup before snapping on the top. "Let's eat at the table. I'll get the iPad and you can finish watching your show while you eat."

Fauna watched CeCe obediently follow Snake's directions and envisioned the fight she would have experienced had she suggested such a thing as dinner at the table. She went over and fixed her own plate and carried it towards the seat she always sat in. Snake had gone to retrieve the iPad in the family room.

"No sit." CeCe pointed at the chair Fauna usually sat in. "For Snake."

"No, CeCe. Snake will sit on the other side of you. We both want to sit with you."

CeCe squinted her eyes in anger at Fauna.

Snake rounded the corner with the iPad still playing. "Look what I found." He set the device in front of the frowning child and looked at Fauna and mouthed the words. *'I was gone for one minute.'*

Fauna raised her eyebrows in a nonverbal reply *see I told you.*

Snake tried to make light of the deteriorating mood in the room. "I think I could use a great—Big—*GIANT* piece of pizza." With each descriptive word his volume increased.

CeCe…and Fauna both looked at Snake and smiled.

Snake joined them at the table and CeCe became engrossed in her program.

Fauna spoke softly, "I wanted to talk again with you before Isabelle comes back to the center about what we talked about." She lowered her voice more and said, "Adoption."

Snake looked up from his plate and glanced at CeCe. "You think we should talk about that later?"

"Things have been so crazy with…" Fauna nodded her head to the side towards CeCe. "…that I'm so exhausted at night we haven't talked again about—you know—it."

Snake swallowed the pizza in his mouth, "You have my attention."

"Have *you* thought anymore about it?"

Snake froze in mid-bite, pulled the pizza from his mouth, and looked at CeCe then back at Fauna. "I thought about it a couple of times and…it might be a lot to handle right now. When is she due?"

"About the same time as Emily? Maybe two months or less."

"How would something like that work? I mean we have CeCe to consider."

"There would be a lawyer involved. We would have to do a lot of talking with Isabelle to really see how she feels about it and how open she wants the adoption to be. These things are never a done deal until the waiting time is over. In Michigan, however, once the papers are signed at the hospital—it's done. There is always a chance, if she decided now for us to adopt that she would change her mind when the baby is born. It happens all the time. Once the mother holds her baby, she can't go through with it." Fauna expression looked grave.

Snake glanced at CeCe watching her program, then back at Fauna. "It seems we have a bird in the hand here." He smiled at the little girl munching pizza.

Fauna put down her fork. "There's something in me that would like to at least see where the adoption might go. The thought of having a child that we could raise from birth without any baggage is appealing."

Snake took a long drink from his pop can, then spoke. "It sounds like a whole load of pain and awkwardness to me. The Hayes family is part of our lives through church, and you have counseled Isabelle for years. How would that work? How much would they be involved in our lives? It seems a bit too close for comfort. The potential for issues is too numerous to count."

Snake continued without reading Fauna's nonverbal communication.

"There was a private adoption at work between two employees that caused so much friction that the couple who adopted the baby had to change jobs to get away from the birth mom."

Fauna's reply came quick—too quick. "Well—hey, don't hold back there!" She looked down at her plate as soon as the words exited her mouth. Tears burned her eyes.

"We're just talking about it. Right? No one's making any decisions tonight."

Fauna laid her napkin over her half-eaten pizza and pushed back from the table. "I'm sorry. I need some alone time. You got CeCe."

Snake reached out for Fauna's hand as she passed by him. "Fauna. Wait."

She pulled her hand away from him before he touched her. She didn't reply or stop. The sound of a door closing and a clicking sound followed.

CeCe looked up from her show. "Pizza good."

Snake smiled at her and said, "Yes, it is." He glanced towards the hallway in the direction of the bedroom and replayed the last few minutes in his mind. Fauna was carrying a big load with work, CeCe, their own lives, infertility, Emily being pregnant and now the possibility of adoption. He felt helpless.

A soft touch on his hand brought his attention back. CeCe tapped the top of his hand with her index finger. "Show over."

CeCe had been with them for well over two months. She had never initiated touch with him, Fauna or anyone that he knew of. But now, right now, at this moment, she picked to connect.

15

With a fistful of enemies in one hand and a fistful of haters in the other,
You radiate with such brilliance that they cringe as before a furnace.
Psalm 21:8 (MSG)

Helen Franko had done a first-rate job sowing seeds of discord among the staff of Christian Family Services. With Christmas break behind them, the office was running at full capacity from the high volume of children removed over the stress of the holiday season. Following the verbal outburst between Helen and Ms. Klingburg before the Christmas break, the tension in the office could not be ignored.

The Monday following Laura and Tom's meeting with Pastor Rey and Callan was definitely not her finest moment. She had allowed Helen to play her. The raised voices between Helen and her were heard by the whole team. Helen had pulled out all the stops to manipulate the other employees over to her side. The office was soon divided into pro Helen or pro Ms. K camps. Things seemed to be in Helen's favor. Stress and discord abounded within the walls of CFS and it made Ms. K physically sick.

Ms. K was aware that she should have taken a cooling off period before tackling the issues that Gina brought to her attention, but this time she could not look the other way nor muster up even one of the fruits of the Spirit that should have been present in her life. The sting of the words spoken to her and also her lack of control with her own response caused Ms. K a profound sense of personal failure. She was depleted. She knew she walked right into Helen's snare. The defensive words she spoke—yelled—made her sound guilty of all charges. She sounded like a fearful kid on the playground trying to stand up to a bully, but in the end, she was still the loser. She felt it.

Ms. K carried two large boxes of donuts through the main office heading in the direction of the breakroom. She fought her way through the pudding-thick tension. As she neared Helen Franko's desk, Ms. K glanced in Helen's direction. Helen was turned in her chair just enough for a grin to be seen. Office drama was Helen Franko's Zen place.

Ms. K hoped the boxes of donuts would be a peace offering, a mending of hard feelings. She hoped the office would return to a stable place of business without the awkward side glances and downcast eyes. Ms. K felt the eyes of all the workers on her as she walked through the office with the brown boxes stacked on top of each other.

Ms. K forced a smile and nodded a few times at a few different social workers who actually attempted eye contact. Once she arrived at the breakroom door, she turned and made an announcement. "I bought donuts as a small token of appreciation for the fine job you are doing to help better the lives of hurting children."

Helen said under her breath, but loud enough for Ms. K to hear, "Like a donut could solve the problems we all face on this job." Helen's expression of disgust was seen by most of the staff.

Ms. K felt the dig. She stepped into the breakroom, placed the boxes on a table and silently pleaded with the Lord to help her act out her Christianity in a way that would bring glory to His name.

Gina was the first to step away from her desk and follow Ms. K into the staff lounge, near the main office. She opened the top box of donuts and eyed the selection of sugary delight. Her fingers wrapped around the powdered sugar, cream-filled long john. She laid it on a napkin and sat down at the other table in the breakroom.

No one else followed Gina into the lounge. Ms. K knew her presence was keeping the other employees from enjoying the treats. She selected a donut for herself, went to her office, left the door open and sat down at her desk. Ms. K watched as the staff, one by one, began to move towards the breakroom. Between phone chatter and conversation amongst the staff, lively voices filled the office.

Ms. K smiled as she watched the positive effect of her peace offering unfold. She opened her laptop computer to check her inbox. The first email on the list was from Tom Brown.

Hi Laura,

The appointment for Helen and you to meet with the board is in 10 days. Would you like to meet beforehand to discuss what is going on in the office and the difficult work conditions that Helen is causing you? I want you to know you are doing a fine job and it will be my recommendation that Helen be terminated or at the least reprimanded for making accusations against us that are unfounded. It borderlines on defamation of character and that is a criminal offense. I'll call you later today, and we can set something up if you'd like.

Tom Brown

Laura hit the reply button and began typing then abruptly stopped and deleted the text of the email. She closed her eyes and with her index finger, she massaged the area between her eyebrows. There were two well deserved vertical wrinkles that had formed between her eyes from years of frowning. The unconscious massaging had become a nervous habit she had developed when she was troubled.

She ran a few options over in her mind. Should she meet with Tom, or shouldn't she? Laura breathed out a loud sigh. "Darned if you do. Darned if you don't," she said out loud as she pondered her next step.

"What's that you said?" Standing in her doorway was Helen Franko. She looked like Bette Davis descending the stairway in that old movie. The one where she says, "Fasten your seatbelts. It's going to be a bumpy night."

"May I help you Helen?" Ms. K looked directly at her

nemesis standing boldly in her doorway.

Helen smirked. "Nope. Your days are numbered here. I'm just wondering about furniture placement once I'm the director." She spoke softly, but there was an ugly tone in her voice that sent a shiver down Ms. K's spine.

Ms. K folded her hands and placed them on her desk. "If you don't mind, I have work to do. You will not provoke me again. This is a matter for the board to decide. I don't know what you think you saw, heard, or what information you have in your possession, but in regard to Mr. Brown and myself, we have a purely professional relationship and that will all come out at the meeting."

Helen winked and nodded her head in an all-knowing way. "Yes, it will."

Ms. K stood up from her desk and walked to the office door. She stepped around Helen who still held her Bette Davis pose, semi-blocking the doorway. Ms. K cleared her throat, then clapped her hands loudly to get everyone's attention. "I have something I'd like to say. If you are on the phone, please put your client on hold for a moment." Ms. K waited until all eyes were on her. "Thank you. I have something I need to say, and I thought it best to say it to everyone at once."

Glancing around the room, Ms. K saw many expressions of trepidation. She pressed on. "I owe you all an apology. I acted badly a week ago when I raised my voice to Helen in my office. Helen Franko and I have had some personal and work-related differences."

Ms. K plunged ahead. "She had made an accusation against me that will be brought to the board in 10 days. I want you to know, I am truly sorry for not acting in a professional manner and allowing myself to become emotional in my response to Helen." Ms. K held the staff's full attention with her words, "Also, I did not represent the actions of a Believer. You all know that I am a Christian. I've made no secret of that over the past 18 months." Ms. K stopped talking for a moment.

Helen had been standing close behind her, but now she was sidestepping away. Helen's movements had the appearance of trying to get as far away from someone who revealed they had an incurable and highly contagious disease. It was obvious Helen did not want to be contaminated.

Ms. K continued, "I would like to see our office be a workplace that is free of offenses. My door is open to anyone who would like to talk or has ideas on how we can operate more efficiently in expediting the care of children in crisis. You may return to your work now. Thank you." Ms. K walked back into her office and proceeded to answer Tom Brown's email.

Tom,

Thank you for your kind email regarding the meeting in 10 days. I appreciate the offer to meet, but as Pastor Rey told us, we need to flee every appearance of evil. I trust this will pass quickly and without incident. Also, I appreciate your kindness in regard to my reputation and the level at which I execute my job as the director of Christian Family Services. I love helping children in need. When all else fails and families can't be reunited, it is a joy to place children in their forever homes with loving and caring foster and adoptive parents.

I look forward to seeing you at the board meeting.

God Bless,
Laura Klingburg

Laura pushed the send arrow. The words vanished with a swishing sound. The email was sent. She looked up from her desk and saw Helen watching with taut eyes. Laura gave a friendly smile, nodded and returned to her work.

Laura's email pinged, signaling a new email had arrived. It was a quick reply from Tom Brown. She opened the email and read the five words.

Yes, Laura. You are right.

Tom

It was Laura's idea not to meet, yet she felt strangely disappointed and wasn't sure why.

***

Samantha eyed Isabelle from where she stood at the kitchen island. Isabelle checked her cell phone yet again which made 10 times since Samantha started counting 20 minutes ago. Curiosity won, and Samantha blurted out, "Issie, are you expecting an important call?"

Isabelle shifted in her seat on the short end of the sectional sofa. Her feet were elevated on the big footstool with a blanket covering her from her waist down to her toes. The movie she was watching was a necessary distraction as she waited for Griffin to text. Isabelle watched her mom leave whatever she was doing in the kitchen and walk in her direction.

Isabelle felt her nerves surge as she tried to deflect her mom's attention. "I'm waiting for a friend to text me and it's kinda important. The text will give me a 30-minute window before we're supposed to meet. I don't want to miss it and make *them* wait for me."

"Oh, who are you meeting?" Samantha's question was more out of boredom than snooping. Her mom was standing at the back of the sofa looking down at Issie.

Isabelle sensed no matter how many questions she answered, there would be a follow-up question. Her mom was always full of questions. The questions seemed more conversational than intrusive—but at this moment she wanted the inquisition to end. Issie added, "From youth group—you don't know them." She kept trying to be gender-neutral in her description, but she wasn't sure how much longer she could continue the ruse without it becoming an outright lie. She had already blurred the lines between meeting one person as opposed to multiple people. Isabelle knew if there was any mention of meeting a boy—there would be no end to the questioning or the follow-up when she returned home.

"Where are you meeting them?" Samantha didn't seem overly interested in the answer but still stood next to the sofa looking at her child—with child.

Isabelle's phone made a ping sound. "Oh, here's the text. I've gotta go. Be back later. If you need me, I'll be available by phone." Isabelle wiggled herself to a standing position and walk-waddled towards the back door that led into the garage.

Samantha followed Issie as far as the kitchen then waved, "Okay, have a nice time with your friends."

"Thanks mom. I will." Isabelle pulled on her largest coat. The one that she could still zip up in front. She imagined sitting down at a booth and Griffin being none the wiser to her condition from the table up. If she leaned forward and rested her arms on the tabletop, maybe, just maybe, he wouldn't notice immediately, and she could tell him in her own time and in her own way.

Isabelle backed out of the garage and headed south towards the expressway. She played out different scenarios in her mind how she would tell Griffin she was pregnant with his child. The thoughts ran through her mind as quickly as the numbers on the speedometer climbed. She scrutinized every possible way to tell him everything that had happened since their last meeting—starting from the unreturned calls all the way to putting their own flesh and blood up for adoption—and everything in between.

Isabelle coasted to a stop at the Exit 57 gas station. She didn't see Griffin anywhere in sight, nor the car he drove last summer. She picked a parking spot close to the restaurant entrance and cautiously opened her car door looking in every direction before exiting the vehicle. She slammed the door behind her and strolled towards the remote little dive she had chosen for their meeting place.

A bulky man held the restaurant door opened for

Isabelle to enter. The smell of fried food greeted her like a slap to the face. A wave of nausea grabbed her stomach and tightly squeezed. She breathed deeply and slowly, walking to the back of the eatery. She selected her seat at a booth far away from anyone who may be interested in their conversation. She looked around the square diner but didn't see Griffin anywhere. Relieved to have a moment to get her stomach under control, she was thankful to be alone. She breathed in slowly through her mouth and exhaled. It seemed to be working for the moment.

Isabelle pulled out her phone to check her messages. There were none. She scrolled through her Facebook account and checked out a few new notifications. The churning in her stomach was a combination of nerves and pregnancy. This was not a great combination when she was trying to look and act like a woman in control of her emotions and life.

She glanced up from her phone screen to scout the area again. A nice-looking young man stepped into the restaurant. He stopped at the entrance to the boxy diner and scanned the nearly empty room. Then his eyes locked on Isabelle and a smile of recognition formed on his face.

Isabelle nervously returned Griffin's smile as he walked in her direction. His eyes never left her face and the nausea returned with a vengeance. She felt sick—really sick.

No! No! Not now—she thought as she tried with all her might to focus on the handsome man walking towards her. She drew in a deep breath through her nose this time, but her stomach was not cooperating. The smiling young man was almost to her table when Isabelle leaned over the side of the booth and vomited on the floor.

Griffin froze in his tracks. He seemed unable to move— or speak.

Isabelle wasn't sure, but a little spray of vomit may have landed on his shoe. She wanted to disappear, vanish, evaporate. She tipped her head up slightly from her position hanging over the end of the booth and fumbled around with her hand on top of the table until she came in contact with the paper napkin. Still bent over the booth seat, she wiped her mouth as Griffin looked on with an expression of horror.

A large, motherly waitress hurried across the diner waving a dirty dish cloth in the air as she spoke loudly, "Don't worry, dear. We'll clean that right up. I saw you come in and I told Sue." She pointed to the other waitress in a matching outfit who was a few steps behind her. "I told her you looked like you were gonna hurl. I was the same way with my second."

Isabelle wanted to hide under the table or maybe she could make a run for the exit. Of all the ways that Isabelle imagined telling Griffin—not one of them involved a waitress or vomit.

Griffin collapsed into the booth across from Isabelle. His eyes were wide, his expression—confused.

Isabelle pulled herself to a sitting position in the booth and looked across the table at a face that held a million questions. She lifted her clenched hands in front of her, forced a smile, and burst opened her hands while saying, "Surprise! We're having a baby."

***

Zander laid his cell phone on the end table in the family room. Callan watched her son from the kitchen. A mother knows when her child is hurting, and Callan was certain Zander was going through some kind of emotional difficulty. It had been awhile since her 15-year-old son had chosen to confide in her, but she hoped today might be different. Callan prayed in her heart for direction and wisdom as she stepped into the family room and sat down on the opposite end of the sofa.

Zander glanced in his mom's direction then back at the quiet cell phone within a moment's reach.

"Hey, Zan. It's been awhile since you and I had a moment to talk. I was just wondering how you're doing."

Callan wanted to say at least 500 more words but forced herself to stop talking. Silence was not a bad thing. She chided herself to be quiet and give the child time. Callan met her son's eyes and his hurt was evident. A twinge of pain pricked at her heart.

Zander's phone vibrated on the table next to him. He snatched the phone up in his hand and scanned the incoming text message then returned it to the table. A frown formed on his brow. His mood moved from worried to dark in a moment.

Callan asked, "Everything okay?"

Zander turned away from his mom and looked out the glass sliding door to the backyard. It was a sea of white snow. He wished for just a touch of green to add a variety to the gloomy winter day.

Callan decided the silence thing wasn't working. "Hey, I know it's been hard these past few months. I've noticed your friendship with Isabelle has grown. Was that text message from her?"

Zander jerked his head towards his mom. His expression revealed shock that she was aware and in tune with his personal life.

"Come on Zander. I'm not blind. I've seen you two at church together, and she's picked you up to go to the mall. Dad and I haven't wanted to push. We haven't said a word since we all talked over six weeks ago, but now I can see you are upset about her. We're here if, and when, you need to talk."

Zander's face softened when he spoke. His eyes were downcast. "She's pulling away."

Oh, boy, Callan thought. Now he was opening up and she had nothing. Where was Rey? Callan said the first thing that came into her mind. "Everything between the two of you has just been a friendship—right? Nothing serious?"

Zander swiped with his big hand at the hair in his eyes while he blinked back tears.

Callan looked away. Lord, help me. It took everything

in her not to jump up from her place on the other end of the sofa and throw her arms around her hurting child. She was sure she could still cradle her big boy-man like a baby if she had to. She tried to inwardly take hold of her emotions and thought. Whatever you do, don't move. Don't touch him.

With a broken voice, Zander spoke again. "Mom...I really like her...a lot! Something's happened. I think she's not interested in me anymore. I think I was just security for her during the worst of it. She's been thinking about putting the baby up for adoption. I think she will regret it forever if she does. Something's changed, but I don't know what."

Callan battled her own thoughts. This was a discussion that she never could have dreamed having with her 15-year-old son a few months ago. "Zander, we know you're not the father. Have you talked about this with Isabelle? I mean about the possibility of an adoption."

Zander sat up taller and pushed his shoulders back. "We've been friendly for about three months now. Nothing too serious, but I had hope that once the baby was born, that we would come to an understanding."

Callan shifted in her seat. "Honey, this thing going on with Isabelle is way outside your scope. I know you want to rescue her, help her, be a strong arm to lean on, but you aren't ready to be that for her. If she chooses adoption, she will need to be in contact with the baby's father and that could lead to all sorts of possible outcomes. I hate to see you hurting. These kinds of conversations and concerns are not things a 10th grade boy should be a part of." Callan scooted down the sofa and placed her arm around her son's shoulder. He leaned into her and rested his head on his mother's shoulder. Callan held Zander, and for the first time in a very long time, patted his back while he cried.

***

Helen Franko circled her finger on top of the small notebook on her desk. The direct line to her desk phone rang. She checked the caller I.D. to be sure it wasn't one of the whiny foster parents again or a desperate birth parent calling to make demands. It was the call she'd been waiting for. Looking around her to be sure no one was in earshot, Helen picked up her phone and answered with a pleasant voice. "Hello. This is Helen Franko. How may I help you?"

A female voice responded, "I am returning your call regarding a job reference for Laura Klingburg."

"Wonderful. I've been waiting on your call to finalize all the references for our candidates. I have a few questions regarding Ms. Klingburg's personal and professional performance while working with your company."

The female voice replied, "I personally was not employed here when Ms. Klingburg was here, however I pulled her file at my boss's recommendation. He said that I could talk to you as the Human Resource representative. Basically, her performance reviews are rather good. However, there are two performance reprimands in her file for being overzealous in her behavior towards birth parents who she believed were unfit, even though the proof to remove the children from these homes was considered insufficient."

A smirk formed on Helen's face. "And may I ask who brought these reprimands?"

The sound of paper rattling came across the phone line. Then the phone was silent, and the female voice resumed. "It looks like the complaint was made by one of the state's psychiatrists. He's called in to meet with the children to do assessments. Evidently, they had a couple of professional disagreements regarding children remaining with the parents against her wishes."

Helen darted her eyes to the right and left. This was easier than she thought. Don't these people even check to see who they are giving all this personal information to? I should have done this years ago to collect information on all my foes. She continued with her sweetest voice. "Was that the only complaint against her?"

"There is something else here that implies there was misbehavior between she and one of the male employees."

Helen's back immediately straightened, and her shoulders lifted. "Can you elaborate on this? We are a Christian agency."

The female voice began to cough and then the speed of her talking increased. "Oh, my. I'm so sorry. That was sealed information." The tone of the Human Resource person changed quickly as she verbally backpedaled. "Based on what I'm seeing in her file, I'd say overall, she is a hard worker and has showed herself to be an advocate for children in crisis. I'd say above all else, she seems to work and play well with others."

Helen's voice held concern. "Yes, but what are we to do with that other information. I can't unhear that."

The female voice sounded worried. "I would recommend if you want more detailed information that the director of our agency will be back soon. He may be the right person to address all personal questions in regard to Ms. Klingburg." There was a slight pause, then the woman added in a low tone, "I believe at one time the two of them were an item *so to speak*. At least that was the scuttlebutt around here after I hired in, but you didn't hear it from me."

Helen's smile returned with a vengeance. "You have been most helpful. Thank you. Could you put me through to the director's voice mail?"

"I most certainly will. Goodbye." The female voice sounded relieved to be passing the call on to someone else.

Following the voicemail message she left for the director, Clay Tarpon, Helen opened her notebook and began writing.

16

Energize the limp hands, strengthen the rubbery knees.
Tell fearful souls, "Courage! Take heart!
God is here, right here, on His way to put things right
and redress all wrongs.
He's on his way! He'll save you!"
Isaiah 35:3-4 The Message Bible

The waitress set two glasses of ice water on the table and handed Griffin a menu. "How about you dear? Are you interested in looking at the menu?" She looked at Isabelle and dangled the one-page laminated menu between her index finger and thumb.

Isabelle reached for the menu and laid it on the table in front of her. Looking at the waitress she said, "I'm sorry about the mess."

The waitress responded as if she cleaned up vomit from the floor multiple times a day. "Are you kidding me? We've cleaned up worse than that, dear. Wave at me when you're ready to order. I'll be back."

Once the waitress was gone, Griffin looked up from his menu and asked the question that had been hanging in the air for a few minutes. "Why didn't you tell me?"

"Well, I tried. You never got back with me. I figured you weren't interested...I thought I was some summer fling for you and that I was all on my own."

"Isabelle. That's not true. I tried to contact you. It was your idea to keep everything so secret that I didn't even know where you lived or who your family was." He took in a deep breath, then blurted out, "I left in a hurry because my sister was in an accident. She almost died."

Isabelle felt sick again. She breathed deeply through her nose and slowly out her mouth. "I didn't know—I'm sorry."

She shook her head in disbelief.

"It was a terrible time for our family, but she's almost 100% better." Griffin randomly ran his finger over the menu then added in a quiet voice, "That said, I think we have a more pressing discussion before us. So, why did you try calling me again a few days ago? What changed?"

Isabelle closed her eyes hoping if she didn't look at him she could get it all out in one breath. "I wanted you to know that I'm considering adoption. I've talked to my counselor. You may remember them from church, she and her husband are the people with the tattoos."

"The snake guy and the butterfly lady?"

Isabelle bit her lips then spoke. "Snake and Fauna Parker are their names. I wanted to talk to you because you will need to sign off if I choose adoption."

Griffin looked out the window at the woodsy area behind the diner, then back at the beautiful girl he had met only eight months ago. At that moment, he realized that their lives would forever be linked no matter what decision was made about the baby. He asked. "How far along are you—like six or seven months?"

"Seven. I'm due in the spring. April 4th is the exact date."

Griffin's eyes shifted back and forth. He was doing the math in his head. "Yup. That would be right."

Isabelle slowly shook her head. "Once. It was just once. Then you were gone."

"I tried to contact you. Even my aunt and uncle didn't know your family. When I tried to explain who you were with the tiny bit of information I had, they had no idea. Plus, I knew you wouldn't want them to know too much about you. I just wanted to contact you before I left. I wanted you to know why. It wasn't over for me." Griffin abruptly stopped, "Adoption?"

"Yes—adoption. It really is the best thing for all of us. Think about it. You're in college. I'm 17 and you're what—19 or 20 now?"

Griffin didn't answer.

Isabelle didn't like the direction the conversation was going. Her voice became very controlled. "We don't have to make any decisions today. I need to know—from you—that if adoption is what I choose that you won't fight me for the baby. Will you sign off and allow me to move forward with the adoption?"

Griffin tried to touch Isabelle's hand, but she pulled it off the table when he reached for it. His eyes reflected the rejection. He asked, "Do you know what you're having?"

Isabelle spoke softly. "It's a boy."

Griffin thoughtfully repeated the words. "A boy."

***

The third Sunday in January big puffy snowflakes fell, covering the Community Outreach parking lot. The guidelines for parking were completely hidden. Laura maneuvered her car into what looked like a parking spot. She looked at the sloppy parking of those around her. She felt uncomfortable, being the rule follower that she was, knowing her car was not in an actual parking spot. She turned her car off and shrugged her shoulders. It was the best she could do since the car that started the line was off by at least three feet.

Laura opened her car door and a blast of cold air pulled at the front of her coat. She clung to the buttons with her gloved hands to close the open spaces. With her head down and her teeth beginning to rattle, she walked towards the church entrance. She was fully focused on dodging the slippery spots and didn't notice Tom Brown walking beside her until Tom reached past her to open the church door.

Laura let out a startled yelp.

The sound brought a quick response from Tom. "I'm sorry. You looked so cold. I just wanted to help with the door."

Laura laughed as she loosened the grip on the front of her coat. She dusted the snow from her shoulders and shook her head to remove the snow that had attached to her brunette hair.

Tom followed Laura to the coat rack and helped her with her coat. He hung it up then placed his own on the hanger next to hers.

Laura wasn't sure what to do next. Should I wait for him? How can I just walk away? He hung up my coat. Walking away would be rude. But I should, I should flee. Move feet. Go feet. Her feet didn't work. She was motionless. Why couldn't she move?

Tom turned and said, "Would you care to join me in the service?"

The expression on her face communicated more than words ever could.

Tom quickly assessed the situation. "I mean, if you're comfortable with that. If not, I certainly understand."

Seeing Tom's attempt at trying to make her feel at ease melted away her concerns. "No, I mean yes." Laura stopped talking for a moment and took in a deep breath then released it and said, "I'd love to join you."

As second nature, Tom extended his arm to Laura, and she took it. They walked into the service together, down the center aisle and sat in the right section near the front. Laura felt like every eye in the room was on her. The moment she was able to casually release Tom's arm, she did.

***

Griffin Walsh walked into the foyer of the Community Outreach Church. He stomped his boots a few times near the door and looked around for even one familiar face. There were none. He had only been in Hillbrooke for six weeks last summer, but he had hoped someone might remember his name and greet him. He would have settled for anyone. His eyes darted around but no one spoke to him. No matter, he thought. It's Isabelle I came to surprise.

When Isabelle ended their conversation at the Exit 57

diner, Griffin had told her that he'd be leaving early in the morning. But after a night of reflection, he wanted to see her one more time before leaving Hillbrooke—maybe forever. Griffin did another visual sweep of the large foyer but didn't see Isabelle. He walked towards the entrance to the sanctuary and sat in the back row. He placed his arm across the back of the pew and positioned himself towards the back-entry doors. He began to people watch.

Griffin saw a few familiar faces, but no one he wanted to talk with or be questioned by. A group of teen girls walked in whispering and laughing. They pointed at another group of their peers sitting near the front and proceeded to walk in that direction like a herd. He directed his focus back to the entrance just as a younger version of Isabelle walked through the doors followed by a very pregnant and lovely Isabelle Hayes.

He remembered seeing Isabelle's younger sister last summer, but it was Isabelle's wish that no one knew they were seeing each other. He had never spoken to her sister and couldn't even remember her name. Griffin watched as two very well-dressed and distinguished adults stepped up behind Isabelle and her mini-me. The man leaned in to whisper something to Isabelle. She nodded her head and smiled. Then she turned in Griffin's direction and the beautiful smile faded.

Isabelle made eye contact and slowly moved her head side to side. Griffin read her nonverbal communication. She had made it very clear to him yesterday that she wasn't ready for him to meet her parents—yet. He would continue to do things her way—at least for now. He knew that an introduction to her parents in the aisleway at church was not idyllic for any of them.

Griffin nodded and turned away.

Isabelle walked past the row where Griffin sat alone. About halfway down the aisle, Isabelle felt a tap on her shoulder. A knot formed in the pit of her stomach. She turned, half expecting to see Griffin behind her, but it was

Zander. Relief and disappointment were all wrapped up together in her expression.

Zander looked down at her with a questioning look then pretended nothing had changed between them and said, "Would you like to sit with me?"

Isabelle thought 'well this is just perfect.' She turned her head just enough to peek past Zander. She had to see if Griffin was watching, and he was.

"Zander, can we talk later? I'm going to sit with Baylee this morning and my parents." Isabelle turned to join her family.

Zander touched Isabelle on the shoulder. She turned back to look at him. He said, "I'll sit with you then."

Isabelle glanced past Zander again to view Griffin. He had leaned forward and rested his folded arms on the back of the pew in front of him. He was frowning.

Zander followed the direction of Isabelle's eyes to the back of the church and saw him. It was Griffin. He was sure of it. The realization of all his worries, all his concerns, the unreturned calls, the short text messages and the awkwardness between them came full circle. Isabelle was in contact with Griffin. She had not told her parents either. Zander looked past Griffin and noticed Ty standing by the back wall of the church. He was watching the whole thing play out. Zander felt all his anger pool towards his brother. Until he looked closer, Ty wasn't gloating or wearing an 'I told you so' expression. He just looked concerned.

Zander looked back at Isabelle and with a soft voice spoke, "Griffin's here."

Isabelle conjured up her best fake smile and with the skill of a ventriloquist, she spoke through her teeth, "I can't do this right now. Not here. Later."

Zander turned to walk away. Ty met him in the aisleway. He touched his brother's arm and said, "Sit with me—right over here."

Zander looked at his brother but kept moving towards the back of the church. He said, "No. I'm going to sit with

Griffin. He's alone."

***

Fauna opened the back door of the passenger side of her car and spoke in a soft but firm voice. "CeCe, it's slippery so I'm going to carry you into the church."

"No!" The response was curt and matter-of-fact.

"I understand that you want to walk, but it's not safe for you. Snake and I don't want you to get hurt." Fauna tried to keep her voice even—without a hint of the internal frustration that was bubbling up. Everything in her wanted to grab CeCe and carry her into the church like a sack of potatoes. She tried another approach. "You can unlatch your seatbelt then I'll carry you in."

"No!" The stern reply from CeCe was followed by a chilling scream that reverberated around the interior of the car and echoed in Fauna's ears.

Fauna took a step back from the car door, shook her head and massaged the ear that took the brunt of the scream. After the fight she had getting CeCe ready for church, she passed off the trauma of carrying the child into the church to Snake. He stood a foot behind Fauna, ready to be tagged in.

Fauna felt a chill from the January Michigan winter as she stood exposed to the elements. In this weather, no one stood around arguing with a child. Normal people would bolt from their cars to the warmth of wherever they were going. Yet, here she was yet again, trying to convince a child to do something that was for her own good. Fauna sighed deeply, watching Snake with his head inside the car. She could only make out a few words that he spoke to CeCe.

In what seemed like seconds, Snake was hoisting CeCe up on his shoulders. He had convinced the child that sitting up there would give her a chance to touch the clouds and CeCe believed him.

Fauna wanted to scream.

The Parker family drudged through the snow towards

the church. When they reached the church canopy, Snake lowered CeCe from his shoulders and opened the door for the two women in his life to enter.

Fauna followed behind CeCe. With her head slightly turned back towards her husband she said, "Snake, you take CeCe to her class. I'll get our seats." Fauna didn't stop to hang up her coat but eased her arms out of the sleeves while she walked directly into the sanctuary.

CeCe stood close to Snake, waiting for direction. Snake took a few steps towards the coat rack and CeCe followed. He took a hanger then bent down and whispered to her, "Let's hang our coats on the same hanger." The mischief in Snake's eyes produced a tight smile on CeCe's lips. There was a non-verbal agreement between them that this was something sneaky—maybe even breaking the rules.

CeCe didn't respond with words, but her eyes communicated loudly—let's do it!

CeCe watched Snake put her little coat on the big hanger and then cover it with his big coat.

Snake watched CeCe's expression as his coat completely covered hers. Then he said, "CeCe, see how my coat is covering yours?" He didn't wait for a reply and continued. "That's the same way that I'll always protect you from harm. If anyone wants to get to you, they will first have to go through me. Never again will anyone hurt you. I've got you covered!" Snake pointed down the hallway. "Time to go to your class. You know where it is."

CeCe asked, "William there?"

"I'm sure he's already there. Let's go see." Snake tried to keep his strides small so not to pass in front of CeCe. She walked next to him and glanced up. Snake tried not to be pushy as he offered her his little finger by stretching it in her direction and wiggling it. CeCe didn't accept the small gesture. She refocused her attention in the direction of the classroom.

"See William." CeCe bolted ahead to the classroom where William stood by the door waiting.

"I was looking for you E-cc." The two children walked into the classroom together.

Just inside the door, CeCe stopped and looked back at Snake. With a touch of concern in her voice she asked, "Get me 'ater?"

Snake's smile was hidden behind his full beard, but no one could deny the twinkle in his eyes when he answered. "Yes, CeCe. Fauna and I will be back to pick you up later."

***

Fauna chose a seat near the center of the sanctuary. Since taking CeCe in, she had learned the hard way that it was a long walk of shame up the center aisle when the preschool volunteers would call her out of the service to assist with CeCe's behavioral issues.

Fauna settled into her place and chose not to make eye contact with anyone. She allowed the pre-service music to wash over her like healing oil. Her soul was battered but being surrounded by her church family and the presence of the Lord was therapeutic.

Fauna replayed in her mind the sleepless night they all had. She and Snake had concluded weeks ago that there was nothing they could do to relieve CeCe's night cries—only time—and of course the Lord, could help whatever haunted the child. Fauna shuttered at the thought of another night. She hated to see darkness come because she knew what was ahead. The worst was that feeling of drifting off to sleep only to be awakened over and over again throughout the night with agonizing screams. It was a nightly cycle without an end in sight.

Fauna's shoulders slumped forward, her head turned down towards her lap. She was holding in all the negative feelings she had towards CeCe. It had been awhile since she had talked to Callan or Emily, or even Marilyn, who was the best listener ever. In the weeks after CeCe arrived, she had shared some of the trauma with each of them, but of late, she couldn't muster up the strength to share her feelings in friendly conversation with anyone. The pain was *real*. The failures were *real*. The doubts were *real*.

Snake had been there for Fauna the best he could. He was obviously smitten, head over heels in love with Fauna and now CeCe too. When Fauna did try to talk to Snake about her insecurities, she could see Snake's pain. This caused Fauna to file away her own pain to be dealt with another day. She knew that day needed to be soon or she was going to explode.

The counselor within Fauna was wagging an imaginary finger in her face yelling *talk-talk-talk to anybody—just talk*. Fauna felt a touch on her arm and looked up to see Laura Klingburg slip into the pew next to her.

Laura kept her hand on Fauna's arm as she spoke. "I saw you sitting here, and you looked a million miles away." Laura patted Fauna's arm in a motherly way and continued to talk. "I'm not going to ask how it's going because church is starting in a few minutes, and I know that question would require longer than mere minutes to answer. That is, if you would even be honest."

Fauna wasn't sure if it was Laura's touch, her lack of sleep or the atmosphere of worship in the air, but a prickly burning began in her eyes. Before she had time to file her emotions, the tears spilled out, one after another. There was nothing--NOTHING she could do to stop them. Get a grip, she scolded herself, but there was no pushing the spilt milk back into the cup. Fauna knew she was moments away from the tears turning into air sucking sobs.

Laura wrapped her arms around Fauna and held her close enough to whisper a prayer. "Lord, carry Fauna through this. Don't let go of her, Lord. Hold her. You're a good Father to all who are motherless and fatherless. When we become paralyzed with fear that is the precise time that we must put our trust in You to carry us through." Before she could finish her prayer, the worship pastor beckoned everyone to stand and sing. The volume of the music ended any chance of Laura's prayer being heard.

Laura ended the prayer by giving Fauna an extra tight hug. Fauna pulled away and wiped her tears. Sometime during Fauna's release of emotion, Snake had joined her. Laura returned to her seat. Fauna watched Laura move a few rows ahead of her and slip into the row next to Tom Brown. Fauna had no control of her face as her eyebrows immediately lifted upward as far as they could go.

Across the aisle, Fauna met the gaze of Isabelle Hayes. Isabelle knew she was caught gawking. Her face held an expression of concern followed by a weak smile.

Fauna nodded and returned Isabelle's smile. Isabelle slowly turned her attention to the worship service at the front of the church.

Fauna thought, what must Isabelle think of her counselor, the woman she is considering to mother her child. She probably thinks I'm having an emotional breakdown in front of everyone. Could my life be any more of a mess? Fauna felt like every eye was on her and she was naked and alone—until she felt the touch of Snake's hand against hers. He mingled his fingers with hers and leaned in until there was no space between them.

***

The worship music faded. Pastor Rey stepped up to the pulpit. It was out of place for him to interrupt this part of the service. The music played softly while Pastor Rey spoke. His tone was reflective. "The money that was given to Judas when he betrayed Jesus was used to buy a place called the potter's field. The potter's field was the dumping ground for clay that was unyielding to the hands of the potter. This throwaway clay was worthless and within days of being discarded would harden to a cement-like substance, thus devaluating the land by rendering it useless. Nothing could grow there, not even a weed could press through this hardened ground."

Pastor Rey took a thoughtful pause then continued, "It was this worthless potter's field that was the first thing purchased through Christ's death, and in this, there's a lesson for all of us. Jesus willingly takes what others have abandoned as worthless. He'll take the unyielding clay and give it a second chance. Jesus always sees value where others see hopelessness."

Choking back emotion, Pastor Rey spoke, "Jesus will take those that society has rejected, labeled as useless, the good-for-nothings and He will transform them. Our Lord is able to take the dark destructive story of our lives, and completely rewrite the ending if we are willing." Pastor Rey scanned the faces of the Community Outreach congregation, "Are you willing?"

Fauna's eyes were focused on Pastor Rey and her heart opened to every word he spoke. Was she willing? Could she keep chiseling away at the hard ground of CeCe's heart? The feelings of hopelessness she felt moments ago were gone, and just like that, she felt it. She was being whisked off her feet into the arms of *Someone* much taller and much stronger than she. Her feet were firmly planted on the floor, but her Spirit soared.

17

*"For My thoughts are not your thoughts
neither are your ways My ways,"*
declares the Lord. Isaiah 55:8 (NIV)

Pastor Rey ended his message by inviting the altar workers to come. Tom Brown looked at the prayer team assembling across the front of the church. The youth pastor, Eli, caught Tom's attention and motioned with a nod for Tom to join him.

Laura stood next to Tom with her head bowed. Tom touched her arm. Laura's eyes widened and something akin to fear gripped her gut. She moved her legs as close to the pew as possible to allow Tom to freely pass. Once he was past her, he paused, leaned in close to her ear and whispered, "Wait for me."

Laura bowed her head and closed her eyes looking the part of a person very much in reverent prayer, but her mind was no longer reflecting on the message nor the invitation by Pastor Rey to come to the altar. Her prayer time was replaced by one nagging question—Why did Tom want her to wait?

Normally, Laura would have gone to the altar to pray, but not today. She couldn't. She couldn't move. She couldn't think. Laura sat down in the pew and began to massage her forehead with her index finger. She watched the prayer line dwindle down to a young man. Callan motioned for him to go for prayer with Tom and Pastor Eli.

Laura dreaded what Tom wanted to talk with her about. They had less than a week before the board meeting, and now was not the time to begin a cozy friendship with the chairman of the board. She knew that Helen was a scary person. Whatever evidence this woman believed she had, Laura would not underestimate Helen's ability to take innocent things and turn them into something ugly.

Laura's thoughts were interrupted when Tom sat down next to her in the pew.

"Laura, I wanted to speak with you before you go because I know we are days away from the board meeting. I was wondering if you have any ideas where Helen may have gotten the idea that you and I were involved in some way?"

Laura shook her head side to side without speaking.

Tom turned towards her as he spoke. "I was thinking last night about this whole mess and I wondered if it could be something from your past, when you worked for the state. Is there something there she may try to bring up?"

Laura sighed. "I'm not the same person now that I was two years ago. I can honestly say that justice has always been my driving force, but I was not beyond making things move in the direction that I thought they should go—even if I didn't have the evidence to prove it." Laura pointed at Pastor Rey and Callan who were talking with a small group at the altar. "I think Pastor Rey and Callan could testify to that." She looked right at Tom and asked, "Did they ever tell you about how we first met?"

Tom nodded and said, "Yes. We walked through that ordeal with them. That was during the time my wife Jean was dying." His voice drifted off.

Before Tom could continue, Laura interjected. "I'm sorry about your wife. I've heard wonderful things about her. I wish I could've met her."

Tom continued. "Thank you. I am grateful to the Lord that I followed my gut that day and hired you. I knew about your past when I recommended you to the board. I watched your life those few months following the healing of Baylee Hayes, and I saw for myself the Lord changing you from the inside out." Tom changed his position from facing Laura to facing forward. He pressed his back against the pew. "Do you think Helen Franko might have dug up dirt on you from one of your past cases? I mean before you came to Christian

Family Services."

Laura pondered the question, then thoughtfully replied. "It's possible. I'd be the first to say that I didn't do everything right back then, but my motives were always in the best interest of the children...or at least I thought they were." She shifted in her seat uncomfortably, "I can't say the same about Helen. I've personally witnessed her wake of destruction wherever she goes, and she doesn't care who gets hurt; parents, foster parents or children."

***

From the back row of the church, Zander watched the slow-moving mass of people exit the sanctuary. He stood a few feet from Griffin Walsh but had not spoken even a word of greeting to him through the whole service, but now was his chance. He had to take it.

Zander turned towards Griffin and waited for him to make eye contact. "Hi. It's Griffin, right? I'm not sure if you remember me but..." Before Zander could complete his sentence, Griffin interrupted.

"Sure, I do. You played the guitar for the youth group and your dad's the pastor. But I don't remember your name."

"It's Zander. Zander Douglas." As soon as Zander said it—he regretted the *James, James Bond* tone he used.

"Yes. I remember now. I didn't have much time for socializing last summer. I had a summer job." Griffin paused before adding, "Well, it was supposed to last for the whole summer, but my plans changed rather suddenly." Griffin's focus changed from Zander to Isabelle as she walked up the aisle. She never turned her head in his direction, and then she was gone. Griffin looked back at Zander. "Hey Zander, do you know Isabelle Hayes? I saw you talking to her before the service. I remember her from last summer. What's going on with her?"

Zander wasn't sure what Griffin knew about him or

about Isabelle's condition. He wasn't sure exactly how to proceed without violating Isabelle's trust. He thoughtfully said, "I guess you'd have to ask her." He felt like he was in a game of cat and mouse with Griffin. And in this game, he wasn't sure if he was the cat or the mouse.

Griffin had an urge to run after Isabelle but stayed where he was. If he followed her on a whim, it could potentially bring down the wrath of a hormonal woman on him. She had made herself clear when they parted ways at the restaurant that all she wanted from him was his signature on the dotted line. Then he could go away, and they could both move past this unfortunate situation. Griffin sat down in the church pew.

Zander followed Griffin's lead. "Everything okay, Griffin?"

"No. Not really. I have a long drive back home today and I'm not excited about the snow. I'm going to wait for the traffic to lighten up, then I have to head home."

"And where is home for you?" Zander wanted to know everything he could about Griffin Walsh without showing one card in his own hand.

"I live seven hours south of here near Evansville, Indiana. It's a small town nobody up here has ever heard of."

"Are you in college now?" Zander leaned his arm across the back of the pew and turned his body in Griffin's direction.

"I go to a local college near where I live. I'm a freshman, how about you? What year are you?"

Zander's smile broadened. "Wow. Thanks for the compliment. I'm still in high school—10th grade."

Griffin laughed. "No way. You're so tall and mature looking."

Zander tried to act nonchalant. "What brought you up this way in the winter?"

Griffin scanned the dwindling crowd in the sanctuary, then glanced at the exit door. He kept his eyes on the door as he answered, "I had to meet with someone about a private matter."

And there it was, Griffin had met with Isabelle. Zander was sure this guy knew that the baby was his. But, would he encourage the adoption or make a play to win Isabelle back? Zander mulled over his options. What if he just blurted out that he and Isabelle were dating—well sorta dating. That might send him on his way.

A quiet buzzing sound caused Griffin to pat the pockets of his jacket that was draped over the back of the pew between them. He pulled his cell phone from a pocket and proceeded to read a text message.

Zander wondered if the message was from Isabelle. Right that moment he wished he had a talent for reading upside down. If only Griffin would tip the phone forward a tiny bit, he might be able to make out a word or two.

A smile brightened Griffin's face. "I'm gonna have to go. I have to meet someone. It was great talking to you. Maybe we can talk again sometime when I'm back up this way."

"Do you have plans on coming back—soon?" Zander inquired.

Griffin stood up and grabbed his winter jacket. "Maybe." He began to walk towards the exit doors, then turned back. "I guess it will depend on this meeting. We'll see."

Zander watched him leave and wished he was old enough to drive.

***

Fauna stood shoulder-to-shoulder with the other parents outside the church's preschool classroom. Moms and Dads were all waiting for their turn to pick up their little one. Even with all the chaos that CeCe had brought into her life, it felt good to stand with this group and be counted as one of the parents. She liked having someone other than an adult to care about and care for. If only her feelings could be reciprocated. Life would be nearly perfect.

Fauna spotted CeCe standing near the doorway and made eye contact with her. The child's lips turned outward like a duck. It was an expression that Fauna was accustomed to. CeCe was showing her disgust at seeing her. Then CeCe saw Snake pop his head up above Fauna's. A happy smile formed on CeCe's face. Fauna returned the smile and CeCe made the duck lips again.

Fauna waved her hand and said, "Come on CeCe. Let's go."

CeCe did not move.

This was a battle Fauna did not want to fight. Her inner monologue questioned, why? Why now? All these parents watching me. Just once, CeCe would it kill you to follow directions. Fauna decided not to make an issue of the child's disobedience. This time she would walk away. With her head cast downward, she took a few steps and ran smack dab into Emily's extended belly.

"Oh, Emily. I'm so sorry. Are you okay?" The remorse was evident in Fauna's voice.

Emily rubbed her middle section and said, "I'm fine. What's the rush and where is CeCe?"

"Snake's gonna get her." She waved her hand over her shoulder.

Emily scrunched up her face. "Everything okay with you?"

Fauna forced a thin-lipped smile and replied, "Oh, of course. I'm fine." Fauna moved past Emily down the hallway in the direction of the exit doors. What she really wanted was to fall on the floor and cry uncontrollably. How could she soar spiritually, moments ago, in the service, then feel like she was being beaten against the rocks by crashing waves?

Snake nodded his head and smiled a toothy grin at CeCe. He dropped down to one knee as CeCe joined him outside the classroom. "Should we go out to eat?"

"William come too?"

"Well, I don't know. That sounds fun. Let's ask Aunt Emily if they want to join us." Snake pushed his tall frame upward and turned around to see Emily standing behind him. "Hey, Em. You guys want to go out with us to the fast food place? The one with the play area for the kids?"

Emily replied, "As long as I'm not the cook, that would be a—YES!

"Awesome. I'll go tell Fauna and we'll meet you there." Snake began walking down the hallway and extended his little finger again to CeCe. She didn't accept his gesture, but half ran, half jumped to keep up with his stride.

Snake was determined that one day he would win this little girl over. Looking down at CeCe's bobbing head as she tried to keep pace with him, he slowed his pace and CeCe followed. In that moment, an inner peace settled on him as he repeated the words in his mind that he knew were from the Lord.

The thick walls that CeCe has built to keep herself safe, I am carefully deconstructing, one brick at a time. Slow down—don't be discouraged. It's going to take her time to catch up with you. Move slow and don't give up.

Snake glanced down at the top of her two-tone curly mop of hair that bounced with each step she took. An excitement rose up within him. He couldn't wait to share with Fauna this nugget of hope the Lord had dropped into his heart.

***

Tom glanced back over his shoulder at the empty sanctuary and said, "Looks like we're locking up."

Pastor Eli stood at the back of the church and flicked the lights. Laura and Tom stood up. They walked side by side as they exited the sanctuary into the empty foyer.

Tom proceeded to the coat rack and reached for Laura's coat. "Thanks for staying to talk with me. I'm going to give some thought to this before the meeting. May I call you if I have any questions?"

"Of course, Tom. I want this all to go away as quickly as possible. There has been a strain in the office. Everyone can feel the strife. We've got to get back to focusing on keeping kids safe and building strong healthy families."

Tom held Laura's coat out for her to slip her arms in. Once her arms were in the sleeves, Tom lifted the coat up to her shoulders. Laura turned, and watched Tom pull his coat from the hanger.

She questioned again whether she should leave or wait for him. It was the same awkward feeling she experienced before. She felt like a silly teenager on the phone saying no, you hang up first. What had changed? In the past, she didn't have a problem saying goodbye to Tom Brown. Why did this feel so strange now?

***

Ty's words from a few months ago rang in Zander's thoughts. *You're gonna get hurt.* Zander wanted to scream out the car window at the sky, but he sat silently in the backseat. He could hear the soft chatter of his parent's conversation as they talked about all aspects of the church service.

Zander usually loved hearing their thoughts and insights into the lives of the people at church, but today, he was consumed with Isabelle. He could feel her slipping further away from him by the second. He questioned if he really *ever* had her. If they were both in their twenties this would not be happening, but a seventeen-year-old mother-to-be and a fifteen-year-old with a learner's permit were two puzzle pieces that were not fitting together.

A splash of self-pity slapped Zander in the face like cold water. His lip snarled, and his thoughts tortured him. Isabelle never cared about me. I was nothing more than a shield to deflect the insults and gossip. She let me take the blame. She led me on. She held my hand. She picked me up for outings. She didn't resist my advances. He thought about the private texts they shared. She has them—all my words and feelings in print. She knew how I felt. She let me bumble my way around her and knew we were going nowhere. She probably laughed about me at night. Now, two months from the finish line, she's casting her net in another direction.

Zander felt his heart race faster with each injustice he felt. Maybe this had been her plan from the beginning?

Zander side-glanced at Ty who sat less than two feet from him. Ty was looking out the window at the fast-moving winter landscape. Then he turned and caught Zander's eye. Without saying a word, Ty put both of his hands together to make the universal sign of prayer, then he pulled them apart and pointed a finger directly at Zander.

Immediately, Zander's shoulders rose up as he inhaled a deep breath. That was the last straw. Ty was praying for him. How dare he! Zander pulled back his arm and landed a punch to his brother's upper arm with an ample amount of force.

Ty yelped and massaged his arm.

"Hey, boys. We're almost home. Settle down back there." Callan cranked her head to see who started what, but both boys were now looking out their individual windows. There were no accusations passing between them, so she gave this one a pass.

Zander pulled out his cell phone and typed a message to Isabelle.

Can we meet later? I spoke with Griffin.

***

Isabelle's phone vibrated on the coffee table. She snatched it up and read Zander's text. She exhaled a quiet sigh. Great— just great! She considered her next move. She didn't want to lose Zander's friendship. He was handsome and maybe in five years or more—he could be someone she was interested in, but not right now. Her life was a tightrope act. She couldn't balance one more thing or she would plummet.

Isabelle gave Zander a generic reply. *Sure, but it can't be today.*

She glanced at the time on her phone. If she didn't leave now, Griffin may think she stood him up. Isabelle walked through the kitchen where her mom was putting the last touches on Sunday dinner. "Sorry, Mom. Don't fix me a plate. I'm meeting a friend for lunch."

"Wait. It's Sunday. We were going to eat together." Samantha looked like the dinner she had been slaving over was lying in a pile on the floor.

"Save mine. I'll have it for supper." Isabelle called back over her shoulder, "When I get back, I need to talk to you and Dad."

Samantha looked like she was standing in front of a firing squad with guns drawn, ready to fire.

Isabelle paused at the mud room door, "It would be good if Baylee was there too." She reached for her coat on the hook just inside the doorway.

Samantha walked into the mudroom where Isabelle struggled to get her coat on, "Wait. What do you want to talk with all of us about? Should I be worried?" As the words exited Samantha's mouth she knew that she was way past the 'should I be worried stage.' She had tried her best to hide her worry over the past months, but letting her pregnant daughter leave the house alone was at times frightening. What if she slipped? What if a crazy person kidnapped her to steal the baby? What if she went into labor prematurely and had the baby in her car?

Isabelle's voice interrupted Samantha's anxious thoughts. "Mom, I'll be back in less than two hours and I'll have my phone with me at all times." Isabelle tipped her head to the side and smiled back at her mom.

Samantha pushed the air in front of her like a Jewish mother. "Fine. Go. Go. Have Sunday dinner with a friend and not your family—unless you want to invite her to eat with us?"

Isabelle smiled at her mom. She was relieved that Samantha didn't even suspect her lunch was with a boy. "No can-do Mom. See ya later." Isabelle shut the door quickly and speed-waddled to the car.

She wedged herself behind the steering wheel, pulled her phone from her pocket and typed out a one-word message. *Coming!*

18

I came to you in weakness—timid and trembling.
I did this because I wanted your faith to stand firmly upon God,
not on man's great ideas. 1 Corinthians 2: 3 & 5 (TLB)

The music coming from Zander's room was louder than Callan remembered it ever being before. There was the occasional strum of Zander's guitar accompanying the canned music. Everything in Callan wanted to march down the hallway, throw the door open and yell some obvious statement like, are you kidding me—turn the music down or off. Off would be better. But she knew he was suffering. She saw Isabelle send Zander away at church. At least that's the way she interpreted what she saw. Then Zander in turn pushed Ty away and joined another young man that looked equally rejected in the back of the church.

Rey looked up from a sports program he was watching and said, "Do you want me to tell him to turn down that music?"

Callan tried her best to look unaffected by the rattling dishes on the counter and spoke in an extra loud voice. "No. Don't bother. He's struggling with the whole Isabelle thing. I think she has finally come to her senses that a 15-year-old isn't what she needs right now." Callan tacked on to her last statement, "Thank God." But just as she yelled the words, the music stopped, and her voice reverberated across the room, quickly followed by an embarrassed giggle.

Rey added, "Thank God is right!"

***

Ty entered his brother's room without knocking and stood in silence.

Zander turned the music off and with anger in his voice spoke. "What—here to gloat?"

Ty closed the door behind him. "Of course not. I never wanted to see you hurt."

"Yea, right. You never wanted Isabelle and me together either."

"Zander were you *really* together. She's having a baby with someone else and you're in the 10th grade."

Zander's voice raised a bit as he spit the words out. "You have no idea. You're a kid."

"I'm not gonna fight with you. I know you're hurt. I just wanted to tell you—you're my brother and..." Ty thought the words, *I love you*, in his head, but decided not to say them out loud. Zander wasn't ready to hear anything cliché or mushy.

"What? What? You're praying for me—you love me— you don't want me to make a fool of myself. I guess the list could go on and on. I guess it's a bit too late for all of that."

Ty prayed silently. *Help me Lord. Help Zander. Speak peace to his pain.*

"Hey, how about if you get out of here. In case you haven't noticed, you're not welcome." Zander reached for the knob on the speakers, but before he could turn the music back up, Callan called them for dinner.

Zander placed his guitar on the stand next to his bed and stood up. Towering over his younger brother, he pushed him to the side and exited his bedroom.

Ty laid the folded piece of paper on Zander's desk. Maybe later he would be ready to see the scripture that Ty wrote down. He felt it was from the Lord. He was also reasonably sure that Zander wouldn't want to hear that either. Ty placed his hand over the paper and prayed, "Lord, in your perfect time."

***

Griffin reread the one-word message from Isabelle. *Coming.*

202

He wondered what was taking her so long. He still had a seven-hour drive home and classes in the morning. Why did she want to meet again? Had something changed? Is she second-guessing her decision to give *their* baby up for adoption?

Griffin decided he was going to tell her how he felt—come what may. When he and Isabelle met yesterday, she controlled the conversation. This time, he was going to tell her. She had built something up in her mind against him and he had to make his feelings clear. She had to at least hear him out.

The waitress pushed a menu in front of him. "Hi. I'm Selena. I'll be your server today. Are you waiting for someone?"

"Yes. She'll be here any minute. We'll each have a Coke. No, maybe she'll want water. Bring us both."

The waitress laid another menu on the table across from Griffin and leaned in to point at the specials on the menu. "You may want to check these out. This one is my favorite." She tapped her finger on the menu and smiled a brilliant white toothy grin at Griffin.

He returned her smile and said, "Thank you." He knew she was flirting with him, but he wanted to be kind without sending any signs of encouragement her way.

Griffin looked over the menu while he waited for Isabelle.

The waitress returned with the four beverages. She placed them on the table and asked, "Do you live around here?"

Griffin looked up at the attractive waitress and began to answer when he saw Isabelle walking towards them. "Excuse me. My girlfriend is here."

The waitress gave Isabelle a glance and walked away.

Isabelle scooted into the booth. With a frown on her face she asked, "Did I interrupt something? Looks like you were having a moment." Isabelle didn't smile or give any indication that she was kidding.

Griffin swallowed. "She's just a waitress being friendly."

"Looked to me like you liked it."

Griffin's eyes opened wide. He had to salvage this and fast. He changed the subject. "I'm glad you contacted me again. I have something I wanted to tell you, but it seemed yesterday was not a great time."

Isabelle interrupted him. "I wanted to talk one more time before you left town to hammer out the adoption. When can you come back to sign the papers with the lawyer? I'm going to tell my parents everything tonight and then we'll make the appointment with the lawyer."

Griffin sighed. "What if I don't want to push through with the adoption?"

Isabelle rolled her eyes. "You think you can raise a baby or make me raise a baby because you won't sign. If you don't sign, there will be no adoption. Do you want to ruin this baby's life? For what?"

"Isabelle, this is all too fast. I just found out yesterday that I'm going to be a father and I'd like to take some time before I sign my rights away—forever."

Selena the waitress stopped at their table and asked, "Have you decided what you'd like?" She kept her eyes on Griffin and didn't make eye contact with Isabelle.

Isabelle spoke to the side of the waitress's head. "I'll have the soup and salad special with the house dressing on the side and the French onion soup."

The waitress still smiling at Griffin asked, "And you?"

Griffin glanced across the table at Isabelle, winked at her in a way that sent a message to anyone watching and replied, "I'll have the same plus a cheeseburger with everything."

The waitress wasn't smiling or flirty when she asked, "You want fries with that?"

"No, thank you." Griffin still held Isabelle's gaze, and he was pretty sure she was fighting a smile.

Selena walked away. Isabelle suddenly felt a bit worried what that waitress might do to the food she ordered.

Griffin laid his arms on the table in such a way that if the person across from him was his girlfriend, she would have been inclined to hold his hands.

Isabelle looked at Griffin's hands. Did he expect her to hold hands with him? He had to be kidding. This was over-the-top. There was a pleading in Isabelle's voice. "Can you at least think about the adoption? The couple I told you about are praying about it. You could meet them if that would help. Maybe when you come back up we could do it all at once—meet the Parkers and see the lawyer."

Griffin shifted in the booth and thought about Isabelle's suggestion. "I have a break coming up that would give me a four-day weekend. I'll text you those dates and we can talk more then."

Isabelle looked at the table as she spoke. "My parents may want to meet you. How would you feel about that?"

"I think that's the least I can do."

"It may not be pleasant. I'm guessing my dad especially will have a few choice words for you."

"...and I deserve every one of them. I know sorry isn't enough, but I'm sorry how this has all played out."

Isabelle looked up. "You know it wasn't just you."

"Yes, but I knew better. I knew things were..." Griffin's sentence was cut off by Selena sliding a plate of food in front of him and then another in front of Isabelle. Selena had a smug expression on her face when she looked at Isabelle.

Isabelle tried to muster up her sweetest voice. "Thank you."

Selena turned and walked away.

Isabelle pushed her food to the side. "I'm not brave enough to eat any food that waitress handled."

"Here, let's share mine." Griffin cut the cheeseburger in half and gave Isabelle the whole salad. "She must know there isn't gonna be a tip with that kind of service."

"I'd like to think I'm overreacting, but just the thought that she may have done something to my food makes my stomach turn." Isabelle felt a comradery with Griffin who moments ago was the enemy. A slight shiver ran up her spine. She fought the urge to get too comfortable with Griffin. She spoke to her heart. Don't you trust him under any circumstances!

The baby boy within her stretched a foot or hand under her ribcage and Isabelle pushed back in her seat. A quiet yelp escaped her lips.

Griffin's eyes widened. "Are you okay?"

In a breathless voice Isabelle said, "It's the baby. His foot is under my ribs. I can't breathe."

Griffin jumped out of his seat and slid into the booth next to Isabelle. "What can I do?"

Isabelle gently pushed down on the top of her enormous belly. The pain stopped. Isabelle took Griffin's hand and placed it on her stomach. "Can you feel him?"

Griffin didn't move and didn't speak. Then he felt his son push back on his hand. He smiled. "Yes. I felt him."

Isabelle quickly realized what she had done and pushed Griffin's hand away. "I'm sorry. I don't know what I was thinking."

Griffin returned to his side of the table. They finished their lunch with generic conversation. Each knowing that one inch under the surface of their chat, they were forever united by a little boy who just moments ago connected them.

***

Snake and Fauna's house looked warm and quiet as they pulled into their driveway after their Sunday lunch at the fast food establishment. Fauna knew she had been quiet—more quiet than usual, but she hoped between the chaos of ordering food and the busyness of the play area that maybe her dark mood had gone unnoticed. At least she hoped it had. She had no intention of sharing her feelings across the table in a packed eatery with screaming children running everywhere.

Fauna opened the front door for CeCe to enter. She

watched the child sit on the little stool they had placed by the door in order for her to put on or take off her boots. She placed her boots neatly by the front door and hung her coat on the hook that Snake had lowered to make her coat easily accessible. Over the past few months, Fauna couldn't deny that she was seeing little, tiny, rays of hope.

CeCe walked past Fauna into the family room and occupied herself with a pile of books. Fauna removed her outerwear and walked into the living room and plopped down in her favorite place. She could see and hear CeCe in the event the angel turned demon. Snake joined her but didn't say a word.

Fauna looked at her husband's face and read between the lines. He wanted to talk. It was going to be a serious talk, she could tell. But the last straw had just landed on her back and she had a few things to say herself. "Snake. We need to talk."

Snake started to form the words in his mind—oh that's not good, but he chose to remain quiet. Snake kept his eyes on his wife and nodded for her to continue.

"I'm not sure if I can do this. There is nothing I can do to win her over. She hates me—and all I've ever done is try to improve her life. I know I'm the adult here—but I'm really at the end of it. I don't know how much more rejection and feelings of personal failure I can endure before I explode." Fauna took a thoughtful pause.

Snake kept his full attention on his wife and knew better than to give a word of advice. He softly stroked her arm and nodded his head.

Fauna looked wide-eyed and divulged her inner feelings, "Should we talk to Laura about giving her back? If we aren't helping her, then maybe we should give her to someone who can. And what about Isabelle's baby?"

Snake moved his body to position himself to glance at CeCe playing quietly. His heart was breaking for both his wife and the child that had been placed in their care. He knew in his heart CeCe needed to stay with them. Now Fauna needed that same assurance. Snake moved his hand from his wife's arm and placed his big hand over hers. "I hear every word you're saying. I think a chat with Laura might be just what we all need. After all, she's there to encourage foster parents when they hit rough patches." He tried to read Fauna's expression. He was dancing on thin ice and he knew it.

"Are you really hearing me Snake? Because I'm ready to quit and it sounds to me like you are not." Fauna slipped her hand out from under Snake's and crossed them tightly over her body.

Fauna didn't see Snake roll his eyes in frustration. He spoke to himself to remain calm. CeCe's life depended on him right now. He could turn the tide against her *forever* if he didn't guard his words. *Lord, help me. Give me the right words or no words—if that's the better plan.* Snake waited, then began to cautiously speak. "Fauna, outside of the Lord—you are the most important person in my life. I can't begin to understand how a mother feels when a child rejects her. I went into this thinking it would be me that any child we got would reject. I never once thought of blaming the child. I knew if the child didn't like me or was fearful of me—it would reflect the child's past—not me." Snake waited for his words to land.

Fauna's response was softer. "I never expected it to be me either. I was not prepared for this."

Snake decided to go for it and took the opening. "I felt like I heard from the Lord today. It happened when I was walking down the hallway at church. I was unconsciously moving at my usual speed and CeCe was hop-running to keep up with me. When I looked down at her bobbing curls I felt a little guilty for not considering her baby-sized legs. I immediately slowed down—she followed."

Fauna listened to Snake unfold his story.

"I knew without question it was—the Lord. It was something like this...CeCe has built a thick wall around her to keep safe. But I (the Lord) will deconstruct that wall one brick at a time. It will be a slow process—so slow down—

don't be discouraged. She needs time to catch up. Don't give up." Snake's voice quivered at the end. He reached for Fauna's hand and she did not resist this time.

Fauna leaned into Snake and began to cry—sob. He held her with both arms. The sound of Fauna's moans drew CeCe's attention. She walked towards the living room but stopped at the entrance and looked at Snake. He tried to smile the best he could, but tears were dripping from his eyes as well. CeCe took a few steps closer and stopped again. "No cry. Me bad?"

Snake mustered up a few words best he could. "Oh CeCe. Sometimes it's good to cry. We're having a good cry."

"Cry bad." CeCe looked worried—very worried. Like her world was being shaken to the very core.

Snake tried again. "It's not bad to cry. Sometimes crying can be a good thing."

"Good?" CeCe questioned—but her face showed her unbelief.

"Fauna and I were just talking." Fauna was still safe inside Snake's embrace and didn't even attempt to try and fix what seemed broken.

"No hurt Fauna." CeCe's finger was pointing at Fauna with a command in her voice.

With those three words, Fauna pulled away from Snake. With emotion present in her voice, she said, "CeCe. I was crying because I'm sad about something. Sometimes the only way to feel better is to cry."

CeCe made her duck-lip face and sighed.

Snake asked, "CeCe would you like to sit with us. I bet that would help Fauna to feel better."

CeCe moved slowly towards the sofa and crawled up on the far end and sat down. No one touched her, and she touched no one. Snake reached for one of CeCe's books that had been left on the end table and handed it to Fauna.

Fauna's eyes widened, and she shook her head no. Snake nodded in the affirmative and laid the book in her lap. She reluctantly picked up the book and held it as close to

CeCe as she dared. The words of the story floated from her lips. "My name is Dove but I'm a turtle. Everyone laughs at me because turtles can't fly, but my name is Dove. I feel sad when the other turtles say mean things to me. 'You're not pretty like a white dove. Why did your parents give you that name? You're not a Dove." Fauna ran her fingers over the raised page that showed the rough shell of the green turtle.

CeCe leaned in as close as she could to see the turtle named Dove. His legs were short. He had no wings or feathers. His back was rough and scaly. She liked this story. Dove's mommy and daddy were not turtles, but they loved him anyway. They gave him the name Dove so he would one day soar.

CeCe heard this story many times and sometimes she wished her name was Dove too.

***

Isabelle pulled into the garage and pushed the button in her car to close the garage door. She was more than ready to put this day behind her. The garage was dark and cold just like her thoughts. As much as she wanted to walk above the fray, she was coming face to face with issues she could not control. Self-doubt nipped at her confidence. Was she doing the right thing? Had she judged Griffin too harshly? Did he want to be a part of her life and their son's?

She eased herself out of the car and shuffled into the house. Regardless of her inner confusion, she had to tell her parents about Griffin—and the plan was still to press through with the adoption. The brief moment that she and Griffin shared at the restaurant had been unfortunate yet amazing. She wondered if this was how it felt when moms and dads were together and excited about bringing a child into the world. She shook her head to clear her thoughts. She was not the happy mom sharing her pregnancy with a loving husband. That was not going to be her life at 17. She still had a whole lot of life to live before becoming a parent—for real. At least I'm proud I chose to give this little boy his life and maybe if Fauna and Snake adopted him—I'll still get to see him grow up from a distance.

In the mudroom, Isabelle hung her coat on an open hook. She considered the truth-bomb she was about to drop on her unexpecting family. There was no way to tell how her parents would respond when they heard who the father was. The past two months Stuart and Samantha had been unwaveringly supportive, but once she introduced a real life, flesh and blood father into the narrative—it's possible things could change.

After all, she thought, a single pregnant-repentant daughter was one thing, but the guy who did this to her, even if it was consensual, that was a whole other story. That's why over the past seven months she hadn't told anyone who the father was, even though a few people had guessed. Isabelle assured herself that if it wasn't for the plan to give her baby boy up for adoption, she never would have told anyone who the father was—ever.

Isabelle walked past the kitchen, through the dining room. The sectional sofa divided the two rooms. Isabelle stood at the back of the sectional sofa and announced, "I'm home."

Samantha looked up from the iPad she held on her lap, and Stuart clicked off the television show with the four news anchors bantering back and forth about sports trivia.

Stuart said, "I hear you have something you want to talk about with us. Samantha—have Baylee come down."

Samantha texted her on her iPad. *Iss is home, come on down.*

Isabelle walked around the sofa and sat at the end of the loveseat giving her the best angle to speak with her family. "I had an interesting lunch at that diner, the one near the expressway. Warning—don't ever eat there."

Samantha looked concerned. "Are you sick? Did you eat something bad? Was it dirty?" The questions were shot at Isabelle like a spray of bullets.

Isabelle laughed. "Oh, no not that—well a little bit of that. The waitress was super rude to the point that I was scared to eat the food she brought to the table—so that said, I hope you saved me some leftovers."

Samantha looked at her very pregnant daughter and said, "Yes—in the fridge. But that's just terrible about your lunch. I have half a mind to call that restaurant to lodge a complaint."

"Mom, I can fight my own battles."

Baylee strolled into the room at the end of Isabelle's sentence. "Who's in a battle? What did I miss?" Baylee sat next to Isabelle on the loveseat and looked completely out of the loop and as always, got right to the point. "Ok, what's this family meeting all about?"

Isabelle cleared her throat more from a nervous habit than because it needed clearing. "I'm not going to sugarcoat this. I've spoken with the father of the baby about adoption—today. That's who I met for lunch."

Samantha looked confused. "I thought you were with a girlfriend."

"Ya, I kinda let you believe that, so I wouldn't have to get into any long discussions before I met with him." Isabelle took a breath and continued. "He hasn't decided if he's willing yet to sign his rights away. I can't sign first, or he technically could take the baby and raise our son himself."

Baylee interjected, "No man is gonna want to raise a baby. I hope he doesn't sign because I want you to keep the baby. If this is a voting meeting—that's how I'm voting."

"Thanks for the support Bay!" Isabelle rolled her eyes.

Stuart sat silent and listened to the women throw the verbal ball around the room but never once did any of them connect with the basket. "Ladies!" Everyone looked at Stuart. "Who's the father?"

All eyes were on Isabelle.

Isabelle knew this was why they were all there, but suddenly she was finding it hard to speak. "Ummmn. He will be back up in a few weeks when he has a break from college. He is willing to meet you." She looked at her father and asked. "You *will* be kind?"

Stuart leaned forward, almost to the point of standing. "His name!" There was a certain amount of demand in his voice.

Isabelle felt her shoulders go up and a familiar spirit of rebellion fanned her raging thoughts. How dare he demand anything from me! I came here to include them not exclude them—and he's going to get demanding with me. I don't think so. Well—

Samantha's voice of reason chimed in, "Stuart, give her a moment. I'm sure this has been a difficult day with seeing him and discussing adoption with him." Samantha asked Isabelle, "Has he known about the baby for very long?"

Isabelle's heart pounded. She tried to bring her thoughts under control. "I told him yesterday. Before that, he didn't know anything. I tried to contact him when I first suspected that I was pregnant. After three failed attempts, I thought he wasn't interested in talking to me." Isabelle saw the anger on her father's face. "But don't judge him too harshly. He said he never got the messages and that he also had tried to contact me. Turns out, he thought that I wasn't interested in talking to him, and he had a wrong phone number for me."

Stuart's face grew redder and did not show any signs of fading.

Isabelle decided to tell them everything beginning with his name. "His name is Griffin Walsh. He's a freshman in college in Indiana. We met at youth group and it was my idea not to tell anyone we were dating because I didn't want to deal with all the questions from anyone. So, first we started talking, then meeting and then things moved faster than either one of us expected. Then he was gone."

"He left you after…" Samantha's voice trailed off.

"Yes. At least that's how it appeared to me until we talked on the phone last week. Why he left had nothing to do with me—in fact he tried to reach me." Isabelle felt a little twinge in her heart like a missed beat. She was defending

Griffin. Why?

Stuart decided to ask one more question. "Why did he go without talking to you?"

"It was a medical emergency in his family. His sister was in an accident."

"Did you check out his story to see if he's being truthful?"

Isabelle pushed the swirling rebellion back down. "I believe him. But even if I didn't—it doesn't matter. I just need him to sign off—that's all!"

Samantha fought to keep her voice pleasant. "We would definitely like to meet him next time he's in town."

Baylee stood up to leave the room then turned back and looked at Isabelle with all seriousness in her 13-year-old face. "Issie, you won't be able to give the baby up. You might as well buy a crib and begin to make plans for him. And don't give some adoptive parents false hope. I know you. That baby is part of you and even if you haven't gotten there yet—you will. Congratulations Isabelle—you're gonna be a mom."

"Like I said, thanks for the support BAYLEE."

"Girls. That's enough. Baylee, stop. Your sister has enough to deal with."

Baylee walked out of the room and Isabelle watched her leave without responding.

The baby kicked. She placed her hand on her stomach and massaged the area. For a moment, she remembered the feeling of Griffin's hand under hers and over their son.

19

We are afflicted in every way, but not crushed;
Perplexed, but not driven to despair;
Persecuted, but not forsaken;
Struck down, but not destroyed...
2 Corinthians 4:8-9 (ESV)

Fauna set her coffee mug in the sink and walked to the family room to check on CeCe's progress. "CeCe, put the toys away. We're leaving for preschool in 15 minutes."

"No go." CeCe stood in the middle of the room surrounded by toys.

"It's your day to bring a snack. I picked up strawberry pop tarts for all your friends." Fauna pointed in the direction of the kitchen.

CeCe didn't move but looked past Fauna half expecting to see a box of strawberry pop tarts floating in the air.

Fauna lowered herself to the floor and pick up a half-clothed Barbie doll and a few odd pieces from the doll house. She tossed them into the box for doll house toys while she sang the song CeCe learned at preschool for cleanup. When she came to the part about...*everybody do their part*, Fauna pointed at CeCe playfully but misjudged the distance between them and landed a poke to the center of CeCe's belly.

CeCe immediately swiped at Fauna's face with her open hand landing a stinging blow.

Ding Dong.

Fauna stood up, rubbing her stinging cheek. "Great. Just great. Who could that be?"

CeCe yelled in defense of her actions. "You poke me."

Fauna yelled back, "You hit me!" She immediately regretted her childish tone. She opened the door to a middle-aged lady holding a badge of some sort. Swinging the door open she asked, "May I help you?"

"Hi. I'm from Christian Family Services. I'm here for the surprise evaluation to see how things are going with..." The lady looked at the little notebook she held in her hand then looked back up and said, "CeCe Jefferson."

Fauna opened the door wide enough for the social worker to enter. "I'm Fauna Parker and CeCe is in the family room. We were having a little stand-off just before you came over picking up her toys."

She extended her hand and smiled. "I'm Helen Franko. I've known CeCe since she was born. Nothing surprises me concerning that child."

Fauna was conflicted by Helen's harsh remark about CeCe. On one side she wanted to agree wholeheartedly with this stranger. Her face still smarted from the sting of CeCe's slap, yet she felt a twinge of protection for her child rise up within her. She did not reply.

Helen walked into the family room like a relative coming over to chat. She went over to CeCe who stood stock-still where Fauna had left her. Helen stayed outside the circle of striking distance. "Hi CeCe. Do you remember me?"

CeCe scowled at the intruder and said nothing.

Helen backed away. "Yes. She's just as I remember her." Helen sat down on the sofa, opened the small notebook with one hand and dug for a pen in her shoulder bag with the other hand.

Fauna sat down in the chair to the side of the sofa and said, "Ms. Klingburg has been working with us. Did our social worker change?"

"No. She's still in charge *for the time being*, but I'm just doing an evaluation. That's how it's done sometimes."

Fauna relaxed back in her seat. "Ms. K has never done anything this formal. How does an evaluation work? What is the purpose?"

"We want to make sure everyone is adjusting and answer any concerns you may have." Helen held her pen in hand ready to assess. "Is there some place the child can go while we talk?"

"That would be nice, but we've found it best not to leave her unsupervised or out of earshot." Fauna cleared her throat nervously. "I could put a show on for her. We could move to the living room. I can watch her from there." Fauna stood, and Helen followed.

After CeCe was safely occupied with a purple dinosaur on the television, Helen asked her first question. "It's been a few months since you opened your home to the child. Do you feel all your concerns are being properly addressed by the agency?"

"Mmmm, I did call once with a behavioral concern and I felt it was handled well by Ms. Klingburg. We are very happy with Laura. We know her from church, and she's an amazing, knowledgeable and caring person."

Helen's eyebrows lifted. "Oh. You know her socially. That's nice. Has that made things better in dealing with your concerns or more difficult?"

Fauna contemplated the question and hesitantly answered. "That's hard to say. If I were being perfectly honest—it may be a bit harder. I'm sure you know that CeCe has behavioral issues. We don't touch her except when it is necessary for something like dressing or lifting. When we do touch her, when it's imperative I mean, it's a blood bath." Fauna extended her hands to show many scrapes, some healing and some new. "There's more on my arms but they're hard to see because of the tattoos."

"How would your social relationship with ah-mm—Laura—make it hard to talk with her about issues with the child?" Helen tipped her head to the side and her voice dripped with concern.

There was an unspoken 'awe you poor thing' in Helen's tone that caused the professional counselor to open up. "I guess in some ways the relationship aspect makes it better and in some ways it's harder. I guess because I know her, I want her to be proud of the job we're doing. But also, because we are Christians—we can pray together about issues that arise."

"And exactly what are your issues of concern?" Helen leaned towards Fauna, almost touching her.

Fauna crossed her legs to the other side. "It's been a challenge. I'm a counselor, but I still wasn't prepared for the things I've faced with CeCe's behavioral issues."

"It's been rough. Huh?" Helen's voice was sympathetic. "Have you wanted to have the child removed from your care?"

Fauna suddenly felt emotional. "I've thought seriously about it, but my husband feels we could still be of some help to her. I guess we aren't on the same page about that."

"Are you seeing any progress or positive signs? I know not everyone would, but with your professional training, I'm sure you'd spot it." Helen nodded in such a way that Fauna began nodding with her.

Fauna's voice cracked as she spoke. "I may be going through some of my own stuff, so I don't want to project it all on CeCe."

Helen stood up and shook hands with Fauna. "Okay. Thank you. I think I have enough here to submit my evaluation. You were a tremendous help."

Fauna followed Helen to the door. "Now, how again are these evaluations used?"

"We're mainly looking for any red flags that would show the child or foster parents are in need of intervention." Helen's eyes widened in anticipation of a big reveal. "Do you think you are in need of intervention at this time?"

Fauna leaned her head against the door that she held open. The words ran through her mind that Snake had shared with her from the Lord. "Ahh. I guess I'd say, we're moving slowly. CeCe has a long way to go. Whether it's with us or not—time will tell."

Helen pushed open the screen door and said, "Yes it will. I have one other question. The chairman of our board at Christian Family Services is Tom Brown. Do you know him?"

"Of course. He is also the director of the non-profit I work for and he goes to church with us."

"Us?"

"Laura, Tom and Snake and I all go to the same church."

"Really? How interesting. So, do Laura and Tom know each other socially too?"

"I don't know how well they know each other outside of church, but they sat by each other this past Sunday. They are both amazing people. We love them so much. But you must know that working with both of them as you do."

"Yes—wonderful people. Good bye Fauna—it was very nice to meet you."

Fauna closed the door and glanced at her watch. Oh—great. She was running late now.

Helen slid into the driver's seat of her company car and began writing in her little notebook while her thoughts were fresh.

Foster mom is struggling. Behavioral concerns regarding the child. Couple not in agreement about keeping the child. Foster mom overly concerned about pleasing Ms. K more than her own regard for the child or her own well-being. Ms. K and foster parents attend same church. Is this a conflict? Foster mom having personal issues that are bearing down on her emotional well-being. She did not elaborate on this but referred to her own personal "issues" being of an equal concern with the child's bad behavior. Tom Brown and Laura Klingburg go to the same church as well. It's all getting very cozy.

Helen laid the notebook on the seat next to her and smiled. I think the board will be very interested in all this.

***

Baylee's bold statement still rang in Isabelle's ears. "You will not be able to give away your baby." Still, Isabelle was determined to proceed with the adoption. How could a mere child, like Baylee, speak to her with such boldness—even assurance. What did she know about anything?

The responsibilities of raising a child would fall entirely

on her and no one else. I'm not a bad person for considering adoption. Why can't Baylee understand that? And Griffin, he's turning into a *wild card*. He could ruin all my plans if he decides to retain his parental rights. Maybe I shouldn't have told him. Maybe if I hadn't, he would have stayed away from Hillbrooke forever.

Isabelle fought the urge to rub her middle. It had become a second nature to her to rest her hands around, on top and under her expanding belly. As hard as she tried to disconnect from the baby boy within her, he was persistent with his hourly messages—*Hey, Mom. I'm in here.* Not with words, but with his movement, hiccups and kicks.

Isabelle placed her foot on the first step to the Hillbrooke Family Counseling Center. The door was slightly ajar even though it was 18 degrees outside. She continued up the steps and pushed the door open the rest of the way. Wet footprints marked the way to the receptionist desk. A family of four blocked her view of the middle-aged lady at the desk.

Isabelle moved closer until she caught sight of the receptionist, who immediately waved her back to the offices behind her. Isabelle nodded and mouthed the words 'Thank you.' When she reached Ms. Parker's office, she lightly rapped on the wood with her knuckles while easing the door open.

Ms. Parker was sitting on the sofa with a book on her lap. She looked up with a smile and said, "Come in Isabelle. How are things going?"

Isabelle chose the seat on the opposite end of the sofa from Fauna. She braced herself with one hand on the arm of the couch while feeling behind her with the other hand for the cushion. "I've had an interesting week to say the least!" There was a hint of suspense in her voice.

Fauna laid the book she was reading to the side and turned her body towards Isabelle, giving her full attention to whatever was coming next. "Do tell. It sounds like you had some excitement."

"I finally contacted my *baby-daddy*." Isabelle waited, giving Fauna opportunity for gasps and awes. Fauna didn't disappoint. Isabelle proceeded. "I had tried to reach him early on but couldn't connect with him. I decided to try one more time and was very surprised when this time he actually answered. As we talked, he claims he'd never received any messages from me. He said that he tried to reach out to me too and when I didn't reply he assumed, as I did, that there was no interest on my part."

"How was your first meeting, his reaction to parenthood and how was it seeing each other again?"

"First impressions were not great. I threw up on the floor in front of him. He had no idea that I was pregnant, of course. How could he? We hadn't spoken. I wasn't going to spring that on him over the phone. Over all, I'd say it was okay seeing him again. I mean, I was unaffected by it." Isabelle watched the expression on Ms. Parker's face change. "I told him that I was going to put the baby up for adoption, and all I needed from him was his signature."

Fauna listened, trying to keep her own feelings at bay. "How did he feel about adoption?"

"At first, Griffin said that whatever I wanted he would do. Then he said he needed time to process the information before he could do something that would be as final as adoption. He did say he'd meet with you and Snake."

Fauna's jaw tightened. "His name is Griffin?"

"Oh, yes. His name is Griffin Walsh. I never told you that. I told my parents last night. Baylee knew who the dad was from the beginning being the observant stalker that she is."

Fauna's heartbeat increased when she asked, "How do your parents and Baylee feel about the idea of adoption?"

The next words Isabelle shared were completely unguarded. "My parents aren't saying much—pro or con, but I kinda feel that my dad is for the adoption, my mom against, and Baylee is very against." Isabelle pondered her own answer, "At least, that's the way I'm reading my dad. He's fooled me before though."

Fauna shifted her focus from Isabelle's eyes to her

midsection, then quickly returned her gaze to Isabelle's face.

Isabelle's voice was soft, "Baylee told me that she believes I won't be able to push through with the adoption." Isabelle jaw tightened. "Which makes me want to prove her wrong."

A pain hit Fauna in the center of her chest. Breathe, she told herself. "Isabelle, this isn't something you can undo. You need to be very sure for yourself and…" Fauna's voice trailed off, "…for your son."

"Ms. Parker, you're still considering doing the adoption aren't you?"

Fauna looked at Isabelle and saw a child—a mere child making a lifelong decision for herself and her unborn baby. She wanted that baby so bad—but at what cost to those in her own circle. "I've talked with Snake and we're still willing to discuss adoption with you." Fauna hesitated, "But we're only having dialogue. We know that nothing is final for you or us until after the baby is born and you make your final decision."

Isabelle sat up with a straight back and looked at Fauna. "I know it's the very best thing for me and for the baby. I'm sure too that I won't change my mind if that's what you're worried about. Griffin will come around. Really, what can he do? He's not able to raise a baby any more than I am."

"Have you thought about how it might work if you had the help of your families? Have you talked the details out with your mom about how they might help you still fulfill your goals and raise your son?"

Isabelle rolled her eyes. "Everyone says they'll help now, but it will all be on me. All my plans will be postponed—my life will be changed forever."

Fauna stood up and went towards her desk. She opened the drawer and pulled out a folder. Walking back to the sofa she held the file out in front of Isabelle. "This folder holds a series of articles written by women who have given their babies up for adoption. Some of them are pro and some con—you need to read them all and become very familiar with every issue that could arise. Knowledge is power. Once you have read all these, we can talk again. Share them with Griffin too. I also would like you to consider speaking with a therapist who specializes in adoption." Isabelle did not take the folder. Fauna laid it on the table in front of her and sat close to Isabelle.

Isabelle's voice was troubled. "I don't want to talk with anyone else."

Fauna took Issie's hand and held it inside of both of hers. "If Snake and I are going to be the ones to adopt the baby, there will need to be some separation between us. It can't look like I've persuaded you in any way or not given you adequate information before the adoption." She squeezed Isabelle's hand, "It's to protect all of us, Issie."

Isabelle's eyes reddened. "I thought we were going to walk through this together. The thought of telling all my personal stuff to someone else is too painful to think about."

"I'm sorry Issie. It has to be that way—without exception."

Isabelle leaned forward the best she could and lifted the folder from the table. She opened it and looked at the title of the first article. Typed in bold print was the title *Adoption is Forever*. This one was clearly an article against adoption. If the title wasn't obvious enough, the picture of the woman with a single tear on her cheek was crystal clear. She closed the folder and placed it next to her on the sofa. "One mistake—it was once and now my life will be altered forever with this one decision. Just when I think I have a plan, and everything is going to be great for my baby, for me, and even for you, everything gets all mixed up again."

"Isabelle, this is exactly how you should be feeling. If you could just give your baby away without any pain—I'd be far more concerned about that. Remember, this is not an easy thing you're doing. Adoption *is* Forever.*"

Isabelle's face showed her concern along with her voice. "Will you still meet with Griffin and me in a few weeks?"

"If that's what you want. We can meet again after you

have one session with the adoption therapist and read the articles."

The defeat Isabelle felt was easy for Fauna to see. Isabelle's head fell forward until her chin touched her chest. Fauna leaned in and embraced the child-mother giving her time to cry out all her disappointments.

20

Remember me, O Lord, when You show favor to your people!
Pay attention to me, when You deliver...
Psalm 106:4 (NET Bible)

Helen Franko rested her hand on the top of her computer monitor then tipped it slightly forward. The fluorescent office lighting caused a glare on her screen that was interfering with the proofreading of her email. Just one more edit, and it would be ready to send. The email had a comprehensive list of every offense past and present that Helen could remember from her meticulous notetaking. The email was going to each board member—except for Tom Brown. He was unduly influenced by Laura Klingburg and she didn't want to tip her hand too soon giving Laura opportunity to come to the meeting prepared to rebut these charges. A surprise attack is always best in these types of situations. The board will see the shock on Laura's face when each allegation is read aloud.

What Tom Brown ever saw in Laura to begin with was something Helen could not comprehend. She had heard the saying before, the heart wants what the heart wants—but really. When Helen looked at Laura Klingburg, she couldn't believe they were close in age.

Laura Klingburg's hair was cut short in a bob with natural streaks of gray running though it like highlights. Laura obviously wasn't concerned about her weight or for that matter make-up—or the lack thereof! Helen's thoughts continued the assault on Laura. She must have a mirror at home, but then again, maybe not. Who could find that woman attractive? It's beyond my knowledge to guess what draws people together. Laura usually had a pair of reading glasses pushed up on her head like a headband. Her clothes were a sad attempt at fashion. Even with all this against her, there was something about Laura that drew people in and set them at ease.

Helen gritted her teeth at the thought of Laura's people skills. Her smile was disarming, and her eyes twinkled. I hate her.

Helen wiggled the cordless mouse causing the cursor to circle above the send button on her screen. She was sure this email would give her the advantage at the board meeting. Even though the meeting was a few days away, the members of the board would have time to consider these accusations before the meeting. She skillfully added the part about Laura having a relationship with a past employee just like she now was having with Tom Brown. That information was a real stroke of luck—even if it happened years ago. It shows a pattern of behavior.

Helen reread the entire email making a few adjustments. Her plan was to read it verbatim at the meeting. The image of Tom Brown and Laura squirming in their seats while she read her charges against them caused a smile to form on her face.

The phone rang on Helen's desk and startled her back to reality. She clicked the mouse, and the email was sent. Now she would let the truth resonate with the six men on the board.

With this important task finished, she answered the phone. "Hello. This is Helen Franko."

Laura Klingburg fought the urge to speak in anger. "Helen, I had a call from Fauna Parker who told me a social worker stopped by her house a few days ago to do an *evaluation*. She said she didn't remember the social worker's name—no business card was left. However, she did describe you to a tee."

"If you're asking if I went to her home to check on her—I fully admit I did." Helen spoke with plenty of accusation in her voice as her words spilled out, "Someone needed to. You left that poor family to sink into a bottomless pit of despair."

Laura responded, "Helen, you have no idea what I've been doing behind the scenes to try and make the Parker's home a permanent one for CeCe."

Helen raised her voice enough to be heard both on the phone receiver and all the way into Laura's office. "You must know that some children can't be saved. I'm trained to see that. Evidently, you are not."

Ms. K breathed in deeply before responding. "Helen, we'll be addressing this type of aggressive behavior at the meeting."

Helen huffed into the phone. "Aggressive? Don't you mean proactive?"

"It's not proactive to interfere with another social worker's clients. It's unprofessional, unethical and dishonorable."

"Well, we can talk about professional behavior in a few days at the meeting!" Helen laid the receiver back on the phone base. She felt her breathing increase along with her pounding heart. She used her inner voice to calm herself. *I can only hope that the board will vote to terminate that woman on the spot. That would be the sweetest thing if Ms. K was escorted to her office by a board member and asked to gather her belongings. Then they would accompany her out of the building.* The picture Helen imagined in her mind helped calm the pounding in her chest and her smile returned. She whispered under her breath, "Just two more days."

***

The nature park had smooth dirt walking trails that cut through the woods. There was the occasional root sticking above the path that gave Fauna a touch of concern for CeCe who ran ahead. Fauna cautioned her charge. "Slow down CeCe. That's too far. You have to stay closer to me."

CeCe didn't listen. She kept running until she came to a

wooden bridge. A chain was draped across the entrance with a warning that the bridge was not passable. Below the bridge was fast moving water. CeCe ducked under the warning sign and ran onto the bridge.

Fauna was too far away to stop her. She screamed with all her might. "No, CeCe! Stop."

CeCe bolted onto the rickety bridge. Then she suddenly stopped in the middle. There were missing planks in front of her. The child looked down and saw the rushing water. CeCe turned back and looked directly at Fauna. The fear on the child's face was intense.

Fauna placed one foot on the bridge and began to move cautiously forward, but the bridge creaked out an eerie sound. Another plank fell from the bridge making a splash in the water below.

CeCe screamed out in fear.

Fauna backed off the bridge as she tried to reason with the child. "CeCe—can you walk towards me? It'll be okay. Don't let go of the rope. Hold on tight."

The child was frozen—unable to move.

Fauna tried one more time to plead with CeCe. Her heart was pounding. Beads of sweat formed on her forehead. Someone was touching her arm. Someone was pulling her back and shaking her.

"Fauna wake up. You're having a nightmare." Snake was tapping her arm gently.

Fauna slowly opened her eyes. Was it a dream or was it real? For a moment, Fauna wasn't sure.

"You were yelling, 'Stop!' Over and over again. It startled me. I thought you were being attacked or something. What happened?"

Fauna sat up. Her pajamas were wet with sweat. "It was terrible. CeCe ran from me at a park and she was trapped on a rickety old bridge, frozen with fear and she wouldn't come to me no matter how much I pleaded. I couldn't help her. I couldn't get to her." While Fauna retold her dream to Snake, she stopped talking.

Snake asked. "What? What happened next?"

"You woke me up. But I think that dream was from the Lord."

"Why?" Snake questioned.

"The problem isn't between CeCe and me." With relief in Fauna's voice she said, "It isn't about me. The problem is that trust has been broken. Even facing death, she was unable to trust me. I know the Lord can heal that. He can most definitely reestablish trust in CeCe's broken life. I can see it now. I get it."

Snake saw that the dream had changed something in Fauna's whole outlook. "Well Counselor, how should we reestablish trust in our little girl?"

"It's no longer about me. I'm not saying it hasn't been hard—all that rejection, but we're going to put on display for CeCe what trust looks like, and we're going to bring in a team of prayer warriors to partner with us."

"Yes. Yes. I like what I'm hearing." Snake laid down and propped his head up on his bent arm. "Who's on our team?"

"It has to be Tom Brown, Laura Klingburg and Pastor Rey and Callan. How does that sound to you? I'm going to fast one meal a day until I see CeCe reach out and begin to trust us." The relief in Fauna's voice was obvious. "It's not me. It's not about me."

A reverberating scream shattered the peacefulness of the moment. "I'll go to her this time. My own dream has adrenaline pumping through my veins. I'll be lucky if I get any sleep the rest of the night."

Snake laid his head back on the pillow and yawned. "Are you sure?"

Fauna smiled. "Yes. You go back to sleep. I'll check on CeCe, then sit quietly in her room and pray." Fauna swung her legs out of bed and glanced at the clock. It was 3 A.M. CeCe is predictable if nothing else.

***

End of term exams had kept Zander busy the past week. He had tried a number of times to connect with Isabelle, but she seemed distant and beyond reach. Zander pushed his bedroom door open and with his foot kicked the door closed behind him. With one motion he pulled his phone out and plopped his body across the bed with phone in hand. He strolled through his messages checking for one name—Isabelle. But her name did not appear.

His thoughts were full of self-pity. Why am I throwing myself at her? If she doesn't want me—then it's time to move on. Who does she think she is? She can't use me and then throw me away like garbage. Zander ran his fingers through his thick hair, closed his eyes and shook his head to clear his thoughts.

He looked at his desk and noticed a folded note. His curiosity got the better of him. He stretched his arm as far as he could reach, but the note was still beyond his fingertips. He stood, took a few steps, then snatched the paper from his desk. When he unfolded the message, the page held only a scripture reference. It was in his brother's handwriting, of that he was sure.

Zander crumpled up the paper in a ball and threw it across the room hitting the closed door. A scripture! That's just like Ty to think a Bible verse is going to mend all that is going on here. Zander looked at the crumpled ball of paper lying on the floor. The verse was Romans—something. What could Romans say that would make this all better? And what did Ty even know about that book of the Bible? That kid drives me crazy.

The ball of paper was mocking him. The desire to know what scripture the paper held grew until all the words rushing through his mind couldn't hold him back. He crossed the room in two large steps and retrieved the paper. He opened it and read the scripture reference—Romans 8:26-28. He couldn't immediately remember what that scripture said, but the numbers were familiar.

Zander reached into his backpack and pulled out his laptop. He opened it and did an internet search for the scripture reference. He clicked on one of the options to open the verse and read the words.

Meanwhile, the moment we get tired in the waiting, God's Spirit is right alongside helping us along. If we don't know how or what to pray, it doesn't matter. He does our praying in and for us, making prayer out of our wordless sighs, our aching groans. He knows us far better than we know ourselves, knows our pregnant condition, and keeps us present before God. That's why we can be so sure that every detail in our lives of love for God is worked into something good. (MSG)

Zander read the verses in a few different versions, but only the first one said, *knows our pregnant condition.* He read the verse in the original version again. This time focusing on the last part. *Every detail in our lives of love for God is worked into something good.*

Zander sighed and mulled over the words, *something good.* What good could come out of this mess? Leave it to Ty to always think that around every corner, God is there looking to make bad things better.

Zander's phone pinged. It was a message from Isabelle. *Can we meet. I'll pick you up in 10-minutes.*

Zander replied. *Absolutely!*

***

Time was of the essence and everyone's schedules were filled to capacity. Fauna wondered how she could get six busy people to try and squeeze in one more meeting. Pushing the meeting back until all the schedules coordinated seemed pointless considering that Fauna needed prayer covering and she needed it now. Fauna reached for her laptop next to her on the sofa. She could see CeCe playing quietly and knew that now was the time to act. Fauna sat down and began typing her email to Pastor Rey, Callan, Tom Brown, and Laura Klingburg.

Dear Friends,

This is Fauna. I have a request that I hope you will consider.

I had a dream last night that has brought me to this moment. As you all know, we have had a difficult time the past months with our foster child, CeCe Jefferson. She has been unable to trust us—mostly me.

This is difficult for me to say, but I have been struggling with deep soul searching feelings of inadequacy. In my internal struggles, I felt the problem must be something with me. I believed that I was somehow less than worthy to be a parent. I didn't want to keep trying with CeCe. I had personally and inwardly given up on her.

That said, the dream I had last night has stirred and moved me to ask for prayer.

Snake and I have decided to fast one meal a day and pray for CeCe's heart to be open and for her to trust us. If you would be willing to partner with us in prayer on a daily basis, please respond to this email with a simple one-word answer. PRAYING! I am sending this email to only four trusted people in my life and you are one of them. With Snake and me there will be six of us praying.

> God bless,
> Fauna Parker

Fauna read and reread the email then pushed the send button. It was gone. No bringing it back, at least four people now knew her struggle. She closed her eyes and laid her head on the back of the couch behind her. The realization of her actions sunk in, and a weariness settled on her. For the moment, it was quiet—even if it lasted for only a moment—it was quiet.

***

Zander glanced at his watch as he peered out the picture window for Isabelle's car. He thought about the scripture again that Ty left on his desk. He wanted to believe that everything was going to work out the way he wanted, but he knew in his heart that what he wanted wasn't what God wanted for him.

Isabelle pulled into the driveway and Zander nearly tripped over his feet getting to the door. He yelled to the quiet house, "I'm leaving now. Be back later." There was no reply. He wasn't sure if anyone heard him, but he did have permission to go—so he left.

Zander bolted down the steps then slowed when he eyed the slippery pavement. Keeping his focus a few feet in front of him, he walked carefully to avoid taking a spill in front of Isabelle. That would be humiliating.

Zander reached the car without incident and slipped into the passenger seat. He didn't feel the same freedom he did the last time they were together. No way was he going to put his arm around Isabelle's shoulder. He turned his head and looked at her. She kept her eyes on the rearview mirror while she backed out of the driveway.

"Is the coffee place in the strip mall okay with you," she asked Zander.

Zander didn't drink coffee. He imagined himself ordering hot chocolate like a child and having a whip cream mustache—not very manly he thought. His reply to Isabelle didn't match his thoughts. "Sure! That sounds great."

The car seemed too quiet—awkwardly quiet.

Zander decided to get to the point. Why wait? "What's been going on with you?"

Isabelle's reply was slow. "Not so much."

Zander tried to draw her out. "Would you care to elaborate on that?"

Isabelle sighed. "Sure. It's been an emotional and busy few days. I've been in communication with Griffin about the adoption. I've talked to my parents about Griffin. Also, I've talked with Ms. Parker who is sending me to an adoption counselor. She doesn't feel it's ethical to talk to me about the adoption anymore."

Zander looked ahead and asked with a lack of interest, "I thought that was Ms. Parker's job. Why can't she talk to you anymore?"

That's when Isabelle remembered that Zander didn't know that she had asked Snake and Fauna to adopt her baby. She tried to repair the damage that was lurking. "I guess Ms. Parker wants me to be sure that I won't have any regrets if I push through with the whole adoption thing."

Zander kept his eyes forward and asked, "Did you give her some reason to believe you weren't serious about it? Does she know you've been talking to Griffin?"

"I've told her everything." Isabelle wanted out of this line of questioning before she said something she couldn't take back.

Zander rubbed his hands together to warm them, then he cupped his hands near his mouth as if he was going to whistle, then he blew warm air into his cold hands. "Are you really sure about the adoption thing? You, of all people, do have options."

Isabelle jerked her head to take a quick look at Zander. "What are you talking about? Do you think Griffin and I are getting back together?" She turned her attention back to the road.

"Wow. Where did that come from? I was talking about your parents being supportive." Zander frowned.

"Zander, do you really want to go to the coffee shop?" Isabelle slowed her car to a stop at the traffic light.

He didn't respond. They sat in silence until the light changed.

Isabelle turned into the strip mall and parked but didn't turn the car off. "We need to talk…"

"Nothing good ever follows those words." Zander crossed his arms like a pouting child. He knew his body language wasn't radiating 'I'm here for you.'

Isabelle turned her head and looked directly at Zander. "I'm really sorry. You have been a great support to me over the past few months. I couldn't have managed the gossip and rejection if you hadn't been at my side."

She breathed in deeply, "But now I have to face some really difficult decisions and it would be wrong to lean on you any longer."

Isabelle looked directly at Zander, "Especially, when I know this can't go any further." She looked down at her belly that was pushing against the steering wheel. "What's ahead of me, you can't be a part of." She knew her words were harsh. What choice did she have? She had to end her attachments with Zander.

Zander decided he had nothing to lose. "Are you getting back with Griffin? He sure was hoping that was the case a few weeks ago when I talked to him at church."

Isabelle looked surprised by Zander's words. "He said that?"

"In so many words—he did." Zander could see by her response that getting back with Griffin was not on her short list.

Isabelle tipped her head back and exhaled. "I'm feeling overwhelmed. Would you mind if I took you back home?"

Zander was relieved. "No. That's okay. I'm not feeling like coffee today."

The ride home was two people sitting side by side in quiet reflection.

Isabelle pulled into Zander's driveway and put the car in park. "Thanks for being so understanding. Who knows what the future holds?"

Zander replied, "I think I do. Before I go, I'd like to read you a scripture." Zander opened the Bible app on his phone and looked up Romans 8:26-28. "Someone gave me this verse a few days ago. I'm still thinking it over myself, but I thought I'd share it with you." Zander read the verses. "Meanwhile, the moment we get tired in the waiting, God's Spirit is right alongside helping us along. If we don't know how or what to pray, it doesn't matter. He does our praying in and for us, making prayer out of our wordless sighs, our aching groans." He paused and turned to look at Isabelle. "I thought this next part was interesting. It says, 'He knows us far better than we know ourselves, knows our pregnant condition.'" Zander stopped reading again to see Isabelle's expression.

"That's what the Bible says? He knows our pregnant condition?"

"Yes. And there's more." Zander repeated that section of the verse again. "He knows us far better than we know ourselves, knows our pregnant condition, and keeps us present before God. That's why we can be so sure that every detail in our lives of love for God is worked into something good."

Isabelle's expression changed. "Are you saying that something good could come of all this?" She waved her hand in front of her tummy.

Zander said, "I didn't say it—the Bible did."

21

"For the Lord your God goes with you to fight on your behalf
against your enemies to give you victory."
Deuteronomy 20:4 (NET Bible)

The Family Christian Services board gathered in the conference room of the agency for their quarterly meeting. The members met briefly to address the issue of the staff members Helen Franko and Laura Klingburg.

Helen arrived for the board meeting and went to her desk to occupy herself with some unfinished paperwork while she waited. She glanced at her watch to see if Laura was late or was she early. It turned out, she was early. Helen glanced at Laura's office window. The room was dark. Good, she thought. I'm here first. Helen jerked her head at the sound of Laura's office door opening.

Laura walked out of her darkened office towards the staff lounge. Her eyes squinted a bit from the overhead lights. Her eyes were red and her skin blotchy. As she passed by Helen's desk, she said, "Good evening, Helen."

Helen did not respond nor acknowledge Laura's presence. But she couldn't help but notice her sloppy attire for such an important meeting. Helen thought, doesn't she have any pride in her own appearance? The least she could have done is touch up her makeup. She didn't even take time to change her clothes.

Helen followed Laura into the breakroom. Both ladies sat in silence as they waited to be invited to join the board meeting.

Helen looked down at the professional navy blue pantsuit she had purchased for this occasion. Her shirt was a crisp white with a coral and navy plaid neck scarf swooped around her neck with a clever knot. She crossed her legs revealing coordinating high heels. She kicked at something on the carpet hoping to draw Laura's attention to her fine footwear. On her lap she held a matching handbag.

Laura Klingburg stood and walked over to the coffee station to fix a cup of coffee. Helen examined her from head to toe. She wore simple black slacks, a sweater vest and collared shirt with no jewelry or fancy shoes. Helen's eyebrows arched upward with a smug expression imprinted on her face.

Laura turned back from the coffee station and walked back to her seat. She could feel Helen examining her and she felt a bit underdressed. Laura tried to keep her focus and remember the reason for the meeting. They were not fashion models preparing to walk the runway. They were boss and subordinate coming to discuss workplace ethics with the board of directors.

Helen opened her purse and pulled out an iPad. She opened a document and scanned the content by moving her finger across the screen in an upward direction. Her lips moved slightly as her eyes scanned the screen.

Laura looked at the sloppy dog-eared folder she had brought with her. It laid on the table mocking her. She slipped it off the table and held it in her lap and wondered if she should have tried to present her case in a more technological fashion. At least she had the spreadsheet which showed Helen's cases over the past six months that revealed a blatant disregard for the children in her care. This was all tucked inside her well-used folder.

Most of what she planned to say was in her head—and heart. She didn't dare open the file in front of Helen. She would look both worried and desperate. Instead, she prayed in her heart. *Lord be with me. This is for the children. The children—Lord—let these men's eyes be open to the truth and not be tricked by sleight of hand or word.*

A stocky middle-aged man stepped into the breakroom and announced. "Ladies, you may come back now. We're ready for you."

Helen bolted out of her chair, clutching her iPad and fancy purse. She was two steps out the door before Laura moved.

Inside the board room of Family Christian Services, the group of distinguished men looked on as the two ladies entered. Helen took one of the two vacant seats at the end of the table. Laura sat in the other open chair and looked directly at Tom Brown, who sat at the head of the table. His face was somber. Laura felt a sinking feeling in her chest. Whatever these men had been discussing before she and Helen came into the room had not been favorable for her. She could see that written all over Tom Brown's face.

Tom opened the dialogue. "Ladies, we took a few minutes before calling you in to review an email that Ms. Franko sent to the board a few days ago. Some of the men had a few questions for you, Laura, regarding that email. But first I'd like Helen to read the email aloud, so we can all hear it, since I was not included in that correspondence."

Without shame, Helen placed her iPad on the table and tilted it with her hands to bring the words into view. She cleared her throat and began reading.

Dear Board Members,

In the 18 months that Laura Klingburg has been working as the director of Christian Family Services, it has come to my attention that there are some deep concerns that either require your intervention or at worst, her termination. I have been working here since this agency began in 1992. I was a wide-eyed dreamer fresh out of college. In the 26 years of dedicated service I have given to Christian Family Services, I've worked under people with varying degrees of concern, commitment and discretion.

Laura Klingburg has caused me great concern both for the good name of this agency and for the safety of the children placed in our care by her reckless disregard for the established protocol for placing and removing children.

I can cite over 20 cases that I have worked on personally

where there was blatant indiscretion. Even when I took it upon myself to give her warning, Laura would not listen to counsel. Also, when it became known to the other social workers in our office that I would be speaking to the board, I received no less than six emails with a list of cases that brought to my attention similar concerns. I can make these files available for review upon request.

Laura has acted cavalier regarding the mental well-being of our foster parents. She has placed children in severe trauma with unqualified foster parents who are ill-equipped to handle these traumatized children. This usually results in the foster parents refusing to take any more children for long periods. Some drop out of foster care completely. She subjected the children in our care to unnecessary home changes causing them even more trauma. Often, they are returned to their birth parents before the parents have adequately shown they are ready. She does not follow protocol or show concern for the safety of children entrusted to our care."

Helen glanced slightly to the side to see how Laura was handling a good dose of reality. Laura's ash-colored face did not disappoint. Helen assured herself that this wasn't personal. It was business—well, maybe it was a bit personal. Helen glanced back at the screen. The good stuff was about to hit the fan.

Before Helen could resume, Tom Brown cleared his throat to draw the focus from the two ladies at the end of the table to him. When Laura looked up, Tom's lips formed a flat smile. He gave Laura a reassuring nod. In his heart, he hoped it would be enough to hold her head above the swirling waters of accusation he knew was coming.

Helen continued.

"With all respect, it grieves me to bring these concerns to the attention of this board of directors and the most grievous is yet to come. For some time, I've been concerned about the ongoing phone calls and visits from the director of the board to the office of Ms. Klingburg. Women have a sense when something is amiss."

Helen looked up from the iPad and spoke from memory, making eye contact with the members of the board. "We know when an office indiscretion is happening and that is what I saw with my own eyes."

Tom kept his eyes on Laura, her head bowed low. He knew the information from Laura's past that was about to be shared could draw a reaction that might be her undoing.

Helen continued.

"The flirty smiles between Mr. Brown, our director, and Ms. Klingburg were too obvious to deny. As I watched them from my desk, my concern for the integrity of this agency grew. This led me to follow up on Ms. K's past behavior while employed by the State of Michigan. Their Human Resource person did not disappoint."

A confused frown formed on Laura's face.

Tom watched with concern and prayed silently.

"It was during this inquiry that it came to my attention that Laura had an inappropriate relationship with a younger male subordinate. It was his accusations against her that caused her to seek employment with us. And now we see her worming her way into positions of power by having another illicit relationship with none other than our own chairman of the board.

Please know that it grieves me deeply to bring such allegations to this committee for review, but it is for the sake of the children. We can't allow this agency to be slandered by rumors, improprieties and distractions that could interrupt the fine work we do at Christian Family Services.

Respectfully Submitted, Helen Franko."

Helen leaned back in her chair and drew in a deep breath. She folded her hands circumspectly in her lap giving the appearance of contrition over bringing this information to the attention of the board.

Laura's heart rate had passed the safe zone and was pushing 911. If she dared open her mouth in defense of these false accusations, it would be disastrous. It would surely make her look guilty of every charge that Helen leveled against her. She silently prayed. *Lord, I need your peace to flood my heart. Please calm me from the inside out. Don't let my enemies' triumph over me.*

Tom needed to give Laura time to absorb the untruths spoken against her. Hearing them for the second time in less than an hour had not made it any easier for him to swallow. "We are going to take a 10-minute break and meet back here to resume our discussion. At that time, Laura, you will have an opportunity to respond to these allegations."

The movement of chairs filled the otherwise quiet room. The sound of friendly chatter was like a faraway echo in Laura's ears. No one spoke to her. No one attempted to reach out in friendship or kindness. Tom stayed at the head of the table and looked at the notes laid out in front of him. Laura slowly stood and walked to her office to distance herself from Helen, the board, and Tom.

***

Emily Edwards sat at the kitchen table with her head propped in her hands. She rocked back and forth in her seat softly moaning. Her cell phone was on the table in front of her.

The front door opened, and Kota rushed in. "Did you call the doctor? Should we go to the hospital?"

Emily looked up from her hands and responded, "Yes, and yes. The doctor said to go to the hospital to be examined. Fauna said we can drop the kids off with her. I couldn't reach my mom." Emily couldn't mask the fear on her face.

Kota took her hand and helped her to a standing position. "Let's go."

"But I still need to pack the kids' stuff." Emily stopped talking and arched her back in pain. She held up one hand in the air signaling Kota not to speak.

He followed her warning and did not speak nor move from her side. When the pain had obviously passed, Kota spoke. "Snake and Fauna both know how to get into the house. They can get what they need. We're going to the hospital right now." Kota yelled, "Kids! Get in the car!"

Maddie and William came running. The urgency in their father's voice prompted them to move without question and within minutes of the last contraction, they were backing out of the driveway.

Emily glanced at Kota. The worry on his face for his wife and unborn child caused her lips to quiver. She whispered in a low voice only Kota could hear, "It's too soon."

Kota reached for his wife's hand and held it with affection. "Em. It's going to be okay. We're 15 minutes away. Fauna and Snake will pick the kids up from the hospital. I already texted them."

Emily arched her back again. Her face looking upward, she pushed shallow puffs of air through her pursed lips. She didn't want the kids at the hospital. She didn't want them to see her like this. She felt helpless. Between the pain, the worry, and the fact that their baby's life was hanging in the balance, right now she had to trust her husband and the Lord.

Kota glanced at the dashboard clock. The contractions were close and strong.

Emily screamed. "No!"

Kota pushed on the accelerator raising his speed to 15 miles over the limit. "What? What's happening?"

Emily lifted a bit off the seat. "My water broke. This is bad. Very bad." She clutched her middle section and groaned. It wasn't a labor pain groan, but a Spirit-led groan. She could no longer hold back her tears. She could no longer put on a strong front for her children.

The sound of Emily's groans came from deep within her. Kota was shaken to the core by the sobs of his wife. He joined Emily in prayer the best he could. "Lord, breathe into our baby's lungs. We put our hope and trust in you. You brought this child into existence, now we ask you to preserve our baby's life. Calm our fears."

The red letters of the hospital emergency sign came into view. Kota turned the van into the drive and slowed to a stop at the hospital door. A rather large man assessed the situation from behind the warmth of the glass sliding doors. Kota waved his arms for help and the guard quickly responded by pushing a wheelchair to the side of the car.

Kota spit out the words in staccato rhythm, "Seven months. Water broke. In labor."

Kota forgot for a moment that his van was blocking the driveway and that his children were in that van as he clung to Emily's hand.

The hospital guard's eyes darted between Kota and the van as he spoke, "Sir, you need to move your van. I'll take your wife to labor and delivery. You can meet her there." The uniformed man looked at Kota clinging to Emily's hand.

Kota's eyes were on Emily and he was not able to process the guard's words.

The door guard raised his voice. "Sir. You can't leave your vehicle in the driveway."

Emily arched her back and cried out in pain.

"Sir. I'd park it for you, but there are children in your van. I can't do it with children in the vehicle."

The sound of a horn drew everyone's attention.

Kota's fog cleared. "They're here. They'll take the kids, and you park the car." He directed the guard.

Snake and Fauna jumped out of their SUV and ran towards Emily and Kota.

Emily couldn't speak but waved her hand at the van.

Kota interrupted, "The kids. Take the kids. We'll call as soon as we know something."

Kota hurriedly pushed the wheelchair into the hospital with Emily clutching her stomach and disappeared out of sight.

Snake and Fauna took the children. Maddie clung to Fauna like a baby and William held tightly around his uncle's neck. When they got to the car, CeCe looked at them all with an equally horrified expression. Fauna and Snake helped the children into the car and they pulled away.

Fauna looked at Snake and said, "I'll pray."

His voice was filled with worry. "Yes. Please. Right now—I have no words."

* * *

The Christian Family Service's board meeting was painfully silent as each person found their seat and carefully avoided eye contact with anyone else. The wood grained table top became the favorite point of interest for most in the room. All present tried not to focus on anyone or anything too long. Tom Brown silently spoke a prayer in his heart. *Lord, have your way.*

Everyone waited on Tom to resume the meeting. He looked at Laura and asked, "Are you ready?"

Laura nodded her answer then drew in a deep breath before starting. "It has been my joy to be the director of this agency for the past year and a half. I have witnessed both the dark side of this business and the pure delight of seeing families reunited. When all else failed, it was a thrill to see children adopted into new families with great success." Laura looked around the room. No one was looking at her except Tom.

Helen Franko rolled her eyes while her lips formed a pinched line across her face. The men in the room gave Laura opportunity to tell her story without benefit of facial expressions, but she wasn't a fool. She knew whoever drew first blood had the higher ground and Helen struck a near fatal blow to her character. Slinging mud at Helen now would only make her look like she had something to hide. Telling her side of this had to be done in a calm, controlled and professional manner. And she didn't want to rule out whatever the Lord's purpose might be in what seemed to be pure madness at this very moment.

Laura continued looking around the room at no certain person too long. "I have appreciated the leadership of each of you as I have endeavored to do my job in a professional and ethical manner. Helen has leveled some very serious charges against me with the promise of producing evidence upon request. I, however, have come to this meeting with evidence." Laura opened the shabby folder and pulled out a stack of papers.

"These are the office phone records for the past six months. If you see anything of concern in these records, you would be welcome to pull the previous year's records for review to accompany these. I have an Excel spreadsheet showing the amount of calls I receive on any given day and the length of these calls. There is also a pie chart showing the most reoccurring numbers. This chart shows that Tom Brown has never called me from his home number. In the past six months he has called, from his cell phone, less than 15 times. Seven of those calls were made after this meeting was requested. None of these calls lasted more than five minutes with the average call being two minutes." Laura stood and passed out a single piece of paper to each board member and one to Helen as well.

Laura remained standing as she resumed. "Helen also charged me with being unconcerned about the placement and removal of children." Laura looked at Helen quickly who began to nervously reposition herself in the uncomfortable office chair. "This is my review of Helen's work over the past six months. I reviewed these numbers with Helen which sparked a flagrant disregard for my authority. This is the reason I asked for this meeting." Laura pulled another stack of papers from her folder and passed them out to each person in the room.

"I won't go over these numbers with you. I'm sure you can see by the headings above each column and the totals speak for themselves." Laura returned to her seat and allowed the men a few moments to review the pages.

Helen laid her set of papers on the table without looking at them. Within moments of examining the spreadsheets, a few men looked up from their papers directly at Helen then returned to reviewing the pages.

Laura had sat silent during the accusations leveled against her, but not Helen. With denial dripping in her voice, she rebuffed. "Those numbers are an outright lie." This was followed by a grunt.

When the board members looked up from the papers Laura had given them, she resumed. "Now, in response to the accusations of improprieties at my last place of employment..."

Helen's position changed from pouting child with arms locked across her chest to shoulders back and head lifted. She could not hold back her sarcasm when she uttered, "Finally, the truth will come out!" She looked directly at Laura as a sneer unconsciously formed on her lips. Under her breath, Helen took one more jab. "Bet you don't have a spreadsheet for this."

Laura kept her focus on the group of men gathered around the table. These men would soon choose her fate. She decided against making any response directly to Helen's snide remarks. She would keep her wits about her as she unfolded this shameful chapter of her past.

"I know that we call ourselves Christian Family Services and that was the true draw for me when I stepped down from my director position at my previous place of employment. This could be a long story with many moving parts, but because of time, I will address the accusations that Helen has leveled against me in two areas. First, with a previous subordinate, and second, with our own chairman, Tom Brown." Laura gave a nod in the direction where Tom sat.

All eyes followed her nod and glanced for a moment from Laura to Tom then back to Laura. She continued. "Five years ago, I went through a rather nasty divorce that left me both angry and alone. I never had children, so when my marriage ended I was in a free fall. I threw myself into my work with a vengeance. In my zealousness to change the world, I allowed myself to be sweet-talked by a younger man whom I had hired. I won't put all the blame on him. I was a silly woman swept off my feet by the attentions of a young man. In my imprudence, I made decisions that were later interpreted as sexual harassment."

Helen Franko fought with her face to control the vindictive smile that tried to push up the sides of her lips. She tried to massage the muscles at the corner of her mouth with her index finger and thumb. Hopefully, this would relax the urge to smile or make any unwelcomed noise while trying to stifle a laugh.

Laura continued, "Six months before these charges were brought against me, I was recklessly pursuing a pastor and his family in the attempts of having their children removed from their home. My heart was full of hate and I had made a predetermined decision without the proper evidence that this family was evil and causing great harm to their innocent children. When I thought my attempts to remove the children from the home were beyond my control, I tried to gather evidence outside the usual means by attending a special service they had regarding healing. I thought their crazy beliefs alone should be grounds to remove a child. However, what I wasn't expecting was to see a physical healing and also experience a spiritual healing in my own wounded soul." Laura breathed in deeply. The emotions of that night stirred within her.

Laura Klingburg looked down at her lap to regather her thoughts. When she looked back up, Tom Brown's face was the first one she saw. His eyes were closed. His lips were barely moving. Not a sound could be heard by anyone in the room. Laura knew in her heart, Tom was praying for her. His prayers gave her strength.

Laura glanced at Helen. Her focus changed from the board members to her nemesis. Her voice softened. "It was at that church service that my life was changed forever when I invited Jesus Christ to be Lord of my life. I ended the affair with my subordinate and I made a determined decision to live and act in a way that I felt was pleasing to the Lord. It was all new for me, but I could not deny what I saw and heard at that meeting. From that day forward, my whole world changed. I tried to stay at my job and do it with honor, but my past was creeping up on me. Unbeknownst to me, the young man had been using me the whole time to take my job. He had been a meticulous notetaker." Laura didn't mean any offense by the remark, but Helen's lips were twisted, and she wore an expression of 'is anyone here believing a word of this.'

"When the young man made his move against me, I had six months of trying to make my wrongs right. The state was not interested in the past six months but focused more on the threat of lawsuits and settlements. It was easier for them to be done with me than to try and salvage my years of service."

Helen snorted, then slapped her hand over her mouth and whispered., "Oh, excuse me." Her eyes narrowed.

Laura took the brief interruption by Helen as a reprieve then resumed. "When I saw there was an opening at Christian Family Services, I decided to apply. It has been a joy to work here, and I've never looked back at my past since arriving. I love the freedom you've given me here to put the needs of the children above all else because we are a nonprofit working only to help focus on the reunification of families—at least that is my goal, but not at the sake of ruining children for profit."

Laura glanced around the room before adding, "Regarding our director, Tom Brown, I did not know him personally, but I did recognize him from church when I came in for my first interview. In our 18 months of working together, we have not socialized privately or in a group setting. What has pushed us together recently was the accusations that there was something improper between us. We did discuss that and reviewed our past actions to try and figure out how Helen could have come to this assumption.

We even met with our pastor for advice because we didn't want this to become something that would cripple the work we are doing at this agency. I trust this information will assist you in bringing an end to all the allegations leveled against me as you assess what is best for the future of this agency."

A hint of sadness was evident in Tom's voice as he took back the meeting. "Thank you, Laura, for your honesty. I'm sure that was not easy to share." Tom looked around the table at the other men on the board. They would not make eye contact with him. "I think the board would like some time alone to discuss what action we will take. Ladies, you may go. We'll contact you in the next week with a decision."

Helen Franko and Laura Klingburg stood, then left the meeting room without saying a word to the board or to each other.

***

The young nurse snatched the baby from the doctor's hands and whisked her into the air. "Emily, take a quick look at your little girl. We're moving her to the NICU to get her stabilized. The doctor will be back to talk with you both soon."

And after one hour of labor, Baby Girl Edwards was no longer safe within her mother's womb. Kota leaned in to kiss the top of Emily's head. "It's early, but she'll be okay. I just know it."

Emily couldn't speak but nodded her head. A few tears rolled down her cheeks.

Kota tried to reassure his wife. "As soon as the doctor says you're okay, I'll call Snake and your parents—Your parents, they are going to be so upset they weren't here." Kota paused then thoughtfully added, "Maybe, I better call them now." He pulled his cell phone from his pocket and tried Marilyn's number again. The phone rang twice before Marilyn answered.

"Hey Kota, I saw Emily called earlier, but there was no answer on her phone when I tried to call her back. Everything okay?"

Hearing his mother-in-law's voice messed with his emotions. He'd done a great job being strong for Emily, but right now—he was feeling like he needed a mommy himself and he couldn't find one word to say.

"Kota? What's going on?" Marilyn waited for a response but all she heard was a gasp and a man fighting tears.

Kota finally collected himself and spoke. "Emily had the baby. It's a girl."

"But...she was only seven months. Is the baby okay? Is Emily okay? Where are the kids?"

The onslaught of questions caused Kota's adrenaline to kick in. "The kids are with Snake and Fauna. The baby is being evaluated. We don't even know how much she weighs. Please come. Emily is okay physically, but she needs you."

James Fields stood close to his wife to try and hear the voice on the other end of the phone. He kept mouthing the words for Marilyn to put Kota on speaker, but Marilyn was processing all the information and was unable to do anything but listen to her son-in-law's concern. The next thing James heard was Marilyn saying, "We're coming now."

When she took the phone away from her ear, her husband looked at her with a questioning expression, then asked with both his mouth and arms, "Well?"

"Emily had the baby. We need to go now." Marilyn hurried around trying to get everything she thought she would need and then calmly placed books, music and food snacks on the kitchen table and said, "Forget all this, let's go."

James was already at the door holding it open, and as Marilyn passed by him, James touched her hand. She stopped, and he embraced her. Her head rested on his chest and he whispered, "Em and the baby are going to be fine—both of them. I feel it with every ounce of faith in my Spirit. That little girl will live."

***

Snake was unusually quiet while he waited for news of Emily and the baby. Fauna tried to comfort him with words of encouragement, but her own emotions were raw. Emily wasn't flesh and blood to her, but it seemed like she was. She had welcomed Fauna into their family and had stood with her through every up and down. She'd even been there for Fauna with all the issues and concerns she had with CeCe and that was no small task. In all the months since CeCe came to live with them, Emily never said no to watching CeCe when Fauna called—not once.

Fauna watched Snake. He held his cell phone in his hand and looked at it with a blank expression. The children had gone to bed an hour ago. Amazingly, CeCe didn't fight them at bedtime like she usually did. She liked the idea of a sleepover with her "cousins" as she had begun to call them. The house seemed unnaturally quiet after the hurried evening of rushing to the hospital, herding three children home and trying to keep spirits high and worries low. She was exhausted.

A sudden blast of worship music burst the bubble that Snake and Fauna were in. Snake quickly answered his phone to stop the music, "We're here. Any news?"

Marilyn answered, "Dad and I are at the hospital. The doctor just left. I told Kota that I'd call you with the update. Their emotions are pretty raw right now. The baby is three pounds and one ounce. The doctor said that she is doing great considering how small she is. She's on oxygen and there are a few other drainage tubes and wires on her. Oh, and she's in an incubator. I guess the important thing is she's doing well for now. It's the lungs they are most concerned about and are watching closely."

Snake had put his mom on speaker phone after his initial question. "Fauna and I are both here. Let Emily know the kids are fine. We can keep them as long as needed." He shot Fauna a questioning look and she nodded in agreement. "Thanks for letting us know. I feel like I can breathe again." Snake's relief could be heard in the tone of his voice.

"Marilyn, please tell Emily we're praying and believing the baby will be fine. Did they name her yet?"

"Not yet. Right now, she's Baby Girl Edwards."

22

But the wisdom from above is first pure,
then peaceable, gentle, accommodating,
full of mercy and good fruit, impartial, and not hypocritical.
James 3:17 (NET Bible)

Fauna stacked the remaining breakfast dishes in the dishwasher and turned to see the children playing in the family room. A knock at the door as it eased open drew Fauna's attention. Marilyn poked her head into the kitchen and smiled. "Are Maddie and William ready?"

Fauna looked concerned and answered her mother-in-law with trepidation. "Yes, but I'm not sure I'm ready to see them go."

The past 18 hours, CeCe's behavior had exceeded Fauna's expectations. She went to bed without a fight, slept through the night without a nightmare and didn't fight her when it was time to remove the morning pull-up. Whatever was causing this sudden change in behavior, Fauna was not complaining, but praying that she would continue to see flashes of hope—for CeCe's sake and for Snake. And maybe even a little bit for her too.

Marilyn took a few more steps into the house and followed Fauna's line of vision into the family room. "There's nothing better than seeing kids play peacefully—and nothing worse than kids fighting." She smiled at her words of wisdom.

Fauna replied. "Too true. Having Maddie and William here has been a blessed distraction for poor CeCe. The house will seem empty when they go. And I know this—she won't be happy about it."

Marilyn placed her hand on Fauna's back. "I wish I could take her too, but I have errands to run which would require a lot of in and out of the car."

"Marilyn, no. I'd never ask you to do that. She probably needs some down time now after all the excitement anyways." Fauna feared that she would reap the whirlwind of Maddie and William's departure for the rest of the day.

Fauna stood next to CeCe at the door and waved as Maddie and William piled into their grandma's van. The rest of the morning passed without incident. When Fauna looked at her watch, she was surprised to see it was time for CeCe's nap. Fauna checked her watch again dreading the idea of breaking the peaceful interval she had had with the child, but if CeCe didn't take a nap they would all pay dearly.

With her sweetest voice, Fauna mustered up the courage to ask, "CeCe, it's nap time. Are you ready?" This was usually the time she expected the yelling, kicking and biting to begin, but instead CeCe picked up a pile of books and walked towards Fauna. She half prepared herself to be pelted by flying books, but instead CeCe dropped the books in Fauna's lap.

CeCe crawled up next to Fauna and waited. Dare she dream that they were about to have a moment? Fauna lifted the first book and opened the cover. She began to read the books one at a time, carefully pointing to the pictures using funny voices and asking questions along the way. CeCe's head relaxed against Fauna's arm. It was more wonderful than words could express. CeCe rested it there for the longest time, and Fauna felt something deep inside her for the first time since CeCe's arrival—affection.

* * *

Isabelle responded to the text message from Griffin with three emojis of a face laughing with tears. They had been texting daily since his last visit. It began slowly, but now she found it a blessed distraction from her growing size, monotonous school work and mounting internal conflicts.

Isabelle typed out the words—*Are you still coming on Friday? I'm one month from my due date. The doctor said I could go early because the baby is big. I've set a time for Saturday to talk to the Parkers. You still good with all this?* Isabelle pushed send and waited for Griffin to respond.

The phone vibrated in her hand. She looked at the incoming call. It was Griffin. They had been sending text messages, but up to this point, they had not spoken on the phone since Griffin left three weeks ago. A phone call was taking it to the next level in her mind. She cautiously answered. "Hello?"

"I'm sorry. I'm so tired of texting. I'll be up on Friday evening. I'm planning on being at the meeting with the Parkers, but I'm not saying yes just yet. When did you want to meet with the lawyer?"

"Can you stay over on Monday?"

"I'll see. Go ahead and make an appointment and I'll arrange things here." Griffin's words said one thing, but his heart felt something different.

Isabelle wished she was texting instead of talking. It still felt surreal to be having a conversation with the father of her child after all these months of pretending she wasn't pregnant then trying to escape the reality that she could do this without including him. Hearing his voice made her heart feel raw. She responded, "Griffin, we're running out of time. I pray we can come to some resolution this weekend."

"Me too. See you then." Griffin hung up and looked at the call ended button on his screen. He didn't want this to be over before it even began. He didn't want it to end with his own child being given away to someone else to raise. But he wasn't stupid. What choice did he have? He wasn't fit to raise a child on his own or even help share in the responsibility of supporting a child.

Griffin spoke out loud to the only other person in the room. "Jesus, help me do the right thing."

***

Laura waited out the week and still no response. She wondered why Tom Brown had not called her with an update. She would die of old age before she would ask—but she did want to know the decision of the board regarding Helen's accusations and what they thought of Helen's job review and unethical behavior.

Laura knew that Tom had known about her past. She shared it all in her first interview with him. Why the silent treatment now? What had changed?

Laura glanced out the window of her office. She wished at times that Helen's desk wasn't visible from hers. Her mind was occupied by every possible scenario when she realized she was looking directly at Helen. Helen responded with narrow eyes and angrily mouthed the word—*what!*

Laura quickly looked away but felt like she was caught doing something bad. She turned back to her laptop and opened her private email. There were 23 emails in her inbox. The first few were junk mail, then her eyes landed on Tom Brown's name. He had never used her private email. She didn't even know he had that address. She clicked on the email to open it and read the content.

Laura,

Sorry for the delay in contacting you. I know you must be concerned about your future with the agency. After you left, the board had a lively discussion that resulted in a split decision. I am contacting you on your personal email because I wanted to give you an update without a trail for anyone who is snooping where they don't belong—enough said.

It seems that some on the board like the idea of making money regardless of the welfare and safety of children. These same men, although they know my character well, have been trying to remove me as director for some time. We decided to table the matter for another month or more until we can compile all the files and review them for both you and Helen.

At least for the time being your job is safe. But we will

have to wait and see.

My prayers are with you as you work with Ms. Franko. Let me encourage you to do the job the Lord called you to do and don't worry about looking over your shoulder. God has a way of making things work out according to His plans above all else.

God Bless you my friend,

Tom

My friend...what in the world? Are we friends now? *Oh, Lord help me. I'm so confused. Should I stay and fight these charges against me or...run?* Laura rubbed her index finger on the frown lines between her eyes with more force than usual, but it didn't stop the unsettling emotions that ran through her thoughts.

***

Given the wild week of activities that Snake and Fauna had experienced with the premature birth of their niece, watching his sister's children at a moment's notice and dealing with Fauna's emotional swings, Snake was left with less interest in adoption than before. None of it seemed right to him, especially adopting a child from a family they went to church with and Fauna had counseled. He was determined to be a good listener and not agree to anything today.

Snake felt Fauna's fingers touch his hand and slowly intertwine with his as they walked up the front steps of the counseling center. It was a Saturday and the center was quiet. This place would give them the freedom to discuss the adoption without prying eyes or eavesdropping customers at a public restaurant. Isabelle had read all the articles after her meeting, met with the adoption counselor, and had a preliminary meeting with her parents and the adoption lawyer. Snake could practically feel the earth moving under his feet. Everything was set in motion, and now for Fauna's sake, he had to keep moving forward no matter how bad he wanted to turn and run.

"Snake, they'll be here in a few minutes. When we see them together, we'll have an idea how the baby will look. He'll be a blend of the two of them."

Snake tightened his jaw and tried to guard his words. "Let's move slow here. Really slow. We're just talking."

Fauna dropped his hand to unlock the front door. "Believe me I know. I've walked this road with many clients..." Fauna fumbled with the lock, rattled the doorknob, then pushed the old wooden door open. She stepped into the warm reception area and gave room for Snake to enter behind her before shutting the door to the cold February morning. "...as much as I want a baby, I don't want to take Isabelle's baby if she's not ready to deal with the emotions involved with adoption."

Snake questioned, "Are we really prepared for a baby? I mean, we're beginning to see little signs of promise with CeCe. I think she should have our first line of attention...maybe we should talk about adopting her."

Fauna walked to the back of the center and unlocked her office door. She avoided Snake's question and suggestion. "I think we'll meet in here. It's a cozy arrangement. It sets the right atmosphere."

Snake looked around Fauna's office. A dread gripped him in the center of his chest. He wondered what emotional harm awaited each of them in the moments to come. In his estimation, they were entering into a very dangerous discussion that could harm Fauna, the person he loved, or Isabelle, a person he cared about. Griffin he didn't know, but if this was his unborn child being bantered about like grain at an auction, he would be infuriated.

Snake sat in one of the side chairs across from the sofa.

Fauna sat on the sofa and patted the place next to her. "Sit here. They would probably be more comfortable sitting in the chairs."

Snake stood and moved to the sofa that faced the door when the bell on the back of the entrance door jingled announcing the arrival of someone.

Fauna jumped to her feet and walked the long hallway back to the waiting area. "Welcome."

Snake could hear the glee in her voice. He wasn't feeling it, not one little bit. A moment later, two very young-looking people joined Fauna as she returned to the office.

Introductions were made, everyone took their assigned seats and the uncomfortable small talk began. Surprisingly, it was Isabelle who brought the conversation to task.

"I know you both are busy. I heard Emily had her baby early." Isabelle looked at Snake for a response.

"Ahh...yes. They're both doing fine. The baby will stay in the hospital for a few more weeks."

"I think we were due about the same time. That's crazy that..." Isabelle's hands rested protectively on her expanded belly and she looked down. "...this baby could already be born."

No one spoke. Then Fauna broke the silence. "Griffin, can you tell us how you're feeling about all this?"

Griffin looked at Isabelle then back at Fauna to answer. "Processing. I'm still processing."

Snake didn't like Griffin's answer nor the way he looked at Isabelle. That was not the look of someone who was willing to step away from the girl or the baby. A picture of Fauna racked with grief over these children changing their mind flashed through Snake's thoughts. This whole situation felt hopeless to him.

Snake felt Fauna's hand touch the top of his. "Did you hear Isabelle's question to you?" Fauna looked at Snake who was obviously a million miles away. "She asked how *you* were feeling about the adoption?"

What could he say? If he told Isabelle what he was really thinking Fauna would freak. Inside, his heart was yelling, you'll never be able to go through with the adoption so please stop now before my wife is heartbroken and I'm left to pick up the pieces. But instead he followed suit with the other traumatized male in the room. "I'm processing it all. It's a lot to take in."

Fauna squeezed his hand tightly and Snake knew that was not the correct answer.

Snake stood up. His 6'5" frame towered over all those in the room. "You know. I think I'd like to talk to Griffin alone for a few minutes. If you ladies will excuse us. Griffin—follow me."

The young man looked relieved to leave the cozy setting as he followed the tattooed, bearded, giant man out of the office.

The two men sat in the waiting area and talked for 20 minutes. The chat ended when the girls joined them. In that short discussion, Snake found out what he needed to know and without a doubt what he had to do.

23

A joyful heart is good medicine, but depression drains one's strength.
Proverbs 17:22 (GW)

Samantha stood outside the bedroom door of her eldest daughter, Isabelle. She had tried, on a number of occasions, the past few weeks to have a meaningful conversation with her moping daughter, but the girl was acting like a lovesick teen. Samantha was over it. Something had to give. She rested her hand on the door then tapped the door softly with her open hand. There was no response. She rolled her hand into a fist and tapped a bit harder and longer with her knuckles. Still no response.

Samantha wiggled the doorknob. It was locked. "Issie. Are you in there?" No answer. "Issie, if you don't at least answer me, I'll get the key and come in."

"Can't a person be alone in this house without everyone going crazy?" Issie's voice was loud and her irritable emotional state was coming through.

"I want to talk with you. I'm not leaving. We can do it face to face or through the door—your choice." Samantha waited. She heard movement in the room. The door rattled then it opened.

Isabelle made a grand gesture with her hand to sarcastically invite her mom into her domain. "Please do come in."

Samantha wedged herself around Isabelle who didn't mean to completely block the door—but she did. As she struggled to pass she tried not to infuriate her daughter any more than she already was. She remained standing to allow Isabelle to pick her seat first. Issie chose the window seat and Samantha rolled the desk chair close to the window to be in the proximity of her daughter. "I can see you are struggling with something and I know you don't want to discuss it with me…that's fine. But, I want to say this one more time. Dad and I are willing to help you. You don't have to give up your child. I don't work. I'm home every day. It would give me great joy to help as little or as much as you need. These past few weeks, I've felt that Griffin is not in favor of the adoption either."

Isabelle's gloomy face changed to rage. "Of course, he's not in favor. But, the best he'd ever be is a weekend distraction possibly for years to come, if not forever. It's all on me. I mean us, if I were to keep this baby."

"You may want to cut that boy some slack. After all, at one time there was something about him that drew you in and he has been driving up here seven hours one way every time you ask him to. It just seems to me, if he were a deadbeat, he would be a deadbeat now. And you've treated him pretty rude sometimes. I mean…"

"Really, Mom. Just really!" Isabelle threw her arms in the air and let them fall at her round side. Her expression revealed the dissatisfaction of the state of her body. "No one will ever want me again. I'm ruined forever…and fat!"

Samantha fought a smile and a condescending tone. "Issie, every woman in history who has had a baby has been where you are. Things will come back to a near normal state soon enough."

Tears began to cluster in the corners of Isabelle's eyes. She pointed at them. "…and this. I can't seem to make them stop. I still have three weeks until my due date and…" She half laughed as she asked. "Can your water break through your tear ducts? Because I think my water breaks on a daily basis right here!" She pointed at her eyes again with great emphasis.

Samantha broke into deep rolling laughter. Between laughs, she said. "Oh Issie. You're a hoot."

Isabelle fought a smile. Her mom's laugh was contagious. "I'm glad you're getting such a kick out of my misery."

Through her laughing Samantha tried to speak. "I'm so

sorry. I just can't stop."

Soon Issie was laughing too. They laughed together for what seemed like an hour, but it was mere minutes.

Then the room grew quiet.

Issie asked, "What about the Parkers?"

Samantha saw it. It was the first crack in her armor. She inwardly warned herself—proceed with caution.

***

A feeling of relief filled Laura Klingburg as she closed the email. For months she had been sitting on the possibility that CeCe would be available for adoption. Now she had great news to give them without any false hope. It was all in writing before her eyes. The wheels of government bureaucracy move slowly, but eventually they do move. Laura dialed Fauna's cell phone. It went directly to voice mail.

"Fauna. This is Laura Klingburg. I have some great news. I'd like to speak with you and Snake at your earliest convenience. You can pick the place and time. I'll make it work for my schedule. Call me."

Laura silently prayed, asking the Lord to continue the work He was obviously doing behind the scenes. This had to be the Lord—the timing couldn't be more perfect.

Laura looked at the open file on her desk. Finally, a success. She closed the file and laid her hand on top of the cream-colored folder. That uneasy feeling of someone watching caused Laura to look up from her desk. Helen Franko stood in the doorway. Laura held her jaw tight while trying to speak with a professional tone. "May I help you?"

Helen stepped inside the office and closed the door behind her. "Actually, I may be able to help you."

Laura fought the urge to roll her eyes and sigh. Instead she gestured towards the seat in front of her desk. "Please have a seat and tell me what's on your mind."

Helen moved into the office with a swagger and sat

down. She met Laura's eyes and smiled. "Can we put this messy-mess behind us while we're both on a kind of a probational period?"

Laura didn't respond. They had received the final report from the board that had basically said that they should both tread lightly. She was not going to discuss this with Helen— no way. Laura asked again, "Was there something I can help you with? Otherwise, I have work to do."

Helen used a voice that was thick with sweetness. "You know, we've both made mistakes here. I'm willing to let bygones be bygones." Helen's words were paramount to an olive branch of peace being extended.

Looking at Helen's smile, Laura heard the music in her head to the song, *Never Smile at a Crocodile*. The tune rolled around in her head and almost brought a smile to her lips. "Helen, I'd like to keep things between us on a purely professional level. If you don't have something work-related to discuss, I'll have to ask you to leave."

"Fine. Fine. It's CeCe Jefferson. I'd like to ask if I could see her file. I believe there is false information in there about me and it needs to be corrected."

Laura was quick to answer. "You mean the part about you being her first social worker and how you dropped the ball and returned an infant to a drug addicted mother without proper aftercare or follow up?" Laura spit out the words without taking a breath. Why did this woman continue to take out her mistakes on an innocent child? Was she trying to get rid of her mistake by erasing the child from the system, by losing her in a group home? Laura knew without a doubt that God had a plan for CeCe's young life. She believed it included parents who loved her in spite of her past, and she hoped those parents would be Snake and Fauna Parker.

Laura silently asked the Lord to guide her before she spoke another word. "You know Helen, good things are in store for CeCe. Stop trying to ruin her life by protecting yours. Let her thrive."

Helen's face grew red with anger. "How dare you, Laura

Klingburg, try and blame me for that child's issues by dropping all her baggage at my door. I did my job. That child was damaged goods from the get-go. You can't blame that on the social worker."

Even after her prayer and a quickening in her Spirit, Laura still responded, "You can if the social worker isn't doing her job."

"How dare you!"

Laura stopped herself before their voices seeped out into the workplace. She would not allow this woman to ever cause her to lose her temper again. Laura's voice changed from argumentative to consoling. "I don't want to get into a battle of words. I'm asking you kindly to step back from CeCe. She's no longer your case. She's in a place of hope. God is on the verge of doing something wonderful in her life. Don't try to interfere with the good that is beginning to happen for that little girl."

Helen pushed herself up from the chair with such force that the chair where she sat tipped over and landed on its side. "I won't tolerate this one more day. I'm calling the board and letting them know."

Laura didn't move from her seat and in a calm voice said, "So, let me get this straight. You're going to tell the board how you removed a baby from a safe home with caring foster parents and placed her back into the care of a drug addicted prostitute who failed to show up for mandatory drug screening. And this family was not followed up on for two more years because of your negligence. By then the baby had experienced such neglect and abuse that it would be difficult to read her file in mixed company." Laura drew in a deep breath and continued. "If you feel the need to take this to the board, I want you to know that these men will hear the whole story this time, not just an email read out loud to them. I have the files and the reprimands that were written by your former director."

Helen tightened her lips into a thin line and picked up the toppled chair. She stood silent.

Laura leaned forward resting her folded arms on the desk top. "CeCe is going away soon. She will be out of the system. And with her, goes her file. But be assured, it will be through adoption, not by being institutionalized or lost in the system."

Helen walked towards the closed office door and laid her hand on the knob. She turned back and looked at Laura. "You think you've won, but I will not have my job jeopardized by that child."

"Let it go Helen. And you both survive. Push it, and you will be the only one damaged by the contents of this file." Laura patted the top file on her desk.

Helen's eyes narrowed as she looked intently at the file under Laura's hand.

24

You will show me the path of life;
In Your presence is fullness of joy;
At Your right hand are pleasures forevermore.
Psalm 16:11 (NKJV)

The scurry of events following the arrival of Emily and Kota's baby girl left all their families in a perpetual state of flux. The children had been strategically moved between parents, grandparents, aunts and uncles. Even a few church friends had stepped up to help with transporting kids to school and bringing meals. Emily was exhausted. This was not the way she had pictured the arrival of the final member of their family. The stress of seeing her newborn daughter tethered down with wires and tubes broke her heart. The past six weeks had completely consumed Emily's life.

They had named their baby girl Eve, which means 'life.' Now that Eve was finally gaining weight, she was moved to a room where they could receive visitors. If all went well over the next few days, baby Eve would be able to go home exactly three weeks before her original due date.

Rocking her newborn baby, Emily wondered how things were going with CeCe. She made a mental note to ask them the next time she saw either Fauna or Snake. Emily enjoyed her skin-on-skin time with Eve. Her heart was overcome with gratitude for the love and support of her family and church. As she batted her eyes to hold back the wave of emotion, she noticed Fauna outside the door of the hospital room. She was putting the required mask and gown on before entering the room.

Fauna eased the door open the rest of the way and smiled at the picture of mother and child in front of her. "I just love seeing you hold her, Emily. She's so perfect." Fauna moved into the room and took the other seat near the baby bassinette that had been little Eve's home the past six weeks. Eve's tiny foot dangled out from under the blanket Emily had loosely draped over her. Fauna reached out and touched Eve's foot. It was warm and soft. Her unfulfilled desire for a baby of her own caused her heart to ache.

"Fauna, I wish you could hold her. We will be home soon and then you can."

"I'd be scared to hold a baby so small." Fauna placed her hand on the blanket that covered little Eve's back. "She's gaining weight, right?"

"Oh yes. Soon our lives will get back to normal."

Fauna choked on a laugh. "Ha. We left normal behind months before Eve's surprise appearance." Fauna released Eve's tiny foot and leaned back in her chair. "Can I get you anything? I can't stay long. I just wanted to check on you before going to pick CeCe up from childcare."

"I'm good. Thanks for stopping by. Go home now and love on your little girl."

Fauna frowned. "My little girl?"

"Yes, CeCe is *your* little girl."

Fauna sighed. "I'm not so sure about that. I'll admit, we've seen glimpses of hope, but I'd hardly call her my little girl. We don't even know what her situation is regarding adoption. We've never asked."

Fauna wondered if she should tell Emily about the private adoption they were discussing with Isabelle Hayes. Fauna decided to tell, but nothing about the birth mom. "Well, I do have some kinda good news. Nothing is for sure yet, but Snake and I have been talking with a couple who want to place their baby for adoption."

Emily's eyes widened at the announcement.

Fauna continued. "Actually, we've been talking for months about it. The thought of raising a baby from birth without dealing with the damage inflicted by someone else is very alluring. Even more so now, after what we've endured with CeCe." Fauna swallowed hard then cleared her throat and spoke in a soft voice. "I'd be lying if I said it has been anything but grueling with that child."

"I know it's been hard, but how could you ever let her go after investing all these months in her?" Emily rearranged the sleeping baby against her chest and baby Eve let out a pitiful squawk like a little bird. Emily rested her open hand on the baby's back. "Snake cares so deeply for her. Even if you didn't adopt her—at least you'd keep her. Right? I already feel like she's family."

"Honestly, I don't know how CeCe would be with a baby in the house. It would be scary. And the attention and care a baby needs would probably cause her to act out even more."

"I'm sorry you guys are going through this." Emily glanced down at her sleeping baby's face then looked up at Fauna and declared, "I've got a lot of time on my hands right now—I'm gonna pray that God will step in and make a way that will be crystal clear to both of you."

Fauna stood up to leave and leaned in to hug Emily. "Thanks, Em. We need the mind of the Lord for the decisions ahead of us. Now I've got to go face the wrath of a 3-year-old. She's always pretty angry when I pick her up after being in the structured childcare environment. I think she knows that Snake and I are pushovers for the most part." She stood to leave, "You know your brother. He's in love with that little green-eyed girl." Somehow saying the words out loud caused a stir in Fauna's heart that was familiar, yet new in her feelings towards CeCe.

Emily chuckled. "Hang in there. Something wonderful is coming, and sooner than you think. I just feel it. And...I know you love CeCe."

"From your mouth to God's ear. I could use *wonderful* anytime now. The love thing—I want it, but I'm not feeling it as yet." Fauna turned back and waved as she left the room and discarded her gown and mask in the bin.

Fauna reached into her pocket and moved the mute

button on her phone to ringer mode. She opened her phone. There were two missed calls and two voicemails. She touched the voicemail key on her phone and waited for the first message from Snake.

The message played in her ear. *Hey Fauna, I'll be home later. Don't fix dinner for me. I've got a meeting. I'll tell you all about it when I get home.*

Huh? Fauna snorted, forgetting her elevator etiquette. A stranger shot her a questioning look and she replied, "Oh, I'm sorry. Just thinking out loud." Fauna smiled and returned her focus to her mobile phone. Being mindful of her surroundings, she moved to the second message. It was from Ms. K. *Hi Fauna. I have some great news I want to share with you. It would be good if you and Snake are both there, but I'm too excited to hold it another moment. I'm stopping by your house at 7 P.M. tonight. Call me only if this is a bad time. If I don't hear back from you, then I'll see you later tonight.*

Well that's just great, she thought. Who's Snake meeting with, and what does Ms. K have to tell us that is exciting and can't wait? She glanced at her watch. She'd have to wait for the news from both of them until later. For now, a curly haired little monster was waiting for her. Uh!

***

Snake moved uncomfortably in the booth at the restaurant. He felt a twinge in his chest like he was being unfaithful meeting with someone in secret without Fauna knowing. He assured himself that he did leave the voicemail so maybe his deception was only a half-truth. He didn't give her all the facts. But soon—he would.

"Mind if I sit down?"

Snake looked up and nodded his head in the affirmative.

Griffin Walsh slid into the booth seat across from Snake and did a quick examination of the man he'd only met briefly once before. He's huge, Griffin thought. How are those massive hands gonna care for a tiny baby? Griffin looked down at the table and spoke. "I'm glad you called. I know you must have a million questions—and so do I."

Snake tried not to be intimidating but every move he made could be interpreted by someone who didn't know him as just that. He leaned inward and rested his forearms on his side of the table and spoke. "Griffin, I'll tell ya this from the get-go. I'm not a man of many words and I'm gonna be straight with you." Snake scratched his bearded face with his hand and looked to be pondering his next statement before he spoke. "So, let's just be honest with each other. No females here this time."

Griffin relaxed his shoulders. "I'm glad you said that because Isabelle and I are not on the same page."

"Okay. Let's just say what's on our mind and move on, shall we?"

Griffin pointed at Snake and said, "That sounds great—you go first."

"After Isabelle's baby is born, I don't think she'll be able to give it up, and the longer my wife gets her heart set on that baby, the harder it is going to be when the baby is born."

"I hear ya. If it were up to me, I'd move back here and stay with my aunt and uncle. They already offered it to me and said that I could finish my college here and look for whatever work would allow me to go to college."

Snake thought over Griffin's words, then said, "I'm not an expert on women, but I think if you showed your willingness to be involved, this could give Isabelle hope for a future with her child—and possibly even you, Griffin." Snake kept his eyes focused on Griffin's face the whole time he spoke.

"I want to but…"

"No buts here boy. You're in or you're out. A child's life depends on it."

Griffin didn't try to complete his unfinished sentence nor start a new one.

Snake looked sternly at the young man. "Did you have a father at home while you were growing up?"

Griffin nodded his head. "There was fighting, but we all lived under the same roof."

"Would your life have been better without him?"

Griffin pondered the question before answering. "No. He was there for me when I needed him."

"Do you think your son deserves the same?"

Griffin looked away, then down at the table. "She already said no. She said that it would all be on her to raise our son. She thinks I won't be there for the long haul. She's the one who kept me out of the picture."

"Well then, all the more reason to move here before the baby is born. Show her you're committed now before it's too late. She won't sign the adoption papers—if you don't sign. Actually, you have more power than you think." Snake felt a twinge of guilt for that last remark. That was crossing the line to manipulation. He knew his motives were not pure. It would be easier for him if the decision was made by someone other than him. He didn't want to be the voice of reason and say no to the adoption. He was moving the chess pieces in such a way that it would not fall on him—but it was wrong.

"Griffin, you do what you think is right. Sign or don't sign. Just know that you can't change it once it's done."

Snake looked at the boy who was trying to process things that were far beyond his nineteen years of life. He felt sorry for him. With his own reckless past, that could have been him sitting on the other side of the table ten years ago. "Are you okay?"

"I think I need to talk to my parents before I make any decisions. They already said that they'd help. Maybe it's time to step up and take action." Griffin choked back his emotions, but not before the moisture in his eyes spilled over.

"Listen Griffin, the Lord brought you into my life for a reason, and if there is anything I can do to help you become the man of God you want to be—well, I'm good with that. I will be a listening ear and give advice when asked. I have one more very important question—how are you doing in your relationship with the Lord?"

"I'd say things have been better. This mess has created a distance between me and all things spiritual that I can't seem to bridge. Ever since Isabelle told me, God has seemed so far away. I can't even pray about it."

"You do understand the whole concept of what forgiveness is—right?"

"Yeah, but I got a girl pregnant. A whole life is forever affected by my sin."

"True. But is it unforgivable? Let me answer that for you. Absolutely not!" Snake pulled his phone from his pocket to open his Bible app. "No time like the present for our first talk. You got a few minutes?"

"If I could truly understand God's forgiveness—I'd give you all the time you need."

Snake turned his phone around towards Griffin and pointed. "Read this verse out loud to me and then we'll talk."

Griffin took the phone in his hand and began reading. "Come now, and let us reason together, says the Lord: though your sins be as scarlet, they shall be as white as snow; though they be red like crimson, they shall be as wool."

"We don't have to carry our past mistakes. Jesus did that for us when he died on the cross. When we ask for forgiveness, it's done. Here, read this one." Snake quickly moved his finger on his phone screen a few times and handed the phone back to Griffin.

"And I will forgive their wickedness, and I will never again remember their sins." Griffin handed the phone back to Snake. "How can God forget this? I sure can't. How could He ever forgive me?"

"We have to take him at His word. If it's written in the Bible I believe it as truth. I don't question His love, His death, His resurrection nor His forgiveness. I wouldn't be sitting here today if I didn't believe. I've made some pretty big mistakes and hurt a lot of people, but this I do know, that God removed my past from me and gave me a new beginning. You could say that I wrote my story for the first 24 years of my life. Then I gave God the pencil and He erased all of it and began to write a new story. And *God's rewrite* is a masterpiece."

With his head down, Griffin said, "God's gonna need a pretty big eraser on that pencil for me."

"No bigger than mine. You're looking at a life that God rewrote, and His rewrites are breathtaking. The best thing is when I mess up—and I still do sometimes—I just ask Him to forgive me and that big eraser comes out again and the rewrite begins."

"You think God can rewrite my story?" Griffin asked.

"Absolutely. Would you like to start by saying a simple prayer with me?"

"Yes."

***

Fauna looked at the clock for the 100th time. Snake wasn't answering his phone or text messages. This was not like him. Dinner was a fiasco with CeCe actually throwing her food at Fauna. The edge of the plate hit her on the lip and that area still smarted. Fauna rubbed her lip as she remembered the moment. CeCe was sent to bed early but Fauna could still hear her talking to herself. Once she heard a familiar song from preschool echoing down the hallway with an 'e-i-e-i-o.' The few times Fauna went to CeCe's bedroom to check on her, CeCe would quickly turn towards the wall and not move or make a sound.

Fauna sighed as she thought of her seemingly hopeless situation; a child that hated her, a husband who was MIA and a social worker on the way to the house to talk. Yeah, her life was fabulous.

Headlights shined into the kitchen window signaling someone was in the driveway. The snow was gone but the days were still short. At 6:45 P.M. it was dark. Fauna went to the window to check who had arrived—husband or social worker. And it was Ms. K—still no husband.

Fauna stood at the door while Ms. K gathered her things from the car and walked towards Fauna with an unusually broad smile. "Everything okay with you?" Fauna asked.

Ms. K stepped up to the door with ease and embraced Fauna with a bear hug. "I'm so glad to see you Fauna. It's been a rough day and your face just makes me happy. I can see the love of Jesus all over you."

Fauna felt the red rushing to her face. She didn't feel like Jesus was all over her—quite the contrary. Fauna mustered up her best tone of sincerity. "I'm so sorry. Snake's not home yet. He should be arriving soon. Is this something you need us both here to talk about?"

Ms. K removed her shoes and walked into the living room to sit down. She plopped down the briefcase she was carrying, then sat. "What a day! It feels so good to just sit for a moment."

Fauna asked, "Can I get you something to drink?"

"Oh, no thanks. If I drink one more drop of anything I'm going to float away. Did you say when Snake was coming?"

"Soon I hope, but I can't reach him right now. It's actually quite unlike him."

"Oh no worries. I have some amazing news that I wanted to share with both of you, but you can relay the message. Where is CeCe?"

"She's in her bedroom. We had a little incident at dinner." Fauna pointed to the puffy area near her lip. "A plate took flight and hit me in the face."

Ms. K's face looked like her life's dreams were suddenly dashed against the rocks. "Oh. That looks painful."

"Nothing I haven't had to face before. CeCe and I are still finding our way."

"Thank you for not giving up on her. I know there is good in her that is trying to get out and she's still so young. I have hope for her."

"Yes. That's exactly what Snake keeps saying on a daily basis. He—and I have not given up. But it's been tough."

"Well, maybe you won't think my news is so great after all." Ms. K looked at Fauna.

"No, please tell me. I could use some good news." Fauna sat back on the sofa and looked directly at Ms. K.

"CeCe's birth mother's parental rights have officially been terminated. She is actually in jail and she won't be coming out for a very long time. CeCe is officially up for adoption. Is that something that you and Snake might want to consider?"

Fauna couldn't mask her shock or the widening of her eyes.

"Ooo-kay. I see you may need some time to process this information."

Fauna looked away and shook her head. "Adopt CeCe? She hates me."

"Well, it can seem like that sometimes, but hate is a strong word. She's only three."

"No. I'm pretty sure it's *hate*."

"Take a week to think it over and talk to Snake. God created the world in six days. I bet he can do a miracle for all of you in the same amount of time."

"We have been praying, as you know. But the good memories are hard to remember when you get hit in the face with a plate. That will cancel out a lot of good stuff."

"Kids like CeCe have so much trauma. Just take this week. I'm going to continue to pray as I have been and see what God can do. Who else is praying?"

"Pastor, Callan, Tom Brown and you."

"Tom Brown? How did you come about picking him?"

"We've known him for a long time. He believes, as we do, in the power of prayer."

Ms. K nodded her head in agreement with Fauna, but her head was tipped to the side like she was thinking about something else.

Headlights shone through the kitchen window and Fauna jumped to her feet. She looked out the window and said with relief, "He's home."

Ms. K stood and walked towards the door. "You go ahead and fill Snake in on what we talked about. Let's plan to meet at the office next week."

Fauna held the door for Ms. K as Snake hurried to greet her. "What did I miss? I was in a meeting with someone and couldn't stop to call or text."

Ms. K touched Snake on the arm as she passed by him. "No problem. Fauna will fill you in. See you next week in my office."

Snake looked back and forth between the two women to see who would give him more information. Ms. K descending the steps made the final decision. He would wait for Fauna to tell him whatever information she held. He stepped into the house and Fauna closed the door.

"So? What'd Ms. K want?"

Fauna decided not to drag out the information and blurted it out. "CeCe has become eligible for adoption and she wanted to know if we were interested."

Snake stood still. He fought a smile and lost. "Really? Truly?"

"Snake, I'm just not sure. I'm not. I don't know if I want to take on a lifetime commitment with someone who hates me."

"She's getting better. Remember she laid her head on your arm that one day. That was huge. And she let me pick her up last week without fighting. She walks close to us when we insist that she does."

"She threw a plate at me tonight and hit me in the mouth." Fauna pointed at her lip.

Snake drew her into a hug and kissed the top of her head. "All kids throw things. She has to learn that kind of behavior won't be tolerated by her parents. Her parents— that could be us."

"Snake I know you want this, but I'm gonna need more. Just a sign. Something from the Lord to me and I'll know in my heart that this is the right thing to do when I feel that assurance in my heart and not before."

"Okay. We have a week. Right? That's what Ms. K said. God is going to do this. Now where is CeCe?"

"She's in her bedroom. I'm sure she's still awake."

Snake went into CeCe's bedroom and talked with her. A few minutes later CeCe walked out and Snake followed behind her. CeCe stopped in front of Fauna. Fauna had her legs tucked up under her and was leaning on the arm of the sofa. She looked at Snake, then CeCe.

CeCe said, "I sorry."

Fauna looked again at Snake towering over the child, then back at CeCe. "And what are you sorry for?"

"Da plate. No like that."

"You know CeCe, if you don't like something, you can just tell me, and we'll see what else we have. You don't have to throw your plate at me."

"You 'eft me."

"I had to go to work. I always come and get you after work."

CeCe tightened her jaw and looked away.

Fauna slipped off the sofa and knelt down in front of CeCe. "Thank you for saying sorry, CeCe. Snake and I care about you very much and want you to learn to be a kind person. Throwing things at people is not kind."

With more force than before, CeCe said it again, "I sorry!"

Fauna replied., "I forgive you. Can I hug you good night?"

"No hug." CeCe turned and ran back down the hallway to her bedroom.

Fauna laughed. "Well, I will admit. That was promising."

The rest of the evening Fauna and Snake talked about adopting CeCe, adopting Isabelle's baby and Snake's encounter with Griffin. As they walked down the hallway to their bedroom that night, Fauna felt like she was three steps from happiness, but two steps from falling off a cliff.

25

For His anger is but for a moment, His favor is for life;
Weeping may endure for a night, But joy comes in the morning.
Psalm 30:5 (NKJV)

G riffin turned into the circular driveway of Isabelle's house. He had only been here one time before. That was the day Isabelle introduced him to her parents nearly two months ago. He had come up as often as Isabelle asked and he was trying to be supportive and available to her. They had gone out a few times socially, but not romantically. She had put him in the *friend box* and it was going to be a long time before she would trust him outside that box.

Griffin wasn't sure why everything was his fault. Last he knew—it took two. He had tried to contact her and she him, but neither one got through. It was a freaky thing that it took so long, but why that was on him, he wasn't sure.

It was spring break and he had only four more weeks of college. In the next few weeks, he would have to decide if he was moving to Hillbrooke or if he would be an absentee father—if he was permitted at all to even be a father.

Isabelle's due date was in two weeks and she hadn't bought a single thing for the baby nor had her parents or the Parkers. Everyone was in a holding pattern waiting to see what Isabelle would decide. There had been loads of talking, but nothing drawn up or put in writing. No one believed Isabelle could go through with it once the baby was in her arms.

Griffin tapped lightly on the horn and a very pregnant Isabelle opened the front door and waddled down the steps. Griffin opened his car door and hurried around the car to open Isabelle's door. He looked up at the house and saw Dr.

Hayes looking out the window by the door. He let out a sigh of relief that he had at least opened the car door, but he knew he should have rung the bell and helped her down the steps. What was he thinking?

"How are you feeling?" Griffin extended his hand to allow Isabelle to take it as she lowered herself into his car.

"Really? How do you think I'm feeling?"

"Sorry, just trying to show some interest. Exactly what time is your doctor's appointment?"

"I have to check in by 10 A.M. so we have plenty of time. Could we stop at the coffee place next to the doctor's office? I'm craving one of those chocolate frozen coffees."

"Sure, we can do that. Are you still having that false labor stuff?"

"Yes. It was most of the night and I also lost this plug thing. It was gross. I'm thinking the baby may come before my due date now. I hope the doctor has some encouraging news and not the usual. *Everything looks great, see ya next week!*"

"Well, I know you won't believe me, but you look beautiful."

"Are you trying to pick a fight with me?"

"No. I'm complimenting you."

"Well stop it!" Isabelle laid her open hands on the sides of her stomach and breathed in slowly.

"Is it a contraction?"

Isabelle didn't speak.

Griffin kept his eyes on the road and kept quiet.

After a minute, Isabelle let out a deep breath, leaned her head back on the headrest and turned towards Griffin. "Have I told you today how much I hate you?" She let out a little chuckle, then added, "No really—I hate you!"

***

Tom Brown sat on the deck of his new condo and looked at the golf course view. It wasn't the beautiful water view he had shared with Jean at their home on Deer Lake, but it would do. The March weather was cool, but sunny. One of the fun surprises about Michigan weather in March and April is that you never knew what to expect from day to day. The nice weather had brought the golfers out of hibernation. Tom watched a few men take their swings at the 9th hole.

He glanced at his Bible on the table next to him. His coffee was still hot. There were a few streams of steam rising in the cool air. His life was busy, but also lonely. It had been over two years since Jean passed away. He was still strong, healthy, and had a growing desire not be alone for the rest of his life.

Lately, he found himself thinking about Laura Klingburg in more than a business-related manner, but he was more than 10 years her senior. Would she even consider him as a companion? He pushed the thought from his mind and picked up the Bible and lifted the string attached to the book spine to open the place where he left off his reading yesterday.

His eyes fell on his last reading. It was Proverbs 30. He looked at the heading for chapter 31. It said, A Wife of Noble Character. He shook his head in disbelief. He read the chapter and his heart leapt when he read verse 10. Who can find a virtuous and capable wife? She is more precious than rubies.

Okay, Lord, are you trying to tell me something? If I put my neck out there You better be with me to be sure it doesn't get chopped off. Am I too old for this? Lord help me.

Tom picked up his cell phone and searched through his contacts until he came to Laura Klingburg. He held his finger for a moment over her name then lightly touched her name and placed the call.

"Hello."

"Hi Laura. It's Tom. I know you're at work, but I wanted to ask you something quickly. Would you be available for dinner tonight?"

"I am. Is this in regard to something at work? Did something else come up with Helen and the board? She did threaten me that she was going to report me to the board." There was apprehension in Laura's voice.

Tom quickly responded, "Oh, no. This is not work related. It's personal."

"Personal? You mean a *date*?"

"Yes. I can pick you up at 6:30 P.M. at your home. This is my treat."

"Ahh-mmm. Is that something we can do? I mean with the accusations of Helen. Would that be wise?"

"I'd like to take you out, if you're willing. I'm not concerned about gossip. Are you?"

Laura took a moment to think. She was concerned about gossip. It could cost her—her job. A warm feeling hit her in the center of her chest followed by peace. She'd felt that peace before and it was like an assurance that everything was going to be okay. "I'd like that very much. I'll see you at 6:30."

They said their goodbyes and Tom hung up the phone. "This is gonna happen." A smile formed on his lips as he imagined how their evening would go.

* * *

"Isabelle Hayes." The nurse called into the crowded waiting room of expectant mothers of various sizes.

Griffin touched Isabelle's hand. "Can I come in?"

Isabelle rolled her eyes and said, "Fine."

Griffin walked beside her. A feeling of contentment filled his heart. For the first time since their meeting at the restaurant along the expressway, he felt like they were a couple—even if they weren't. He was sure at least everyone there knew he was the father. He held his shoulders a bit higher as he held the door for Isabelle to pass through into the examination room.

The nurse looked Griffin over like he was an interloper. Isabelle saw her expression and quickly said, "This is the baby's father." She gestured towards Griffin. His smile emitted pride. She had said it. He heard it. He was the baby's father.

The nurse padded the table. "Can you scoot up here? The doctor will be in soon."

Isabelle stepped up on the stool then slipped onto the high table. As she swung her legs up in the air to lay back on the table, she yelled, "Oh, no! Oh, no! Oh, no!"

The nurse came to her side. "What is it, dear?" Then the nurse jumped back as water began to drip from the tabletop on her shoes.

"My water just broke, and I'm soaking wet."

"Looks like somebody is having a baby today."

Isabelle glanced at Griffin whose face looked like he was far—far outside his comfort zone. "Griffin are you okay?" Isabelle asked. Then she immediately bent forward and let out a groan. "This is a bad one. It's bad."

Griffin shot out of his seat and stood next to her. He wasn't sure if he should talk or touch her, so he silently prayed the best he could.

The nurse looked at them and questioned if she should call a more reliable family member. Once the contraction passed, she said, "You two go directly to the hospital. You're only five minutes away. Go now and let them examine you there." She looked at Griffin, who had lost most of his color and asked, "You can do this right?"

He nodded and helped Isabelle off the table. He took off his large coat and she tied his coat around her the best she could to cover her wet pants. "This was not the way I imagined I'd have the baby, but it will make a story to laugh at someday."

Griffin grinned, "...and tell our son."

Isabelle bit her lip and didn't reply.

In the car, Isabelle tried her house number—there was no answer. She tried her mom's cell phone. Samantha answered. But before Isabelle could speak, she was hit by another hard contraction. She handed her phone to Griffin.

He said, "Hello. Who is this?"

"Griffin. Is that you? Why do you have Isabelle's phone? Is she okay?" Samantha's voice was full-on panic.

"She's fine. She's having a contraction. We're on our way to the hospital. Her water broke at the doctor's office before they could even examine her. She'd like you to pick up her bag at the house and bring it with you to the hospital. Oh, and please call whoever else she wants to know. I think you'd know that better than me."

"Oh my gosh! Okay! Can I talk to her?"

Griffin looked at Isabelle, then replied, "I'd say you better get up here fast and talk then. We're almost ready to get out of the car."

"Okay-okay! Thanks Griffin. Please, take care of her!"

He felt very protective of her in a strange way at that moment. With brokenness in his voice, he answered, "I will! I won't leave her side. I promise."

"Okay. Tell her I'm coming!"

"I just put you on speaker."

Trying to stay calm, Samantha spoke, "Issie. I'll be there soon. Very soon. I'm so excited. Hang in there. Get the epidural! This isn't a contest of endurance."

Griffin shouted, "Okay. We're here. Hurry—Mrs. Hayes!"

Griffin hung up the phone and rushed around to open the car door. The guard came with a wheelchair and Griffin handed him his keys. "Her name is Isabelle Hayes. We're going to maternity."

Isabelle wasn't talking at all. Just moaning with a grunting pushing sound.

Griffin had never heard anything like it. He pushed her as fast as he dared and followed the signs to the maternity admitting area. They took one look at the situation and Isabelle bypassed the admitting area and was taken to a room.

Griffin followed behind.

The nurse asked, "Are you the father?"

Griffin answered with confidence, "I am."

***

Samantha Hayes broke the law multiple times between the trip home to pick up Isabelle's bag and then rushing to the hospital. Speed walking down the hallways towards labor and delivery, she whispered a thank you to the Lord that she was not pulled over by the police. The whole trip had taken longer than she expected. She breathed in deeply and told herself to relax. Soon she would be standing at Isabelle's side. It had only been a bit more than an hour since Griffin called. *Lord, I hope she's not going crazy wondering where I am.*

Griffin texted her the room number and she was searching the hallways when she saw Griffin standing ahead of her in the hallway. A panic feeling filled her body from head-to-toe. Griffin was crying.

Samantha approached, and apprehensively put her hand on Griffin's shoulder. "What happened? Are Isabelle and the baby okay?"

Griffin was emotionally broken. He couldn't speak.

Samantha couldn't hide her concern. "Griffin. Griffin. What happened?"

With his face still pressed against the wall he spoke in low tones. "It was bad. The blood. The pain. I-I-I-had no idea. She was brilliant. Isabelle was…"

"She had the baby?"

Griffin turned from the wall and looked at Samantha. "He was too big. She hemorrhaged. I didn't leave her until the doctor said she was okay. I didn't want her to see me break down."

"How in the world did she have the baby so fast?"

"The doctor said she was probably in active labor last night but was tolerating it until her water broke then it was full-on crazy fast."

"Where is the baby? Did she see him? Did she hold him?"

"She's holding him now. You should go in. I'll be right in."

Samantha stepped into the room and pulled back the curtains. Nothing can truly prepare a mother for the moment she sees her child for the first time—holding her child. It was a surreal and beautiful picture that she hoped would be imprinted in her memory forever.

Isabelle looked up from her baby's face to meet her mom's gaze. "Mom. Look he's perfect."

Samantha stood next to Isabelle's bed and looked at her grandson. "Yes, he is." She pulled back the blanket a bit and took a better look. "Issie. He's just like you were. Lord, I hope he's not as strong-willed."

Isabelle held the baby a bit closer in a protective way. "He'll be perfect in every way." There was a motherly protection evident in Isabelle's voice.

Everything in Samantha wanted to ask if she had made the decision to keep the baby, but she didn't. The picture of Isabelle holding her son and protecting him spoke louder than words. Samantha's lips relaxed into a knowing smile. Now Samantha was truly happy for the stash of baby things she'd been buying and hiding in the basement. She could have Isabelle's room ready for the baby within hours after she got home. *Lord, let it be so.*

Griffin pulled back the curtains of the hospital room. Isabelle looked up at him and could see he had been crying. Her heart melted just a bit at the sight of him trying to put on a tough front.

Griffin walked across the room and stood on the opposite side of the bed from Samantha. He rested his hands on the bed's guardrail. "That was intense to say the least. How a woman can bounce back from what you've just been through is far beyond my comprehension. Birth is not for the weak." He looked at his son and his son's mother. A contented smile settled on his face. He winked at Isabelle and she reached over and rested her hand on top of his.

Isabelle kept her hand on Griffin's and looked back at Samantha. "Mom, Griffin helped me get through this. I wouldn't have wanted to do this without him."

Samantha smiled. She wasn't crazy about the boy, but he did step up to the challenge, and he didn't seem to want to push through with the adoption. In Samantha's book, that moved him to the front of the class.

26

"The Lord is near to the brokenhearted and saves the crushed in spirit."
Psalm 34:18 (ESV)

Laura didn't want to seem anxious, but she couldn't help looking out the window for the umpteenth time. Where was he? She checked the clock in the kitchen. He wasn't late, but she thought he'd be early. She pulled back the curtains again and peered out into the darkness. Her face was illumined as headlights shined on her like a deer. She dropped the curtain and felt her face flush. Great, just great. I've been caught. He'll probably think I've been standing here for hours gawking out the window.

Laura went to the closet and pulled her coat off the hanger with a little extra force. She rolled her eyes as she thought how she must have looked. She was disgusted with herself for being caught. She slipped her coat on and started to open the front door when the doorbell chimed. She quickly realized that Tom Brown was not some teenage boy who honked his horn for his date to run to the car.

Laura opened the door, and Tom greeted her with a smile. Her self-loathing vanished as she looked at the distinguished gentleman standing on her doorstep. It had been over two years since she kept company with a man socially, and there were butterflies in the pit of her stomach— lots of butterflies.

Tom waited for Laura to lock the door and then extended his arm to her. She locked arms with him and they walked in unison. "Laura, I know this is new for both of us, but I want you to understand something from the beginning. I open doors, pull out chairs and I don't split the check. I pay. I treat women respectfully and follow the guidelines of God's Word in all I do. I want you to know that I'm a gentleman. If these things would be acceptable to you, I think we may have a future."

A million things rushed through Laura's mind. She would have been repelled by such a statement ten years ago. She would have slammed the door in the potential suitors' face without so much as a word, but now it felt wonderful to be treated with respect by a suitor who was a believer and who obeys God's Word and wouldn't ask more of her than her own beliefs would permit.

Once Laura was safe inside the car, Tom closed her door and walked around the car. He eased into the driver's seat and said, "I've planned a nice evening that I hope you will enjoy."

Laura glanced at Tom in the dim light and searched the outline of his face. Was this for real? Was this a dream? Eight weeks ago, she wasn't sure if she would have a job and now she not only had a job, but someone who was interested in her, without the fear of ulterior motives. Life was good for the first time in a very long time.

***

"We can't take CeCe to the hospital with us." Fauna's voice was split between wishful thinking and a demand.

"Honey, we don't have a choice. If we want to see the baby, then we have to take CeCe with us. We can take turns I guess, but CeCe may enjoy seeing the baby too."

"Snake, you don't understand. New moms are highly protective of their babies. Isabelle is going to look at us like we have some plague, but to bring a preschooler in the room with us is unthinkable. Trust me on this one. We have to take turns."

"Fine. You can go in first."

Snake herded CeCe to the car while Fauna put the baby gift in a bag and stuffed some tissue paper on top of the two outfits and little pair of baby sneakers. She grabbed the bag and headed out the door. CeCe was yelling from the car.

"See babies."

Snake was trying to explain. "No. We aren't going to see any babies. Just the new mommy."

"No—me see baby too."

"Really, CeCe the baby won't be there. It's in another room with all the other babies. We're going to wait, and Fauna will go see the mommy first, and then I'll go. One of us will be with you all the time."

Fauna pulled herself into the car and laid the present on the floor by her feet. "Let's do this."

"Present for me?" CeCe asked.

Fauna answered, "No. It's for the new little baby that Isabelle had."

"I give it."

Fauna looked at Snake. He responded by shrugging his shoulders while keeping his eyes on the road. Fauna took a stab at it. "Maybe when the baby comes to church for the first time you can see him then."

CeCe didn't reply. She processed the information, then blurted out, "Me want a baby."

"Snake."

"What?"

"You answer her." Fauna turned her head towards the passenger window and closed her eyes.

Snake glanced in the rearview mirror to see CeCe's face. Her head was cocked to the side in thought. "CeCe, maybe someday we'll have our own baby, but for now we have you."

"I not baby."

"Well, in a way, you're our baby. Or you could be. Would you like that?"

"I no want to be baby."

"Would you like to be our girl?"

Fauna reached over and squeezed Snakes hand and shook her head for him to stop this line of questioning. She had not decided if she wanted the arrangement with CeCe to be permanent. She needed time to process one disappointment at a time. That was all she had the strength to handle with grace.

***

Griffin stayed at the hospital for the whole day. He knew it wouldn't be right to spend the night and Samantha would not allow it even if Isabelle wanted him to, and she didn't, as far as he could tell. Samantha had checked her watch too many times to count and he could no longer pretend that his presence was needed. Isabelle was tired but unable to rest. Maybe if he left she would.

Griffin stood at the side of Isabelle's bed and looked at his sleeping son resting in her arms. "Isabelle, I'm going to go now. I'll be back in the morning. I think we have a lot to talk about, but we'll take a few days to let things settle down." Then Griffin said the thing that had remained unsaid since their baby boy breathed his first breath early that day. "I want you to know I can't sign the adoption papers, and I'm moving to Hillbrooke."

Samantha's ears perked up, but she didn't speak.

Isabelle laid her head back on the pillow of her bed and smiled, "What adoption papers?"

Stuart had been sitting in the corner of the room reading something on his phone. He looked up, and a thin smile formed on his lips.

Baylee jumped up from her seat and yelled, "I knew it!" Then her voice turned sad, "The poor Parkers. Have you told them yet?"

Griffin leaned in and kissed Isabelle on the top of her head, then he kissed his son's forehead. "What's his name?"

"I have one picked out, if you like it."

Griffin's eyes widened, and he waited.

Isabelle turned the baby around to allow everyone in the room to see him. "Meet Stuart Griffin Walsh."

Samantha spoke first. "Really? Really? Ah Stuart. She named him after you." She looked at Griffin standing next to her daughter's bed, "Oh, and you too, Griffin."

Griffin's face lit up. "You're giving him my last name."

"Well, you are his father."

"Yes! I am."

The door opened, and a female voice spoke from behind the door curtain. "Is it okay to come in?"

Isabelle answered, "Sure. Come in."

Fauna Parker pulled open the curtains on the sweet family moment. An awkward silence filled the room. Fauna held the bag out as she walked towards the bed. "I brought *your* baby a gift."

"Thank you, Ms. Parker. I guess you've figured out I'm keeping him?"

Fauna answered quickly, "There were some signs along the way that were undeniable, but I was open for whatever you wanted." Her voice was confident, but inside she was wearing black and in mourning. She had known it was a long shot, but the heart wants what the heart wants. "Can I see him?"

Isabelle showed the perfect little bundle of pink flesh and brown hair to Fauna.

"He's precious. Now remember, I'm here for you, if you need to talk along the way. I have no doubts that you'll be a wonderful mommy." Fauna looked around the room at Isabelle's family. "And you are blessed to have this kind of support." Fauna handed the gift to Isabelle. "Snake would love to come in for a moment. We had to take turns because of CeCe and she didn't handle it well. I'll go and relieve him." Fauna turned to walk out of the room.

Stuart broke the silence. "Thank you, Fauna for all the excellent counsel you gave our girl. I know this must have been a roller-coaster ride for you too. We are extremely grateful to you."

Fauna didn't turn back but nodded and whispered as she pulled back the curtain to leave, "It was my pleasure."

***

CeCe's knees were drawn up in the waiting room chair. Snake's phone resting in her lap and a cartoon played on the phone with the volume turned low.

Snake kept his eyes on the doorway that led to the patients rooms, watching for Fauna's return. When she finally walked into the room, he could see the red eyes. Without putting much thought into his next question, he blurted out, "How did it go?"

Fauna nodded and tried to get the words out, but only one came out. "…keeping…"

Snake stood up and hugged his wife. "We knew it though…didn't we?"

Fauna swallowed hard and agreed with a nod. "You go. They're waiting."

Fauna sat down next to CeCe and without thinking, patted the child's arm.

CeCe yelped. "No. You bad." and pulled away from Fauna. The words were like a dagger to her already wounded spirit.

Fauna was numb and deep in thought when Snake returned sooner than expected.

"Are you two lovely ladies ready to go?" His words were cheerful.

Fauna felt a void in her soul that she wasn't prepared for. It was raw and painful. *Lord, help me,* she thought as she stood up. *I need You. How I need You.*

"Fauna are you okay?" Snake placed his arm around her shoulder and waited.

Fauna spoke reflectively. "It's final—that's all. The little dream of having a newborn we could love and instill our values in—is gone. I guess I'm just mourning something I never really had, and in truth never really believed I would. Yet, I still feel the loss." She glanced at CeCe who was fixated on the video she was watching.

Snake replied, "Well, who are we to question what God has put in our lives right now? Maybe she needs us even more than we need her."

Fauna slipped out from under the protection of Snake's arm and walked towards the elevator.

Snake reached for his phone. "Come on CeCe. Time to go."

She looked up at Snake with a questioning expression. "But where baby? See baby."

"Not tonight. We have to go home. We'll see the baby another day."

CeCe stuck out her lips like a duck in protest but slipped out of the chair. She walked ahead of Snake and behind Fauna.

Snake watched from behind as Fauna led the procession of disappointment. CeCe's little shoulders slumped forward and her head cast downward. She was the picture of Fauna walking a few steps ahead of her.

Snake fought a giggle as he watched his depressed girls step into the elevator. He followed them in and pushed the button for the lobby. The elevator doors closed them in; the man with a snake tattoo, the woman with the butterfly tattoo and the little girl with the mop of curly hair. Snake looked away from the depression and smiled at the wall. He thought they made a nice-looking family indeed.

***

The Tower Restaurant came highly recommended to Tom Brown by his former employer. It was a bit of a drive to get there, but the view was breathtaking. The city skyline at night was a sight to behold.

Tom escorted Laura to their table and pulled out her chair. This particular table was in a coveted location near the window.

Laura looked around the elegantly designed establishment. From the moment they arrived, she had felt a snobbish attitude that radiated from the hostess, to the waitstaff, to the patrons. This added to the uncomfortable small talk she and Tom had in the car on the way to the restaurant. Everything was beginning to press in on her. She was feeling claustrophobic. They placed their orders and waited.

Laura checked her watch again and only five minutes had passed. They were both feeling awkward after using all their best conversation in the car on the long ride. Sitting with someone on a first date and not talking was the kiss of death. And besides that, Laura was starving. She hadn't eaten since noon and it was pushing 8 P.M.—closer to her bedtime and hours past her usual dinner time.

Tom saw Laura glance down again at her lap. He knew she was hungry, tired and uncomfortable in this place, but the orders were made. "Laura, I'm sorry. It was thoughtless of me not to consider that you've been at work all day. This type of place should have been more of a weekend date."

Laura felt horrible that he could see she was uncomfortable. "I hope you don't think I'm ungrateful for such a lovely evening, but it has been quite a day ranging from high to low. I'm sorry, is it okay to talk work? I don't want to ruin your evening."

"Of course. I want you to talk about your day." This was the very thing that Tom had missed since Jean's death—table conversation. Eating in silence was not enjoyable, but sharing daily experiences with someone was highly fulfilling.

Laura felt chatty for the first time since their date began as she described her day. "The low part of my day was, of course, Helen coming into my office demanding a file that has incriminating information about her handling of a past case. First, she tried to manipulate me with sweetness, but I'm not going there with her. I have zero trust for that woman."

"What file was it?"

"It's actually pretty bad stuff. I alluded to that file at the meeting. I sincerely hope I won't have to bring this past offense out in the open. She's already paid for her mistake, as has the poor child. I've talked with her about it privately, but she wants the file purged and her name cleared of all wrongdoing. I really have tried not to make a point of it with the board because I believe the Lord is even now redeeming the situation."

"So, you involve the Lord in your work?" A fondness formed in the expression on Tom's face.

Laura felt her face begin to blush. She smiled and looked away. "Didn't you talk about the Lord when you worked at that solar energy place?"

Tom smiled and nodded. He waved his hand at the waiter passing by. "Could we have our coffee warmed and how much longer before our dinners arrive?"

The waiter looked bothered by the interruption and spoke as he continued to walk, "Yes sir. And I'll check on your order."

Tom looked at Laura and rolled his eyes. "Well, that didn't sound very promising."

Laura shook her head and replied, "Nope." She took another roll from the breadbasket and spread an ample amount of butter on it. She lifted the basket towards Tom. "You want another roll?"

Tom said, "No, I'm looking forward to that steak. I don't wanna fill up before the main course."

Forty minutes after their arrival, a young man carrying two very large plates placed them on the table in front of the couple. Laura bit her lip to hold back a gasp. Tom was speechless. They were looking at the tiniest portions either one had ever seen in a food establishment. The small portions of food rested in the very center of the enormous platters. The whole amount of food could fit in the palm of a child's hand with room to spare.

The waiter proudly said, "Bon Appetit," then clicked his heels and walked away.

Laura held in the laughter the best she could until a full-fledged snort escaped her nose. She looked up at Tom in horror. Did she just snort in a fancy restaurant on a first date? Without saying a word, the worst date ever had just turned into roaring laughter.

The looks from the other customers spoke volumes. It was time for them to go. Tom waved his hand in the air again and best he could through his laughter said to the waiter, "I'm sorry but we have another pressing engagement. Could we have these boxed and please bring the bill?"

After another 20 minutes wait, they both walked out of the restaurant with tinfoil swans the size of small dogs. Tom pressed the down button on the elevator and said, "There is a Coney Island down the road that I feel compelled to stop at. Would you care to join me?"

"I most certainly would." Laura replied, and she slipped her arm inside of Tom's and stepped into the elevator.

***

CeCe fell asleep in the car on the way home from the hospital. This had happened once before and when they tried to carry her into the house, she woke up. It was ugly.

Snake put the car in park and looked at Fauna. "Should I honk the horn or something?"

"Well, I don't think the neighbors should be punished because we're afraid to touch our foster child—do you?"

Snake sighed, "Well, I can try waking her up."

"Maybe we should. If she doesn't wake up, then carry her. Maybe—just maybe you won't be clawed to bits if she realizes she's being touched."

Snake jiggled CeCe's shoulder. She didn't move. "CeCe, wake up!" He moved her around a bit more. She responded with a quiet moan. Snake unbuckled her seatbelt and lifted her over his shoulder. She laid her head down. He felt her body relax against him.

He pointed with one hand at CeCe's back and mouthed the words without making a sound. *This is awesome.*

Fauna ran to the house and held opened the door. Once Snake was safe inside with CeCe in his arms, Fauna ran down the hallway and pulled back the covers of CeCe's bed.

Snake had managed with one hand to remove CeCe's

boots and coat.

"Should we just let her sleep in her clothes?" Snake asked.

"I have to put a pull-up on her. She has never had a dry night in the five months she's been with us. And I don't want to clean that up. Do you?"

"But we'll have to wake her."

Fauna let out a thoughtful moan as she considered her options. "Okay, lets lay her down and see if she wakes up."

Snake gently laid the sleeping child on her bed. She curled up in a ball making it impossible to get a pull-up on without an enormous amount of effort.

Fauna got a pull-up off the dresser. "Okay, let's do this thing." She pulled CeCe's legs down and with the skill of a gymnast moved around the sleeping child with grace and speed. The job was done, and the child was still sleeping.

Snake stood at the door and whispered, "That was very impressive."

As they walked out of the room, CeCe rolled over and said, "We pray."

Fauna turned in surprise and said, "Yes dear. We can pray. We thought you were sleeping."

Snake knelt on the floor and Fauna sat at the foot of the bed, careful not to touch CeCe.

Snake prayed, *"Dear Jesus, please give CeCe a good night's rest tonight. Let your angels encamp around her all through the night. Give her good dreams about good things and let her sleep be sweet. In Jesus Name we pray. Amen."*

Snake and Fauna said together, "Good night CeCe, sweet dreams."

CeCe rolled over and said, "Nite-nite."

27

"Be joyful in hope, patient in affliction, faithful in prayer."
Romans 12:12 (NIV)

The sun cast streams of light into the hospital room. Samantha sat up on the cot where she had rolled and tossed the night away. She looked around the hospital room then wiggled her feet into her slippers and stood up. A cup of coffee sounded amazing right now, but there was no way she would leave the room before Isabelle woke up. Nothing could budge her from that room until she assessed for herself what Isabelle's mood would be today towards the baby.

Little Stuart slept peacefully in the hospital bassinet and Isabelle was sleeping soundly with the child only a few feet from her.

In 24 hours, their whole lives had changed. Today, they would bring a baby home, and Isabelle would be a full-time mother. Samantha hoped and prayed that the emotions of yesterday were real and not just a rush of adrenaline. The thought of Isabelle waking up and changing her mind about keeping the baby was still a very present thought in Samantha's mind.

Samantha quietly straightened up the room, trying to be as quiet as she could. She spotted Isabelle's overnight bag that she had hurried home to pick up yesterday. She had never even checked inside to see if Issie had remembered to pack her bathroom necessities. Samantha tiptoed towards the open bag on the countertop. Clothes had been left hanging over the sides of the bag. Samantha shook her head at the mess and glanced behind her at the two sleeping babies—Isabelle and her son.

Was Isabelle prepared for what lay ahead? Up until

yesterday, she was planning to give her baby away and come home empty-handed. Now, she was a mother. What issues were they going to face with a newborn in their home? Samantha wondered if Isabelle had considered keeping the baby at all over the past 9 months? Did she really understand all the things that would change in her life? And Griffin's? They would be forever connected now. Samantha's concerns caused a deep frown to form on her face.

The clothes Isabelle wore yesterday were thrown on top of her overnight bag in a heap. Samantha busied herself by arranging the discarded items of clothing. The overnight bag was open, and a pair of clean jeans had been hurriedly tossed inside the bag.

Samantha reached into the bag and pulled out the jeans to refold them when she felt resistance. She tugged harder on the jeans. As she lifted the pants higher, Samantha saw it. Hooked to the pocket of Isabelle's jeans was a little onesie still on the hanger with the price tags still in place.

Samantha's heart melted as she turned the words on the front of the onesie into view. The khaki green material read, *Hi, I'm new here.*

Samantha's lip quivered as she held the little shirt in her hand. She reached into the bottom of the bag and discovered it was filled with baby things: diapers, creams, sleepers, a blue fuzzy blanket and little track shoes. As she carefully returned each item to its original place, Samantha's eyes pooled with tears. Isabelle had thought of keeping the baby after all.

A contented sigh caused her shoulders to rise and fall. The knowledge that Isabelle had been preparing for her baby's arrival brought an unexpected peace to Samantha's heart. They were all going to be okay. She knew it. They would face whatever came without fear—as a family. A smile formed on her lips as she thought—even Griffin.

Samantha sat down in the hospital chair next to Issie's bed and looked at her daughter's sleeping face. This moment was an answer to her prayers. She had hoped and believed that Issie would change her mind, but her own faith was rocky. But not Baylee's—she never wavered and wouldn't even join in any family discussions that didn't revolve around keeping the baby. Maybe there is something to be said about childlike faith.

28

But when I am afraid, I will put my trust in You.
Psalm 56:3 (NLT)

The events of the past evening had been emotional for Snake and Fauna. After putting CeCe to bed and praying with her, the couple collapsed in their own bed to talk about their long-term fears in regard to adopting CeCe. Snake was still pro-adoption while Fauna was firmly planted on the fence of indecision.

Fauna reached across the bed in the dim morning light and patted around on the mattress. Snake was already up, but the house was quiet. She continued to drift in and out of sleep.

Fauna ran toward the rickety bridge. Her voice was hysterical as she yelled, "CeCe stop. Don't go on the bridge. STOP!" Her heart was racing. She was having difficulty breathing. She huffed, "Please, CeCe stop!"

The child had gone halfway across the bridge and was frozen in fear. "Help! I scared." CeCe looked back at Fauna.

A peace came over Fauna as she spoke, "CeCe, listen to me. Hold the rope and walk back to me slowly."

CeCe began to cry. "No—move."

"CeCe, please come to me. I can help you. Just take one small step at a time. You have to trust me."

CeCe turned towards Fauna, grabbed the rope bridge, and took one very small step. "You're doing great Honey. I know you're scared, but you can do this. You're a strong and brave girl."

CeCe took one more step, then another and another. She was almost within Fauna's reach. Their fingers were almost touching.

Fauna's eyes opened as she felt the blankets of her bed being pulled.

She rolled over and CeCe stood at the side of her bed. It was the first time since she arrived at their house that she had ever entered their bedroom.

"Potty. I need go potty."

Fauna sat up in the bed looking at CeCe wiggling about from foot to foot.

Fauna quickly recouped her bearings and jumped out of bed. "Let's go. Hurry!"

Fauna rushed ahead of CeCe opening the bathroom door and in one seamless motion pulled out the stepstool for CeCe to climb up.

With surprise in her voice, Fauna shouted. "CeCe, you slept all night. No nightmares and your pull-up. It's dry!" The corners of CeCe's mouth turned up slightly to reveal a modest amount of pleasure in her success.

"Remember, today we go see Ms. Klingburg. She's a nice lady."

CeCe scooted off the toilet and tugged on the pull-up. "I no go there. It baaad." She drew out the word *bad* almost to the point of humor.

Fauna fought the urge to laugh. "CeCe it's a good place. That's where we first heard that you were going to come here to live with us."

CeCe's lower lip went out at the same time her top lip went in. "Baaad place. It bad."

Fauna sighed and decided not to try and convince her of something that wasn't happening for another seven hours. Their appointment was at 4 p.m. Snake was coming home from work early to ride with them. Ms. K was waiting for their decision about adoption. They needed to be on the same page by then.

Fauna whispered a quick prayer as she went to the kitchen to start breakfast. "Lord, I have to know in my heart I can do this. It can't just be a momentary good feeling. Show me. Let me see with my own eyes the way to go."

***

The front door slammed shut behind Snake. He checked the time on the dining room clock. They would need to leave soon to make their appointment with Ms. K at Christian Family Services. The house was quiet. That could be good or bad. He ventured into the family room to see if he could find either Fauna or CeCe. He saw Fauna curled up on the sofa with a pile of kid's books resting in her lap. Slumped over on Fauna's arm was CeCe—sound asleep. Fauna put her index finger to her lips but didn't speak. She moved the books to the sofa, reached for a couch pillow and gingerly wedged the pillow between CeCe's sleeping head and her arm. Then she lowered her onto the couch.

"Don't we need to go?" Snake asked.

Fauna waved for Snake to follow her into the kitchen. "I just couldn't wake her. We've had quite a day. It started out with CeCe pulling on the blanket in our room. She woke me up."

"What? She came into our room?"

"Yes, I know. I was shocked. She woke me from that same dream I had before about the bridge. Only this time when I called her to come to me, she trusted me. She was almost in my arms when CeCe woke me!"

"Wow! You should have called me."

"No time for phone calls. She asked to go potty and her pull-up was dry."

"I'm sorry. I'm gonna have to call you a liar." Snake's voice dripped with sarcasm. "That can't be."

"Well, it gets better. She obeyed me in everything today, and at naptime about an hour ago she asked me to read her that pile of books. She fell asleep on my arm and I didn't move her. I couldn't. But I know we have to go. I pray we aren't waking her before she's had enough sleep. This could be an ugly finish to a beautiful day."

Snake looked longingly into the family room. "Well,

wish I could have seen the CeCe you saw today. That must have given you hope for the future." He sheepishly questioned, "Right?"

"One good day does not make a lifetime commitment." As soon as the words left Fauna's mouth she felt a bitter taste. "I'm sorry, I'm still processing. I'm hoping for more time. I don't understand why we are being rushed to make a decision."

"Ms. K must have her reasons. She's been good to us. I believe CeCe was placed with us for a reason. Let's walk this thing out and see what comes next. But first...who's gonna poke the bear?"

Fauna smiled and walked to the coat hooks and pulled CeCe's coat down. "You may have the honor. I'll help with the coat and shoes."

The ordeal of waking and dressing CeCe was not uneventful nor was it as traumatic as it had been in the past. It was the typical three-year-old stuff when you wake a child too soon from a nap.

As the car backed out of the driveway, Fauna heard CeCe ask, "Go to William's?"

Snake responded, "No. Remember. Today we need to go visit Ms. K at the Christian Family Service building."

CeCe had not been back to that place since she came to live with the Parkers. Fauna dreaded CeCe's reaction when she saw the building. She knew it held bad memories for the child from what Ms. K had told them.

"CeCe, I know you don't like to hold hands, but if we have to park across the street then we'll have to hold hands. Let's pray there is a spot near the door."

CeCe clenched her teeth tightly. She didn't respond.

Snake glanced back at CeCe in his mirror, then at Fauna, "Oh, I think she can do it. How about if CeCe doesn't want to hold hands, she can hold the edge of my coat when we walk into the building?"

Fauna turned to look at CeCe who was obviously contemplating Snake's proposal. They turned the corner, and the Family Christian Service sign loomed in front of an old three-story office building. Snake parked near the front door and quickly got out. When he opened CeCe's door, she had already unbuckled her seatbelt and was standing up.

Snake smiled, making a gentleman's bow while offering his hand to CeCe. She reached out and took his hand. Fauna let out a gasp and Snake smiled. Then Snake, CeCe, and Fauna walked into the building together. As they stood in the elevator, the doors slowly closed, and CeCe reached up and found Fauna's hand.

29

Behold, children are a heritage from the Lord…
Like arrows in the hand of a warrior…
Happy is the man who has his quiver full of them…
Psalm 127:3,4,5 (NKJV)

In the waiting room of Christian Family Services, Ms. Klingburg talked with the foster mom of two elementary aged girls. The children sat stone-faced in chairs across the small waiting area. The elevator doors opened, and Ms. K glanced in that direction to see who was arriving. With a shocked expression, her head jerked at the sight of CeCe standing between Snake and Fauna holding their hands.

The expression on Ms. K's face was priceless to Fauna and Snake. No one said a word, but Snake and Fauna nodded their heads like bobblehead dolls and smiled.

Ms. K turned to the foster mom and said, "Excuse me for just a moment."

She turned towards the open elevator and greeted the Parkers. "Well, don't you all look very friendly today." She winked at CeCe, who looked away, and pressed her face against Fauna's leg.

Snake whispered while pointing down with his free hand at CeCe. "I think she's concerned about coming here. Not good memories."

Ms. K nodded, then turned towards the security window. "Gina, could you come and take CeCe to the playroom while I speak with the Parkers in my office?"

Gina buzzed open the security door and looked at CeCe whose eyes had narrowed and looked ready for a brawl—at least as much as a three-year-old could. "CeCe, you want to come with me to the playroom? We have some new toys. I think there is a doll in there you will like." Gina wiggled her index finger in the air for CeCe to follow.

Fauna felt CeCe's grip tighten on her hand. The squeeze was felt more on her heart than her hand. Fauna dropped down to one knee but did not release CeCe's hand. "CeCe, we're not leaving you here. We just need to speak to Ms. K for a few minutes in private. I bet you'll be able to see us from the playroom if Gina keeps the door open." Fauna looked at Gina for assurance.

"Sure, I can do that. How about if you all follow me to Ms. K's office and then I can show CeCe how close we'll be."

Snake and Fauna walked hand in hand with CeCe to the office. At that moment, neither Fauna nor Snake could imagine breaking the grip that CeCe had on their hands.

Ms. K said her goodbyes to the family in the waiting room, then followed behind the unbreakable human chain called the Parker Family.

Once inside the office, Fauna turned, and for the first time, tried to break CeCe's grip on her hand. "CeCe, we'll be right here, and won't leave this place without you."

Slowly CeCe's tears began. They were big tears, followed by a pitiful plea. "No leave me."

Snake looked at Fauna and shook his head. "I can't do this. I won't. How about if I stay with her while you share your heart with Ms. K? It's your choice. I'll stand with you whatever you decide." He scooped CeCe up in his arms, and she clung to his neck. He looked back at Fauna as he followed Gina out of the room. "I guess we should have brought her back here a long time ago. Who knew the effect it would have?" Snake followed Gina to the adjacent room.

Fauna watched Snake sit down at a kid's table with CeCe clinging to his neck. It was what they had longed for all these months. Just a little sign that they were making a difference. Just a little bit of hope that she could grow fond of them. Just a little bit of love from her to them. Just a morsel of trust.

Fauna didn't expect it all to happen in a matter of minutes. But it did—oh how it did.

Ms. K pointed at the chair across from her desk. "Have a seat Fauna. So, tell me what's going on. That was quite a display of emotion from our closed off, tight as a drum little girl now—wasn't it?"

Fauna's face was flushed, and her heart was pounding. "Hey, I'm just as shocked as you." As soon as the words exited her mouth she thought again. Am I? After all that prayer, am I really shocked?

Ms. K said the words moments after Fauna thought them. "It seems our prayers have been answered. We wanted a sign that she was bonding with you and we wanted to see her show some affection to you both. This is fantastic. How long has she been doing this?"

"I'd say five minutes ago when she took both our hands in the elevator. That was the first time *she* has initiated any touch with us at all—*ever*!"

Ms. K shook her head and let out a giggle. "This is too wonderful for words!"

Fauna looked confused. "I don't understand."

"Well, I mean. How are you feeling about the whole adoption thing now?"

Fauna pushed her back against the chair and sat up very straight. Her internal dialogue was shouting. How can we be expected to make a lifetime commitment to CeCe based on this one positive action? She could turn ugly again in a flash and then what—a plate to the face. Fauna didn't answer.

Ms. K's voice was soft and sweet. "I know it's a difficult decision and I don't want to push you but there are some extenuating circumstances. I am going to need a decision today and we'll need to start the paperwork today as well."

Fauna bit her lips. "If we were to sign the papers and things didn't go well, would we have any recourse?"

Ms. K grew somber. "She's not a puppy, Fauna. She needs a family that will strive with her through the good and bad. And I promise you this, there will be bad and lots of it. I won't sugarcoat it for you. What I saw today was as near to a miracle as I've seen in this business. But you could sign these papers today and when you get home be hit upside the head with a flying doll the moment you don't do what she wants. It's the nature of the beast. But she's young—so young—only three-years-old. What do you remember from being three? I know it's not much for me. She needs stability and someone she can trust for the long term. If it's not going to be you and Snake, we'll have to move her very soon to a new home."

Fauna leaned forward and rested her hands on Ms. K's desk. "Why? Why can't we keep going like we are and take some more time to see how things play out?"

"There are reasons. I need your decision."

Fauna leaned her head into one of her hands and massaged her forehead. Then she turned her face to looked over her shoulder into the playroom. That was when she saw it. The picture that sealed the deal in her heart.

CeCe, still clinging to Snake, was moving her finger over the outline of the hissing snake tattoo on the side of Snake's face. Then she leaned in and began to kiss the snake. She kissed it over and over again.

Fauna laughed. "I can't believe it. Look." She pointed towards the playroom. "Look at that."

Ms. K jumped up from her desk and went to the large window in her office. "Oh, my goodness! Lord never let me forget this picture." Ms. K turned back to Fauna. "Well?"

Fauna tightened her jaw, and her lips began to quiver. "We're ready to sign."

Ms. K walked back to her desk and opened a file. "Would you like to ask the rest of your family to join us?"

Fauna walked across the office to the playroom. "Ms. K can see us now—all of us." She tried to mask her excitement, but she couldn't hide her tears.

Snake took CeCe's hand and followed Fauna back across the office. Concern was evident on his face.

Helen Franko sat at her desk with a scowl on her face. Her eyes trailed them—especially *that* child.

CeCe held tight to Snake's hand and pointed at Helen

with her free hand, "You bad."

Helen looked away as if the child did not exist.

Snake scooped CeCe up and whispered in her ear. "Remember, we need to be kind."

Inside Ms. K's office the Parker family sat down. She opened the file and pulled out a stack of papers and turned them towards Snake and Fauna. Looking at Snake, she said, "Fauna said that you were ready to make an adoption application for CeCe. Is this correct?"

Snake reached for Fauna's hand with CeCe still clinging to him. He couldn't speak. He bit at his lips to fight the emotion. But his eyes betrayed him.

Ms. K leaned back in her office chair. "Now there is just one more thing I need to make you aware of before you sign." Ms. K had the Parkers full attention. "A week ago, as we discussed, CeCe's mother lost custody of her children. All her parental rights are now terminated."

Fauna tipped her head and asked, "Did you say children?"

Ms. K chuckled. "I thought you might notice that. We like to keep biological children together in the same family unit."

"We would have taken CeCe's siblings from the beginning, but we thought she was an only child." Fauna looked confused.

"She was an only child until one week ago. Now, she's a big sister."

Snake and Fauna looked at each other and didn't know whether to laugh or cry. Snake said, "You mean we're going to get the baby too?"

"Yes, you are. It's a little boy. I needed to know you wanted CeCe before I could tell you that she comes with some extra baggage."

Fauna looked at CeCe sitting in Snake's lap. "CeCe, you have a baby brother. You're a big sister now and we have a baby."

Ms. K slid a picture across the table towards Fauna.

"Meet your son. His birth mom named him Blu, but you can change that once the adoption is final. I'd recommend that you begin now to call them by the names they will have once the adoption is final. Why confuse them for another moment?"

Ms. K looked at CeCe. "Well, you finally have your very own mommy and daddy."

CeCe looked back and forth between Snake and Fauna. She reached out and touched Fauna's arm. "You Mommy?"

Fauna nodded her head. There were tears. Lots of tears.

Then CeCe turned around in Snake's lap and touched his beard. "You Daddy?" Her voice cracked a little when she said his name.

It was the sweetest name he'd ever heard, said by the sweetest little girl he ever knew.

"Yes CeCe, no more Snake and Fauna—God has rewritten your story, just like he did mine. You have a Mommy and Daddy now, and we love you very much."

30

(Eighteen Months Later)

*You have put more joy in my heart
than they have when their grain and wine abound.*
Psalm 4:7 (ESV)

Fauna laid the banner on the dining room table and pulled out the chair. She stepped up on the chair and then the tabletop. She yelled into the family room, "CeCe, can you help Mommy? I left the tape on the counter." Fauna pointed at the tape dispenser across the room.

CeCe hurried into the kitchen and reached for the tape dispenser. She lifted it as high in the air as she could reach. "Here Mommy."

Fauna took the tape and finished taping the banner on the wall. "Can you read the words CeCe?"

CeCe stood back from the table and looked at the banner and sounded out each word. "It says. Wel-come to you-r for-ev-er home. CeCe and Atlas Parker—We Love You."

"Very good, CeCe."

"I like ta read."

"I know you do. And I'm proud of you for all your help taking care of your brother too."

CeCe pushed out her lips as she pondered her mom's remark. "Well—sometimes Atlas is bad. He wrote on the wall with a crayon and that's bad." CeCe nodded her head in agreement with what she'd said.

"Yes, it is bad. Do you remember when you were little that you also wrote on the walls with crayons?"

"No Mommy. I don't write on the walls. I know that's

bad. I would not do that."

"Yes, you know it's bad now, but once you were little, too, and I'm glad we were patient with you just like you are with Atlas."

CeCe looked at the cake on the kitchen island. She inched her finger towards the corner where a bit of frosting was on the edge of the cardboard. "Can I pleeez take just one little taste?"

"Sure, go ahead. Today you are the guest of honor." Fauna pointed at a spot that was hard to see. "Right there. I think someone should take a taste right there."

CeCe looked at her mommy and smiled, then slid her finger across the edge of the shiny cardboard that held the cake. "Mmmm. I love da frosting."

The doorbell rang, and Fauna looked at her daughter. "CeCe, go tell Daddy to bring Atlas so we can welcome the guests."

CeCe ran to fetch her father and brother and was back before Fauna had the door open.

"Welcome!" Fauna said as she stepped aside to allow William and Maddie Edwards to run past her. Two steps behind was their little sister Eve.

Fauna watched the kids run by, then she turned back to her brother-in-law and sister-in-law and said, "Thanks for coming—you guys. It means so much to have a supportive family."

"We wouldn't miss this day for anything. But it's just a formality. CeCe and Atlas have been your children from the very beginning. No piece of paper can change what is already in our hearts." Emily hugged Fauna who was as dear to her as any sister could be.

Kota was a few steps behind Emily, carrying two very large gifts, wrapped with excellence. "Where do you want the gifts?" he asked.

Fauna pointed in the direction of a small table, where a few gifts were arranged with a box for cards. Kota walked over to the table and dropped off the gifts.

Snake held 18-month-old Atlas as he spoke, "You guys didn't have to do that—money would have been fine!" He tipped his head back and laughed.

Kota smirked. "Not funny!"

"Really! Thanks for coming. This is a very special day for our family and it wouldn't be right if you guys weren't here with us."

Atlas's big brown eyes were locked on the presents. He was a handsome little boy. Snake and Fauna were amazed that wherever they went, without fail, someone would remark on their beautiful children. And they never tired of hearing about CeCe's beautiful eyes and curly hair or Atlas's sweet face. His hair wasn't as curly and unruly as his sister's, but there was no denying they were related.

Before Fauna stepped away from the door, Marilyn and James Fields, her in-laws, were walking towards the house. Fauna left the door open and yelled towards the family room, "Grandpa and Grandma are here!"

All the children came running—a total of five. They stood in the kitchen anxiously awaiting their grandparents to cross the threshold. When James walked through the door, it was CeCe who jumped into his arms first. Then, one by one, each grandchild hugged Grandpa then moved on to Grandma.

Marilyn asked Fauna, "Now—who all is coming? This looks like a lot of food!" She scanned the array of foods on the table, countertop and kitchen island. "Why didn't you ask us for help? Emily and I could have done something."

"No—we wanted you to come and celebrate with us. Grab some food and go sit down."

Marilyn began fixing food for the children and getting them settled when Pastor Rey and Callan rang the doorbell.

Fauna greeted them with a question, "Where are the boys? I thought they were coming."

Callan sighed. "Hum. Those boys! I can't keep them home for a minute. Ty is on the soccer team and they practice nearly every day and Zander took a job to earn money to buy his own car—that boy."

Callan shook her head and twisted her lips to the side. She lowered her voice, "He thinks he's in love with this girl who works at the store with him. He's invited her to church and she's come a few times. We're praying about the whole situation. I'll save the rest of that story for another day."

Callan winked at Fauna. "The food looks great. Especially the cake!" Callan wandered over to the cake and looked it over with great interest. "I hope you already took pictures of this cake, because I'm gonna want a piece of this ASAP." Callan laughed. Then got serious and said, "I'm not kidding. I never kid about cake."

The doorbell rang again. Fauna opened the door, and Isabelle Hayes walked in carrying a gift.

Isabelle announced in a loud voice, "I've got something for the Parker children. Where are they?"

Fauna gave Isabelle a side hug and said, "I'm so happy you came. Are your parents and everyone coming?"

"Oh yes. They are all right behind me." Isabelle pointed back at the door.

Griffin stepped through the door carrying their son Stuart. The baby squirmed out of Griffin's arms and ran directly through the kitchen into the family room where the other children were eating.

Isabelle gave Griffin a stern look. "Griffin, go get him! Stuart can't be trusted for a moment. He'll destroy the Parkers house."

Griffin hurried after Stuart, their little ball of energy.

Fauna chuckled. "Don't worry Isabelle. This is a kid-friendly house. What's one more 18-month-old child running around?"

From the kitchen, Fauna could hear CeCe yell, "Look it's baby Stuart. Come here baby. Sit with me." Fauna thought how CeCe had become such a loving child over the past year and a half since they added Atlas to their family. Just as Ms. K had promised, there were a few dolls that hit Fauna upside the head, but with each day that Atlas grew—CeCe grew more loving. It was a metamorphosis that happened so gradually, even Fauna couldn't mark the day that things changed for the better.

Fauna felt a hand at the small of her back. She turned around to a glowing sun-kissed face.

"Fauna. This is the day we prayed about, dreamed about, and fought for, and now it's here. You have your family all around you. What an incredible day this is. It's days like today that make every difficult day I face at work—all worth it." Laura Brown pulled Fauna in for a hug. "What a blessing to be here for this celebration."

Fauna slipped her arm into Laura's and held it there while she spoke. "If it wasn't for you, we wouldn't have these two amazing blessings from the Lord. To say thank you just wouldn't be gratitude enough for all you've done for us—but thank you!"

Tom Brown joined his bride. Laura let go of Fauna's arm and took her husband's. Tom smiled down at her, then at Fauna. "She insisted that we were back for this celebration. I can't deny her anything. Only married for two weeks and I'm putty in her hands."

Laura sighed then smiled. "Come on let's get something to eat."

Snake stepped close to his wife and slipped his arm around her shoulder, pulling her in for one of his bear hugs. He put his lips close to her ear and whispered, "Look how the Lord has blessed us. Look at the people he has brought into our lives. Me, a rebellious son, a law breaker, angry and hateful. And you, abandoned, alone, hopeless and helpless. Then God stepped into both of our lives, took an eraser and wiped the pages of our messed up lives clean and look..." He turned Fauna around towards the full house of people then leaned in close again and whispered, "...just look how the Lord has filled those blank pages with this. This is God's rewrite, and we are truly blessed."

***

Snake stood at the kitchen sink looking out the window. The days were getting shorter as fall drew near. Everyone had left hours ago and Atlas and CeCe went to bed without a fuss following the busy day. The house was quiet and peaceful as he finished putting the last few dishes in the dishwasher.

Fauna had disappeared to another room.

Snake closed the dishwasher and wiped his hands on the dish towel then returned it to the hook under the sink. As he turned, he saw it. He thought it was one more thing to throw away. He took a few steps towards the rectangle box on the table—then he stopped. He had seen boxes just like this one before—but not for a very long time.

He took another step closer and snatched the box from the table with a quick swipe. He turned it around in his hands a few times then drew a deep breath in and yelled, "Fauna— FAUNA where are you?"

From the bathroom, Snake heard Fauna scream. "Oh— my—God!"

Discussion Questions

Fauna is desperate for a baby and has experienced many heartbreaks in the waiting process. Have you ever been in a holding pattern waiting for God to answer your heart's cry? How did you cope during your time of waiting?

Snake and Fauna were not on the same page for most of the book about adopting CeCe, their foster daughter. When a husband and wife are not in agreement on a major life decision, what steps should they take to find common ground?

Callan Douglas, the pastor's wife, had a big heart but often blurted out things she later regretted. Have you had people in your life with great hearts but were clumsy maneuvering through life? How do you extend grace to someone like this? Or how have others extended grace to you in situations like this?

Dr. Stuart and Samantha Hayes were in the midst of a life altering situation with their teenage daughter. If you were giving the Hayes family, the Parker family (Snake and Fauna) and Laura Klingburg a report-card grade in the following areas what would they be and why:

Good Listeners
Accepting Without Condoning
Bring Resolution Without Dictating
Restoring What is Broken to Wholeness

Isabelle didn't blame Griffin Walsh for her condition, but she seemed unforgiving towards him. Did this affect her ability to trust God? How would you have handled this situation differently if you were Isabelle?

CeCe Jefferson was a wounded child lashing out in her pain. Could you handle a child with all the trauma like CeCe's in your home? Have you ever considered foster care?

Laura Klingburg had a life-changing event in *Hillbrooke The Healer* that rewrote the outcome of her life story. How were the lives of the main characters in this book changed by God's Rewrite?

In the Christian Family Services' board meeting, Helen mixed enough truth with unfounded accusations to cast doubt on Laura Klingburg's reputation. Have you ever fallen prey to another's false accusations? Have you ever believed a bad report about someone only to find out later the facts stated to you were without evidence? What process do you use to decipher if the information you receive is creditable?

Fauna was steadfast in keeping her emotions in check throughout the book regarding the adoption of CeCe. Yet, it was a very emotional thing that put her over the top while watching CeCe interacting with Snake. When can you trust your emotions and when should you be on guard?

About the Author

Beverly Roberts is married to Bob Roberts, senior pastor of New Life Christian Fellowship in Grand Blanc, Michigan.

Since 1977, the Roberts have served in full-time ministry filling the positions of youth pastor, senior pastor, and missionaries.

Beverly was an at-home wife and mother to her three children until 1998. Then she began working part-time in the ministry. She loves her family and has no regrets using her energy to train and serve them. The Roberts have ten grandchildren.

If you enjoyed Beverly's writing, check out her weekly devotionals at www.beverlyjoyroberts.com.

And remember to leave a comment on Amazon.com or Good Reads about this book.

Made in the USA
Columbia, SC
08 July 2020